G000109662

Summer Cruising

Summer Cruising

a novel by

Dave Benbow

palari
Publishing

www.palaribooks.com

A Palari Trade Paperback Original

Summer Cruising
© 2006, By Dave Benbow

Published by Palari Publishing LLP
www.palaribooks.com

All rights reserved. No part of this book may be reproduced or utilized in any form or by any means, electronic or mechanical, including photocopying, recording or by any information storage and retrieval system, without permission in writing from the Publisher.

This book is a work of fiction. Names, characters, businesses, organizations, places, events, and incidents either are the product of the author's imagination or are used fictitiously. Any resemblance to actual persons, living or dead, events, or locales is entirely coincidental.

Inquiries should be addressed to: Permissions Department
Palari Publishing, PO Box 9288, Richmond, VA 23227-0288

Library of Congress Cataloging-in-Publication Data

Benbow, Dave.
  Summer cruising : a novel / by Dave Benbow.
      p. cm.
  Summary: "Fictional account of a gay cruise on The Princess Diana that includes romance, mystery, and a disaster at sea"--Provided by publisher.
  ISBN-13: 978-1-928662-07-5 (pbk.)
  ISBN-10: 1-928662-07-2 (pbk.)
  1. Gay men--Fiction. I. Title.
  PS3602.E657S86 2006
  813'.6--dc22

                                                                    2005034705

ISBN-13: 978-1-928662-07-5
ISBN-10: 1-928662-07-2

Printed in the United State of America
10 9 8 7 6 5 4 3 2 1

Front and back cover photos © DAVID MORGAN www.dmny.com
Model: Brandon
Grooming: Jorge Vargas
Cover design: Dave Benbow

For Rich Campbell.
Without his generous help
this book could never have been written.

Acknowledgments

First, I must thank Rich Campbell and his awesome, talented and really good-looking staff at Atlantis Events, Inc. for all their amazing help during the writing of this novel. All of you went above and beyond, and I will be eternally grateful. And just so you know, dear readers, all those fabulous, fun and adventurous gay cruises I took were purely for research. Honest. I mean it. Really.

I want to express deep appreciation to the staff and crew of Royal Caribbean's *Splendour of the Sea,* Norwegian Cruise Line's *Norwegian Dawn*, and Carnival Cruise's *Carnival Pride.* The dedicated men and women of these great ships treated me like royalty and patiently answered my million annoying questions.

I have to give a big thank you to Photographer-of-the-Gods David Morgan for his phenomenal cover shots. If you want sexy photographs of stunning, hunky men, David's the go-to guy, trust me. And of course, deeply envious thanks go to our stunning cover guy, the hot, handsome, and amazingly down-to-earth Brandon. No one will pick up this book because of me, that's for damn sure, Brandon!

And last, but certainly not least, I'd like to say thanks to Dave Smitherman and Ted Randler for welcoming me into the Palari family so warmly. Let's do it again!

1

The Mediterranean Sea, off the coast of Italy

Jorge Camarillo staggered up the metal staircase, gripping the sea-sprayed teak banister tightly with each rise up the steps. There was a gentle rocking motion coming from the slowly moving cruise ship, and Jorge didn't trust his feet to land where he wanted them to.

Shouldn't have had that last martini, he snickered to himself.

There was a stiff warm breeze, and his open shirt flapped around his chiseled torso like a flag on a pole. The metal dog tag around his neck chinked gently in the wind. It was dark out, but the illumination from the deck lighting along with the three-quarter moon above allowed him to see where he was going.

That is, until he managed to get to the top of the stairway.

The long, narrow raised bridge of the Compass Deck was seductively dark. Apparently the lights were shut off at midnight to discourage visitors from venturing up to see the three large compasses that displayed the latitude, longitude and position of the *Princess Diana* on her cruise through the Mediterranean sea. Quickly discovered by the more adventurous men on board, this area had become one of several late-night assignation spots on the ship where randy couples could make out, or more, in relative darkness.

Sometimes two men became three. Or four. Or more.

Grinning as he remembered the awesome sex he'd had up here the night before, Jorge hoped the same would happen again tonight.

At 29, Jorge Camarillo was at the peak of his considerable physical beauty. His Cuban blood gave him flawless dark skin, and a deep reserve of animalistic passion. His square jawline, stunning jade-green eyes and straight nose were not the first thing men noticed about him. Nor was his perfectly cut and carefully tended black hair. No, it was his amazing physique, unbelievable ass and full crotch that held most men transfixed.

A part-time swimsuit model from Miami, and last year's winner of South Beach's "hottest man" contest, he spent hours at the gym toning, refining and building up his six-foot frame. Spin class-toned, long legs connected to the perfect bubble butt, a bubble butt seen on packages of Hombre underwear all over the country. He had a sensual and hairless torso, complete with the required six-pack of abs and flawlessly pumped up pecs. His large back flared out in a perfect V-shape, and his wide shoulders led to big arms that were the envy of many.

Happily single, he had decided to take the cruise at the last minute when his buddy Marco was suddenly called home for a family funeral and couldn't go. After telling Jorge it was an all-gay cruise traveling to several exotic Mediterranean ports of call, on a ship packed with over thirteen hundred gay men, Marco sold the model his ticket at half-price. Now Jorge was sharing an oceanview cabin on deck three, the Pearl Deck, with a hot fitness instructor from Dallas who'd already fucked him three times.

Standing at the top of the stairwell, Jorge looked around, straining to see in the dim light. The sexy buzz from the ecstasy tab he'd taken earlier had been replaced with a warm fuzziness due to the three martini's he'd had at his disastrous dinner date.

He wandered to the railing that overlooked the wide stern of the *Princess Diana*, a wake of white foam and churning water trailing behind her. His eyes adjusted to the dark, and he found he was alone. Slightly disappointed, he was nonetheless content to simply gaze out over the moonlit water.

Oddly, tonight he wasn't bothered that much by the surrounding sea. Jorge normally hated and feared large expanses of water. In his altered state now, however, he found he could enjoy the view.

He suspected his phobia was a result of the treacherous ocean crossing he, his mother and father, two uncles, and three cousins had made from Cuba to Miami when he was barely six years old. The ropes they had used to lash the inner tubes together had come apart, and the sodden refugees had barely made it ashore alive. Jorge's deepest fear now was one of drowning.

He closed his eyes and enjoyed the sensation of wind blowing wildly through his hair, his shirt still whipping around him.

"Hey."

Surprised by the deep voice, he opened his eyes and looked around. He spied a male form by the stairwell. "Hey," he called back.

"Beautiful night, huh?" asked the stranger, in a seductively soothing tone.

"Yeah. I love the hot breeze."

The man came closer, and Jorge could see his outline a little more clearly. Tall, with broad shoulders and obviously thick, hard legs, the man was definitely well built. "Me too," the stranger said softly, coming even closer. "Though, I have to admit, the warm air makes me horny."

Jorge smiled. All right! Now completely interested, though still inebriated, he turned to face the man who was now only about five feet away. The man was wearing a tight lycra boxcut bathing suit that fit him perfectly. Jorge couldn't see his face clearly in the extremely dim light, but he could tell the man had dark hair. The pale moonlight bathed the stranger's hot body in a faint white glow. Heavily worked-out arms, beefy pecs and what appeared to be a promising, thick bulge between his legs were all that Jorge needed to see.

His heart began to race slightly as the man kept coming closer and closer, until he was mere inches away. Jorge couldn't take his eyes off the huge erection straining at the thin fabric of the man's small swimsuit.

"Does the warm air have that same effect on you?" the mystery man whispered into Jorge's ear. He reached out and brazenly grabbed Jorge's crotch, squeezing hard.

"Oh, yeah," Jorge groaned.

"Yeah?" The hot man sexily questioned, licking Jorge's ear and then jamming his tongue deep into the canal. Jorge spasmed and moaned louder. The man trailed his hand upward, letting his hot fingers lightly touch and stroke Jorge's six-pack. The hand continued north and gently gripped and pinched one of Jorge's nipples, again getting a favorable reaction.

"Oh, Papi," Jorge sighed.

"Mmm, you're such a handsome man. You know, I first noticed you at the Bon-Voyage T-Dance yesterday, shaking that hot ass of yours," the man breathed. "I knew I would fuck you eventually…" His warm, wet tongue traveled down Jorge's neck.

"Keep doing that, Papi, and I'll let you," Jorge gasped, sucking in his breath in pleasure as the man dug his hand down inside Jorge's loose jeans. Jorge wasn't wearing underwear, and the stranger's hand clamped around his hard manhood and began to gently pump it.

"Mmm, I'd like that a lot. You'd like it, too…"

Unable to stand it anymore, Jorge reached out himself and slipped his hand into the elastic waistband of the stranger's swimsuit. He, too, clamped around a massive hardness and deftly snapped the bathing suit down, in effect cupping the man's truly impressive package with the stretchy fabric.

"Yeah, that feels so good," the man whispered, coming around only millimeters away from Jorge's face. He leaned in the short distance and began to deep kiss Jorge with such ardor and passion that Jorge felt faint.

This guy knew how to kiss!

Jorge gave in to his baser needs, and he clumsily shucked all his clothes and tugged down the stranger's swimsuit as well. Now both completely naked, the two men pressed up against each other, and Jorge marveled at what a hot body the stranger possessed.

They lowered themselves onto a convenient deck chair and soon Jorge found himself on top of the hard man, and in seconds had the man's huge piece jammed eagerly in his mouth.

"Fuuuuckkk..." the stranger groaned, stretching back, subtly jutting his hips up in the process, allowing Jorge to take him further down his throat.

"Mmmm..." Jorge garbled, busily bobbing up and down. His right hand joined in, sliding up and down the spit-slicked tool in opposite rhythm to his mouth.

"Fuuuck! You're gonna make me come," the stranger gasped, pushing Jorge's head away from his throbbing member.

"I want you to," Jorge said, moving back in to take the immense erection into his mouth again.

"No, not yet..." The stranger suddenly gripped Jorge's shoulders, hard, and in a surprising feat of strength, spun him around, and then under him.

Jorge, slightly dazed by the quick move, bucked up in pleasure when the man abruptly took a hold of his cock and parting his thick lips, sucked it into his moist mouth. "Oh, yeah!" Jorge said loudly, his fingers clutching at the stranger's head.

Never deviating from his erotic and ferocious head bobbing, the stranger deftly spun his big body around, and soon was inverted, his large hanging piece slapping up against Jorge's face. Pleased with the sixty-nine position, Jorge happily retook the man's nine-plus inches into his open mouth.

The slight rocking motion of the ship added to the pleasure of the act, and soon both men were close to climax. The stranger suddenly stopped, and quickly shifted his body around so that he was now positioned firmly between Jorge's upraised legs. He pressed himself against Jorge's opening, teasing the writhing man beneath him.

"You want it, don't you?" he implored, pressing in again and again.

"Oh, Papi, yeah! I gotta have it," Jorge nodded, closing his eyes. His head was swimming with the last traces of the X, alcohol and sexual hunger, and he quite literally felt like he was in another dimension. Not entirely responsible for his actions, he found himself reaching down, and grabbing the hardened cock that was teasing him mercilessly. "Fuck me, Papi!" he gasped, not releasing his grip.

"Do you have a condom?" the man growled, pressing forward yet again.

"In...Ohhhh!...In my pants pocket," Jorge moaned, arching his body back.

After a quick moment of fumbling, the stranger, now sheathed, hawked up a large wad of spittle, and Jorge guided him in. Within seconds, the stranger was fully extended inside the sexy Cuban, filling him with a painful pleasure that quickly became all consuming. Jorge stroked himself as the man began to push in and out.

The stranger became a fucking machine. He plowed away, slowing down when he sensed Jorge needed a change in rhythm, then quickly speeding up again. The two men were in perfect sync, and the stranger grinned, knowing that he was giving the handsome dark man beneath him the screwing of a lifetime.

His eyes shut in the throes of ultimate passion, Jorge thought he would go out of his mind. It was the absolute hottest fuck he had ever received, and he didn't want it to end. Unfortunately, because it was the hottest fuck he'd ever gotten, he knew he'd come soon. "Oh, sweet Jesus…I'm so close…" he moaned, not wanting the pumping to end.

The stranger got Jorge's drift. He stopped his thrusting and gently slipped out. "Stand up," he ordered. "Against the railing. I want you from behind."

Jorge obediently obeyed, and rose from the chaise. He went to the railing, overlooking the stern, and gripped the wet teak with both hands. "Come on!" he urged, wiggling his hungry ass at the man approaching him.

The stranger came up tight behind and slipped back inside as a short gasp burst forth from the Cuban's lips.

Under the faint light of the moon, the two men were connected as one, and the stranger expertly slid in and out, back and forth. He let his hands roam across the great plain of Jorge's broad back, the feather light touch driving Jorge even more crazy with desire. He spread his legs, widening his stance so he could take as much of the man inside him as possible. Frenetically stroking himself, Jorge felt the sweet pressure build, and soon he simply could not contain his orgasm any more.

"I'm cooominggg…" he moaned through gritted teeth, as his huge load pumped out, wave after wave, over the deck and down into the swirling water below.

"Oh, God! Me too!" the stranger shouted, quickly pulling out, and tearing off the condom. He let loose all over Jorge's back.

Both men had to grip the railing, and catch their breath.

"Fuck!" Jorge finally managed to croak. "That was so intense!"

"No kidding," the stranger replied, nodding his head.

"Man! I needed that," Jorge began to giggle. "Damn! I don't even know who you are. He turned around and faced the stranger, looking him eye to eye with a clear head for the first time. "Fuck! It's you," he gasped, recognizing his sex partner. His broad grin clearly showed his excitement by the revelation.

"Yes, it's me." The stranger shrugged, pushing away a sweaty lock of hair from his forehead.

"I can't believe it!"

The stranger's mood began to subtly change. His red-hot passion now sated, he was forced to deal with the consequences of his rash actions. It was something he hated. *Why do I do this?* he wondered. *I have absolutely no self-control.* Sighing, he made the decision he'd had to make far too many times before. *I slipped, and now I have to make this right.*

He stared solemnly at Jorge. "I'm really sorry."

Confusion crossed Jorge's face. "What? Why?"

"Because it would have been better if you hadn't recognized me. I don't want anyone to know I screwed up."

Jorge laughed. "Papi, fuck me like that again, and I'll never tell anyone about this."

"Well, that's true."

Jorge cocked his head. "What's true?"

"You'll never tell anyone about this."

In a flash, the stranger reached down and grabbed Jorge's legs. In a burst of almost superhuman strength, he lifted and flipped Jorge up and back-wards. Jorge was too stunned to scream; he could only feebly try to grab at the railing. He got a tentative grip, but his fingers slipped off the wet teak. Finally finding his horrified voice, he began screaming as he flew over the railing and down sixty-five feet into the churning white water of the *Princess Diana*'s wake.

He was knocked unconscious by the concussion of hitting the water and was quickly pulled under. Tumbling around and around in the swirling water, he came dangerously close to getting sucked into one of the giant spinning propellers, but a freak underwater current caught his nude body, pushing it up and away from the slicing steel.

He didn't surface for a full eight minutes. When he did, he gently bobbed face down in the dark water as the *Princess Diana* sailed farther and farther away.

Six Days Earlier...

2

Barcelona Airport, Barcelona, Spain

Zack Barnes staggered off the SwissAir plane, and ambled up the sleek, covered ramp leading to the waiting area. Trying to shake the fatigue from his body, he blinked several times and stretched his head first to the right, then to the left. He pulled up on the strap of his overstuffed carryon and followed the crowd of passengers down to customs, and queued up, waiting his turn to get his passport stamped. He spent his time in line trying to figure out what time it was back in L.A.

"Did you just arrive from Zurich?" asked the handsome customs official when Zack got to the glass booth.

"Yes," Zack nodded wearily. His trip here had actually involved two flights. One 11-hour flight from L.A. to Zurich, then after a two-hour layover, a 90-minute flight from Zurich to Barcelona.

The customs man gave Zack a quick once-over, then officially stamped his passport and handed it back. "Buenos dias" he said, smiling brightly, showing white, even teeth.

"Buenos dias," Zack parroted as he turned away and headed towards baggage claim.

A few minutes later he was standing in front of an empty luggage carousel waiting for his bags to come tumbling out, and he felt yet another wave of despair overcome him. Everywhere he looked he saw the happy gay couples that had been on his flight from L.A.

Some of the men he recognized, such as the L.A. newscaster Rick Yung and his partner, the millionaire heir Kurt Farrar. They had flown to Spain up in first class, so Zack hadn't yet gotten the chance to say hello. Now he could, but he didn't feel like it. One or two other faces were familiar from the gym or parties he'd attended, but his head hurt from fatigue and loneliness.

Everyone except Zack looked so excited to be here, despite the fourteen-hour flights they had all just been on.

In fact, Zack still couldn't believe he was standing here, in the Barcelona airport, alone. He just couldn't believe it. He'd planned and saved and looked forward to this trip for a year. He'd thought it would make a great anniversary trip for him and Bayne.

Finally, it was something he could do for the two of them. He had seen a big ad for Titan's Mediterranean Gay Cruise in the glossy gay magazine *OutPride* and had been instantly entranced. He'd always wanted to take a cruise, but the thought of screaming kids and complaining AARP members had always turned him off the idea. An all-gay cruise was the perfect solution. And this one was going to be amazing.

The newly refurbished cruise ship *Princess Diana* would leave from Barcelona on a Sunday afternoon and arrive in Cannes, France the next morning. She would sail again that night and steam to Civitavecchia, the gateway to Rome. The day after that would be a day at sea while the ship crossed to Mallorca, then Ibiza. After two days on the party island, there would be a one-day stop in Florence, then back to Barcelona. All meals were taken care of in the passage price, as were the endless parties, cocktail receptions and shows. Guided tours to the various cities were also available for a small additional charge.

The 69,130-ton, 867-foot-long *Princess Diana* was the pride of the Lassiter Line, a family-held shipping company that specialized in luxury cruises throughout the world. Of the seven ships the Lassiter Line possessed, the *Princess Diana* was arguably the most beautiful. She had been named, obviously, after the striking and glamorous Princess of Wales, who curiously enough had never sailed on her.

After the Princess's divorce from Prince Charles, there had been many Lassiter Line interoffice discussions about changing the name of her namesake cruise ship. But public opinion seemed to demand that the elegant liner remain named after the most elegant woman of the day. Lassiter Lines ultimately caved to public pressure and kept the name. Then, after Diana's untimely death, the very thought of changing the name of the ship was beyond comprehension to all who sailed on her. Passengers rabidly felt that the ship was a beautiful monument to the radiant, late princess.

The striking liner had recently been put in dry dock for over a year while being refitted and improved in a hundred different ways. New furnishings, high-tech gadgets and improved passenger comforts had been the order of her refit. She was now truly a floating palace with numerous restaurants, a complete casino, two pools, a fully equipped gym, a mini putt-putt golf course and more.

A sunny, romantic cruise to European ports on one of the world's most luxurious cruise liners sounded like a great idea to Zack. Bayne had been less than thrilled, but had begrudgingly gone along with it for Zack's sake. Bayne was used to first-class travel, and he didn't think he would get that on a gay cruise.

Zack had proudly paid for the entire trip, from the business class airline tickets to the hotel reservations for the four-day pre-cruise tour in Barcelona and, in what was supposed to be a big surprise, an upgraded ocean-view cabin on the ship. He had worked many extra shifts at the restaurant in order to come up with the money, but he hadn't minded.

In addition to his part-time job of waiting tables, Zack was also a budding photographer. For real world experience, he worked freelance as a photographer's assistant, and had spent the last year working for Trevor Barbados, the top fashion photographer in L.A. Zack also created headshots for aspiring actors and actresses when he could. To earn extra cash for the trip, he'd booked himself up solid for two months prior.

He and Bayne were having some relationship problems, and this was exactly what they needed. A romantic cruise through the Mediterranean! A trip where they could just relax, take in the sights, party with their own kind, and reconnect, getting to know each other again.

Quickly tiring of Zack's cruise-related, heavy work schedule and wanting his boyfriend to be home more, Bayne had eventually tried to give Zack money, as usual, to help pay for the trip. But it became a point of pride to Zack that this was one thing Bayne Raddock wouldn't finance.

Bayne was the scion of the Raddock family of tony Newport Beach. His highly prominent family owned Raddock Communications, a consortium of newspapers, billboards, radio and TV stations and the hip magazine *Trend*, which Bayne was now editorial director of.

Bayne also was the man who, fourteen hours earlier, at the Thomas Bradley terminal at LAX, had told Zack he wasn't going on the trip after all because he had fallen in love with another man.

Zack had stood there in disbelief as the man he loved told him he'd been having an affair with his home features editor, a man named Sean Gleason, for the past eight months. He and Sean had decided they wanted to live together. Bayne was so insensitive, and so wrapped up in his own needs, that he actually told his stunned lover that Zack should be happy that he'd finally found true love.

Bayne also told Zack to go ahead and go on the trip. He knew how much Zack had been looking forward to it, so he should go, enjoy himself, and not worry about anything back home. He then quickly added that he had already put down a deposit on an affordable apartment in West Hollywood for Zack, and would have his stuff moved out of the Hancock Park house before he got back. Sean had some redecorating ideas he wanted to try, and he wanted to start as soon as possible.

Typical Bayne. He always covered every angle, leaving nothing to chance. The ultimate control freak, he had even decided where his now ex-lover was going to live.

Zack had been in such a state of shock he didn't know what to do, but some instinct told him to turn around and get on the plane. If Bayne didn't want to go, fuck him. Zack had never been to Europe, and he had worked so hard to be able to go on this trip. He'd cleared his schedule at the restaurant, school wouldn't start back up for another month, and he had nothing else to do. He could tell from Bayne's determined expression that his decision was final, and nothing Zack did or said would change it.

Somehow, Zack had seen it coming. He just hadn't been prepared for it on the very eve of what was to be their anniversary. As he stumbled back away from Bayne and away from the life he'd known for the past three years, Bayne stepped forward and shoved a thick envelope in his hand.

"It's my share of the trip. I'm sorry, little man. But the heart wants what the heart wants," Bayne shrugged before he quickly walked away. When Zack finally opened the envelope, somewhere over Canada, he saw it was filled with hundred dollar bills. Fifty of them.

Now bags were starting to arrive, and Zack waited to see his come down the chute. The passengers all pushed forward to claim their luggage. Zack took a step back, and wiping away his tears with the sleeve of his shirt, he tried to focus on the multicolored bags spinning around.

Fifty feet away two young men stood impatiently waiting for their luggage to arrive as well. Andy Caruso and Frank Thomas, both 34, were tired, cranky and ready to get to their hotel and take a shower. Preferably together.

They had been stuck at the back of the plane, in coach, for fourteen hours, and neither of them had been thrilled about it. Even the rushed blowjob Frank had given Andy in the cramped aft lavatory somewhere over the Atlantic hadn't broken the tedium of the long flight.

They were lovers from the Castro district of San Francisco, and they too were in Barcelona to take Titan's gay cruise. Andy, the taller of the pair, nudged his partner. Frank, an African-American with startling, powder blue eyes, looked up at him, and Andy nodded his head in the direction of a lone man standing forlornly aside from everyone else staring at the arriving bags.

"He's fucking hot," Andy said in a low voice.

Frank gave the lone man the once over.

What he saw was indeed hot. The man was in his late 20s, and probably about 5'11" with a solid hardbody under the loose long-sleeve tee and sweats he'd worn as travel attire. He had a sexy, boy-next-door quality about him that undoubtedly hid deeper passions. His sandy blond hair was cut in a shaggy, hip cut and it framed his square face perfectly. He had large hands and big feet, something that *always* interested Frank. His cornflower blue eyes seemed to be filled with tears, and Frank wondered what could possibly be so awful in this handsome man's life.

"Yeah, he is hot," Frank agreed. "I'd let him fuck you, no problem. I get to watch, though. Then it's my turn."

Andy grinned. "My thoughts exactly."

"Go give him our card." Frank reached into his pocket and pulled out a business card that had a color photo of the two of them and their Jack Russell, Duke, on it, along with their names and cabin information on the ship.

Andy took the card and sauntered over to the hot man. "Hey," he said, sticking out his hand.

Zack looked away from the carousel and was surprised to see a good-looking stranger speaking to him. "I'm sorry?" he asked, confused.

"I said, 'hey,'" laughed Andy easily, still extending his hand.

"Oh. Hey." Zack shook his hand.

He has a good firm grip, Andy noticed. "I'm Andy. That's my boyfriend Frank over there," he indicated Frank, who waved.

"Oh, hi. I'm Zack."

"Well, Zack, you're on the cruise, right?"

"Yeah."

"So are we. I just wanted to give you this." He handed over the business card. "Look us up on the ship. What hotel are you staying at in Barcelona?"

"Umm, the Hotel Royale."

"Us, too! We should share a cab. Whaddaya say?"

"Uh…Okay. Sure. Good idea." Zack glanced at the spinning carrousel and saw his bag. He reached over and grabbed it. Soon, all three men had their proper luggage, and they headed out into the warm, late afternoon air of Barcelona to hail a cab.

A dark blue Mercedes pulled up and the driver hopped out and began loading their bags into the trunk. They barely fit. Zack, Andy and Frank all piled into the back seat. When the driver got in himself, Andy instructed him, in halting Spanish, to take them to the Hotel Royale.

"I love the cabs in Spain," Frank declared after they had gotten underway. "A Mercedes! How cool is that?"

Back at the luggage carrousel, Kurt Farrar easily pulled the heavy bags his lover Rick had carefully packed off the moving platform and stacked them casually on a chrome baggage cart thoughtfully provided by the airport. A huge, powerfully built man, Kurt spent half his waking hours at the Gold's Gym in Hollywood working out his competition-worthy body, and the remainder of his time at his small press, Atlantis Books, a prestigious publishing house of art books. He'd only owned the publishing business for two years, but had taken to it like a duck to water.

In fact, he'd initially balked at leaving L.A. for this vacation, because he had three new books going through the publication process, and he wanted to oversee each step personally. A veteran of previous Titan Tours cruises through the Caribbean, Kurt had finally agreed to go on this cruise when Rick pointed out that there was a newly installed cyber cafe on the ship, and he could stay in constant contact with his office via e-mail.

Kurt also had felt slightly guilty about the lack of time he and Rick had been spending together lately. Their extremely busy lives left little room for romance, so Kurt and Rick made the promise to each other that this trip was going to be a golden opportunity to reconnect, focus solely each other and fuck their way across the warm seas.

"Is that everything, honey?" asked Rick. "Is my small green bag there?"

"Yup. It's here," Kurt said, lifting a black duffle to show his partner the bag underneath. "You have the passports?"

Rick patted his carryon. "Right here." He reached out and rubbed his boyfriend's back in a soothing motion. "Hey, thanks for this. I know you really didn't want to come. I just want to say thanks. It means a lot to me."

Kurt felt a rush of emotion for his partner and leaned over, tenderly giving Rick a kiss on the lips that was a silent message of love. "I'm glad you talked me into it. Honestly," he said, reaching a large hand up to gently caress his lover's face.

Rick beamed. Rick Yung was the highly respected six and eleven o'clock news anchor for the local UBC television affiliate in Los Angeles. He'd just been offered a position on the network's prime-time national newscast as a roving correspondent and weekend anchor, and he had to give an answer when he got back to L.A. after this vacation. He hadn't broached the subject with Kurt yet. Kurt's thriving business was in L.A., and Rick knew he wouldn't move. And if Kurt wouldn't move, Rick didn't want to go.

Unfortunately, Rick had been working all his professional life for the opportunity to work in network news. How could he turn his back on a dream held since childhood?

Rick sighed and reached up to brush his straight black hair out of his eyes. At 6'1", his striking Asian features contrasted sharply with his lover's blonde California look. Contrasted, but complimented. Rick was often referred to as the Asian Brad Pitt due to his undeniably good looks and his physically perfect body. He was extremely photogenic, and the ratings for his newscast were 12 full points above the competition.

Rick had always been in top shape, but since living with Kurt, he'd also developed a monster routine as his lover's workout partner. Under Kurt's tutelage, Rick's body had expanded and grown to truly jaw-dropping proportions. Men routinely, and unabashedly, propositioned the two lovers when they were out together, often asking just to be able to lie between two such glorious visions of masculinity. Those offers were always politely declined by the two built men. They were one-man men, and they had already found their one man.

Kurt gave the luggage one last look-over. "Well, I think we're set then. Let's go try and find Hayden," he said, gripping the handle of the luggage cart and wheeled it to the front of the airport.

Rick scanned the milling crowd, but didn't see Hayden Beasley anywhere, and he hoped he'd recognize him when he did. They had only met once, during Christmas last year at the Sunset Plaza home of their good friends, the actors Travis Church and Clayton Beasley. Hayden was Clay's twin brother, though the two men couldn't look more different. Fraternal twins, Clay was fair and blond, yet Hayden was dark. The one thing they did share was uncommon good looks.

Rick felt a firm hand on his shoulder, and turning around, faced Hayden, who was smiling broadly. He'd cut his hair in a shorter, different style and trimmed off a few pounds, but Rick was relieved to see he'd have recognized him anyway.

"Sorry I'm late," Hayden said in a rush, giving Rick a big hug. "I couldn't get away from work! They just kept saying, 'One more thing, Hade, one more thing.' Sorry!"

"Don't sweat it. We just got here. You look great!" Rick grinned. It was true.

At 5'10" Hayden had warm brown eyes that were flecked with green. He sported a somewhat crooked nose, a family trait, that his famous brother had had fixed years before. The slight bump didn't bother Hayden, and his nose suited his face. He had a rakish, manly air about him, despite the ruddy patches of red that sometimes covered his cheeks when he was flushed or nervous. A solid, square jaw line lead to a thick neck and broad shoulders.

He had an extremely fit body, though he was no gym rat. Instead, Hayden was a competitive tri-athlete, and he preferred to run, swim and bike for his exercise. He had a lean, tight body that looked amazing in the gray Prada suit he was wearing.

Kurt joined the group hug, giving Hayden a couple of powerful pats on the back. "So this is your city, huh? Not much to rave about so far," he dryly cracked.

"Well, let's get out of the airport. Then she'll dazzle you." Hayden had lived in Barcelona for the past three years, and was very proud of his beautiful adopted city.

The three men caught up with each other's lives as they left the building and went to the parking structure to find Hayden's car.

"…So, I told them give me the time off or I'd quit. That shook 'em up, so they gave me the time off," Hayden was saying as they walked up to his silver Land Rover Freelander. "So, I'm officially free for the next two weeks. Thank God. This cruise idea is brilliant! I really need the break."

Hayden popped open the tailgate, and he and Kurt began to load in the luggage. "Well, contrary to what your brother warned us about, you don't look like you've been wallowing in post-relationship grief," Kurt grunted as he lifted the impossibly heavy bags into the car. *What the hell had Rick packed*, he wondered. "You look like you've been out in the sun. I didn't know international banking could make a man so fit."

Hayden laughed. "Clay. I love him to death, but he worries too much about me. I bike every morning and run every night. Since the breakup, I've been really glad to have my training to focus on. It's made it easier for me."

Rick gave him another hug. "Clay told us what happened. I'm sorry."

Hayden nodded, accepting the condolences. "It's for the best. Pedro was a great guy…just not the right man for me."

"Good attitude! Besides, in four days you're going to be surrounded by thirteen hundred gay men, all of whom would be lucky to have you..."

"And, lord knows, I'm willing to be had," Hayden cut in, deadpan.

They all laughed and got into the SUV. Kurt took up almost the entire backseat.

3

Hotel Royale, Barcelona, Spain

When Zack, Andy and Frank got to the hotel, they almost had to force their mouths shut. Barcelona was so much more beautiful they any of them had imagined, that they had stared, drop-jawed, at the passing scenery until the arrived at the impressive hotel.

Ten stories tall and built in a classic Beaux-Arts/French Normandy style, complete with wrought iron balconies and stone pillars, the Hotel Royale was an architectural jewel anchoring the corner of the Passeig de Gràcia and Avenue de Valencia like the proud sentinel of a more gracious time. Just across the wide boulevard from the equally luxurious Hotel Majestic, the Hotel Royale was a favorite of pampered travelers the world over.

The Royale looked like something you would find in Paris, or at least that's what Zack thought, having never been to Paris. Barcelona was a decidedly European city, which truly surprised the dazed man. As he walked into the spacious and beautifully understated lobby, Zack was relieved he'd decided to book his accommodations there.

A a small gaggle of gay men were milling about waiting for bellhops to come take their bags up to their rooms, and Zack barely noticed all the interested stares he got. He just wanted to get into his room, shut the door, and allow himself the luxury of the good cry he'd had to keep stifled for the last fourteen hours.

He wearily handed over his credit card when it was his turn at the front desk. "Zack Barnes," he said to the harried looking clerk.

"Ah, Senior Barnes. Welcome to the Hotel Royale. I trust your flight in was pleasant?" The man officiously punched up Zack's reservation on the computer.

"Yes, it was long, but fine."

"Ah, bon. Good," the clerk said absently in accented English as he took Zack's credit card and ran it through the machine. In a few moments he was done. He handed over a small booklet that contained hotel information and two plastic keycards. "Here you are, sir. You and Mr. Raddock are in suite 415, as requested, on the fourth floor. There are two banks of elevators, one set there," he pointed behind Zack to a small alcove. "And one set directly behind this counter, through the mezzanine. Do you need a porter for your baggage?"

Zack had cringed unconsciously at the mention of Bayne. "Oh, no, I can manage, thanks. It's just these two." Zack picked up his bags, took the booklet and left the counter, quickly replaced by Andy and Frank.

"Hey, Zack, we're going to dinner in an hour. You're going to join us, right?" Andy called after him.

Zack smiled politely. "I don't know. We'll see how I feel in an hour, okay? I'm pretty beat. I may just go to sleep."

Andy, who, in his mind's eye, had already planned an erotic evening involving a steamy three-way with the handsome fellow Californian, tried not to act too disappointed. "Well, meet us down here in the lobby in an hour if you want to go. I hope you join us…"

"Okay. Thanks." Zack smiled feebly and got in a waiting elevator.

The ride to the 4th floor was surprisingly long, which normally wouldn't have been a problem except for the fact that the elevator was truly no bigger than a linen closet. Four people maximum could fit in it, and Zack got slight pangs of claustrophobia just standing in it.

Mercifully, the doors finally opened and Zack practically raced out of the closet to search for his room. He walked down the hall, passing men along the way, not noticing the appreciative glances cast his way.

He found 415 soon enough and was a little confused. Instead of an ordinary door set along the hall, like the other doors, this one had a fine mahogany frame around it. Thinking perhaps he'd made a mistake, he tried his keycard in the slot and was almost surprised when it clicked and unlocked the portal. He pushed the door open and was taken aback by what he saw.

Mouth agape, he walked into a large, luxurious entry hall with a small powder room off to the right. He walked, dazed, through the hall to enter a sumptuous sitting room complete with velvet down sofa and two extremely comfortable looking club chairs. A real antique desk anchored one wall, while a large TV and mini-fridge took up places scattered about the large room.

Through a set of open double doors was an enormous bedroom that was actually larger than the living room. Another large bathroom was found, complete with tub and shower. Sitting on the coffee table Zack noticed a chilled bottle of champagne on ice resting in a silver bucket and a card, which he tore open. The note, neatly written on heavy card stock, read:

Sr. Raddock,

The senior staff and I wish to extend to you
and your guest a warm welcome to
the Hotel Royale! Please do not hesitate to
contact me if I can be of any service.
Enjoy your stay in Barcelona...
Juan de la Torre, Manager, Hotel Royale

Well, that explained it. Bayne must have made a phone call to upgrade the room Zack had already paid for. He hadn't trusted Zack to get a good enough room. He probably gave them his credit card over the phone to pay for the difference. Typical. For some reason this really made Zack mad, and he considered going back down to the front desk and getting a regular room.

Then he got a hold of himself. Was he crazy? It was a great space, and if Bayne was stupid enough to dump him and pass this up, then screw him. He'd stay here and enjoy the suite, even if he was alone.

After absently checking out the two amazing balconies overlooking the city, Zack flopped down onto the bed and suddenly felt very alone and very far away from home. His tears came quickly and in seconds he was sobbing and hugging one of the pillows, curled up in a fetal position. He cried for over 20 minutes before exhaustion overtook him and he drifted off into a deep, dreamless sleep.

The bellman slid the keycard through the lock, and let Kurt and Rick enter first. While the two lovers wandered about the two-room suite, the bellman brought their bags in and placed them in the bedroom. He briefly explained the necessities of the suite and, after Kurt gave him a ten-euro bill, left them, quietly closing the door behind him.

"Alone at last," Rick sighed, taking Kurt in his arms and kissing him deeply.

"Eww. I need to brush my teeth!" Kurt protested, albeit weakly.

"Then go, go brush your teeth, wash up, and then come back here and fuck me. We only have 40 minutes till Hayden gets back!"

Kurt slapped his lover on the ass and trundled off to the bathroom to freshen up.

Rick wandered over to the window and looked out over the city. They were in suite 615, and since they were located at a corner of the building they had commanding views of both the Passeig de Gràcia and Avenue Valencia. Rick was entranced by the sweeping vista their suite offered. All the buildings near them had an old-world look to them that could have been found in any major European capital.

He noticed that about a half a block away, down Passeig de Gràcia, a roundly modernist building was bathed in uplighting, and a small crowd of people were standing at its base staring upwards, gazing at its beauty. Rick figured it must be one of the Gaudi buildings - spectacular, visionary buildings designed and built by the Spanish architect Antoni Gaudi over 100 years before.

He was so intently staring at the scenery, he didn't hear Kurt sneak up behind him and wrap his massive arms lovingly around him. Rick arched his head a bit, allowing Kurt to kiss his exposed neck.

"Mmm, I needed this," Rick sighed, loving the touch of his partner's tongue gliding around his throat.

"Me too, baby. Me too."

Kurt let his hands slide slowly down Rick's chest, and he stopped only when he was clutching Rick's hard-on through his chino trousers. Rick let out a slight whimper and pressed his ass back into Kurt's crotch. He was rewarded with a firm, telltale bulge that was begging to be set free.

"You know," Kurt whispered between kisses. "I was thinking…"

"Yeah?" Rick gasped, feeling waves of pleasure course through his body.

"How about I fuck you later tonight…" Kurt teased Rick's earlobe with his darting tongue.

Rick twisted around, and faced his lover. "Aww, baby, but I want…"

"Shhh…" Kurt silenced him with a tender kiss to the mouth. Then he pulled slightly away. "I'll fuck you so damn good later you won't walk for a week, if you'll fuck *me* now," he said, gazing straight into his lover's eyes. "I've been craving it all damn day."

Rick grinned. "Smooth talker."

Kurt's excitement continued to grow. He pulled Rick back into the bedroom, and the two men fell on the bed.

All his sexual life, Kurt had been a top. Not out of any particular desire or inclination, it's just the way it always worked out. Men had not been able to ignore his mammoth cock, and upon seeing it revealed for the first time, every sex partner he'd ever had instantly begged to have it slide up inside them.

Kurt had only been too happy to oblige.

Rick, too, on their first night together, had gasped in delight when presented with Kurt's massive tool, and had immediately sat on it, off and on, for over two hours.

Only after they'd firmly established a committed, monogamous relationship, did Kurt first broach the subject of wanting to experience the sensations of being fucked by his lover. He sheepishly warned Rick he'd never been screwed before, and Rick, bless his heart, had been not only been gentle and patient with him as Kurt got accustomed to this new sexual act, he'd actually turned out to be a hell of a fucker. Rick reasoned that it took an awesome bottom to know how to be a great top.

Kurt happily discovered, to his great surprise, that he loved the feel of his lover inside him. He now got almost as often as he gave.

"God, I want this!" he growled, now tugging at the buttons and zipper of Rick's khakis. Rick wiggled out of the pants and helped Kurt shed his own travel-wrinkled clothes.

Soon, completely naked, the two men ravaged each other. Kurt bent over and took Rick's throbbing cock into his mouth, while Rick began to play with Kurt's ass, teasing him, rubbing him, probing him.

Kurt twitched with desire and rolled over onto his hands and knees, shoving his meaty ass up into the air. "Oh, yeah, baby..." he moaned low, as Rick became more forceful with his explorations. "Yeaaaahhhh..."

Rick took only a minute away from his task, to dig into his carryon and whip out a small tube of lubricant. He snapped open the lid and squirted a huge glob directly onto Kurt's pulsating ass. Kurt jerked up and jubilantly cried out again.

"God, sweetheart, I love to see you want me," Rick soothed, as he sank one, then two fingers into Kurt's willing ass.

"Iwantyou...Iwantyou...Iwantyou," Kurt repeated over and over, panting as he pressed his ass back and forth, taking the slender digits deeper into his body.

Rick continued to press in and out, and soon slipped in a third finger. He adored watching his lover enjoying sex. He could see Kurt's thickly ripped arms strain and flex while supporting his hulking upper body weight, his back muscles bunching and relaxing with every movement. Kurt's massive thighs were tensed and flexed as well, the deep cuts revealing themselves with each press back.

No doubt about it, Kurt is the hottest man on the planet, marveled Rick. *And I got him!*

"Oh, please, baby, please..." Kurt begged. "You...I want you! I want your dick! Fuck me hard, now, please...I can't stand it anymore!"

Rick retrieved his fingers from Kurt's body and grabbed the lube. He covered his hard-on with the slippery fluid, and in one long, slow push, slid into his lover's eager ass. He could feel Kurt's muscles tense up at first, but as Kurt grunted in pleasure, Rick felt his lover relax and willingly admit him. Soon, the warm tightness enfolded him, and he was still for just a moment, letting his partner adjust to the invasion.

"Oh, maaannnn," Kurt groaned. "You feel so damn good!" When he was ready, he began to press forward and push back, letting Rick know he was good to go.

Rick picked up the hint and began his pumping. Slowly at first, then building in intensity. He could feel the slight shaking coming from Kurt's frantic stoking of his leaking cock. Rick then felt the constriction on his thrusting pole that signaled Kurt was about to climax.

"Ohhhh!" Kurt gasped, arching his back up. "Ohhhh! Too soon! No! Ohhhh!"

"No, let it fly, baby. Let me hear you shoot," Rick whispered hotly into Kurt's ear.

The closeness of his lover's warm breath on his overly sensitive body pushed Kurt past the point of no return.

"Ohhhh!" Kurt stretched his gigantic body upwards so that he was now kneeling, but this sudden motion caused Rick to press up behind him much closer, his steel cock thrusting up even deeper into the huge man's ass. "Ohhh!…Here I come…Ahhhhh!" Kurt yelled loud enough for everyone on the street, six floors below, to hear. "Fuuuuck!" His load was not only thick and heavy, it was tremendous in volume. The spray shot out of his engorged erection with enough force to literally hit the bedside table opposite the panting couple. It was such a huge release, that it actually hurt Kurt to have so much fluid vacate his body so quickly.

Rick was barely able to survive the clamping of Kurt's excited ass muscles on his now highly worked up cock, and he frantically tried to pull out so he could shoot his own big load. To his great amazement, Kurt reached his large hands around, and clutched hungrily at Rick's sweat-slicked ass, pulling him in deeper.

"Baby, I can't…I'm gonna shoot!" Rick protested, knowing he'd never be able to continue to fuck his partner without climaxing.

"I know," Kurt panted. "In me…I want you to come inside me."

Just hearing the words come out of Kurt's mouth caused Rick's balls to tighten. "Oh, maaannn," he whistled as he let go and pumped into his lover's ass. He'd never felt anything so tender and giving as this act, and his love for Kurt actually grew, though he didn't see how that was possible.

One block away, at the Hotel Barcelona, a different group of weary travelers had descended on the marble front desk wanting to check in. They were exhausted from their various flights. There were 20 men alone that had all come in on the same British Airways flights from New York to London to Barcelona, and several of those men were very disappointed to find their bags hadn't followed them as closely. Crankiness and flared tempers seemed to be *the* accessory in the lobby of the Hotel Barcelona.

Because over 400 men were exploring Barcelona for the pre-cruise tours, they were spread out over several hotels throughout the city. The Hotel Barcelona was not quite as grand as the Hotel Royale, but still luxurious, and would be the sight, the next night, for the pre-cruise welcoming party.

One by one, the tired men checked in and received the keys to their rooms. One man in particular caused quite a stir among the others.

He was only about 5' 6" with a decent gym body that was inappropriately dressed in a snug Versace dress shirt that was unbuttoned one button too many, too tight, low-rise jeans, and Reef flip-flops. He was 39 and had already started to go gray, a fact he tried to minimize by the close crop haircut he now sported. He was aware of the low whispering that followed him now wherever he went. In fact, he was disappointed when he didn't hear it.

"That's Geoff Corbin!" an excited twink whispered to an unimpressed man next to him as Geoff passed them on his way to the counter.

He sauntered up to the front desk and presented his new platinum American Express card. "Hi. Geoff Corbin checking in," he announced to the front desk man.

"Excuse me?" a voice came from behind.

Geoff turned around and saw an unbelievably gorgeous Latin man standing right behind him. The guy was truly stunning. Geoff quickly took in the man's amazing green eyes, his expertly cut hair, and after a speedy glance downward, his full and promising crotch.

"Yes?" Geoff said, trying to keep his voice even in the face of such beauty. He began to feel slightly awkward, knowing he wasn't in the same league as this man.

"You're Geoff Corbin, aren't you? You won *Race Around the World 5*, didn't you?"

Geoff nodded, his confidence returning. "Yes. Did you watch?"

The hot guy smiled the broadest smile Geoff had ever seen. "Oh, Papi!

Every week! It's, like, my favorite show! I knew you'd win! You made good alliances and lied the best. Then when that punta Tasha missed her train, I knew you were safe."

"Yeah, she was a bitch," Geoff nodded.

"Everyone said you were an asshole, but I figured you just played the game better than the rest," Hot Guy shrugged. "You did what you had to do to win."

Geoff had heard much worse before. "What's your name?"

"Jorge. Jorge Camarillo." Jorge held out his hand.

Geoff took it and the two men shook.

"I have to tell you, it made me so proud to see a gay man win the million bucks. I screamed with joy," Jorge enthused, not letting Geoff's hand go.

The Tasha that Jorge had spoken of was Tasha Pearl, a golf pro from Plano, Texas who had gone into the final two with Geoff after they both had spent 45 days running their asses off in an around-the-world race. The television program *Race Around the World 5* had a simple premise. Fourteen total strangers raced to find hidden clues in a global scavenger hunt, with the last participant who arrived at each episode's final destination point being eliminated. The hugely popular program was one of the highest rated shows on the UBC network.

A smash hit right out of the box from the very first episode of the first season, *Race Around the World* had become a Monday night institution, watched by millions of armchair travelers. Geoff had been selected along with 13 others to participate in the fifth season, now generally thought of as the best edition of *RAW*.

Geoff had ultimately won the game due to a sneaky bit of business when he told Tasha that the train for Zurich left an hour after it really did. Tasha stupidly believed him and missed it, giving Geoff the edge in time, and ultimately, the win, the million bucks, and a brand new Chevy TrailBlazer.

"I guess I'm just a big, big fan of yours. Say, how hard was it to get by on no sleep? Did you lose weight?" Jorge said.

"Well, thanks for the kind words, Jorge. Yeah, I lost thirteen pounds, half of which I've put back on. Dammit," Geoff smiled. "You going on the cruise, too?"

"Yeah." Jorge finally let go of Geoff's hand, and shoved his hands into his front pockets, the act pulling down his loose cutoff jeans so low that Geoff could see the beginning of his trimmed pubic hair.

Geoff thought he would faint. "Well, I'm glad," he managed to utter, trying not to look down at the shaved patch of dark hair.

Jorge, aware of the effect he was having on the television person-ality, sunk his hands deeper into his pockets, which popped open the top button on the ragged shorts, pulling them down even lower. He pushed his weight forward on his feet, causing his hips to jut out a bit. He enjoyed seeing Geoff squirm, trying not to glance down, but doing it anyway.

"So, what do you do, Jorge?" Geoff asked, sneaking another peek. Jesus! He could actually see Jorge's pretty cock through the opening in the loose jeans top. He gulped. He couldn't be sure, but it looked like Jorge was aroused!

"I'm a model. You ever see the packages for Hombre underwear?" Jorge flashed another dazzling grin, as Geoff nodded. "Well, that's my ass."

Geoff thought he'd died and gone to heaven. He'd whacked off to that packaging more than once. And here was the actual ass. Live. In person!

"David Morgan shot it. He's the best body photographer in the business." Jorge turned slightly, pushing out his beautiful bubble butt into a startlingly sexy pose. "He really caught the perfect angle to make my ass look totally Hombre worthy, don't you think?"

Staring at Jorge's hard ass, a thousand erotic images flooding through his mind, Geoff found he had no words.

"Mr. Corbin? Sir? Here are your room keys," the front desk clerk said, drawing Geoff's attention away.

After Geoff fumbled about, signing the receipts, and getting his keys, he felt a light pressure on his shoulder.

Jorge.

"They gave you two keys," the younger man noted.

"Yes. Silly, since I'm traveling alone," Geoff responded holding them both up.

Jorge slowly reached over and took one of the keys. "I'll need this for later, won't I?" He smiled slyly at Geoff.

Geoff's heart skipped a beat. "Room 734," he managed to croak out.

Jorge leaned in, close to Geoff's ear. "I'll be up in about an hour, Papi. I'll let you get a real look at my dick. And more, I hope." He then stuck his tongue into Geoff's ear and was gone.

Geoff practically floated to the elevators. As he passed a group of five men waiting their turn to check in, he heard the whispering.

"Look! It's Geoff Corbin!"

"Isn't that the guy who won the million bucks on *Race Around the World?*"

"Ugh! He was such a lying asshole! I hated him!"

"I think he's cute."

"Man, I'm so gonna bag him before this trip is over!"

Geoff smiled as the elevator doors shut.

4

Lobby of the Hotel Royale, Barcelona, Spain

Jebb Miller walked into the expansive lobby of the elegant hotel and smiled. Everywhere he looked he saw happy gay men. They were all dressed and going out to dinners all over town. Most of them didn't know who he was, but they were only here because of him.

Jebb was president and CEO of Titan Tours, the travel company that organized gay events all over the globe. He had set up cruises through the Panama Canal, the Caribbean, Hawaii and even Alaska. Big circuit events in Atlanta and Las Vegas. All-gay biking tours through the French countryside. He was the best at this sort of event, and he knew it.

This particular cruise through the Mediterranean was his biggest challenge yet. It was by far his largest gay event, and the endless list of details that had needed his attention was staggering. He had just flown into Barcelona via London, and thankfully his baggage actually arrived when he did.

He briskly walked through the crowded hotel lobby, nodding at a guest here and there, and went directly to the anteroom of the ballroom where the Titan Tours help desk was set up. He noticed the quick, interested glances the men gave him and smiled.

Jebb was a good-looking man, single and just shy of 45, but with the energy and enthusiasm of a man 20 years younger. He knew his looks helped him in his line of work, and therefore he took excellent care of himself. His personal trainer back in L.A. often bragged to his other clients that Jebb never complained, and was always willing to do an extra set if it got him the results he desired. It was simply the way Jebb went through life. He always went the extra mile.

He had close-cropped hair and sparkling blue-green eyes that drew people in when he spoke. He had a commanding presence and was a natural born salesman. A devotee of pilates and religious about his daily workouts, no matter where in the world he was, Jebb still had the body of the college athlete he'd been. In fact, it had taken 12 years for his NAACA record in shot putting to be broken.

If there was only one disappointing facet to Jebb's life now, it was the fact that he hadn't yet met the man of his dreams. He rarely dated because his schedule was so insane that most men got tired of waiting for him to either be back in town, or to leave the office. It saddened Jebb, because he knew he had a lot to offer, but he didn't let it get him down. He reasoned it would happen when it was supposed to.

Entering the anteroom, Jebb was relieved to see that Nick Stone was manning the help desk. Nick had been with Titan Tours for over seven years, even through the tough years when Jebb didn't know if he could meet his payroll. Nick was highly competent and was second only to Jebb in decision-making. In fact, Nick had come up with Titan's tag line "We Play HARD," which was used liberally in all the promotional materials.

"Hey, Nick," Jebb called out upon entering the large, almost vacant room.

"Hey, boss man!" Nick answered back, looking up from a laptop computer screen. Nick, 34, had the quirky good looks of a lazy surfer dude. He had choppy, heavily streaked blonde hair with dark roots that he gelled up into a greasy tumbleweed. When he was not working, he was usually in the water on his cherished vintage longboard near his ramshackle beachfront apartment in Manhattan Beach, California. Tall, lean and lanky, he was thin almost to the point of being skinny, but he was uncommonly strong, and never lacked for male companionship.

Nick was sitting at a formal desk that had been placed in the center of the room, the computer laptop open and humming in front of him. Another tall, trim young man was with him, going over some detail of his reservation. Several large posters were placed on easels around them advertising the various extra tours Titan guests could take if they choose.

Nick got to his feet and went to Jebb. Genuinely happy to see his employer, he gave his boss a big hug. "How was your flight?"

"Good, good. No delays. Thank God." Jebb went to the desk and looked through the sign-up sheets.

"Jebb, this is Rhett Mitchell," Nick said, introducing the two men. "Rhett's bags didn't make his flight, and the airline says they may not get here until after we sail."

"Oh, no, Rhett. I'm sorry to hear that," Jebb said, shaking the man's hand.

"Well, I have my necessities in my carryon, so at least I can brush my teeth," Rhett said in a thick southern accent.

"If your bag doesn't get to the hotel in time for departure, we'll make arraignments to have it sent to Cannes, our first port. Make sure Nick has all your cabin information, okay?"

"I already have it," Nick piped up.

"Okay, then. I surely do hope it turns up. I packed my lucky charm in it, and I'd sure hate to lose that!" Rhett sighed. "Well, I guess this just gives me an excuse to go buy some new duds, huh?" he said, trying to look on the bright side. He turned around to leave. "Bye, y'all. Nice to meet you. I'm really lookin' forward to this cruise!"

"Bye, Rhett," Nick and Jebb said in unison.

Just as Rhett started to leave, another guy entered the room. As he passed Rhett, the new man gave him a lingering glance, but didn't make eye contact. The new guy was tall, easily 6'2", probably early to mid-forties, and had broad shoulders that strained at the tight pale yellow Lacoste alligator shirt he was wearing. He had long, beefy legs that surely led up to an awesome ass, but since he was walking towards Jebb and Nick, neither man could tell for sure. He walked with the studied grace of an athlete, an unabashedly masculine athlete. But he also seemed to be under tight control, like he hadn't ever really completely relaxed. He had dark, neatly combed hair, a squareish, but very handsome face, and piercing dark eyes. Altogether, one hot package.

There was something else about him, Jebb realized. Something about this man's attitude. Jebb couldn't put his finger on it, but there was a slightly menacing air about him. A rough, menacing air that let everyone know this man could take care of himself in a barroom brawl. It was all undeniably sexy.

Just Jebb's type.

He couldn't help himself. His eyes dropped immediately to the new man's very full crotch, and he breathed in deeply as he imagined the delights hidden by the tight denim.

"Is this the info desk?" the man asked, his voice deep and rich. "The guy at the front desk told me to come here." His dark eyes seemed to bore into Jebb like lasers.

"Uh, yes…Yes, this is the Titan info desk," Jebb managed to say. *Jesus! He is the hottest man I have ever seen*, he thought. *How does my hair look right now?*

The man came closer. He held out his Titan packet. His hands were large, yet surprisingly supple. "I didn't get any luggage tags for the ship in my packet, here." He again looked Jebb square in the eye, his striking face impassive.

"Well, let's get you some!" Nick jumped in. "What's your name?"

"Smith. Dan Smith."

Nick smiled broadly. He'd seen the instant attraction Jebb was feeling for Dan, and he wanted to help his boss out. He loved Jebb like a brother, and he felt Jebb deserved to get laid, just like any other Titan guest. "Mmmm. Well, Smith, Dan Smith," he said, "Let's see what cabin you have." He consulted his clipboard.

"I hope your flight was good," Jebb offered, trying to start up a conversation.

"Who are you?" Dan asked brusquely.

"I'm Jebb Miller. President of Titan Tours." Jebb held out his hand and gave Dan his best smile.

Dan frowned slightly, hesitated, then jutted out his hand. Jebb was surprised by the immense strength in his handshake.

"Well, here you are. Ohh! Diamond Deck, single cabin." Nick looked up at Dan, impressed that he spent so much money for his own private stateroom. "Cabin 7267. And that means you get an orange luggage tag." Nick reached into a large folder and pulled out three orange Lassiter Line tags. "So, Dan. Single, huh?"

Dan's eyes narrowed a hair. "Yeah."

"Well, you're just steps away from Jebb's cabin. So, if you have any questions, don't hesitate to ask him."

Jebb, picking up the cue, nodded. "Absolutely. I'm always available."

"Uh, great," Dan said gruffly. He took the tags from Nick, and without another word, walked away.

"Wow," Nick sighed. "That man is wound tighter than a watch."

Jebb nodded slowly. "Yeah, but look at that ass!"

"Down, boy, down," Nick joshed. "Well, at least he got his luggage, right?"

Jebb pulled his mind away from the sexual thoughts he was having and focused on his duties. "Right. I hate when the luggage doesn't show up," he said. "Make sure Rhett Mitchell gets his bags, okay?"

"I will."

"So," Jebb said, bracing himself. "Any other problems? How we doing?"

"Okay so far. Only a few snags. Does the name Raymond Daggatt ring any bells? No? He says he sent a check in to cover a requested upgrade on the ship, but I don't have record of it here. She threw such a bitch fit, you have no idea." Nick rolled his eyes. "He's a mean girl, and he's looking for you."

"Thanks for the warning." Jebb grinned. "Are there any upgrades available?" He picked up a paper-laden clipboard and searched through the names. Everything looked to be in order, he was pleased to note.

"A few, but you have to approve those. I can't."

"Give the man his upgrade. What else?"

"The tour operator in Cannes called and said he doesn't know if he has enough drivers to cover the number of buses we'll need. He said he'd work on it."

"He'd work on it?" Jebb arched his eyebrows. "I sent that guy a hefty deposit check over three months ago. You call him back and tell him if he doesn't have one driver per bus as stipulated in our signed contract, he forfeits the remainder of his fee." Jebb dropped the clipboard. "He'll dig up the drivers."

Nick nodded, typing in a note on the laptop. "You got it."

"Where's the rest of the crew?" Jebb looked over the display, and straightened some errant papers.

"Willy's at dinner and will be back in 20 minutes. Clive and Baldwin are unpacking their stuff and said if you want to join them for dinner to call them in their room. They're in 612…" Nick then continued to rattle off the various positions of the other Titan staff members who were in Barcelona. Jebb had handpicked his staff for this cruise, and each one of the handsome men he had chosen was both friendly and hardworking.

"I can't have dinner with Clive and Baldwin," Jebb said. "I'm taking Garrett Gardner out tonight."

Garrett Gardner was an openly gay writer, comic and venerable showbiz institution. A talk show circuit veteran and a former regular on the syndicated game show *Hollywood Crosswords*, where he had become famous for his quick-witted quips, Garrett had recently ended a one-year run as Miss Hanagan in the smash hit Broadway revival of *Annie*. His hilarious double-entendre filled, over-the-top, drag performance as the crusty orphanage manager had earned him rave reviews and a Tony award as Best Actor in a Musical.

Garrett was also a beloved and often outspoken member of the gay community. His bi-weekly column in *OutPride* magazine was considered a bible for modern queer living and was on the "must read" list of those-in-the-know. Renowned for his willingness to lend his fame and name to countless AIDS charities, Garrett had also appeared at, or even MC'd, too many fundraisers to count. He had earned the respect and admiration of gays, lesbians and transgenders the world over for his selfless altruism. He was always ready with a great sound bite or quote, and stars knew they could count on him to punch up a speech. The portly comic had also script-doctored more than one Oscar-nominated screenplay, as well as writing the award telecast itself 12 years in a row.

Garrett was going to perform his rarely seen standup routine onboard the ship, and Jebb was thrilled to have booked him for this cruise. He was going to go out of his way to treat Garrett right, as Jebb wanted him to perform on other cruises in the future.

"Oh!" Nick slapped his forehead. "I can't believe I almost forgot. Rex Lassiter is here! He was asking for you earlier, and he didn't look happy."

"Rex Lassiter? What the hell is he doing here?" Jebb was dumbstruck.

Rex Lassiter was the persnickety president of the family owned Lassiter Line, the owners of the *Princess Diana*, the ship they were sailing on in four days.

"I don't know, but you're about to find out," Nick said, pointing behind Jebb. "Here he comes."

Jebb turned around and saw Rex. The president of the Lassiter Line was a pompous man who moved with forced confidence. He was aware of his vaulted position in life, and he reveled in it. Never seen without his thick glasses, his face might have been handsome if it didn't always seem to be pinched in consternation. Even when he smiled, which was rare, it came across like an alien expression on his face, as if the facial muscles just under the tight skin were struggling to adapt to new use.

Rex's company, the Lassiter Line, had been founded by his great-great-great-great grandfather Cyrus Lassiter in 1846 with one leaky ship doing the hazardous transatlantic circuit. One ship led to two, two lead to five, five lead to nine. The Lassiter family held on to the company with an iron fist. Several takeover bids had been unsuccessfully attempted as the company grew through the years. The Lassiter Line became known for punctuality, exceptional service and safety. Certain members of leading European royal families and world famous film stars would either sail on the grand, beautiful old Lassiter liners, the *Queen Victoria* or the *Princess Eugenia*, or not sail at all.

As for safety, it was proudly pointed out, immediately following the tragic Titanic sinking, that all Lassiter Line ships had always carried a full company of lifeboats, with seating for all aboard.

The onset of air travel did severe damage to the black ink of the Lassiter Line, as it did to every other passenger ship company. As the other major transatlantic carriers White Star and Cunard were forced to merge to avoid bankruptcy, other, lesser known lines went under. The Lassiter Line continued to ply the seas, shrewdly turning to cruising travel and eventually completely phasing out its once-heralded transatlantic service.

But other cruise ship lines had risen up through the ranks, and competition for cruising dollars was intensely fierce. Newer, better ships had to be built with bigger, better features and attractions, while older cruise liners had to either be refurbished, sold, or scrap-heaped. The fact that the *Princess Diana*, a relatively young sixteen-year-old ship, had just finished a complete refit and redecoration eight months before was a clear example of how resolute the Lassiter Line was to compete for cruising dollars.

Rex Lassiter was determined to make the Lassiter Line the premiere cruise line in the world. It was his tireless goal, and all his energy was spent on achieving it. To that extent, he had two brand new ships, light years ahead of the current cruising competition in style, comfort and technology, being constructed in the shipyards of Germany.

Whatever pressures he was under at the company's London home office, Rex tried to keep himself under strict control. Constantly in the European society pages, Rex and his Italian-born wife led a glamorous life, jetting around on their private plane to all the grand parties. Rex was tall and had a large body, but was never seen in less-than-complete business attire. Wags that had met the stiff man joked that he probably wore his custom-fitted Turnbill & Asser suits to bed.

As he huffed and puffed his way into the Titan lobby, Jebb noticed that Rex's handmade Italian loafers were shined to within an inch of their lives, and his tie was perfectly knotted. Rex's brown hair was severely parted on the side and slicked back, and the large black glasses he always wore shielded eyes that seemed to miss nothing.

As Nick had predicted, he indeed did not look happy.

"Are you Jebb Miller?" Rex said haughtily as he walked up to Jebb and Nick, no trace of a European accent detectable in his voice. A youth spent in America going to various prestigious schools there, including Yale, with graduate work at Harvard, had erased his childhood's dulcet English tones.

"I am. You must be Rex Lassiter. Hello, it's nice to meet you." Jebb stuck out his hand, but the stuffy man let it hang there. Instead, Rex crossed his arms across his chest and stared at Jebb, anger in his eyes.

"Sir, I cannot believe I am in this dreadful position! If I had been in the office when your charter bid came through, trust me, your tawdry little group would not set foot on my *Princess Diana*."

Jebb started to feel his blood boil, but he held his tongue. He'd heard what an ass Rex was, and now he was discovering the rumors had been true. "So what exactly is your problem, Mr. Lassiter?" he said.

"My problem? Let me tell you what my problem is!" Rex looked nervously around to see if he could be overheard by anyone else. "Thirteen hundred...*homosexuals*," he whispered the word "homosexual" like it was a cursed and dirty word, "doing God knows what on my beautiful ship for one thing! We are a family company! We don't condone this sort of thing! I wouldn't be surprised if we get bomb threats! Believe me, I fired the booking director who accepted your charter," Rex spat out his holier-than-thou attitude, reeking of hatred. "If that wanker hadn't already deposited your check, I would have canceled this distasteful trip immediately!"

Jebb knew Rex was aware that in the travel industry, once a business check was deposited for a service, it was then considered a valid contract and could not be terminated without legal repercussions. "Again, I ask, what is your problem?" Jebb knew his tone was getting nasty, and he took a deep breath to try and calm himself.

"I really just wanted to inform you that I, myself, will be traveling on this cruise. I'll be in the reserved Lassiter suite on board. Both my wife and I will be on this trip, and we will be keeping a sharp eye peeled on your...guests." He said the last word as if he had smelled something bad. "If we see anything, anything, untoward happening on my ship, anything that breaks the contract you signed, then I'll shut you down, and kick every last one of you off my ship. Am I being perfectly clear?" He glared at Jebb, defying him to challenge his dictate.

"Mr. Lassiter," Jebb began slowly. "Not only have I paid for this charter in full, in advance, I have also gotten signed releases from each and every guest absolving Titan Tours of any responsibility regarding their personal behavior. So, according to my lawyer's interpretation of our contract, my guests can butt fuck each other on the Sun Deck in broad daylight if they choose, and as long as they don't impede the safe operation of the *Princess Diana*, there's not a damn thing you can do about it." He leaned in close to Rex, whose face was frozen in shocked horror. "And if you try, even think about trying, to halt my charter, I'll slap you with a lawsuit so huge, you'll need a steam shovel to dig your homophobic ass out. I think you recall the bad press that island in the Caribbean got when they refused us entry? Their tourism rates dropped by fifty percent after that. I don't think you want that kind of publicity for the Lassiter Line, do you?"

Rex turned red, then purple with rage.

"Besides," Jebb continued, perversely enjoying dressing down the pretentious man. "I understand the Lassiter Line is in some financial trouble right now. Two of your new ships under construction are way behind schedule, and the banks are starting to circle."

Rex, flabbergasted, could only sputter, "How...How do you know that?"

"The travel industry is very small, Mr. Lassiter. I know that you're close to receivership. You're in dire need of capital. You can't afford the long, drawn out lawsuit and bad publicity I will cause you if you shut us down. Do I make myself clear?"

Rex barely managed to contain his fury. "Mr. Miller, I'll be watching you. Don't you think I won't!" He spun around on his heels and stormed out of the room.

"Wow," Nick observed dryly. "That could have gone better."

Jebb glared at his assistant, and then broke out into gales of laughter. "Well," he said between giggles, "I hate pompous, asshole Eurotrash like that. He hates gays, and the fact that we're taking over his ship must just kill him. Good."

"Well, watch out for him. His cabin is next door to yours."

"Oh, Christ," Jebb, moaned, his laughter suddenly halted.

"Yeah," Nick smirked. "Not so funny now, huh?"

Zack woke up and rolled over trying to focus on the clock. He'd been asleep for over four hours, and was still dressed in his clothes from the plane. He did a quick calculation in his head and realized he hadn't had a shower in over 24 hours, but he didn't get up. He closed his eyes again and allowed himself to drift back off to sleep.

He was still hugging the pillow.

Hayden, Kurt and Rick were seated at a table at the smart restaurant Bathsheba, located in the old town part of Barcelona. The hip eatery was fast gaining a reputation as an excellent restaurant with astounding personal service. The decor was minimalist, with a splash of red thrown in here and there, punching up the basically black and white space.

Hayden had suggested they all have the tasting menu, which at ninety euros apiece was pricey, but once the food started arriving, turned out to be worth it. Kurt had ordered a compelling Spanish red wine that ended up being superb.

"I can't believe the wine prices here," he said, recalling the unbelievably low prices in the wine menu.

"One of the many secrets of Europe. Wine here is cheap, cheap, cheap. A terrific bottle shouldn't cost you more than 20 euros. In the States you can't touch a good bottle for under fifty bucks," Hayden said, sipping from his goblet. He had changed into a sleek pair of black pants that fit him perfectly and a tight black knit shirt that was open at the collar.

Rick couldn't help but notice Hayden's tasty-looking squared-off pecs that were barely covered by the thin fabric. He looked back at Kurt when he felt Kurt's warm hand land gently on his thigh under the table and caress him. Rick was dressed in a pair of white jeans with a gray, loose shirt that allowed him to breathe comfortably. Since Rick had to wear a coat and tie all day long at work, when he was off-camera he liked to wear loose and comfortable clothing.

Kurt, in gray flat-front pants and a white tee that threatened to burst from the strain of containing his muscular torso, was telling Hayden about the publishing house he owned.

"Well," Hayden said, "I think it's great that you've made a success of it. I remember Clay saying that you weren't sure about it when you took it over."

Kurt nodded. "That's true. I didn't work before this. Didn't have to." This was an understatement. As one of *the* Farrars of Los Angeles, Kurt's family had money. Real money. Kurt was a trust fund baby of the highest order. His parents' messy divorce a few years back had dropped the publishing company in his lap.

His father had originally bought Atlantis Books for Kurt, hoping his proudly out gay son would take it over and quit his wild, circuit boy ways. Kurt had refused, not wanting to have anything to do with a gift from his estranged father. It wasn't until the company had been awarded to Kurt's mother in her divorce settlement that Kurt agreed to a trial run as president. Much to his surprise, he turned out to be a great editor, and two of his books had topped the coffee table book best-seller lists. "I love it now though," he added, before tasting his lobster bisque.

"That's true," Rick nodded. "I almost never see him anymore. He's always at the office. Just to get him to take this trip was a major negotiation," he chided his partner lovingly.

"But so worth it," Kurt smiled, shifting in his seat a bit. His ass hurt just a tad, but he couldn't wait to have Rick fuck him again.

"So tell us about your job. Sounds exciting," Rick said, turning the attention to Hayden.

Hayden shrugged. "It's fine. You know, when I took the position, I thought 'international banking' sounded so glamorous. It's not. I sit at my desk staring at a computer screen for most of the day. I could do this in Des Moines."

"A little homesick for the old U.S. of A.?" Kurt asked.

"I don't know if it's that or just that I'm lonely. Ever since I split up with Pedro, I've just felt a little at loose odds, you know?"

Kurt nodded. "I know exactly what you mean. Before I met Rick I was so unhappy. I had everything, you know? But I had nothing. Now? Well, hell, I just couldn't be happier." He patted Rick's thigh under the table and gazed at him with total devotion.

"Aww, honey! That's so sweet," Rick blushed, thrilled to hear his lover say the words. He was even more thrilled to feel Kurt's hand crawl up his thigh and come to a rest in his crotch, gently groping him.

"Well, one day, I'll have that again," Hayden smiled.

"Damn skippy!" Kurt said.

"So where is your stateroom on the ship?" Hayden asked.

"We're in cabin 7551 on the Diamond Deck. We have a royal suite," Rick said proudly.

"Well, I'm down in the bottom of the boat with the other steerage riffraff," Hayden joked. "Cabin 2076. B Deck. I'm so far down that my deck doesn't even have a name, just a letter."

"But it's a very nice letter," Kurt said.

"It was all I could get on such sort notice. When Clay called and told me that y'all were coming over to do this cruise, I thought, fuck it. Why not? I need to put myself out there again. So I signed up, too."

"We're so glad that you did," Rick smiled. "Means we know at least one other person on the ship."

"Well, a friend of mine is coming as well," Kurt said to Rick. "Bayne Raddock? Remember? You met him at the Equal Rights Campaign gala dinner last year?"

"Oh, right." Rick's tight smile indicated his private thoughts about Bayne Raddock.

Kurt turned back to Hayden. "Bayne is really wealthy." He noticed the glint of a suppressed smile come to both Rick and Hayden's faces. "Okay, okay. I know what you're thinking. I'm wealthy too, but Bayne is really rich. He could buy and sell me five times over."

Hayden and Rick had to laugh.

It was no secret that Kurt Farrar was one of L.A.'s richest gays, due to the mega holdings that his father's company had acquired over the years. Kurt's personal wealth was well into the high eight digits.

"*Anyway*," Kurt continued, deciding to overlook the snickers of his dinner companions, "he and his boyfriend are coming as well. You'll like them. I think his boyfriend's name is Zeke."

"It's Zack," Rick corrected him. "And he's much nicer than Bayne, who's a pompous ass if you ask me."

"Well, they have the cabin opposite us, so be nice. Bayne finagled an upgrade."

"Oh, joy," Rick said.

"Do you know who your cabin mate is?" Kurt asked Hayden.

"No. I just hope his name isn't Jack Dawson. I wanted to get a single, but they were sold out."

"I'm sure it'll be fine," Rick said. "And if it doesn't work out, you can always crash with us. We have two bedrooms."

"Good to know," winked Hayden.

Dan Smith was restless. Nude, he paced around his rather nice room in the Hotel Barcelona, puffing on his third cigarette. He wanted to quit, but the timing was off. Smoking helped quell the other destructive urges he felt, so it was best for everyone if he went ahead and smoked.

Sighing, he looked around the spacious room. He'd stayed at this hotel before, and liked it. It was central to town, luxurious, and full of hot men for the next few days. What was not to like?

He happened to pass by a large mirror hanging over the dresser and stopped cold. His hair was mussed up, and the fact that he'd barely slept in the past 36 hours was clearly written on his face.

"I don't think Jebb Miller would be much interested if he saw me now," he snickered to himself. He had felt the sexual interest coming off the handsome president of Titan Tours, and that might be worth investigating later on.

Realizing he was hungry, Dan quickly began to throw on some clothes. He wanted to go out and find something to eat. Maybe later on he'd go up to the rooftop pool and swim a few laps. Working out always helped control his irrational urges and allowed him to think clearer and act more normally. Dan was well aware that he needed to be as sharp as a tack for the next ten days.

He didn't want to make any more mistakes.

In room 714 of the Hotel Barcelona, Geoff and Jorge lay on top of the tangled sheets, trying to regain normal breathing. Both men had just climaxed mightily, and now Geoff wondered how long it would be before Jorge started asking the questions.

He didn't have to wait long.

"So, how'd you get picked for *Race?*" Jorge asked, leaning up on one arm and staring at the sweaty million-dollar winner.

Geoff stifled his need to laugh. This always happened. Some hot guy would go to bed with him, willingly, and afterwards pump him for info on how to get on the show.

What the hell, Geoff realized. *You have to pay the band sometime*. The awesome blowjob he'd just gotten from Jorge more than made up for a little *RAW* chitchat.

"Well, it was tough," he finally said, reaching over to the nightstand and pulling out a Marlboro. He lit it up and was about to settle back, when Jorge indicated he'd like one too. He handed the stud a cigarette, and after Jorge put it in his mouth, he leaned over and lit it from the burning end of Geoff's. "I sent in a tape like everyone else, and then they called me in for an interview. I didn't think I had a snowball's chance in hell, but Joan Thomas, she's the producer, she thought I'd be controversial, and next thing I knew, I was on a plane to Istanbul."

"Was it as hard as it seemed? Or did they sneak you money off-camera?"

"No way! That was one of the new rules Joan came up with for our season. No money. We had to beg, borrow or steal every dime we needed, except for the airfares. Let me tell you, you haven't lived until you've tried begging in India. I think we had it worse than any other cast. I know we had it worse than the *Race Around the World 4* cast." Geoff exhaled a thick cloud of smoke and idly watched it float up and vanish.

"Wow," Jorge sighed, rolling back on his back and staring at the ceiling. "I want to be on *Race Around the World*. I send in an audition tape for every season, but they never call me."

"Well, they get a lot of tapes. Don't take it personally."

"Maybe you could put in a good word?" Jorge leaned over and let his hand trail down Geoff's belly, until it stopped at his groin. He clamped onto Geoff's flaccid penis and began squeezing.

"Oh, I don't think I can again so soon…"

"Sure you can. You can do anything you want…" Jorge put his cigarette in the bedside ashtray, then rolled over and moved his flawless body down, stopping only when his head was poised right over Geoff's cock. "You can get hard, you can even come again…and you can make a phone call to your producer and tell her about me…" Jorge's mouth was now just millimeters away from the head of Geoff's now growing erection. He looked at Geoff with wide, innocent eyes and licked his beautiful, pouty lips.

Geoff had to see Jorge take him in his perfect mouth again. The man was so damn good-looking!

"I could, huh?" he said, beginning to squirm in anticipation.

Jorge nodded, and then went slowly down on Geoff's piece once, then came back up. "Mmmm, think how hot I'd look on that show. I'm perfect for it! They haven't had a sexy Cuban on yet. And I hear they're going to start in New Zealand next season..." He bobbed down on Geoff once more. "...I've always wanted to see New Zealand..."

Geoff, groaning loudly, made a quick mental decision. He couldn't help Jorge get on *Race Around the World 6*. Those kinds of decisions were made in the *RAW* production offices in Los Angeles, and the last person Joan Thomas was going to listen to was a former cast member. Particularly one who Joan had never gotten along with.

But Jorge didn't have to know that.

"Well...Oh, yeah! Just like that...that's so good! Maybe I could see what I could do for you. Ohhhh! Don't stop that!"

5

Passeig de Gràcia, Barcelona, Spain

Rhett Mitchell wandered down the mostly empty boulevard and casually glanced into the darkened shop windows he passed. He was surprised by the amount of high-end retail shops there were. Chanel, Burberry, and Coach all had shops along this wide boulevard, though they were, of course, closed now. Rhett had never seen so many luxurious goods for sale in one place before. It was almost overwhelming to his country boy eyes.

Coming to a stop, he was slightly surprised to find himself back in front of his hotel. Wandering into the lobby of the elegant palace, he took his sweet time getting to the elevator bank. His Titan selected roommate, a nice enough fellow from Chicago named Steve, was up in their room screwing the brains out of some guy he'd met at the hotel bar earlier that evening. Rhett thought Steve's trick was an underwear model from Miami, but he couldn't be sure.

Rhett himself was from Gatlinburg, Tennessee, and he was beside himself with glee at being in Spain. Hell, he'd never been out of Tennessee before this!

He was 26 years old, and at 6', he was quiet and unassuming. He'd spent a lifetime in swimming pools becoming a state-ranked amateur swimmer, but having grown tired of it, he was now a competitive marathoner. Rhett had the long, lean frame of a distance runner. His coppery hair was bleached almost golden from his daily afternoon runs through Gatlinburg, and his face was as tanned as a Florida retiree's. He worked at a cell phone retailer and had saved up for six months to take this trip.

Just really coming to terms with the fact that he was gay, Rhett had recently ended a two-year engagement to his father's boss's daughter, a rather plain girl named Brenda Jean. He hadn't had very much homosexual experience, basically only a few quick drunken blowjobs in various men's rooms, and he thought a gay cruise would be a great way to meet nice men, and, hopefully, finally get properly laid.

For Rhett, getting laid in Gatlinburg was next to impossible.

He wandered over to the Titan help desk to let them know his lost bag had arrived an hour after he'd spoken to Nick about it. He wasn't surprised to see it empty of staff, seeing as how it was after two o'clock in the morning. Rhett was all messed up time-wise, what with the time change, and had slept earlier, so now he was wide awake. He looked over the tour descriptions displayed by the desk and signed up for one tomorrow to the old city of Barcelona. Across the great hall of the hotel was the bar, and it was still open and going strong. There were several tables filled with clusters of men chatting to each other.

So many men! And all so handsome. It was almost too much for him to drink in.

Rhett wandered into the bar and sat down in a plush chair. He ordered a rum and Coke from the waiter and downed it fast when it came. No one was talking to him, and no one came over. He ordered another drink, then another. Rhett was naturally shy, and he found he just couldn't go over and introduce himself to strangers. He hoped against hope that someone would come to him.

Finally, after sitting in the bar for over an hour and not speaking to anyone except the waiter, he stood up and stumbled over to the elevator. His roommate and his trick surely were done by now, and he would just go to sleep. Tomorrow he would be more aggressive in meeting the hot men all around him. The doors opened and he stepped in. He punched 9 and leaned against the mirrored wall of the incredibly tiny elevator.

He was feeling tipsy, and he giggled. He never drank back in Gatlinburg.

The elevator stopped on the second floor, and a tall broadly built man with dark hair got on. The man re-punched 9. The doors closed, and he turned around and glanced at Rhett.

"How are you tonight?" he asked in a deep, but silky, voice.

"I'm terrific, thank you very kindly for askin'," Rhett giggled. For some reason everything was funny.

"Nice accent," the man smiled. "Where you from?"

"Gatlinburg, Tennessee."

"I've never been there. Is it nice?"

Rhett felt his eyes go in and out of focus. He was really feeling no pain from those drinks.

"Not really," he replied, trying to zero in on the tall man's face but not being able to. He did know he was tall and powerfully built.

The man laughed politely at Rhett's crack. "So, late night for you?"

"Yes, sir. My roommate got hisself lucky. He's fuckin' a guy up in our room. I surely hope they're done by now."

"And why didn't you get lucky? You're a hot man. You should be the one fucking up a storm."

Rhett didn't quite believe his ears. "Wh...what?"

The man took a confident step closer to Rhett. He reached out a hand and pressed the Stop button on the elevator keypad. The elevator came to a sudden halt, and Rhett almost lost his balance in the small space. The man caught him. He leaned in so his face was only inches from Rhett's.

"I said," he whispered seductively, "that you're a fucking hot man, and I think you should be doing your fair share of—" He leaned in closer. "Hot fucking."

"Oh, my Lord," drawled Rhett, as the tall man kissed him passionately on the lips. It tasted so good, so sweet, and it completely turned Rhett on.

The stranger reached down and began to knead Rhett's crotch getting a handful of hard dick as a reward. Rhett groaned and clutched at the man with all his strength, pulling him closer. He could feel the man's rigid cock pressing against his leg, and he wanted to get at it so bad he didn't know what to do. "Let's go to your room," he urgently pleaded, so eager to finally find out what it would feel like to have sex with a man.

The man pulled away for a minute. "No...let's go up to the roof. It's closed now, but I know a way. We'll have it all to ourselves." He re-pressed the Stop button, and the car started moving again.

"Yes, sir! Anything..." Rhett allowed himself to grab at the man's thick bulge and he held on for dear life. It felt so good to hold a man's package in his hands. He'd fantasized and jerked off so many times to doing exactly this, and now it was happening!

They got off the elevator on the ninth floor, and the man motioned for Rhett to follow him. Rhett hoped no one would come down the hallway, as his own huge boner was so obvious.

The two men went to a stairway door, and walked up a short flight of stairs. The stranger pushed against the door at the top and it slowly creaked open.

"They never lock this. I don't know why," he said, allowing Rhett to pass through first.

Rhett stepped out of the darkened stairway onto the rooftop pool area. There was a wide teak deck filled with chaise loungers and tables and chairs neatly stacked up for the night. The pool, a four-foot deep rectangle of about ten by twelve feet looked cool and inviting. There was a detailed mosaic, all in tiny tiles, on the wall at the back of the pool, a clever portrayal of the city of Barcelona and its highlights.

"It's nice up here, isn't it?" said the man as he took Rhett into is arms and hungrily kissed him again. "You can see the entire city from here…"

"Mmm…uh…oh, yes…" Rhett breathed in air in short staccato gasps.

"Look at the lights of the city," the stranger said, leading Rhett to a low railing. They both looked out over the building tops at the center of the Passeig de Gràcia. Even though the hour was so late, there was still a fair amount of bustling traffic on the wide boulevards below. A stone's throw away, the Gaudi designed apartment house Casa Batlló was bathed in its warm uplighting, though no crowd stood at its base admiring the architectural wonder.

"It's so damn beautiful," Rhett said.

"Not as beautiful as you," The stranger said, as he began to unbutton Rhett's shirt. "Oh, yeah, nice chest!…Mmmm…Makes me want to lick it. Bite it."

And he did.

Rhett couldn't believe how good it felt to have this hot man chew on his nipples. He felt passions and desires he didn't know were possible.

"Oh, my Lord," he repeated as the man began to unbuckle his pants. Rhett felt the stranger's strong hand slip into his boxers as he continued to bite and tease Rhett's nipple, which was fine by the lanky Tennessean.

"Nice," the stranger murmured between nibbles.

"Excuse me, sir," Rhett managed to gasp.

The stranger stopped his playing and looked up at Rhett. "Yeah?"

"What's your name? I'm Rhett…"

The man smiled. "As in Butler?"

Rhett blushed. "Yeah. Momma was a big 'ole fan."

"Well, Rhett, that's a sexy name for a sexy man…"

Rhett loved being complimented by the stranger.

"You can call me…" The stranger paused for a beat. "Dante."

"Dante? Ain't that just another name for Satan?"

Dante nodded. "Exactly. Because I'm a little devil…" He went back to his gnawing.

Rhett involuntarily jerked as the pleasure flooded him, and he clutched at the man's head, pressing it harder up against his nipple. "Oh, man! Lordy, Dante, that just feels so good…"

"Mmmmm…"

Before Rhett knew it, they were naked on the teak deck, head to toe, sucking each other madly. Rhett finally got to taste a man's dick, and he loved it. He wanted to try everything. He urged Dante to do anything he wanted to try. Over the course of the next forty-five minutes, Rhett experienced almost every sexual act two men could perform with, and to, each other.

The actual sensation of having a guy slide in and out of his ass was a delight he hadn't been able to image. It was so good with a real live man! Much better than with the "authentic Matthew Rush" dildo he had stuffed under his bed back home.

Rhett ultimately let the hot man have him from behind, from on top, from the side, and finally, with Rhett frantically bouncing up and down on his lap.

The lanky Tennessean managed to hold off his climax until finally, with Dante underneath him pushing up his hips as he sank down, he felt a massive load pump out before he could cry out a warning. Dante quickly slipped out, whipped off his condom and ejaculated, his eyes shutting tight as he came.

"Lordy, that was amazing!" Rhett waxed on, after getting off Dante. They both sat on the teak decking near the pool.

"Yes, it was."

"You know, that was my first time," Rhett said sheepishly.

"You're kidding! You were fantastic. I never would have thought that."

"When can we do it again?" Rhett grinned. "Tomorrow?"

"Hmmmm…That might be a little…complicated. I'm, uh…in a relationship, Rhett."

"Oh," Rhett sighed.

Silence fell between them. Then Dante got up and slipped into the cool water of the pool. "Come in," he called out. "It feels great!" He pushed away from the side, and floated on his back, his still hard penis sticking up out of the water. Rhett, transfixed by the very thing he had waited so long to get, slid into the water and splashed over to Dante.

"Suck it," Dante ordered, and Rhett happily went to work.

He was eagerly going up and down on it, when Dante slowly placed his hands on Rhett's head. Dante regretted that he had slipped again, and he had to make it right.

"I'm so sorry, Rhett," he whispered. "I'm so sorry."

Hearing his name, Rhett looked up, but didn't take his mouth away from his task.

Dante suddenly pushed down on Rhett's head, dunking him under the water. Sputtering, Rhett jerked away from Dante and struggled to get to his feet. Dante quickly spun around, and placed his knee on Rhett's back, and pressed all his weight down on the lanky man.

Rhett began to frantically thrash around under the water. His lungs were burning and he needed to get air. He couldn't comprehend what was happening, and his animal instinct to survive took over. He kicked and struggled, but the man on his back was too strong.

Eventually, Rhett's struggling ceased, but Dante stayed on him for an additional couple of minutes, just to make sure. When he felt comfortable in knowing Rhett was never going to come up for air again, he got off the dead man's back and waded over to the edge of the pool. He pulled himself up and out of the water and picked up a stray towel he had spied by one of the loungers. He toweled off, and picked up his clothing. He spied something limp by his shirt, and delicately lifted it from the teak flooring. With a sigh, he dropped the used condom over the side railing, and watched it fall down to the street below.

Dante looked at the spectacular view of the city as he carefully dressed. He then gave Rhett's floating body one last sad look.

"I'm sorry, Rhett," he whispered softly to the lifeless form in the water. "I screwed up." He turned away, and walked back to the stairwell door, and silently disappeared into the dark stairway.

6

Fourth Floor, Hotel Royale, Barcelona, Spain

Zack opened his eyes and quickly closed them again. The harsh sunlight felt like it was burning his retinas. In a minute, he forced them open and slowly got used to the brightness of the room. He had to pee badly, and he rolled off the bed and went to the bathroom.

He was just finishing brushing his teeth, when he heard a gentle knock at his door. He walked down the hallway and opened the heavy door a crack. There was a pretty young maid waiting patiently by her cart.

"Can I clean your room, sir?" she asked, with a rich, sing-song Spanish accent.

Zack shook his head, and said, "Can you give me 30 minutes?"

"Ah, si, si. Trenta, trenta," she nodded, getting behind the big cart and pushing down the hall to the next room. Zack shut the door and went back into the bathroom.

He gazed at his reflection in the wall-to-wall mirror over the dual sinks. He looked like hell. His hair was all mussed up, he had lines in his face from the wrinkled fabric of the bedspread he'd slept on top of, and he needed a shave.

Sighing heavily, he opened the frosted glass door to the huge standing shower and turned on the nozzles full blast. He quickly stripped off all his clothes and gave his nude, tanned body a once-over in the mirror, as well.

Broad shoulders. Worked out and rounded pecs. A solid four-pack and a tapering waist. A discreetly trimmed pubic area complete with impressive cock and balls. Hard ass. Thick thighs and meaty calves. Zack knew he was in peak shape, having worked out really hard the previous six weeks knowing he would have to be in a small Speedo by the pool with 1,300 other gay men. He'd wanted Bayne to look good for having such a hot boyfriend.

What a joke that had turned out to be.

He stepped into the shower and let the hot water and steam envelope him in a warm, wet cocoon of comfort.

Twenty minutes later Zack, feeling better and slightly more alive than he felt the day before, gently closed the suite's door behind him. He went to the elevator, pressed the call button, and was quickly rewarded with an empty car that was already waiting on his floor. He got in and pressed 0.

The doors opened on the lobby floor, and he got out, only to be greeted by the sight of orderly chaos. There were several policemen standing around muttering to themselves, and shockingly, two EMT technicians wheeling out an ominously full, zippered bodybag. Zack could see a waiting ambulance parked on the sidewalk in front of the hotel's glass front doors.

There were several guys from the tour group standing around talking among themselves in hushed tones. Andy and Frank were there, standing next to a very handsome guy Zack didn't know, and Frank waved Zack over.

"What's going on?" Zack asked, when he reached them.

"Oh, it's awful!" Frank said. "Some poor guy drowned in the pool on the roof last night."

"What?"

Frank nodded sadly. "He was from our group. They don't know what he was doing up there. The pool closes at eight o'clock each night. They say he apparently snuck up there and went swimming alone and…drowned."

"My, God, that's awful."

The four men fell silent. "Oh," Frank said, "This is Dan." He indicated the tall man standing next to Andy. "Dan, this is Zack."

Zack nodded in the direction of Dan, who barely acknowledged him. He was too busy staring intently at the paramedics. His intense interest in the solemn activity before them was slightly unnerving.

Frank glanced at the covered body resting on the gurney again. The EMTs were now loading it into the ambulance. "This whole thing is so Brian Bainbridge," he said,

Andy wrinkled his nose. "Oh, Frank! That's so mean!"

Brian Bainbridge, the good-looking (and rumored to be gay) lead singer of the boy band Back2Boyz had died in a tragic accident the previous spring. Halfway through a sold-out concert tour, his nude body had been found facedown in a Jacuzzi at the Park Sloan Hotel in Manhattan. Teenage girls and gay fans everywhere had been devastated.

Frank shrugged. "I'm just saying. No solo hot tub or late night swims for me."

Andy had seen enough. "Well, there's nothing we can do about it," he said airily. "Let's go eat. I'm starving." He started to lead the other men off to the hotel's dining room where a daily breakfast was part of their package.

Dan Smith hung back. "Uh, no thanks, guys," he said. "I think I'll stick around here." He shoved his hands into his pockets and continued to watch the EMTs through the front doors. His expression was one of sadness, and his eyes never left the bodybag that was being strapped down inside the ambulance.

Andy took his lover's arm. "Suit yourself."

"We missed you last night, Zack," Frank commented as they entered the spacious dining room. A huge buffet was set up on several serving tables in the center of the room, hot food kept warm under large metal covers, with large baskets of fruits and breads stacked at either end. Tables and chairs were placed neatly around the space and most were full of loudly chattering men, excited about their first full day in Barcelona.

"I slept all night through. I just woke up an hour ago," Zack said. "Uh, do they know who the drowned guy was? What his name was?"

"I don't know," Andy answered blithely. "Boy! If you slept all night, then you must have been tired. Well, don't worry. You really didn't miss much. We're going out after the cocktail party tonight, and you have to come with us."

"Cocktail party?" Zack asked, picking up a plate at the buffet.

"Yeah," Frank cut in. "The Titan Cruise welcome cocktail party over on the rooftop terrace of the Hotel Barcelona. Tonight at 8:00?"

Zack suddenly remembered. "Oh, right. I don't know, guys, if I'm gonna go."

"Why not?" Andy asked, sidling up next to Zack, heaping a scoop of scrambled eggs onto his plate. He looked Zack up and down. He liked the khaki shorts and tight navy blue tee shirt Zack was wearing. He would have much preferred that Zack was buck naked, but, in due time, Andy hoped. In due time. "Look," he lowered his voice conspiratorially, "Frank and I have brought with us some X that is just the shit! You won't believe the buzz you'll get from it."

Zack stood still. He shrugged. "Here's the deal, okay? I was supposed to be here with my boyfriend, Bayne, but he dumped me at the airport, just before I boarded the plane to get here."

Frank and Andy both gasped in horror.

"He's in love with someone else, but I came on here anyway. So, you see, I'm just not in a big party mood, I'm sorry. I wouldn't count on me running around to all the hot spots with you. I'm sorry, but I just can't…"

"Oh, poor Zack!" Andy comforted, giving him an awkward hug. "We completely understand. Screw that idiot boyfriend. He's a fool to let you go!"

Andy's mind was already spinning. The guy was on the rebound! Perfect! He'd finagle this hot man into bed before this cruise was over, or he'd die trying.

"I'm so sorry," Frank also comforted.

"Yeah, well, shit happens," Zack said bravely, trying to appear strong and unaffected by the turmoil in his life.

The three men looked around for an empty table and found one a few feet away. They sat down and proceeded to eat their breakfast.

"So what are you going to do today?" Frank asked, after shoveling a fork-ful of eggs into his mouth. "We're taking a tour of the old city."

"I think I'm just going to wander around and explore the town on my own. Take some photos," Zack replied.

"Oh? Are you a photographer?"

Zack nodded his head. "Yeah. I photo assist, do headshots for actors, and I'm taking classes at the California School for the Arts."

"That's great!"

"Bayne didn't think so. He said it was a waste of time."

"Is it your dream? To be a working photographer?" asked Andy.

"Yes, it is."

"Then how could that be a waste of time?"

Zack was about to respond when he caught sight of Bayne's wealthy friends Kurt Farrar and Rick Yung, enter the dining room and go through the buffet line. They were both wearing tight gym shorts and tank tops and were damp with sweat. They must have done an early workout, Zack thought. "Well," he said, returning his attention to his tablemates. "I agree with you."

The three men ate in silence for a minute or two. Kurt and Rick had loaded up their plates and were looking for a place to sit down when Kurt spied Zack. He grinned at him and whispered something to Rick, and the two men came over to Zack's table.

"Hi," Kurt said. "You're Zack, right? Bayne's Zack?"

"Well, I'm Zack, all right," Zack said, starting to stand up.

"No, no, please sit down." Kurt looked around the table. "Hi, everybody, I'm Kurt Farrar. This is my partner, Rick. Can we join you?"

"Sure." Zack motioned for them to sit down.

"Please!" Andy said, too quickly. He hungrily eyed the two men as they eased themselves down into the small dining room chairs. Kurt was possibly the biggest, best-built man he'd ever seen. And his lover was no slouch! They both looked like competitive bodybuilders, and fantasies of being in the mid-dle of a sex sandwich suddenly flashed before Andy's rapidly blinking eyes.

"Uh, sweetheart," Frank nudged his partner. "Put your eyes back in their sockets, and pass me the ketchup."

Frank giggled and passed over the bottle. Introductions were quickly made all around.

"So, Zack, where's Bayne?" Kurt asked, after shaking Frank and Andy's hands. "Still sleeping? That lazy ass..."

Zack, Andy and Frank all glanced at each other briefly. "Well...he...he won't be coming on the cruise," Zack finally said, his voice quiet. He looked down at his half-eaten plate.

Kurt looked surprised. "Oh? Did he suddenly have to work?"

Zack looked up, and stared at Kurt, eye to eye. "No. He suddenly had to fuck his new boyfriend."

"What?" Rick joined the conversation.

"He's left me for some guy in his office. He won't be joining us here," Zack said in a flat tone.

"Oh, Zack, I'm so sorry," Rick compassionately said.

"Wow," Kurt added.

"I told you Bayne was an asshole," Rick said to Kurt.

"I'll agree with that," Zack feebly smiled.

Kurt quickly apologized. "I'm really sorry, Zack. I didn't know."

Zack shook his head. Don't worry about it.

"I never told you this, Kurt," Rick interjected, "but, remember the night we first met you, Zack? At that Human Rights Campaign dinner?"

Zack and Kurt both nodded.

"When you and Kurt went to the men's room, he grabbed my crotch and came on to me so hard, I had to literally shove him away. The guy's a pig."

"What?" Kurt and Zack said in unison.

Rick shrugged, and nodded his head. "Yep. I never told you about it, honey, but it happened."

"Jesus Christ! He hit on you when I stepped away?" Kurt was incredulous. "I can't believe you didn't tell me! I'd have punched his lights out good for that!"

"That's why I didn't tell you."

"Oh, Rick, I'm sorry you had to put up with that." Zack was embarrassed for himself and for his ex-lover's behavior. "I had no idea."

"The point is," Rick said, "is that the guy was a jerk. You are much too good for him, and frankly, him leaving you is the best thing that could happen to you."

Zack shook his head, shame and guilt flooding him. His eyes traveled up. "Then why doesn't it feel that way?"

Rick reached across the table and placed a comforting hand on top of Zack's.

Zack shook it away, pushed his chair back, and stood up. "I'm sorry. I'm not so hungry anymore. If you all will excuse me." He quickly left the table and almost ran out of the dining room.

Rick shook his head. "Well, as far as I'm concerned, Mr. Bayne Raddock is off our Christmas card list."

"I can't believe what an ass he turned out to be! Poor Zack. I feel so bad for him." Kurt chomped down on a piece of bacon. "Hey, let's invite him to join us today. Hayden won't mind."

Rick reached over and rubbed his lover's back. "That's a great idea, sweetheart."

"Let me see if I can catch up with him. Excuse me," Kurt said, raising his massive bulk up from the chair. He left the dining room and headed towards the elevator bank. He saw Zack standing patiently waiting for the doors to open.

"Zack!" Kurt called out. "Zack! Wait!"

Zack looked over and saw the bodybuilder approaching him.

"Man, I'm really sorry if I upset you in there," Kurt said soothingly, reaching a hand out and squeezing Zack's shoulder.

"No, no, you didn't." Zack fumbled to say. "It's just still kinda hard to believe. I feel so stupid and ashamed."

"Why? He's the asshole! Not you. Fuck him!"

Zack smiled a little.

"Listen," Kurt continued. "One of my best friends' back in L.A. is Clay Beasley. Do you know him?"

Zack nodded. "I've met him a couple of times at events and dinner parties. He's with Travis Church, right?"

"Exactly. Well, Clay has a brother who lives here in Barcelona. He's gonna take us on a local's tour of the city today. Come with us."

"Oh, I couldn't, that's kind of you, but…"

"I insist. Please join us. You'll love Hayden, and Rick and I would really like it if you came along."

He looked so sincere that Zack believed him completely. He thought for a minute. Well, what else was he going to do? Mope around the city feeling sorry for himself? Screw that!

"Okay. You talked me into it."

Kurt flashed a broad grin. "Terrific! Meet Rick and me in the lobby in—" he glanced at his watch, "an hour. That's when Hayden will be here."

"You got it."

"Great. I'll go tell Rick. He'll be thrilled." Kurt turned around and started to leave.

"Hey, Kurt," Zack called out after the huge man. Kurt stopped. "Thanks for asking me. I really appreciate it."

Kurt smiled again, came back to Zack, and wrapped his big arms around the surprised man and gave him an affectionate hug.

"You're gonna be fine," he said, squeezing Zack hard once more. "Hell, you're about to go on a gay cruise with over 1,000 horny gay men who are all gonna be after your hot ass. Who knows? Maybe you'll find your true Mr. Right!"

7

Jebb's head hurt. It was bad enough that one of his guests had died, something that had never happened before, but he also had to endure the third degree from the Barcelona police. While the policemen who questioned him were cautious not to completely piss off a tour operator who had brought over thirteen hundred people to the city to eat, drink and shop, and in the process spread a lot of money around, they had no problem grilling Jebb about his limited knowledge of Rhett.

There was nothing that Jebb could tell them that shed any light on how the accident happened, so eventually, they thanked him for his time and left.

Even worse than his tense meeting with the police was the phone call he'd had to make to Tennessee. Rhett had listed his mother and father as his emergency contact number, and they had been shocked to discover that not only had their son left the country for a cruise, but that he was on a *gay* cruise.

Apparently, Rhett hadn't come out to his parents yet, and their stunned silence was awkward to endure. Then Rhett's mother said something to Jebb that bothered him. In a tearful and shaky voice, she wondered how her beloved son could possibly drown when he'd been a high school and college swimming champ. In fact, she proudly told Jebb, he always carried his first place NAACA swimming medal from his senior year as a good luck charm.

After offering what little words of comfort he could and promising to make sure that he would do whatever he could to help them in their time of grief, Jebb had only been too glad to get off the phone.

"Fuck!" he breathed, after hanging up. "That was rough."

Nick reached over the desktop and gave his boss a comforting squeeze on the arm. They were in the anteroom at the Titan help desk.

"What do we do now?" he asked.

"Can you see to it that his personal effects are packed up from his room? Make sure to find a swimming medal. His mother will want that back. Then Fed-Ex those things to his parents." Jebb tore off a slip of paper on the pad in front of him. "Here's their address."

Nick reached across and took the slip of paper. "Okay."

"Mr. Miller!" came a strident voice from the entrance to the room.

Jebb looked up, and audibly groaned. He did not need this now. "Yes, Mr. Lassiter?" he said as politely as he could.

"I'm shocked! Shocked! I've just heard that one of your guests drowned last night!"

"Unfortunately, that's true." Jebb was actually touched that the persnickety man was expressing concern.

"I knew this tour was going to be trouble! I knew it! You people!" Rex spat out, the venom unmistakable. He was dressed for his day in Barcelona in a crisply pressed pair of cream linen slacks and a formal white shirt, buttoned at the collar, where a simple brown tie was smartly knotted. "All you gay people do is party and drink, do drugs and have wanton sex!" he ranted. "This proves that you are all completely irresponsible! How could someone be so stupid as to drown in four feet of water? My God!"

Jebb had to use all his personal restraint not to punch the man in the face. "Sir, a young man has just died. Show a little respect."

"Please. You poufs don't deserve respect! You deserve a swift kick in the ass and a good dose of self-control. You, Mr. Miller, need to watch your queer boys a whole lot better." While Jebb fumed silently, Rex reached into his coat pocket and pulled out a folded piece of paper. "And look at this! Look at it! It was faxed to me from our London office this morning!" He thrust the paper out at Jebb, who took it warily.

"What is it?"

Rex's eyes turned to slits. "A bomb threat!" he spouted triumphantly.

"What?" Jebb unfolded the paper, and Nick leaned over his shoulder to read along. The page was a faxed copy of a letter originally composed of pasted together letters, like the kind a kidnapper would create in a bad movie.

> Mr. Lassiter,
> Faggots must die!
> The Princess Diana will never see home port again
> if you allow those sinners to sail on her! Beware!
> We'll blow her out of the water!

"This is obviously some sort of joke. No self-respecting terrorist would make up such a ridiculous letter," Jebb said.

"Are you willing to risk the lives of your group on that statement?" Rex huffed.

"Did you show this to the police?"

"Certainly not! I don't want to draw anymore publicity to this tawdry tour of yours."

Jebb handed the note back. "Well, I think it's just some gay-hating crackpot trying to cause trouble. I've seen this sort of thing before. A bunch of ultraconservatives sit around thinking up ways to try and scare us away from enjoying the same liberties that they enjoy."

Rex shook the paper in Jebb's face. "This threat gives me the power to cancel your charter!"

Jebb narrowed his eyes and took a step forward. "I don't think so. You'd have to have the authorities investigate first, then they would determine if the threat is viable or not." He reached into his pants pocket and pulled out his cell phone. "The police were just here. Let's call them back, what do you say?"

Rex's confidence seemed to melt away. He nervously looked at Jebb, then Nick, then the phone. He lowered his hand and stuffed the note back into his pocket. "Okay, fine," he spat out. "You win this round. But if I get any more threats like this, you and all your rump ranger passengers will find themselves without a ship! I won't sacrifice my beautiful *Diana* over your kind, no sir!"

Jebb had finally reached his limit with the contentious man. "Mr. Lassiter?" he said calmly.

"What?"

"Get the fuck out of here!" Jebb roared. Lassiter actually trembled at the sudden outburst. "I have never in my entire life met such a complete and total asshole as you are!" Jebb continued to shout. "Get out! Go!" Nick had to physically restrain his overwrought boss from lunging at Rex.

Like most bullies, Lassiter was all bluster and no fight. He quickly turned tail and began backing out of the room. "You're all crazy! Crazy!" he squeaked, before he turned and ran out of the room.

"Jesus Christ! I hate that guy!" Jebb seethed. "I bet he made that note himself just to try and stop the cruise..."

"Man, I thought you were gonna deck him!" Nick said, breathing deeply, and trying to calm his nerves.

"I think *I'd* get a medal if I did."

After a beat, Nick went back to the desk and picked up a clipboard to go through the number of guests taking the old city tour the next day.

"Say, Nick," Jebb wondered aloud. "Just how does a statewide swimming champ drown in four feet of water?"

Zack came back down to the lobby after changing and grabbing his camera bag, and wandered around waiting for Kurt and Rick to come downstairs. He was staring at a glass display case showing off some new Chanel products from the designer's store next door when he felt a slight tapping on his shoulder.

"I'm sorry," said a great-looking guy who was wearing khaki cargo shorts and a loose-fitting Jocko tank top. "Are you Zack?"

Zack nodded, much to the relief of the man.

"I'm Hayden. Hayden Beasley? Clay's brother? Kurt called me and told me you'd be joining us today." He held out his hand.

Zack took it and they shook. Zack liked Hayden's firm grip and found that the handshake lasted a beat longer than necessary.

"So, where are we off to today?" Zack asked, shouldering his camera bag.

"I thought we'd take a brief tour of some of the Gaudi buildings nearby, namely the Casa Batlló and the Casa Milà. Do you like architecture?"

"Oh, yeah! I thought for a while I'd like to major in it at school, but I kept going back to photography." Zack raised up his camera bag.

"Oh, then you're going to love these buildings. So ahead of their time it's scary," Hayden grinned. *Kurt was right*, he thought. *He is handsome! His boyfriend was a fool for letting him go.*

"I saw the one up the street when we checked in. Which one is that?" Zack asked. While he was grinning back at Hayden like an idiot, he was thinking, *He has the most beautiful eyes.*

"That's the Casa Batlló. The Milà is down the street a couple of blocks. After that, I thought we'd go see the La Sagrada Família."

"That's the church that they've been building for over 100 years, right?"

"Exactly."

"They need a new contractor," Zack cracked. Hayden laughed, and just then Kurt and Rick appeared at their sides.

"So," Kurt said giving Hayden a warm hug, while Rick did the same with Zack. "You two have met."

"Yup," Hayden nodded.

"Sorry we're late," Rick said, blushing. "We had to...uh, change."

Zack looked at Hayden and they smirked at each other. By the obvious glow about the two men, they had done a little more than just change clothes upstairs.

"So where we goin'?" Kurt asked Hayden while throwing a beefy arm around Zack affectionately.

"I was just telling Zack. Let's go check out the Gaudi stuff, and then we'll take a bus tour. It's just easier to see everything that way."

"Cool. Let's go!"

The foursome walked out into the warm late-summer air, crossed the congested Passeig de Gràcia and walked up the busy boulevard a few hundred feet. They stopped in front of an Anton Gaudi masterpiece, the Casa Batlló, a wonderfully whimsical apartment building that had been lovingly restored in 2000.

In a surprising twist, Casa Batlló was surrounded by some other equally astounding buildings. Right next door was the Flemish inspired Casa Amatller, and further up the boulevard was the ornately decorated Casa Lleó Morera.

But it was the Casa Batlló that drew the most attention. Several stories tall, it capped out with a sharply raked roofline that was heavily trimmed in blue-green curving tiles. Beautifully colored tiles also had been attached to its street facade in an iridescent pattern that seemed to change color when a gazer happened to move. It was a stunning sight, and it captured the imagination of those that happened upon it.

The daily allotment of tour tickets was already sold out, so the four men couldn't view the interiors. But they were happy just to stand out front and gaze upwards. Zack unsheathed his camera and started clicking away, furiously moving his zoom lens in and out.

"The building was originally designed around 1907," Hayden lectured, sounding like a tour guide. "It's meant to evoke a dragon. Notice the scale-like tiles cladding the walls? And if you look closely, the tiles on the roof look like the spine. The railings of the balconies? See how they look like skull bones? In fact, the building's nickname is the 'house of bones.'"

"It's awesome!" Rick gasped, staring at the intricate tile work of the structure.

"Wow," was all Kurt could say as he snaked his arms around his lover from behind and hugged him close.

"I love the spires," Zack said, snapping off a few more shots. "And the mottled color of the tiles! It's so…modern. I can't believe this was designed a century ago!"

"Pretty visionary, isn't it? Gaudi is now regarded as a genius, but he died penniless and unrecognized," Hayden said.

"Hey, you two," Zack called out to Kurt and Rick, aiming his camera their way. The two men stood stiffly by each other and smiled at him. "Come on, act like you like each other," Zack directed. Kurt impulsively grabbed Rick around the waist and pulled him close. Zack clicked off a few frames as the two men smiled broadly at him. Zack motioned for Hayden to join the lovers. "Now, you get in there, too." Hayden slid in between them and all three hugged as Zack snapped their image.

Next, the happy group went to see the Casa Milà just a few blocks away. Gaudi's Casa Milà was a corner apartment building finished in 1912. Seven stories tall, its gently undulating facade drew huge numbers of gawkers as it was perhaps one of the most striking buildings in all of Barcelona.

It was said that there was not one straight line in the entire building. It curved, dipped and swayed its way across the large expanse of ground it covered. Creamy limestone had been used for construction and its large apartment balcony railings were a fanciful nest of tangled and twisted wrought iron.

The unique and unrestricted design of the building made it look like a wave in motion. Zack was entranced. He peppered Hayden with question after question and was slightly surprised when Hayden knew the answers.

The foursome were luckier here, and they snagged tickets to see the interior. Kurt, Rick, Hayden and Zack gawked at the intricately tiled hallways that seemed to shimmer in the late morning light and charmingly crooked banisters as they climbed floor after floor.

Emerging onto the rooftop they found themselves in a forest of cracked-tiled chimneys that resembled huge soft-serve ice cream cones. The small dormer windows of the upper floors looked like little eyes, and all four men marveled at the stunning vistas of Barcelona afforded from up there.

Next on Hayden's tour was a bus ride through the farther areas of town via the Tourista Bus. The large, colorful double-decker buses made frequent stops at all the highlights of the city and were a common sight in town. They were a cheap and easy way to view the splendors of Barcelona.

The four men decided to take the red line bus, which took a scenic tour through the Northern routes of the city first. They would take the blue route through the southern spots later.

After paying their fare, they trudged up the tight, steep staircase to the open-air upper deck. Kurt had a hard time squeezing his massive frame through the narrow stairwell, but eventually made it to the top. Hayden and Zack were seated towards the rear of the upper deck chatting away about the finer points of Gaudi architecture, and Rick had snagged the only other empty seat, which was further forward. Kurt tried to squeeze in next to him, and managed, though it was a tight fit.

"It's a good thing I love you," Rick joked. "Because you're practically sitting on my lap."

"How about I make an honest man of you later, when we get back to the hotel?" Kurt leered suggestively.

"Yowsa. You're on."

Kurt reached down and patted his lover's knee. He jerked his head towards the back of the now moving bus. "They seem to be getting along, huh?"

Rick turned and looked back at Zack and Hayden. Hayden was pointing out some other facet of Barcelona and Zack was nodding vigorously. "Yeah, I think they are."

8

Lobby, Hotel Royale, Barcelona, Spain

It was chaos in the reception area of the grand hotel. Checkout time was noon, so all the tour guests had to vacate their rooms and suites, but boarding the ship didn't take place until three. So now with three hours to kill, there was much confusion among the men as to what to do in the short span of time. Suitcases and bags were stacked up in every conceivable space of the lobby, and the sweating bellhops were scurrying about trying to keep their charge's luggage straight.

Each Titan guest had been given colored luggage tags with their names, stateroom numbers, and deck level in their Titan confirmation packets. All bags going on the ship should have been placed outside their hotel rooms last night. Special ship porters had roamed the halls picking them up and placing them on special baggage vans going directly to the ship, where they would then be placed in the correct corresponding cabins.

But, evidently, more than one guest had not exercised this option, hence the cornucopia of baggage in the lobby.

Titan staffers were milling through the throngs of men giving information and answering questions. They were easily identifiable by their bright blue polo shirts with the Titan logo on the left breast pocket.

Zack was sitting with Kurt and Rick on one of the comfortable down sofas in the side lobby, watching the confusion. He was dressed for his first day on the ship in a pair of baggy A & F cargo shorts and a new navy tee he'd bought at the huge Burberry flagship store two blocks away from the hotel.

"This is insane," muttered Kurt, as he nursed his latte. His head was pounding, a reminder of the wild night he and Rick had had the night before in one of Barcelona's gay discos. He had drunk far too much Spanish wine, and had ended up dancing on the bar top, doing a clumsy striptease to the cheering chants of the crowd. Only when he got down to his underwear did he come to his senses and climb down. He and Rick had left soon after that, where they had made love hurriedly in their suite before both passed out.

Zack had dinner with Hayden at a fabulous restaurant near the gothic quarter last night, and after giving his new friend a warm hug goodnight, had gone up to his suite, alone, and had fallen into bed. It was the first night that Zack hadn't cried himself to sleep over Bayne since arriving in Barcelona. He'd simply had too good a time with Hayden, enjoying the city and a wonderful dinner, and just hadn't been in the mood to mentally rehash his failed relationship.

Zack was a little surprised at how quickly he was getting over the loss of his boyfriend and the loss of his former life. He was so thankful to have found Kurt, Rick, and Hayden. The four of them had explored the farthest regions of Barcelona in the past couple of days, and Zack was amazed to find himself laughing and joking with them, as if everything was normal.

Hayden had been a treasure to meet, as he and Zack both were nuts about art and architecture, and they had even taken a couple of outings to art museums without the other two men. Kurt had sworn he couldn't look another masterpiece in the eye, and had made Rick lay out by the pool with him yesterday, while Zack and Hayden had taken a tour of the Picasso Museum in the Barri Gòtic quarter of town.

The two handsome men had strolled up Las Ramblas, the main drag of the gothic quarter, and window shopped. They explored the great cathedral and cloisters, stunning in their Catalan designed beauty, located there. Zack had been particularly impressed with the Plaça del Rei, a vast square in the heart of the ancient cathedral, where long ago locksmiths and hay sellers had earned a living. His camera clicking furiously away, Zack captured image after image of the wondrous old brick and intricately carved stonework.

He'd also managed to sneak one or two shots of Hayden as well.

Ah, Hayden.

When Zack thought about him, he smiled. He had been so gracious in showing him around, and Zack was truly thankful. They had an easy camaraderie that was full of laughter and excited discovery.

Not to mention the fact that Hayden wasn't hard to look at.

Zack was surprised to find himself checking out Hayden unconsciously time and time again. Hayden had worn a particularly tight pair of jeans yesterday and Zack found himself stealing lustful glances at his tempting crotch and hard ass all afternoon.

Now, sitting in the lobby of the Hotel Royale, Zack found himself looking around for the handsome man and wondering where he was.

Rick noticed this, and smiled to himself. He had come to really care about Zack, and he thought Hayden was a catch. He wanted the two men to find each other. They would make such a great couple.

"I don't think Hayden's getting here until 2:30," he said, still smiling.

"Huh? What?" Zack asked.

"I said, I don't think Hayden's showing until we need to leave for the dock around 2:30," Rick repeated.

"Oh, I wasn't thinking about that," Zack lied, knowing full well he'd been thinking exactly that.

"Uh huh, right," Rick nodded.

"My fucking head is killing me," Kurt interrupted.

"Poor baby," Rick soothed, caressing his lover's meaty thigh. "Next time, don't order the third bottle."

"Now you tell me." Kurt leaned over and rested his body weight against Rick. Rick just continued to stroke his lover's leg, and soon, Kurt's eyes fluttered shut, and he fell into a light sleep.

Zack observed this and realized he yearned for that. He wanted that intimate connection with another man, where you were so comfortable with him that you could just doze off resting against him. Sadly, he realized that even with Bayne, he'd not yet had that level of intimacy.

He sighed and looked back over the milling crowd, his thoughts again returning to Hayden.

Jebb Miller finished checking out of his room, thanked the counter man for his assistance, and went out into the bright sun of yet another glorious day in Spain. He ran smack into Dan Smith. "Oh! Hey," he said, surprised and slightly ruffled.

Dan stared at him blankly. "Hi," he replied automatically.

"I'm Jebb," Jebb said, hopefully. Why did he feel like he was fifteen again, a geek with pimples and glasses, around this guy?

The corners of Dan's mouth curled upward. "I remember. How are you?"

"Good, good. Big day. Have a lot to do."

"I'm sure." Dan put on his sunglasses, and shielded his eyes from both the sun and Jebb.

"You looking forward to the cruise? Gonna be great!"

"Yeah, I am."

Jebb couldn't tell if Dan was completely uninterested or just playing it cool. His attitude was once of tough-guy nonchalance, but Jebb felt a slight electricity between them. He decided to take a chance. "Listen, Dan, maybe you'd let me take you to dinner one night. There's an awesome private restaurant on board the ship, and I think you'd like it."

Dan thought for a moment and weighed his options. "Yeah," he finally said. "I think that would be great."

Jebb felt like he'd won the lottery. "Well, I'll give you a call when you get settled on the ship and set it up."

"Good man."

There was an awkward silence. Jebb smiled and turned around when a car backfired nearby. He saw Nick standing with Clive Peters and Baldwin Barrows, a couple from New York City that had worked the last three cruises for Titan. When Jebb turned back to say goodbye to Dan, he was already gone.

"Jebb!" Clive shouted out, spying him.

Clive and Baldwin had originally been guests on a Titan Caribbean cruise, and had struck up a friendship with Jebb while on board. Jebb loved their bright, sunny outlook, and their willingness to pitch in and help him set up a T-dance just for the fun of it, when his regular paid staffers had over-slept. He'd hired them for the next cruise, and every cruise after that. They owned a small, thriving floral shop on Madison Avenue in New York City and were able to take off when they wanted. Clive and Baldwin had become cherished Titan team members.

"Hello, boys," Jebb called out to them as he approached their group.

"Jebb!" Baldwin cried out, giving him a big hug. At only 5' 6" and weighing 175, Baldwin was a stocky little fireplug of a man with mischievous brown eyes and a shock of fire-red hair. His compact frame and bowlegged walk made him look a little bit like a bulldog, and that's what most people called him.

"Bulldog!" Jebb hooted, and he squeezed the jovial man hard.

"Hey, baby," said Clive, as he leaned over for a quick kiss from Jebb. Clive was almost the exact opposite of Baldwin. A thin, frail man from Cornwall, England, he was skinny everywhere his lover was thick. They truly looked like the old cartoon characters "Mutt and Jeff." But there was no denying the deep love they felt towards each other. To them, life was a big party, and they had found the perfect dance partner to sail through it with.

"Any major snafus yet this morning?" Jebb asked Nick, who was dressed in a pair of loose fitting board shorts and his blue Titan polo.

"Not really. The usual bitching about mini bar charges, but that's not our problem. So far, so good."

"Good. The shit will hit at embarkation."

"You got that right."

"Nick, let's you and I go on to the ship now and make sure everything is set up okay."

Jebb hailed a cab, and he and Nick hopped in. There were no bags to take with them, as they had set out their baggage the night before.

"Well, I don't feel like sitting around here for a couple of hours. Let's go do something," Zack said, rising to his feet. He was feeling a little cramped in the hotel with all the bodies standing around, and he wanted to get some air.

Kurt stirred, and opened his puffy eyes. "Oh, you go ahead. I don't want to move," he complained, nestling closer against Rick.

"Go on, Zack. We'll wait here," Rick grinned. He reached a free hand up and stroked Kurt's head.

"Okay. See you in a few. I'll meet you here at 2:30?"

"We'll be here," Rick said.

Zack shouldered his camera bag, and worked his way through the crowd. He walked out the front doors, turned right and started to wander up the street when he heard his name being called.

"Zack! Hey! Wait up!"

He turned around to see Hayden paying off a cabbie. He had a few large bags on the ground next to him.

Zack walked back to Hayden and gave him a warm hug. Hayden was wearing faded board shorts and a tight white wifebeater. He looked really good.

"I got bored sitting at home, so I thought I'd come over early," Hayden explained. The taxi driver got back into his car, and drove off.

Zack laughed. "And I got antsy waiting here so I was gonna take a walk. It's a zoo in there."

"Oh. Well, I'll go with you, if it's okay…"

"It's totally okay! Let's get your bags inside." Zack blushed, and realized his heart was beating a little faster. It was something that seemed to happen whenever he was in Hayden's presence.

He liked it.

They dashed inside, checked Hayden's bags at the bell desk, and said a quick hello-goodbye to Kurt and Rick. In minutes they were back out in the sunshine strolling down the Passeig de Gràcia, happy to be in each other's company.

Zack whipped out his camera and took a few shots of some children playing. "My instructor is going to freak when he sees the shots I've taken here. Should help me out when class starts up again."

"You know, you keep talking about school, but you never explained why you're still there," Hayden asked Zack, as he bought glacés for each of them from a street vender. "You're what, 28? I'd have thought you'd have graduated by now."

"I guess I'm on the 10-year plan," Zack joked. He put away his camera and took the cool treat from Hayden. He saw the questioning look in Hayden's eyes and felt compelled to tell him the whole story. "My dad was in the navy. He was captain of a battleship, actually. So, I, of course, had to go to Annapolis. I hated it. It wasn't my bag, but I did what my father told me to do. I always had, you see..."

"Uh huh," Hayden nodded.

"So I worked really hard and passed my plebe year with flying colors. When I went back for my sophomore year, I came under the command of a real hard ass. He was an upperclassman who made it his job to make my life a living hell. He just rode my ass all day, every day. It was intolerable." Zack stopped and glanced into a store window, admiring a sweater.

"Go on," Hayden urged, licking his dripping glacé.

"So, one weekend, I have a pass, and I go into D.C. I knew by then I was gay but hadn't done anything about it. I figured it was time to change that." He glanced at Hayden, who winked. "So, I worked up the nerve to go to a gay bar. I had a drink, not talking to anyone, mind you, then left and went to another bar. I ended up pretty drunk in a leather bar of all places, and lo and behold guess who's there?

"The asshole?"

"You got it. He sees me, freaks out that I've seen him, and tries to leave. I go up to him, I'm drunk, you know, and I say 'why are you such an a-hole to me?' He looks at me, then kisses me. Really hard. Turns out he had a crush on me from the start. Well, I'd never kissed a guy before, and before you knew it, we're in some dingy hotel room fucking like rabbits. It was wild."

Hayden giggled. "I'll bet!"

"So, we kinda start having an affair. He eased up on me at school, and I'd sneak into his room at night, and we'd just screw our brains out." Zack paused.

"Don't stop now! What happened?"

"We got caught. One of his classmates came in to borrow a textbook, and found us. Imagine the scandal! Oh. Did I mention he was the nephew of the then Secretary of Defense?"

"Holy shit!"

"Yeah. 'Don't ask, don't tell,' my ass. Goodbye Annapolis. They tossed me out. Not him, though. He claimed he was drunk and didn't know what he was happening. He said I took advantage of the situation and 'raped' him." Zack laughed. "I love that when we got caught, his head was buried in my crotch, bobbing away, grunting 'Fuck my mouth!' and he had the balls to claim I raped him! And yet, the brass bought it. I guess being related to the head military guy has its advantages. So, I go back home to San Diego, and then Dad kicks me out of the house because I'm gay, and suddenly I was on my own. I went up to L.A., got a bunch of crappy retail-slut jobs and began my thrilling party-boy career. I got hooked on coke, and spiraled down until I checked myself into a rehab. I had one relapse," Zack said heavily, but honestly. "However, I've been clean for five years now," he added, proudly.

"Jesus, Zack," Hayden said sympathetically.

"Yeah, well, sometimes life isn't pretty. I admit to my mistakes, but I know I'll never go back to that life. At my therapist's suggestion, I picked up photography as a creative release and found I had a knack for it. So I wait tables at night, and go to art college during the day. When I can, I work as a photographer's assistant. Remember that whole Cameron Fuller-model thing a couple of years ago?"

Hayden shook his head. "The designer? I remember there was some scandal, but I don't keep up with that stuff."

"Cameron fell in love with one of his male models, and then his wife was murdered at a swank party, in front of hundreds. Then, Cameron killed a cop. It was in all the papers. Don't you read?" Zack joshed.

"I think that all happened right when I had just moved to Barcelona. Like I said, I don't keep up with that stuff," Hayden shrugged. "Why?"

"I worked with the photographer on the shoots for them. Trevor Barbados? He's, like, the top fashion photographer in the world now. He took the most amazing photos of Blake, that was the model's name, Blake. Great guy. Anyway, after the scandal, the photos never saw the light of day. That whole campaign was canceled after the deaths." Zack fell silent for a beat. "Oh, and I also shoot headshots for actors."

"Man! You are one busy boy!"

Zack laughed. "And, when I can find the time, I'm working on a personal project. I'm shooting a series of photographs all around town that reflect what I see as the 'real' L.A. Very architectural. No people."

"That sounds cool."

"Well, I want to get into photojournalism. It has taken me a while to complete the school courses because it's important to me that I pay for it myself. I need to prove to myself that I can do it, you know? It may seem silly, but it's how I want it. Then, no one can take it away from me. It's been tough."

"But you're…ex…was rich, wasn't he?"

"Yeah. He could never figure out why I wanted to do it myself. It was one of our biggest problems," Zack's voice changed tone as he spoke about Bayne. Just talking about him brought back to realization that their relationship was over.

Hayden saw the subtle change come over Zack's face, and quickly apologized. "Oh, man, I didn't mean to bring him up. I'm sorry, Zack."

"Oh, don't worry about it…" Zack said stepping off the curb and absently entering the street. Hayden saw a taxi bearing down on Zack, and he jumped out into the road and quickly pulled Zack back just in the nick of time. The taxi honked loudly as it whizzed past, and both men felt their pulses race.

Hayden didn't know if it was because of the close call or the fact that he was holding tightly onto Zack. He could feel Zack's hard body under his loose clothing, and he had to force himself to let go.

Zack, scared and breathing hard, looked deep into Hayden's liquid eyes, and felt a heated rush flow through his body. The two men stood for several seconds staring at each other.

Zack backed up a feeble step and broke the sexual tension. "Thanks," he mumbled. "Maybe we should head back now."

Hayden felt the subtle change in Zack and put away his erotic thoughts. "Sure. Let's go. I bet we can head on to the ship a little early, anyway."

9

The *Princess Diana*, Port of Barcelona, Spain

Zack was stunned. "Are you sure? Is this right?" he asked the steward, dumbfounded. The efficient cabin attendant, checking a clipboard. "Mr. Bayne Raddock and Mr. Zack Barnes. Cabin 7532, Royal Suite."

Zack shook his head. Bayne had done it again. He'd upgraded arrangements without explanation, even though he knew how important it was for Zack to pay for the trip.

"Okay, fine. Thank you very much."

The steward bowed his head slightly. "You're welcome. I am Guillermo. If you need anything, please don't hesitate to ask. Welcome aboard the *Princess Diana*." He backed out of the cabin and shut the door behind him.

Zack sighed and threw his camera bag on the lavishly made up queen-sized bed in the larger of the cabin's two bedrooms. Surprisingly spacious, the master bedroom also contained a huge dressing table, plenty of closets and a large bathroom complete with a full-sized tub.

The stateroom suite was composed of three main rooms. The larger master bedroom with space to spare, a wide and smartly configured living room, and a separate, smaller second bedroom containing twin beds that could be pushed together to form another queen-sized bed. The color palette used throughout was neutral beige and a warm, pale blue.

Luxurious, rough silk curtains hung in front of a massive floor to ceiling double-glassed panoramic window in the living area that gave a spectacular view of the Barcelona coastline, just beyond the massive pier where the *Princess Diana* was berthed. Rich, highly polished cherry wood cabinetry was used throughout with plenty of drawers, cupboards, and cubbyholes for storage. The thickly piled carpeting underfoot was a subdued mosaic pattern in beige and blue, and all the hardware of the suite was polished stainless steel. A comfortable looking sofa was flanked by two deco-styled side chairs in the living room, and the suite's lighting was provided by frosted glass sconces placed evenly throughout.

There was also a wide, long private patio/deck that was accessible from both the master bedroom and the living area. It was furnished with a table and chair set and two chaise loungers begging to be used.

There was a bar and a mini fridge stocked with goodies. Two televisions, one in the master bedroom and one in the living room, were on and blaring hot dance music videos, a nod towards getting the party started. Zack looked down and saw that his luggage had been delivered, as promised.

Hands on hips, Zack's anger at Bayne rose. The man had always treated Zack like a child and acted like he was the all-knowing father.

"Fuck him!" Zack shouted gleefully, and he jumped on the bed in pure joy. He had an awesome cabin on a beautiful ship, had made some terrific friends, and was seeing an amazing man. He was going to enjoy himself now, and worry about the asshole Bayne later.

On the exact opposite side of the ship, Kurt and Rick were inspecting their cabin as well. Identical in every way to Zack's, they opened cabinet doors and check out the closets.

Rick had been amazed at how easy the check-in process had been. He, Kurt, Zack and Hayden had gotten a taxi at the Hotel Majestic and had been driven to the port.

The four men could see the beautiful and sleek *Princess Diana* tied up to a long dock beyond the streamlined Lassiter Lines terminal. After gathering their bags and paying off the driver, they hustled inside.

They queued up in the "boarding" line inside the terminal building, and were surprised to find that about a hundred other Titan guests had decided to board early as well. They waited about 20 minutes in line, then, when their turn was up, went to the customs desk, presented their passports, and had been checked into the ship's computer.

Each guest was given a credit card sized keycard, which, cleverly, was also their onboard charge card. Then they each had their picture taken for the ship's guest computer system. The purpose for this was whenever a guest left the ship for shore excursions, they would present their keycard, it would be swiped through a large security machine, and their picture would pop up on a monitor. The security detail manning the ID machine could then make sure the right person was exiting and entering the ship, as well as have an electronic log as to who was on board and who was off ship.

Next, the four friends had a group picture taken in front of a painted backdrop of Rome at the corny photo booth set up by the Lassiter Line. Then they ascended the long sloping ramp to enter the ship. After having their key-cards checked one final time by a cute seaman, they stepped on board the *RMS Princess Diana*.

Ascending the main grand stairwell, they all paused when they came to an enormous oil portrait of the real Princess Diana that hung over the wide landing. After discussing how sad it was that the electrifying princess's life was cut so tragically short, they were each directed to their appropriate decks by a helpful staffer. Hayden went to the bowels of the ship, Rick, Kurt and Zack to the exclusive top passenger deck.

The men quickly discovered that the *Princess Diana* was broken up into eight passenger decks. Each deck was easily accessed by multiple banks of gleaming elevators or wide staircases that were spaced evenly throughout the ship. The decks that were comprised mostly of passenger cabins had long, labyrinthine corridors that seemed to go on forever, only to suddenly turn left or right around some obstruction, then continue on forever again. These slightly claustrophobic corridors were well lit however, and had teak handrails along the walls, in case the ship should suddenly lurch to one side or the other.

The lowest deck passengers could access, Deck B, was comprised of economy passenger cabins. Not as luxurious as those cabins on the upper decks, these staterooms still were quite nice and very practical.

The next deck up, Deck A, had more of the same. The companionways on this deck were a bit wider, and the higher viewpoints afforded from the portholes of these cabins offered a better scenic view.

Above Deck A, was Deck 4, the Pearl Deck. This deck was all passenger accommodations as well, only upgraded. These cabins were larger, and had a few extra creature comforts such as wider windows and better bedding.

Deck 5, the Emerald Deck, was also known as the Promenade Deck. This deck was home to the ship's main dining room, the Côte d'Azur, as well as several smaller specialty dining spots such as the Sushi Bar and Hamburger Palace. The Highgrove Casino was positioned here, but was only open for business when the ship was at sea. The main bar of the ship, the Piccadilly Pub, was located just forward of the Côte d'Azur dining room, and just beyond that was the Double Decker Disco. The wide teak outdoor promenade that surrounded the Emerald Deck was also, incidentally, the lifeboat station deck.

The next deck upward was Deck 6, the Sapphire Deck, or Main Deck.

Here, there was a shopping arcade with duty-free shopping. High end jewelry stores and clothing boutiques, as well as a liquor shoppe and a perfume bar, would open their doors as soon as the *Princess Diana* left port, because, like the casino one deck down, they could only operate when the ship was at sea. The Bond Street Theater, the ship's grand showroom, was located forward of all the retail areas. The children's video arcade was located on this level as well as the Union Jack Cafe, a coffee and pastry shop. The Union Jack was at the base of the Grand Atrium, a five-story-tall space flanked by two brass and glass elevators that rose up and down between the open decks. Vast glass skylights in the ceiling of the Grand Atrium allowed sunlight from above to beam into the cavernous expanse.

Above the Sapphire Deck was the Diamond Deck, Deck 7, home to the ship's most exclusive cabins. There were also several public rooms on this level including the cyber cafe, the smoking room and a small pastry shop.

The top two decks were mostly devoted to outdoor activities. The Sun Deck on Deck 8 was home to the ship's two swimming pools, a couple of outdoor bars, the a la carte dining room, a compactly designed Putt-Putt golf course, and a cleverly engineered self-serve ice cream shop. Just forward of the matching pools was the spa and gym area, which overlooked the bow of the ship and gave its patrons wide, panoramic views of the seas ahead.

Above the Sun Deck, was the wraparound Compass Deck. A sports deck that overlooked the twin pools and provided extra sunning areas with hundreds of chaise loungers lined up neatly, this deck was the uppermost area passengers could access. The ship's running track was up here, as well as Notting Hill, the *Princess Diana*'s day care and children's activity center. The ship's exclusive Spencer House dining room was also accessed from this deck.

Perched above the Compass Deck was the off-limits bridge of the ship. Along with the ship's controls, there were numerous practical areas here, including the captain's quarters, the radio room, the radar room, and other vital ship functions.

All in all, the *Princess Diana* was a complete city at sea, fully self-contained and state-of-the-art. She was designed with one purpose: to provide a luxurious and relaxing cruise through sparkling warm waters to glamorous ports and give her passengers the confidence of utmost safety.

After only getting a little lost finding it, Rick and Kurt were now finally ensconced in their beautiful cabin. "It's great," Rick enthused after their steward had left.

"Yeah, it is. It's a lot nicer than I thought it would be." Kurt flopped onto the bed, glad to finally be lying down. Rick dropped his carryon bag and crawled on the bed as well, snuggling up next to his lover.

"Feeling better?" he whispered into Kurt's ear.

"A little, thanks." He pulled Rick close. "At least my headache has gone away. Remind me never to drink again."

"I'll try."

Kurt turned his head and looked deep into Rick's warm eyes. "Look, honey, " he said softly. "I know I fought you over taking this vacation, but I'm so glad you talked me into it. You were right."

"Can I have that in writing?"

Kurt smiled. "I'm serious. I've been so wrapped up in work lately. I know I've been giving you the short end of the stick, and I'm sorry. Being able to spend all this time with you just reminds me how much I love you. How much I need you."

"Oh, baby," Rick sighed happily. He sensually began to grind his arousal into Kurt's thigh.

"Mmmm," Kurt rolled over, ending up face to face with Kurt. "I take it you have something in mind?"

Rick put a look of deep concentration on his face. "Hmm...Let me think..." He pressed his crotch against Kurt's. He leaned in and began to kiss and lick Kurt's neck. "How about..." he continued in a sexy, low voice, "You whip that big, beautiful cock of yours out, and fuck me hard and long?"

Never one to disappoint his lover, Kurt was soon doing exactly that.

Three decks below, Jorge Camarillo arched his head back, and moaned loudly. He was getting plowed, and plowed well, by his new cabinmate, Kirby Dickerson, a short, but truly hunky personal trainer from Dallas, Texas.

"Oh maaaaaannn," Jorge sighed, as Kirby pulsed his hips back and forth.

"This is," gasped Kirby between thrusts, "Crazy!...I fuckin' just met you!"

"Oh, yeah..Ohhhh, move it like that!...Ohhhh!" Jorge said, as he gazed at Kirby's photo-worthy, ripped abs tighten and relax as he rammed his pretty tool in and out of him. Kirby's smooth chest and tight body looked so damn hot between his legs!

"I can't believe I'm doing this...!" Kirby continued.

"Oh, Papi, just shut up and fuck me!"

Kirby fell silent and picked up the pace.

Forty-five minutes earlier, Kirby had been unpacking his stuff in Cabin 4116 when the most gorgeous man he had ever seen entered the room. Introductions were quickly made.

"I'm Jorge. From Miami."

"Hey, Jorge, I'm Kirby." They shook hands, and Kirby noticed the interested glance Jorge gave him, his eyes going up and down him from head to toe. Kirby knew it was a good view.

Though only 5'6", Kirby had worked his body out until it resembled a Michelangelo sculpture. He taught a daily spin class at a high-end health club in Dallas and trained bored Dallas socialites the rest of the day. He had a slightly round face, lively brown eyes and a wide happy smile. His naturally curly blond hair was cut into a super short buzz cut. His bedroom eyes were shielded by the thickest set of lashes in three counties. He possessed thickly built legs and a tight, meaty ass that equaled, and possibly surpassed, his new cabinmate's in its tempting beauty.

They chatted while they both unpacked their bags in the tiny cabin. Twin beds hugged the side walls, with a narrow space between them. One solitary porthole window was over the centered nightstand, the curtains parted and open. A microscopic bathroom was next to the doorway and across from that a closet.

Kirby started to change from his clothes into his swimsuit. He wanted to get in a few laps in the indoor pool before joining the afternoon Bon Voyage T-dance that was already underway by the outdoor pool on the Sun Deck.

For a few brief moments he stood nude in front of Jorge, who licked his lips at the beautiful man changing before him. Without saying a word, Jorge went to his knees and took Kirby into his mouth. The sheer audacity of the brazen act, not to mention seeing such a sexy man go down on him, turned Kirby on and soon, they were sixty-nine on the cramped cabin floor.

One thing led to another…

"Ohhhh!…Yes!…Wiggle it like that, you little fucker!…Maaannn!…How do you do that?! Mmmmm…!" Jorge swooned, knowing he was seconds away from a mind-blowing climax.

Kirby, completely into the sight of Jorge squirming on his back, was unprepared for the mighty gush that issued forth as Jorge came and came and came. He felt his own climax fast approaching, and pulling out of Jorge's amazing ass, he tugged off the condom and let loose.

Afterward, both men were left panting on the floor.

"So," Jorge finally said, rising to his unsteady feet. "Which side of the room do you want?"

10

Diamond Deck, *Princess Diana*, Port of Barcelona, Spain

Zack had just finished unpacking when is cabin phone rang.

"Hello?"

"Hey, it's Hayden. How's your stateroom?"

Zack looked around his plush surroundings. "It'll do."

"Mine's the size of a closet. A *small* closet."

"Well, it's not like you're going to be in it all that much."

"True. What are you doing?"

"Nothing. I just finished unpacking. I was going to go explore this barge. Wanna come?"

"Sure! Where do you want to meet? Where are you?"

"Cabin 7532. Diamond Deck."

"I'll be right up. Bye."

Zack hung up the phone and felt a giddy flush of excitement.

Ten minutes later he heard a knock at his door. He opened it, and let Hayden enter.

"Dayum! Look at all the room you have here!" Hayden was dumbstruck. Zack's cabin was easily ten times the size of his. "Wow. You even have your own balcony!" He opened the sliding door and stepped outside. Zack followed, and the two men leaned against the teak railing and looked at the activity on the pier below them. They could see hundreds of men swarming around, getting into the check-in lines, boarding, getting bags out of cabs. It was a mad scene below them. Both Zack and Hayden began to laugh at the craziness of it all.

"Looks like an anthill," Hayden joked, looking over at Zack.

"My thoughts exactly." He looked up and caught Hayden's direct gaze. There was a spark between them that couldn't be denied. Zack wanted to lean in and plant one on the handsome man next to him so badly, it shocked him.

"You look really good today," Hayden said softly, edging closer.

"You, too." Zack felt weak with desire. But it confused him. He was only five days single, and he was so unsure of who he was now and what he should feel.

Using all his strength, he stepped back from Hayden and went back into the cabin. "Let's go explore," he said, with false cheerfulness.

Hayden, sensing the mood change, struggled to appear easygoing. "Uh, sure. Let's go."

Without another word, they left the suite.

They turned left in the companionway and stopped at a wide balcony overlooking the grand atrium. Looking around the five-story open space, Zack gazed upward and took in the ornate glass sculpture that was the chandelier, and the skylight above it showing the clear blue sky, while Hayden looked down on the various activities happening on each deck below.

"I, like, feel, like I'm sooo at the mall?" he joked, affecting a Valley girl accent.

Zack nodded, looking down as well. "Totally. Fer sure."

A pair of large gold-trimmed glass elevators that glided silently between the floors were packed with excited men coming aboard. The atrium was clearly the indoor social center of the ship and the main focus of the public decks. Even though it did have a slightly Vegas-like air about its decor, Zack and Hayden agreed it was still an impressive space.

At the base of the Grand Atrium they saw the Union Jack Cafe with guests already sitting down, taking in the sights and drinking brightly colored cocktails served up by smartly uniformed waiters moving through the throngs of men.

On Zack's deck, hugging the open atrium on the starboard side was the cyber cafe. Over 25 computer terminals were set up in private low-walled cubicles that allowed guests to check, send and receive e-mail from anywhere in the world. Opposite that, on the port side of the ship, was the Hyde Park lounge, a generously proportioned public area filled with clusters of comfortable chairs and beckoning sofas. Heading aft, the two handsome men took the grand staircase up one level to the Sun Deck.

Zack and Hayden decided to go towards the bow of the ship. They entered the huge glass-covered solarium and swimming pool. Wrought iron chaise loungers were lined up like soldiers on either side of the wide pool and intimate clusters of chairs and tables were placed next to the floor-to-ceiling glass walls that looked out over the sea.

A large sky dome could be mechanically opened allowing the bright sunshine in, but since the *Princess Diana* was in dock, it was now closed. Soothing music filtered through speakers hidden in the ceiling, and the entire space had the feeling of a luxurious retreat.

Passing by the large, twin Jacuzzis flanking the pool, and already filled with hot men in skimpy Speedos, Zack and Hayden entered the spa and gym. They walked by the hair salon, and sailed into the spa. Soft, relaxing music was wafting from overhead speakers here as well, as they passed the massage rooms and steam areas. The air here was scented with the pleasing aroma of eucalyptus, spearmint and other clean scents. Hayden remarked that he had signed up for a massage first thing when he'd entered his cabin.

Wandering through the spa gift shop they came upon the gym. To Zack's surprise, it was reasonably well equipped with many more cardio machines than he'd expected. Set against a wide bank of yet more floor-to-ceiling glass walls were treadmills, recumbent LifeCycles and elliptical trainers. Free weights, bench presses and other workout machines were liberally placed about the clean, open space.

"I think I can get a decent workout done in here," Zack commented as they passed two men already puffing away on the recumbent bikes.

"I think so, too. Though I like to run," Hayden replied.

"They have a track on one of the decks. We could do that together every morning," Zack offered.

"You're on."

They exited the gym and found themselves back in the solarium indoor pool, opposite where they entered the spa area. Passing through the solarium, they soon found themselves outside and strolling towards the outdoor pool area.

All the deck chairs and loungers that normally would be lined up in neat rows around the large pool area had been discreetly stored away, leaving the vast space open. An enormous bar, with barstool seating for easily 20 patrons, anchored the rear of the pool area, and it was filled to capacity with happy, chatting Titan tourists getting to know each other.

There was loud dance music blaring from some heavy-duty speakers that had been added especially for this cruise. Mounted on the railings of the overhang deck that surrounded the pool from above, these massive black boxes boomed out the latest Gwen Stefani dance track.

In a raised-up gazebo area beside the pool, DJ Kenny BamBam, the hottest DJ in the club circuit scene, was busily getting his CDs and records in order. A surprisingly muscular and handsome man, he was wearing only a faded pair of low-riding cargo shorts, an Abercrombie & Fitch visor and a thick padded headset. His beautifully chiseled chest had a slight sheen of sweat on it from the constant gyrating and dancing he did as his music blared out over the crowd.

Over two hundred men were already dancing on the teak flooring next to the freeform pool and again, the duel hot tubs here were filled to capacity. While most were still dressed in their embarkation clothes of shorts and tanks, some passengers had eagerly changed into swimsuits or brightly colored sarongs complete with floral leis around their necks.

A lot of the dancing men were sporting small, flesh colored patches behind their ears. Hayden pointed these out to Zack and explained that these were anti-nausea patches that some of the more queasy fellows used to keep from getting seasick.

The two friends squeezed through the growing crowd, saying hello to guys they had met during the pre-cruise excursions in Barcelona. Zack saw Andy and Frank dancing shirtless up close against a hot young man who seemed to love the attention from the two men. When Andy saw them, he waved. Zack waved back.

"Man, the boys are out today!" Hayden whistled, looking out over the sea of dancing men. Most had stripped off their shirts and had tucked them into their back pockets where they hung, swaying like a banners as their owners danced.

The music was excellent, the bar was open and the party had started.

"Let's get a drink," Zack yelled back to Hayden over the loud music.

"Good idea!"

At the crowded bar, they each ordered a Corona, and taking the cool bottles with them, circled the dance area and watched the show for a few minutes.

"Mmm. I wanna dance," Hayden yelled. "Let's do it!"

Zack, getting into the groove of the music, readily agreed. They worked their way into the mass and created a space smack in the middle of the crowd. A great dance mix of one of Zack's favorite songs came up and soon they were both shaking their groove things.

Hayden swigged from his beer and got hot first. He handed Zack his beer and slowly peeled off the tank top he was wearing. He reached behind and tucked it away in his back pocket. Zack couldn't help but ogle his trim, tight torso and perfectly shredded abs. His baggy board shorts hung low on his hips, giving a teasing view of his super-sexy happy trail. Hayden caught Zack looking and laughed. Zack shrugged and handed him back his beer.

Soon, Zack took off his tee shirt as well, and the two men worked up a sweat. Hayden openly stared at Zack's rounded pecs and hard four-pack glistening in the late afternoon sun.

The music was amazing, and Zack needed this release of letting his tension and unhappiness go. He and Hayden got into a mutual rhythm, and their dancing styles complimented each other. At one point, Hayden reached a hand out and pulled Zack close to him, and the two men playfully grinded their hips together in time to the beat. Laughing with pure joy, they both began to sing along to a hot remix of Kelly Clarkson's "Since You've Been Gone."

Arms waved, legs paced, and heads swayed.

Hayden flagged down a cocktail waiter and ordered more beers. Upon his return, Hayden handed a fresh one to Zack, who took it gratefully. "This is so great!" the investment banker shouted. "Just what I needed! Look at all these guys," he said, waving his arms around to indicate the throngs of dancing men. "Everybody's here to have a good time, let their hair down, and just be gay and accepted…I love it!"

Zack nodded furiously. "I know what you mean! I feel so free…"

Freshly showered and blissful in the afterglow of powerful sex, Kurt and Rick squeezed a path through and joined their friends on the dance floor. The four buddies formed a tight circle and danced as one. Kurt had removed his shirt and the frankly lustful stares he got were hilarious to watch. Rick ripped his tank top off too, and generated much of the same interest. But soon, feeling a tad possessive, Rick began pressing up against his lover. His overprotective behavior was purposely designed to let everyone know that Kurt was taken. This not-so-subtle message was instantly understood by the men dancing around them.

They could look, but not touch.

Dan Smith didn't seem to notice the appreciative glances thrown his way as he casually strolled along the Compass Deck, just above the dancing throng one deck below. The Compass Deck was the overhang deck directly above the Sun Deck, which, besides being home to the shuffleboard courts, contained a half-court basketball area, and offered an elevated walkway around the entire ship. Completely open over the pool area, a passenger could stand up here and gaze down on the activity below.

The running track was also on this deck, as was a neat feature, the namesake compasses. Anchored on an extra, small deck overlooking the stern of the ship, and accessed by a flight of stairs, the compass area was a section where three large brass compasses were displayed, showing the position of the *Princess Diana* on her travels.

But Dan wasn't taking in the ship's architecture right now. He was on a mission. And, as such, he was dressed appropriately.

He was shirtless, showing off his perfectly proportioned and built chest, which was already deeply tanned. He was wearing a snug D-Squared boxer-cut bathing suit in black, flip-flops and nothing else. The bathing suit did little to hide his impressive endowment. By no accident the thin garment also accentuated the muscle tone of his lower body in jaw-dropping fashion. An avid swimmer and cycler, Dan had great legs and a hot ass, and he knew it. He also knew how to use his physical attributes to his own advantage.

His heavily tinted sunglasses were perched on his rugged nose and hiding the fact that he was searching the crowd of gay men relentlessly. There was one man, a man he had seen boarding, who was his prey now. He would find this man and not let him out of his sight again. Then, either through luck or complicated scheme, the occasion would arise where Dan and this man would be alone together...

In order to fulfill his personal objective, Dan needed to be alone with his prey. As the adrenaline rose in his body, Dan was subtly aware that he was actually enjoying this particular hunt.

"Oh, Daddy!" squealed out a slightly built man of about 23. He was with his friends when Dan happened to walk by, and was determined to get the hunky man's attention. "Need any help getting out of those swim trunks?"

Dan, torn from his mission, glanced at the twink and cracked a rare smile. The kid was very skinny and very feminine. Not Dan's type at all. Dan liked them athletic. Built. Hot. "Not today, thanks," he said.

"Well, Daddy, you name the day!" The twink's friends all busted out laughing, and Dan moved on, refocusing on his objective.

Geoff Corbin sauntered out onto the Compass Deck, just across the pool from where Dan was, and took in the scene. He saw the raised deck for the compasses and considered going up there for a better view of the dance. He changed his mind, and instead, leaned against a railing directly next to one of the massive extra speakers.

He had been greatly displeased with his cabin, an inside space, no more than a closet with no windows. After marching up to the Titan Tours desk, he demanded and got an upgrade to a better room, one that at least had a window. Now somewhat mollified, he gazed out over the dancing crowd and began to check out the talent.

He was wearing his lucky shorts, the very same cutoff jeans shorts he'd worn on *Race Around the World 5*. He'd won the million dollars wearing these shorts and had steadfastly refused to put them on E-Bay for the usual after-show charity drive of *RAW* memorabilia.

He was wearing the shorts and nothing else. Barefoot and shirtless, he looked down at the dancing men, and swayed in time to the beat of the dance tune blaring from the speaker right next to him. There were about 75 other men up on this deck looking down as well. More than one of them noticed him and pointed him out to their friends.

Geoff chose to ignore the men near him and instead focused on the dancing throng. He was spellbound by one particular couple. They were two bodybuilders, one huge and blond, the other Asian, and they were practically fucking right there on the deck! Geoff gulped and noticed that another couple of hot men were dancing with them. Damn! He'd sleep with any one of the four!

"Hey, Geoff," came a familiar voice from behind him.

Turning to see who called out to him, he saw Jorge walk past him, waving. Jorge's flawless body was on full display. Wearing only a tiny black Aussie Bum Speedo style bathing suit, his exquisite chest was shiny with suntan oil, and his thick arms were pumped up and clapping in time to the music. His hot, amazing, and perfect ass was teasingly encased in the flimsy fabric of the swimsuit, and as Jorge moved, it swayed enticingly. The hot man picked his way down the stairs to join the action on the dance floor.

Geoff watched him enter the crowd. Men stared openly agog at Jorge's beauty and opened a path for him automatically. Spying a raised section of built-in benches that surrounded the pool, Jorge hopped up, and now elevated slightly above the crowd, started to dance.

Jorge closed his eyes and let go. The Ecstasy tab he'd just taken was doing its thing, and Jorge was enjoying the buzz. He knew he was now the center of attention, and he loved it. He could feel all eyes on him. He could feel them caress him, touch him, stroke him. Even though he had just gotten royally fucked by his new roomie, he was still horned up. Jorge could have sex five times a day and still want more. The waves of adulation that swept over him from the good-looking crowd turned him on, and he felt himself growing hard.

He spun and dipped and waved his arms around, dancing like he had never danced before. He touched himself, slid his hands sexily down his oil-slicked chest, felt his own cut thighs, and cupped his ass teasingly all in full view of the dancing crowd. He knew it would only be a matter of time before the crowd would scream for him to pull down the swimsuit.

Jorge felt so good, so alive, he might just do it, too.

Dan had stopped at a teak railing and was looking down at the dancing men spread out below him. The music was amazing and the air festive. Dan was a good dancer, but was clearly not in the mood to join the party. He was serving a greater need now, and that was what he was focused on. His eyes expertly took in each of the faces he gazed at and quickly dismissed them. He was looking for that specific person, and he wouldn't stop searching until he found him.

A swirling, dipping and prancing Hispanic man, jutting out his hard ass while at the same time tugging at his skimpy Speedo, had caught the attention of many men who stared at him with lust in their eyes. There were whistles and catcalls directed towards him. More and more people found themselves compelled to watch the erotically dancing stud.

Dan's eyes fell on Jorge, too. He lowered his sunglasses slightly to drink in the view.

Just then, Jorge looked up. He saw an incredibly sexy man on the deck above checking him out. *Papi, you can have me anytime, anywhere*, he thought. *And the sooner, the better!*

Jorge flashed Dan a sexy grin and spun around, letting his hands cup his ass, then tug down the Speedo a bit, flashing his ass cheeks. He never took his eyes off Dan, and was secretly thrilled when the corners of Dan's mouth began to curl upward in a slight smile.

Hayden had glanced once in Jorge's direction, but found Zack a more rewarding view. Zack looked over his shoulders to see what everyone was looking at and, giving Jorge the once-over, couldn't help but notice the generous hard-on the underwear model was now proudly flaunting.

He nudged Hayden and, shaking his head, pointed it out to him. "Jesus! I'd be so embarrassed to have a big ole boner in plain view of everyone, wouldn't you?" he shouted over the deafening thump-thump-thump of the music.

Hayden smiled sexily and shrugged. Suddenly, he reached out, grabbing Zack's hand. Pulling it forward and down, he guided Zack's tapering fingers to his crotch, where his arousal was readily apparent.

"That's because of you," he shouted back, winking.

Zack, while caught off guard by Hayden's bold move, found he couldn't take his hand away. He was slightly surprised to find himself throwing his inhibitions to the wind, as he squeezed, felt and tugged at Hayden's nicely packed piece.

Hayden thought he might explode. Zack's hand was making all the right moves, and Hayden wanted to pull him to the floor and pounce on him. The sexual energy in the pool area was palpable and Hayden wanted to give in to it. It felt so freeing to be lost in a crowd of his own kind, everyone celebrating the very fact that they could celebrate. It felt good and natural to be free in his sexuality here, now, and he damn sure wanted Zack. He'd wanted Zack since the day he'd met him in the lobby of the Hotel Royale.

Unable to restrain himself any longer, he leaned in and pressed his lips to Zack's. Zack responded by opening his mouth and letting Hayden's tongue slither in and wrestle his. In seconds, their two sweaty bodies were pressed together. Zack reached his hands up and placed them on either side of Hayden's face and pulled him closer as the two men lost themselves in a kissing marathon that had no equal. Doing this intimate, sensual act in the swarm of undulating men was a complete turn on to both of them, and soon their hands began to roam.

Rick pulled away from his studly lover for just a moment and happened to glance in Zack and Hayden's direction. He saw the passion building as the two men made out.

It made him very happy.

Zack thought he felt the deck tilt, and he clung to Hayden. His head was swimming and he felt drunk. It wasn't the beers, it was Hayden. His kisses were so deep and heartfelt it literally took Zack's breath away. He felt Hayden's hand gently squeeze and tease his painfully hard cock, and the sensations of having this unbelievably hot man feel him up made him think carnal thoughts that would make a porn star blush.

Rex Lassiter and his beautiful Italian-born wife Donnatella arrogantly strode out onto the Compass Deck. Rex and Donnatella were both dressed in expensive designer clothes, Donnatella in a fitted black Gucci cocktail dress that fell sedately to her knees, and Rex overdressed in a Hugo Boss suit that had been custom fitted to perfection on his tall frame. He was even wearing a tie.

The Lassiters had already visited their enormous cabin and Rex had found several things unsatisfactory about it. Three cabin attendants were now busily redoing the bed linens, bringing in better crystal and vacuuming the space to better suit the demanding owner.

Now, impatiently standing on the Compass Deck, Rex started to scan the crowd. He and Donnatella were standing next to a big, built man who had on one of those shockingly tight square-cut bathing suits that only the gays wore, and flip-flops. Rex shook his head in disapproval. He then noticed the man was staring down at the crowd below, yet paying them no attention. Instead, he seemed to be focused on one of the gays in particular.

The man must have sensed that Rex was watching him. He looked up slowly, and even though his eyes were hidden by his sunglasses, Rex knew the man was checking him out. The man grunted an inaudible greeting, then went back to staring at whoever it was who had caught his eye.

Puffing up with disdain, the shipping magnate ignored him.

Rex was a man overwrought with tension. Clutched in his well-manicured fist was yet another newly received bomb threat letter. He repeated his visual search of the pool deck, trying to find Jebb Miller. He wanted to flaunt this latest letter under the tour leader's nose.

Not able to resist the temptation to glance at the hate-filled note one more time, Rex unfolded the sheet of paper and again read the words it contained:

> Lassiter,
> We warned you!
> All the sodomites will die when
> the Diana sinks to the bottom of the sea!
> It's God's will.
> We hope you die too!

Crumpling the hate letter up in his fist, Rex grimaced and continued his visual search for Jebb. Frustrated, he realized that Jebb was not on deck.

He allowed his gaze to become less focused, and he took in the wider scope of the bacchanal happening down on his Sun Deck. "Oh, my God!" he gasped, finally realizing what he was witnessing.

Donnatella's eyes grew large as she gaped at the scene below. "Rex! Rex, those men down there are…kissing!" she said, her lightly accented but throaty voice displaying her excitement. Waif thin and tall, she was the very definition of chic. Carefully tended and expertly colored flaming red hair cascaded down her straight back, and her long legs ended in a pair of custom-made black pumps.

Homosexuality wasn't as shocking to Donnatella as it was to Rex. She had a lesbian half-sister and a gay cousin. It wasn't discussed in her family, but she knew. And she didn't really care. Love was love. Gender shouldn't matter. Rex was the zealot.

She reached up and casually lowered her oversized white Chanel sunglasses so she could see better. Her sparkling blue eyes drank in everything below her.

"My God! Turn away, Donnatella!" Appalled, Rex had gripped the railing so hard, his knuckles turned white.

"Oh, please," she said dismissively. "He's hot!" She pointed to Jorge who was gyrating and tugging his swimsuit down low, exposing a sexy tanline and more taut flesh, then pulling it back up, teasing the chanting crowd.

"Donnatella!" Rex exclaimed, shocked by his wife.

"Oh, pull the stick out of your ass, Rex," she snapped. She continued to stare at Jorge, who had spun around, and was now pulling his suit down to expose his unbelievably hot ass. Donnatella licked her lips. "Oh, my," she said under her breath. She unconsciously unbuttoned the top button on her dress, allowing a glimpse of her ample cleavage to show.

"This is disgraceful! I'm going to speak to Jebb Miller about this! Those men are…My God! Those men are…are…feeling each other!" he thundered, pointing to Zack and Hayden.

Donnatella found she couldn't take her eyes off Jorge. The exotically beautiful man's undulations and overt sexuality had her absolutely spellbound. As if hypnotized, she stared numbly at the thick erection tugging at the silky fabric of his swimsuit, threatening to erupt forth at any second.

At least she *hoped* it would.

"I can't watch any more of this! Let's go," Rex ordered, turning to storm back to their cabin.

"Um…you go on. I'll…I'll be there in a minute." Donnatella never took her eyes off Jorge's crotch. She deftly undid another button on her dress.

My, it's getting warm, she thought.

Zack felt like he didn't control his hands. They seemed to have a mind of their own. They glided over Hayden's body, touching, caressing, squeezing.

"Oh, Zack," Hayden breathed hotly into his ear, "Let's get out of here. Let's go back to your cabin. I want to make love to you…"

Zack wanted to do exactly that as well. So bad he ached. But for some reason he pulled away from the delicious man who wanted him. Hayden looked at him quizzically.

"I'm sorry, Hade," Zack mouthed, shaking his head. "I can't. Not yet." He tore himself away from Hayden and walked briskly away from the party.

Hayden watched him go, disbelief and hurt flooding his face.

11

Diamond Deck, *Princess Diana*, Port of Barcelona, Spain

Zack flopped himself down on his bed and cried anew. He felt so conflicted and confused. He couldn't deny that he was attracted to Hayden. And not just physically. He liked Hayden's mind, his ethics, his personality. He liked the way he smiled when he told a joke. He liked the way Hayden stood when he was listening intently to someone, like they were the most important person in the world. There was so much he liked about Hayden.

But, Zack fretted, *what does that say about me?*

Zack was not a sleep-around kind of man. Sure, in his early 20s, when he was newly out and tweaked out of his mind half the time, he fucked around like a stud. But not in a long time, and Bayne had been the only man he'd slept with for the past three years. Zack had become a hopeless monogamist. When he was in love with a man, that was it for him. That was all he needed.

So how could he be so willing to go to bed with Hayden when he was just barely separated from his ex-lover? Was that previous relationship so meaningless that he could get over it in five days?

But, now that he thought about it, he knew he was over Bayne. Completely. How could that be, though? Zack's head hurt from trying to figure it out.

He knew he'd hurt Hayden, kissing him, feeling him up, then running away, and that bothered him. Hayden deserved better treatment than some guy being a cock tease, leading him on, then pulling back.

And why did I pull back? Zack asked himself, sniffling. *I'm attracted to him. He's a stone cold fox and I'm single now. What's my fucking problem?*

That's when it hit him.

"Jesus!" he said aloud, sitting upright. "I'm falling in love with him." Once said, it was fact.

Zack was stunned by his own personal revelation. In the course of five days, he'd transferred what he had once felt for Bayne, and focused it on

Hayden. It was insane, but there it was.

Now what do I do, he wondered.

There was a terse knock on his door. Getting up sluggishly, he wiped his eyes dry, and crossed over to answer it. He was relieved to find it was Hayden.

"Hey, what was *that* all about?"

Zack let the still shirtless Hayden in and closed the door.

"I'm sorry."

"You're sorry, and I'm confused." Hayden looked at Zack, and his crossness evaporated. "Look, Zack. I like you. It's been months and months since I felt this for anyone. It just sucks that you're still wrapped up in your ex."

Zack smiled helplessly. "I know. I'm sorry."

Hayden now looked embarrassed, like he'd said too much. He waved his hands at Zack. "No, don't be. I'm sorry. I guess I got carried away and pushed you a little too hard." He sighed and looked out the large window of the living room. "Hey!" he said. "We're moving."

It was true. The *Princess Diana* was underway and beginning to leave the safe port for open sea. The four diesel-electric generators deep below Zack and Hayden's feet surged with power.

These power units were capable of delivering 10,395 kilowatts each, enough power to light a good-sized American city, and gave the *Diana* a highly respectable top speed of 22 knots, with a normal running speed of 20 knots. It was the immense power from these engines which drove the twin propeller Azipods into action.

Unlike ships of the past, the *Princess Diana* didn't have an actual rudder. Instead, she was equipped with the latest marine technology, the highly capable Azipod propulsion system. The amazing feature of these giant propeller units was the fact that they could swivel and turn individually, acting as the rudder themselves. When used in conjunction with the four bow thrusters located at the very front of the ship, these pods actually allowed the great ship to move sideways if need be.

Suddenly, as if to solidly confirm Hayden's observation, a loud blast resounded through the ship as the deep basso foghorn blared once, then again. The floor beneath their feet shuddered and a gentle vibration began to build.

Zack went to the sliding glass door of the balcony and opened it. Stepping close to his balcony railing and looking forward, he saw the churning water coming from the bow thrusters. He then looked aft and saw the same churning water coming from the Azipods as the *Diana* moved laterally away from the dock. Suddenly filled with glee, he grinned and beckoned Hayden to join him, and soon, as they lined up at the railing, they watched the city of Barcelona begin to fade away into the distance.

Neither man spoke for a while.

Zack looked down and watched the white-water waves splash away from the ship as she throbbed forward. The wind was picking up and washing over them like a warm blanket.

"Man, that feels good," Hayden murmured, closing his eyes.

"It's really beautiful, huh? I can barely feel the ship moving."

"Me either."

Zack turned to Hayden. "Hade, I am sorry if I've been sending mixed signals." Now Hayden looked down at the slicing water. "The truth is," Zack continued, "I am attracted to you. Very much." Hayden looked back up, hope in his eyes. "Too much. That's what's freaked me out. I was just dumped, and I am at loose ends. I just don't want to make another mistake and get hurt, or even worse, hurt someone else. Hurt you."

Hayden reached a hand up and gently stroked Zack's face.

"Now see?" Zack sighed. "There you go, being all nice and sweet…"

"What's wrong with that? Wasn't anyone ever nice to you before?"

Zack had to stop and think. "Not for a long, long time," he admitted.

"Stop fighting it, Zack. Maybe this will work out and maybe it won't. I know you think it's too fast, but you can't fight what you feel, can you?" Hayden whispered, coming closer. "I know you can't, because I feel it too."

"But, I might…I can't…" Zack floundered, staring at Hayden's beautiful mouth that he wanted to kiss again so badly.

"Oh, shut up, Zack," Hayden barely murmured as he pulled the tormented man's face against his own. He kissed Zack with feather-light kisses that sent tremors through Zack's body. Hayden kissed his closed eyes, his nose, his forehead, and finally stopped at his lips.

With barely-there pressure, he placed his own soft lips on Zack's. Sliding his tongue forward, he parted Zack's mouth open and sensually probed its interior. Zack's breathing became labored and small groans began to come up from deep within him.

Hayden pulled him even closer and their hot bodies were rubbing up against each other. Zack snaked his arms around Hayden's back and held on for dear life. Hayden's kisses had him feeling lightheaded and dizzy.

Hayden continued his kissing assault. His lips now traveled slowly downward, under Zack's chin and to his neck, where his darting tongue licked and caressed the salty skin.

"Oh my God," whispered Zack, as he tilted his head back to let Hayden get at it better.

"You taste amazing," Hayden whispered back, then he dragged his tongue all the way from Zack's chin to his clavicle. His fingers lightly stroked Zack's silky smooth skin, first sliding up his chest, then down.

Zack had felt so bad about himself that the love he was receiving from Hayden was almost overpowering. He felt like he was in a dream, a hazy warm dream that he didn't want to wake up from.

"Man, you have the softest skin..." Hayden murmured, continuing his lick trek down Zack's body as he squatted lower. He allowed himself the luxury of tasting every inch of Zack's magnificent chest. Playfully, he thrust his tongue into Zack's navel, enjoying Zack's sharp intake of breath when he did it. He marveled at Zack's sexy atlas belt, the V-shaped band of muscles where his torso met his hips.

Now on his knees, Hayden was staring right at Zack's full crotch, the hard-on in his shorts a stiff tube waiting to be freed. Instead, Zack went back in, licking Zack's lower abs, letting his tongue slide under the loose waistband of the shorts every now and then. Zack's hands were holding on to his head, and he was watching Hayden work with a look of rapture on his face.

Hayden eventually brought his hands to the tempting erection and began to play with it through the shorts, never removing his tongue from Zack's stomach.

"Oh, my God," Zack moaned again.

"Mmm..." Hayden snickered. He deftly unbuttoned the shorts and slipped his hands inside, brushing against Zack's hot, sweaty skin. He gripped Zack's arousal with determination and pulled it out. Zack actually shivered at Hayden's touch on his manhood.

"Oh, man...it's prettier than I hoped," Hayden smiled, admiring the hard dick in his hands. Zack's shorts, now open and loose, slid down his thighs to his ankles.

Zack couldn't believe he was basically naked, outside on his cabin's balcony, a warm Mediterranean breeze washing over him while perhaps the hottest man he'd ever met was about to go down on him.

Please God, he thought irrationally, *let him be good at giving head.*

He needn't have worried.

Hayden let his tongue lick at the thick mushroom head and then he kissed it. Slowly, and with the utmost concentration, he slid his warm mouth over the dick and kept going. Zack, watching, couldn't believe how Hayden just kept going and going. His entire cock disappeared into Hayden's moist mouth. Then, just as slowly, Hayden pulled back and away from it, covering every inch of the hard flesh with his tongue in the process.

"I have no gag reflex," he whispered, before he went down it again.

"Praise Jesus," Zack sighed, as he watched this beautiful man take all of him.

Hayden's mouth slid back and forth, causing Zack to shudder in ecstasy. To Zack, it felt like his whole body had been enveloped in a warm, wet tunnel. He found himself groaning loudly, something that seemed to turn Hayden on.

Hayden let the wet dick slip from his lips, and he went to work on Zack's balls. Flicking, licking, and sucking them, he actually made Zack twitch in spasms of delight.

"Let's go inside...I want to get you on the bed," Hayden growled, knowing that he could never get enough of exploring this hot man trembling in front of him.

Zack eagerly moved to go inside, but tripped on the bunched up shorts tangled around his feet. He would have fallen if Hayden hadn't caught him. Giggling with embarrassment, he stepped out of them and shucked them aside.

The two men practically raced to the bed.

Zack scrambled up and rolled onto his back. Hayden crawled over and on top of him, his arms pressing into the mattress inches from Zack's shoulders. Their faces were lined up perfectly, and they just gazed at each other for a beat or two.

Zack, flat on his back, with a painfully hard erection jutting up from his crotch, relished these few seconds of yearning without action. Then, unable to contain his passion anymore, he reached up and put his arms around Hayden and pulled him down on top of him.

Jebb walked over to DJ Kenny BamBam, pulled his headphones off, and yelled in his ear.

"You have to shut it down!"

"Why?" Kenny asked, surprised by the request.

"Boat drill!"

"What?"

Just then, there were two deep blasts from the ship's foghorn. Kenny flipped a few switches, and the pool area became unearthly quiet. A split second later, the shouted protests of the dancing crowd began.

Over the ship's loudspeaker system came a series of gentle rhythmic chime tones. In the days to come, the men would discover that these chime tones always proceeded a general ship-wide announcement. The announcement now was somber in tone.

"Attention! Attention!" boomed a deeply-timbered male voice. "This is a lifeboat drill! I repeat, this is a lifeboat drill. All passengers are to return to their staterooms and get their life jackets. Please put the life jackets on, and then report to your lifeboat stations for our legally mandated lifeboat drill. Lifeboat stations are listed on the back of your cabin doors. If you have any questions or need special assistance, please contact your cabin attendant immediately. Thank you for your cooperation!"

After some minor booing, the men on the pool deck began to disburse. Jebb picked up a spare microphone and flicked it on.

"Gents," he said into the mike, "As soon as the boat drill is over, the party will continue! So come on back!"

This was greeted by much cheering.

"Oh, fuuucccckkk! Don't stop...oh, please, Hade!...Don't stop!" Zack howled. His legs were wrapped around Hayden's sweat slicked back, ankles intertwined. "They can have the...ahhhh...drill without us. Fuuuck...don't stop!"

"I won't!...Mmmmm...I'd let the ship sink before I stop...!" Hayden withdrew almost, but not completely, and then slowly glided back in. He repeated the motion, staring in awe at the wondrous emotions crossing Zack's gorgeous face.

"Oh, my God...ahhhh. I love it slow like this! How did...ohhhh...you know?" Zack felt a surge of passion well up and race through his body. The only way he could let it out was to whip his head from side to side in utter rapture. He started to hyperventilate and Hayden slowed down his thrusting some more.

"Zack," he asked tenderly. "Are you okay? Is this okay?"

"Oh, God, yes! Yes!" Zack cried out, his eyes screwed shut. "Grrrrrr! It just feels so good! You feel so good...Mmmmm!...It's just hard to absorb, that's all..."

"Oh, Zack...I feel it too," Hayden stopped his pushes and became completely still, just resting inside the man he had come to care so much about. He relished the sensation of being completely enfolded by Zack, and the tight, hot pressure on his cock was sweet agony. He resisted his impulse to start thrusting hard again. He knew his partner needed a moment to regroup, and he'd give him that.

"God, Hade! Just having you inside me…Like this…Not moving? Oh, fuuucckk! It's driving me crazy! I haven't…I haven't—" Unexpectantly, his eyes filled with tears.

"What is it?" Hayden asked, reaching a gentle hand up to wipe away a tear.

"I…this is what sex is supposed to feel like, isn't it? I feel… so…connected to you! Like I've never felt with another man…Ohhhh! Oh, God! You're moving again!…Ohhhh!"

Hayden had indeed begun to pulse his hips forward and back, just a hair. The slippery, tight pressure on his dick was sweet reward for this, and he felt himself come close to climax again.

"Attention all passengers!" came the stern voice through the room's intercom system again. "Please report to your boat stations immediately. Your lifeboat station is posted on your cabin door. Please proceed as quickly as possible in your life jacket to your assigned lifeboat station! Thank you for your assistance!"

"Ohhhh…no…we're not leaving…oh, fuuuckk!" Zack gasped out as Hayden picked up his pace.

"Damn! You feel so good! I can't believe how good you feel!"

Captain J. Lucard had never seen anything like it—a sea of half-naked men wearing only shorts or bathing suits and bright-orange puffy life jackets.

The Former British Naval Officer was standing primly on the starboard enclosed fly wing of the *Princess Diana*'s bridge, binoculars in hand and looking down at the Promenade Deck. His experienced eyes missed nothing.

The bridge of the *Princess Diana* stretched from one side of the beautiful ship to the other, and actually extended beyond. These extra extended areas, or fly wings, allowed executive staff to walk out over the sides of the ship and be able to look back along the entire length of the *Diana*.

Located forward and two decks above the solarium swimming pool, the bridge was a vast open area kept in tidy trim by a demanding but fair captain. Wide, tinted glass windows wrapped around the bridge while three distinct console centers were located inside. The left console of the bridge held communication and safety apparatus. The right console housed more mundane monitors; tank levels, engine status and such. The broad center console controlled navigation, the ship's speed, and other extremely vital functions.

One of the many areas where the *Princess Diana* was head and shoulders above her competition was her state-of-the-art navigation system. A complicated system that involved radar, a computerized geographical chart tracking and GPS positioning, made sure the *Princess Diana* was never more than ten feet off course at any given time.

In addition, the *Princess Diana* was one of the few cruise ships sailing with "black box" technology. A system very similar to those used by the airline industry recorded computer data, voice commands and radar images. This system could be used not only to record data in the unlikely event of an emergency, but also could be reviewed later for crew training exercises.

Because of her many automated systems, it was a standing joke among the officers of the *Diana* that she could almost run herself. In addition to the numerous navigation systems, she was outfitted with four anti-collision detectors, two digital gyro-compasses, and two auto-pilots.

But Captain Lucard knew that this was all just hardware. A ship like the *Princess Diana* was almost like a living, breathing being. She absolutely needed the gentle and commanding touch of her captain.

Lucard continued to let his binoculars roam over the boat deck as he watched the boat drill take place. He observed that his new passengers all had good haircuts and were very tan. There were a few men here and there who had merrily decorated their life jackets with feather boas or long chains of rainbow-colored plastic beads.

To Lucard's amazement, the gays had humorously turned the tedious drill into a festivity. They were clustered around each lifeboat station, laughing and chatting loudly among themselves like it was a party, and Lucard didn't see any of the fear in their eyes that usually accompanied this procedure.

Normally the lifeboat drill was done before the ship left dock, but there had been some problems with customs, and the baggage stevedores were threatening to strike. Lucard had to leave the port on schedule, so the drill was pushed back an hour.

The ship's officers were dashing back and forth counting to see if the men who'd shown up were the correct number for each boat. The passengers were busy introducing themselves to each other and cracking lame jokes about their new fashion accessory, the life vest.

One by one the reports came up from the officers and even though it seemed like a few of the passengers had not attended this mandatory drill, all seemed to be going smoothly.

Lucard dropped his binoculars and let out a suppressed breath of air. *Maybe this isn't going to be so bad after all*, he thought. *At least the gays are a fun lot, and not complaining about the drill like the regular cruise passengers do.*

Rex Lassiter had been up in arms since he'd boarded, raving about vague bomb threats, cursing this tour group and generally acting like the ass he was. Frankly, Lucard was glad to have overseeing the lifeboat drill to use as an escape from the annoying man. Lucard secretly hoped that Lassiter would get seasick and be in his cabin for the rest of the voyage. But Lucard knew it was never the impossible passengers that got sick. It was always the cool ones.

He was scanning the boat deck again when something caught his eye. His First Officer, a diligent, burly, tough and gruff German named Klaus, was off to one side of the Promenade Deck nearly hidden behind boat number 3. Bringing his binoculars back up to his sea-wizened eyes and adjusting the lenses, Lucard was stunned to see the swarthy, masculine Klaus happily feeling up a very handsome young Latin man in a small black bikini swimsuit that had the words "Aussie Bum" printed across it.

Dropping the binoculars once again, Lucard exhaled slowly.

"Oh, maaaan!" Hayden gushed, arching his back as Zack's hands roamed over his chest and played with his hard nipples. He was sitting on Zack's cock now, and the sensation of having the hot man's sizable dick planted firmly up his ass was just too delicious.

Hayden's runner legs were positioned on either side of Zack's hips, as Hayden raised and lowered himself using his strong thigh muscles. The investment banker was randomly stroking himself with one hand, while the other was placed on Zack's powerful chest, providing support.

"God, Hade! Ride me! Come on, ride me! You look so fucking hot!" Zack enthused, looking up at the god sitting on him.

"Oh, maaaan," Hayden sighed again as he began to buck up in a more insistent tempo. He couldn't get over how right it felt, how earthy, how natural his and Zack's lovemaking was. He had never felt the rush of emotions he was feeling now before. It was as if he had been destined to meet this man. Their connection was that deep, he felt.

Losing himself in the vertical pumping, Hayden heaved himself up and down, ever faster, until the wondrous probing in his ass had changed from an intrusion to a much wanted and welcome need.

Hayden actually needed to get fucked by Zack. He needed to feel back what he had just given Zack. He needed to share this precious act with a man he knew he was falling for. And he certainly needed the gigantic ejaculation he felt building with each push downward.

"Oh my God, Hade! You are so beautiful…so beautiful…" Zack moaned dreamily, watching Hayden pump furiously up and down on him. He felt Hayden's ass relax and tighten, and the constant friction on his cock was getting him close to shooting another big load. The one he'd shot when Hayden fucked him so damn good, not ten minutes ago, would pale in comparison to the one Zack felt brewing in his balls.

"Man, I can't hold off anymore…!" Hayden grimaced, stroking himself mercilessly.

"Me either!"

"Oh! My! God!" Hayden suddenly ceased his stroking, arched back and grabbed at his head with both hands in pure ecstasy. He arched back so far Zack thought he might fall over. Hayden's sinewy, ripped body flexed and grew taut with the back bend, and the vision was a mighty sight to behold. His stiff cock was bouncing in time to his up and down thrashing, and Zack's eyes grew large as he watched Hayden shut his eyes tightly, and then let loose. The hot come spurted out of his bouncing, throbbing cock unaided and splashed on Zack's abs, chest, and arms.

Zack had never seen anything as erotic and powerful as this, and before he could stop himself, he came as well, filling the condom he was wearing with his own hot seed.

Even after he knew Zack had climaxed, Hayden continued to pump up and down on him, causing Zack to twitch involuntarily from the rubbing his ultra sensitive dick was getting. "Oh, God! Stop!" Zack protested, faintly.

Hayden got a sly look on his face. "No. I want to milk every last drop out of you…"

"You have! You have! Oh…!" Zack bucked up as the constant rubbing did something amazing.

It felt like he was going to come again.

"What the fuuuucckkk?…Oh, God!…Oh, God!…Oh, God!" he cried out, as he felt his third climax in an hour pump out.

Hayden watched in disbelief as Zack contorted under him, and his hands clutched at the bedding.

Finally, truly spent and exhausted, Zack completely relaxed and slumped flat down. He couldn't even find the words to express what he'd just felt.

"Can I just tell you," Hayden said, awe in his voice. "That was the most amazing thing I have ever witnessed. Watching you come twice, in like, two minutes! Oh, my God…"

"I think I need a paramedic…" Zack whispered, as he took in deep breaths.

Hayden gingerly slid off Zack, and curled up next to him. He threw a leg over and snuggled up as close as possible.

"Man, that was just so amazing!" he said, still in awe at what he'd done to the man.

"I think I literally felt the earth move."

"Baby, we're at sea. The whole place is moving."

"Oh. Then that explains it."

"Man, I am wiped out! That totally drained and satisfied me," Hayden sighed, giving Zack a loving squeeze.

"Me, too."

They fell into a luxurious silence for a few minutes.

Hayden lifted his head. "Wanna do it again?"

"You bet!"

12

Côte d'Azur Dining Room, *Princess Diana*, North Mediterranean Sea

Jebb looked around the crowed dinning room to see who called him. "Jebb! Over here!" He spun around, and saw Nick sitting at a large table with Clive and Baldwin. Glad to see his staff members, he happily joined their party.

"Take a load off, boss man," Nick joked, pulling out a chair for him.

Jebb sat down, but scanned the room. The Côte d'Azur dining room was the main formal dining room on the *Princess Diana* and was composed of two levels. The main floor was accessed on Deck 5, the Emerald Deck, and easily held 75 tables, in sizes raging from a two-top to a large captain's table that could seat 12. The upper level, which was open over the main part of the downstairs dining area, held another 40 tables. You could only get to the upper level by using the grand curving staircase in the center of the room.

The inspiration for the dining room was clearly the rich and sensual tones of the South of France. The luxurious, deep-piled carpeting was a royal blue, the color of the sea. The table linens and cloths were varying shades of sage greens and delicious blues. The thickly cushioned chairs were in deeper shades that coordinated with the overall theme. Heavy coral-colored draperies hung over the sweeping panoramic windows that looked out over the dark Mediterranean, which was rushing past them at eighteen knots. The ceiling was painted a sky blue and had twinkling lights inset throughout to give the effect of stars peeking out at dusk.

"We seem to be doing good so far, right?" Jebb asked, waving to a group of return guests three tables over.

"We're fine, relax," Nick soothed, giving his boss a friendly pat on the arm. "The Bon Voyage T-dance was a huge success, and check-in was a breeze this time out. Not like last spring with the Western Caribbean cruise.

Remember? Forty-two guests with no cabins?"

Jebb nodded ruefully. That cruise had indeed been a horror. Compared to that, this one was, literally, smooth sailing. A waiter brought over a cocktail and dropped it in front of Jebb.

"G&T. We ordered it earlier for you," Nick grinned.

Like a man dying of thirst in the desert, Jebb gratefully sipped from the cocktail. "God, that's good."

"So, have you seen Dan Smith lately?" Nick had a smirk on his face.

"No, but thanks for asking."

"Who's Dan Smith?" Baldwin asked.

Nick wrapped an arm around his boss. "Oh, just this very, very, very hot man that Jebb here has a thing for."

Clive and Baldwin looked at each other in disbelief. "What?" Clive gasped, "You mean to tell me that the Virgin Mary has finally met someone who has melted her heart?"

Jebb held up his hands. "Guys, please…"

"Oh, you should have seen it!" Nick continued, ignoring Jebb's protests. "I swear to you, there was saliva practically dripping off his chin. He wants Mr. Smith. Bad."

Clive and Baldwin laughed while Jebb blushed. "Well," Jebb finally said, "While I admit to a silly schoolboy crush, I don't know what will become of it. I haven't seen him since this afternoon, and he hasn't returned my message yet, so…"

Nick patted Jebb's back. "Oh, he will. He will. You're a catch!"

Baldwin and Clive raised their glasses. "To Jebb!"

Jebb and Nick raised theirs as well, clinked, then drank.

"Well," Nick said, wiping his mouth. "I'm just glad it's smooth sailing so far. No Rex Lassiter sightings."

"Well, that's not entirely true," Jebb sighed. "I had a meeting with him a few minutes ago."

"Oh, Christ. That couldn't have gone well," Nick groaned.

Jebb took another sip. "He saw some men, gasp, kissing by the pool!"

Clive, Baldwin and Nick began to snicker.

"That's it? Hell, he's gonna see way worse than that before this cruise is over!" Baldwin chortled.

"The guy is a royal pain in my ass. He made a point to show me another one of those ridiculous bomb threat letters."

"Bomb threat letters?" Clive and Baldwin said in unison.

Jebb rolled his eyes. "You should see them. It's like some third-grader made them. It's just some chicken-shit gay-basher trying to scare us and cause trouble. Remember? We had the same thing happen with our Bermuda resort trip two years ago?" His eyes turned steely. "Lassiter's using them to try and stop the cruise. Over my dead body."

"I think you're right," Nick agreed.

"I know I am." Jebb exhaled heavily. "God, I hate that prick. He just gets under my skin, you know?"

"His wife's cool, though." Clive added.

All heads turned to Clive. "What?" he shrugged. "I had a drink with her at the bar during the T-dance. Hot little number. Great style. Good sense of humor."

"Really," Jebb deadpanned.

"Honest. You'd like her. She's got fag-hag written all over her."

Across the dining room, on the port side, Kurt and Rick sat at their table chatting with two very attractive men. One, a model from Miami, was brazenly flirting with Kurt and the other, a short personal trainer from Dallas, was deep into a conversation with Rick about the proper way to do triceps pushdowns.

Jorge was wearing a black knit shirt that was several sizes too small and unbuttoned halfway down. His impressive chest was barely contained by the stretchy fabric. "So, Kurt, listen," he said, sensually working a cherry from his cocktail into his mouth, "I saw *Titanic*, and I asked this nice officer during the lifeboat drill what to do if we hit an iceberg, and he said not to worry. He says there's enough lifeboats on the *Princess Diana* for everyone." Jorge couldn't take his eyes off the hunky man sitting next to him. It was a rare thing to meet a man hotter than himself, but Jorge had to concede that Kurt was a far superior specimen of virile manhood than he was. He couldn't even imagine how amazing the sex between them would be, and he was doing his damnedest to find out.

"Well, that's comforting to know," Kurt grinned. "Though I don't think many icebergs work their way into the warm Mediterranean Sea."

Jorge dramatically wiped his forehead with his hand. "Whew! 'Cause if we do go down, I sure hope you'd come and save me..." He dropped his hand down into Kurt's lap in a seemingly casual motion.

Rick, who was watching his lover's conversation from the corner of his eye, shot his eyebrows up in surprise at the subtle but brazen move by the underwear model. Kurt saw his lover's stunned expression and winked reassuringly at him.

Jorge leaned in close to Kurt and barely whispered, "I hate the water. You see, I can't swim. You'd save me, wouldn't you, Papi?" Jorge asked, all wide-eyed and innocent. "Then, I'd owe you my life. I would be your slave. Anything you wanted me to do, I'd have to do." His voice dropped an octave. "And I mean *anything*..." He managed to let his hand squeeze Kurt's crotch briefly before Kurt gently removed it.

Placing Jorge's hand back in his own lap, Kurt said, "Like I said, I don't think you need to worry about it." He happened to glance over Jorge's shoulder and saw Hayden and Zack enter. They too had changed for dinner. Zack, wearing a fitted white tee and black jeans looked happier than Kurt had seen him yet on this vacation. Hayden, sporting baggy cargo pants and a tight crewneck long sleeve jersey, also had a special glow about him.

Holy fuck! Kurt realized. *They've had sex!*

"Hi," Zack said sheepishly when he got to the table. "Sorry we're late."

"Yeah," Hayden chimed in. "We're just running behind I guess."

"Oh, no problem," Kurt said graciously. "Hayden, Zack...this is Jorge and Kirby."

The men all said hello and shook hands. Zack and Hayden pulled out a pair of chairs next to each other and sat down. Zack leaned to his left and gave Rick a kiss on the cheek.

"So, where did you two go? One moment you're on the dance floor next to us," Rick asked, also putting two and two together. "And the next, you were gone..."

Hayden and Zack suddenly became very interested in their menus.

"Yeah," Kurt teased. "I looked for you both during the boat drill. You weren't there."

"Yeah," admitted Hayden sheepishly. "We did miss that."

Kurt and Rick looked at them with expectant and mirthful eyes. Zack and Hayden glanced at each other and had to laugh.

"Okay. Busted," Hayden said between laughing snorts.

"I knew it!" Kurt almost yelled, slapping his knee.

"What is going on here?" asked a very confused Kirby.

"Kirby, my man," Kurt said gleefully, "I'm afraid I was wrong. Neither one of these two hot men is available. Anymore."

"Whoa, whoa, whoa," Zack protested, holding up his hand. "We're not picking out china just yet, Kurt."

"Yeah, we're not lesbians, you know," Hayden giggled.

Kurt turned to his right and looked at Rick. "You owe me a hundred bucks!" he laughed.

"You couldn't hold out one more day?" Rick razzed the two blushing men. "I'd have won if you'd just waited until tomorrow!"

Zack shrugged. "Sorry."

Hayden threw his arm around Zack. "I'm not." He gave Zack a deep kiss. Even Jorge was impressed by the heat the men generated.

"Down, boys!" Rick sassed. "Or I'll have to hose you off."

Zack and Hayden, suddenly swept away from the table and back into their own world, parted and looked soulfully into each other's eyes for a beat. Hayden slipped his hand under the table and gently caressed Zack's thigh.

"Well," Jorge said, disappointed that these handsome men would be off the market. He'd have let either one have his ass in a heartbeat. "How was it? Did you two rock the boat?" He wanted details.

Hayden smiled at Zack, then bust out into laughter. "Son, it was amazing!"

Slightly shocked, but oddly excited by the praise, Zack simply blushed a deeper shade of red.

Kurt lifted up his water glass. "To Hayden and Zack," he said. The other men at the table followed suit and the toast was consummated.

13

The *Princess Diana,*
Vieux Port de Cannes, France

Got your camera?"

"Uh, duh," Zack teased in a silly voice as he hoisted up the nylon bag so Hayden could see it. "Both digital and film."

"Good. I got the sunscreen and the tour tickets in my wallet. Let's shove off." Hayden felt for his wallet in his back pocket just to be sure he did indeed have it. He was wearing light khaki pants and an old lime-green Cameron Fuller polo shirt. His new Addias ClimaCool sneakers gleamed white at his feet.

Zack, freshly showered and smelling clean, spent a moment gazing at Hayden. *He's so damn handsome*, he thought, *I'm so lucky to be with him.*

Zack had pulled on dark blue cargo shorts and a white Calvin Klein underwear V-neck tee. He also jammed a floppy tan fisherman's hat on his head. He called it his "Gilligan" hat. He quickly checked through his camera bag to make sure he had enough film for his 35mm camera and extra batteries for the digital for their day trip to Monaco and Monte Carlo. While he did this, Hayden peered out the picture window at the French coastline.

The *Princess Diana* was solidly anchored just off the coast of Cannes, France. Much too big a vessel to steam up and dock at a pier in the tiny port, she was forced to stay offshore and use tenders to get her passengers ashore.

Land-bound passengers were to go down to Deck B, exit the ship through an extended platform, and board a tender ship, which was one of the motorized covered lifeboats, and be driven to the pier. There the tourists could go off and wander the friendly streets of Cannes and shop, eat, or just simply people watch.

If a *Princess Diana* passenger had reserved space on one of the tours sponsored by Titan and the Lassiter Line, they would then board one of the many tour buses parked along the pier. The large tourist coaches were specially hired for this cruise, and would then take the sightseers to Monaco, a 45-minute drive away.

Zack dropped the camera bag on the mussed bed and went to Hayden. "Before we go, you need to kiss me," he said.

"Oh?" Hayden cocked an eyebrow. "Is that the price to get off this ship?"

Zack grinned. "Seems to me you've gotten off plenty."

Zack's joke wasn't that far off.

After dinner the night before, the new lovers had returned to Zack's cabin, and proceeded to talk, cuddle, kiss, make out and eventually made love again. They had stayed up half the night, enjoying the carnal pleasures of sensual contact with each other.

It went unsaid, but was so obvious to both of them. They were both so happy to have found each other.

Eventually drifting off to sleep in each other's arms, they had awakened to a stunning sunrise clearly visible through the large windows of the cabin. Hayden was amazed to discover he was sporting a huge morning erection, which Zack had happily gone down on. The quick reward for Zack's expert sucking efforts was yet another gut wrenching climax for his partner.

After that morning wake up, the two men had dressed hurriedly and taken a three-mile run around the ship on the jogging track. The hills of Southern France and the port city of Cannes were clearly visible off the anchored ship's starboard bow. The craggy cliffs and verdant greenery were an inspiring sight, and each lap around the ship notched up Zack's excitement about seeing the country ashore.

After the run, Zack then lead Hayden through a grueling 30-minute ab workout in the gym that had both men panting from the effort. After that, they had popped into the a la carte restaurant, Sloan Square, for a quick breakfast.

Sloan Square was where meals were served buffet-style 24 hours a day. It was an informal place, great for a quick bite before heading out to the pool or the gym. While room service was also available 24 hours a day, and many of the tour's guests simply stayed in their cabins and had their meals delivered, Sloan Square had quickly become one of the busiest hubs of the ship.

Zack and Hayden had been stunned by the amount and variety of buffet food available in the spacious restaurant. Cereals, eggs, bacon, sausages, individual omelet stations, custom-made pancakes and waffles, it was all freshly prepared and waiting, the intoxicating aromas creating even more hunger in the two starving men.

Their eyes being larger than their stomachs, both Hayden and Zack overloaded their trays with far too much food. They got juice from the juice dispenser and began to search for a place to sit down.

Other men, also up early for their tours, had already crowded the eatery, and Hayden and Zack, still sweating from their workouts, were happy to spy Kurt and Rick sitting at a table alone, so they sat with them. They soon discovered they were all on the same tour today. There was much kidding around as the excited men planned their day.

When Zack and Hayden had returned to Zack's cabin to clean up for their day ashore, they jumped in the surprisingly spacious shower together, and things had gotten steamy.

Hayden had been amazed to find he could climax again so easily.

"Come on, we're late," Hayden urged. "I'll kiss you, but don't even think about doing anything else! I don't think I'll be able to come again for a week." He wrapped his arms around Zack and pulled him close. "My balls hurt. I think they're empty. Bone dry."

"God, I hope that's not true! You make the best face when you shoot." Zack scrunched up his handsome features into an imitation of Hayden. "I'm coming! Oh, yeah!…I'm coming!" he growled, in an exact replication of Hayden's performance not thirty minutes earlier.

Hayden leaned back a hair. "Oh? What about you?" He shut his eyes and snapped his head back and forth in an exaggerated fashion. "Oh, God! Oh, God! Oh, God!" he panted.

Zack had to laugh. "Is that really how I look?"

"Yeah," Hayden nodded, in mock seriousness. "But I love ya anyway."

As soon as he said the words, he wanted to take them back. It was way too early to say something like that to the skittish man in his arms.

Zack pretended he hadn't really heard what he'd heard, but his heart started racing.

Talk of love? Too soon!

To end the uncomfortable moment, Hayden leaned in and kissed Zack, who responded happily. To further break the mood, Hayden drew his hand back and smacked Zack's ass and clamped on hard.

Zack did the same.

"Think they'll let us on the tender like this?" Hayden laughed.

"Let's find out."

Zack broke the hug and picked up his camera bag. "We're outta here."

"Monte Carlo, here we come!" Hayden hooted and followed Zack out of the cabin.

Clive and Baldwin were at the Titan Tours shore excursion desk, across the corridor from the Purser's desk on the Sapphire Deck. There was always confusion on the first day ashore. Worried passengers were peppering them with questions, both intelligent and stupid. Clive had a much better tolerance for the dumb questions than Baldwin did, so they had worked out a system. Clive would be the point man for the more difficult guests, and Baldwin would do the paperwork.

Kirby, wearing a pair of lightweight cargo pants, a white Lacoste polo, and a faded navy blue visor from American Eagle, stood patiently in line, but nervously glanced at his watch. He had forgotten to book himself on one of the tours of Monte Carlo, and he desperately wanted to go. He knew that his new friends Kurt, Rick, Hayden and Zack were going, and he wanted to join them. He was hoping there was still space on their bus. While standing in line he thought about the crazy events of the previous night. After dinner, he had strolled the decks, exploring the ship a bit more. He had unexpectedly found more than one secret trysting spot occupied by a groping couple. Embarrassed, yet slightly turned on, he had backed away each time. He thought he'd seen Jorge in one darkened corner with a ship's officer, but he hadn't wanted to get closer to find out.

He eventually ended up back in his small cabin, watching a good movie on the TV. He had gotten drowsy, turned off the TV, and quickly fell asleep. He was awakened a little while later by a slightly drunk Jorge crawling into his bed. Jorge had been so sweet and affectionate, playfully kissing and stroking Kirby, and soon the personal trainer from Dallas was fucking him like a champ.

Kirby wasn't so naive as to think that his relationship with Jorge was anything other than right time and place. But he had come on this cruise to meet some new people, realize a few sexual fantasies, and have fun.

So far, so good.

"How can I help you?" asked Clive when it was Kirby's turn at the counter.

"Hi, I'm Kirby Dickerson, and I forgot to sign up for the tour to Monte Carlo today. Are there any places left?" he asked hopefully.

"Sure. A couple of guys canceled out," Clive smiled. "A little too much party hardy last night, I think."

Kirby smiled back. "Cool! Um, I have some friends I met at dinner last night, going. I'd like to get on their tour bus if possible. Hayden Beasley? Kurt Farrar?"

Clive scanned his lists. He found Hayden and Kurt's names.

"You're in luck. There was one cancellation on that bus. Number Four."

"Great!" Kirby handed over his keycard for the charge, and soon was on his way to Deck B.

Zack was totally enjoying the slap of warm air rushing against his face. He was less thrilled by the occasional splash of seawater that reached up to him from the cutting bow of the fast moving tender. He, Hayden, Kurt and Rick were sitting on the upper deck of the tender with a bunch of other passengers excitedly looking forward to their day exploring the Côte d'Azur. They were racing away from the *Princess Diana* at a good clip.

A sudden gust of wind blew the Gilligan hat right off Zack's head. Despite his quick attempt to catch it, it sailed away and landed in the turbulent wake of the tender, where it floated for a minute before disappearing under the water.

"Damn," he muttered, as Hayden giggled at his misfortune.

"Don't sweat it," Hayden finally said, sliding his arm around Zack's shoulders. "You look better without it."

Realizing the humor in the situation, Zack had to laugh, too. He soon joined his new boyfriend in staring at the approaching coastline.

The view was amazing. Cerulean waters crashed gently onto the gray rocky shoreline. Gently rising from the pebbled beaches, Zack could see the entire town of Cannes nestled against the sloping hillside. Lording over the village was an old castle-like structure. Kurt, who was sitting next to him, and who had been to Cannes before, said it was Mont Chevalier. The whole town was like nothing Zack had ever seen before.

Pastel-colored buildings were stacked one on top of the other up the hillside towards the castle. There was a marina in the port they were fast approaching, and the multiple masts of the boats moored there added a festive air to the whole thing.

Hayden nudged him. He was pointing to a large schooner ship that was docked along a long wooden pier. "Look at that! Wouldn't you love to sail on her?"

"I like ours," Zack replied, glancing over his shoulder at the now distant

Princess Diana.

"So guys," Rick said, "We have about an hour before we have to be on our bus. What do we want to do for that time?"

"I want to just walk around. See everything I can," Zack replied.

"Sounds like a plan to me," Hayden said.

"Then we need to hit the ground running," Kurt said. "The main drag here is called the Boulevard de la Croisette. That's were all the cool shops and stuff are. It's only a few blocks away from the port, right off the town square."

Kurt had been to Cannes five years before with a producer he had been dating. Well, dating was a strong word. Fucking would be a better description. They had come for the Cannes Film Festival, where the producer had a film in competition, and all the madness that that entailed. Kurt had been shocked by the crowds, the chaos and the couture. He was much happier being back now with his lover on a more low-key visit.

"Lead the way, bro," Zack said, checking his camera bag to make sure the overspray wasn't getting on it.

The tender crossed through the rock jetty and slowed down as it approached the dock. There was a gentle bump and the crewmen on the tender threw some lines over to a waiting crewman on the pier. After the boat was secured, the passengers disembarked. As soon as Zack's feet hit the wood of the dock, he felt an elation that surprised him.

Hayden noticed the goofy grin on his lover's handsome face. "What's up?"

Zack shrugged happily. "Just glad to be here. Another country! France!"

"You are too cute," Hayden grinned.

"Well, you live in Europe. Remember, this is my first time here..."

"Then I'm glad I get to share this with you."

Zack took Hayden's hand in his. "Me, too."

Kurt was already halfway up the quay. "Let's go!" he called back to the straggling men. They hurried to catch up.

They walked through an enormous parking lot, passing the tour buses lined up and waiting. They walked into the town proper and passed a beautiful park-like square with inviting benches occupied by senior citizens who were content to sit and watch the world pass by.

Zack spied something that made his heart leap. "A McDonald's! Thank God! I'm so thirsty."

He dragged Hayden in, and they ordered Diet Cokes for everyone. Paying in euros like a native, Zack proudly counted out the correct amount.

They took the beverages outside and passed them out.

Then the four men strolled up and down the streets of Cannes.

At first walking up the Boulevard de la Croisette, but quickly boring of the pricey stores along its route, they dropped back a block and found a wide pedestrian street full of quirky and more original shops. They ran into men from the ship everywhere. It seemed like the small town had been invaded by well-dressed gay men.

After window shopping for an hour, they headed back to the tour buses. Choosing the coach that corresponded to the number on their tour tickets—four—they climbed up and settled into two rows of seats, Kurt and Rick sitting directly in front of Hayden and Zack. Kurt knew that the best views of the French Riviera would be had from the right side, so he had made them all sit on that side.

The bus started to fill up, and a pretty petite woman with heavily streaked blond hair hopped up and took their tickets. She also placed a small round sticker with the number four on it on each man in the bus. She introduced herself as Gabrielle Peiratt, and she was their tour guide. After about 20 minutes the bus was full, and the driver was preparing to shut the door and pull away. There came a frantic pounding on the side of the bus, and a winded Kirby climbed aboard.

"I thought you we're going to leave without me!" he said in a rush to Gabrielle. He picked his way down the narrow aisle, and found a seat across from Zack.

"Hey," Zack said as Kirby settled in.

"Hey! I picked this tour bus because you guys were on it," Kirby said, blushing slightly. He took off his visor, wiped the sweat from his brow.

"Well, that was cool of you. Join the group," Rick cheerfully called out from one row ahead. He squirmed in place, trying to get comfortable sitting next to his huge boyfriend, who was squeezed into a seat far too small for his frame.

"I got all the way to the pier," Kirby said, explaining his tardiness. "And realized I'd left my wallet in the cabin. Had to go back and get it, then come back. Whew! I barely made it!" Grinning a broad, open smile, he tugged his visor back into place on his head.

"Well, you haven't missed much," Kurt managed to lean around and join the conversation. "Zack treated us all to McDonald's. Very European."

Gabby picked up the bus's microphone, and as the coach started to move, she began to give a brief history of Cannes. The passengers half-listened. They were too busy gawking out the windows at the passing town.

"The name Cannes means 'reeds,'" Gabrielle said in heavily French-accented English into the mike. "There were an, ah, abundance of reeds in the marshes around Castellum Marsellinum, the, ah, castle on Mont Chevalier, above the city, in ancient times."

Zack and Hayden were straining to get a look up the hillside at the turret still visible. Zack leaned over so far that his neck was directly in front of Hayden's face. Hayden leaned forward a tad and kissed it. Zack smiled and continued to look out the window.

"There are now approximately sixty-eight thousand people who live here in Cannes today. Oh! On your right, you will see we are passing the Palais des Festivals et des Congrès!"

Everyone craned to view the imposing bunker-like building. It had a wide slanted cement roofline and a grand staircase that lead to its entrance. "This is where the Cannes Film Festival takes place every May. That staircase is where the film stars all stop and pose for pictures during the film festival. Orlando Bloom, Brad Pitt, and Julia Roberts to recall some. It is very famous."

Passing the complex, the bus moved on.

"Now, on your left, you will see the Hotel Carlton. It is very famous. Many famous people have, ah, stayed here."

All eyes were on the striking and sedate building. It had intricate golden filigree on its tall white facade, giving it the appearance of an elaborate wedding cake.

"One day I want to stay there," Rick said wistfully to Kurt.

"We'll do it, then." Kurt agreed. "I promise."

The bus continued on its trek. The pristine town of Cannes fell behind it as the loaded vehicle snaked its way along the French coastline. Zack was amazed at the beaches. They weren't sandy, like the California beaches he was used to. Instead, they were filled with pebbles and rocks. Settling back into his seat, he couldn't see how anyone could lay down on them and be comfortable.

The lush landscape on the left side of the bus was equaled, if not surpassed, by the stunning seascapes on the right. Little fishing village after little fishing village passed by as the coach droned on.

Gabby keep up a constant stream of chatter, giving all sorts of details and data regarding the Cote d'Azur in her charmingly accented voice. Every once in a while she would nervously reach up and tug a nonexistent strand of loose hair behind her ears.

"We are now, ah, entering the town of Nice," she said, as the bustling port city came into view. "This is truly the only major city on the Riviera coastline…"

"It's so beautiful," Hayden whispered as he stared out the large window.

The coach stayed on the road, which began a climb uphill. The town was now below them, and the passengers had a stunning vantage point to view the entire city. Large, low-rise buildings hugged the coastline while smaller family dwellings climbed haphazardly up the verdant hills. The whole town was a wash of warm pastel colors. Pink, salmon, peach, white, pale sky blue. Wide, rocky beaches stretched into the gentle surf, and they were already covered by over a hundred sunbathers.

"Wow."

"What?" Hayden faced Zack.

"Oh, nothing…"

"No, what?"

"Well, I was just thinking…"

"Yeah?"

"How weird life is," Zack confessed. "Two weeks ago, I was with Bayne, in a bad relationship. A week ago I was this pathetic, dumped loser. And now, here I am, with you, the most fantastic man I've ever met, traveling through the south of France. It's a little surreal."

Hayden took Zack's hand and warmly squeezed it.

14

Diamond Deck, *Princess Diana,*
Vieux Port de Cannes, France

Dan paced back and forth in his lavishly appointed stateroom. The large space was comprised of a roomy general area that held a very comfortable queen-sized bed, a small yet elegant sitting area, and off by the door, opposite a full bank of closets and cabinets, a full bath. The color scheme was subdued, and his attentive cabin attendant had already filled up the ice bucket and replenished the minibar.

He reached for the phone. Catching himself, he stopped in midair. Wrestling with his conscience, he was frozen with indecision.

Why not? he thought. *What's the harm? I can control myself for one night. I can. I will.*

Pushing himself into action, he picked up the phone and punched in the four digits. The phone rang twice before being picked up.

"Jebb Miller."

Dan cleared his throat. "Uh, Jebb, hi. It's Dan. Dan Smith."

In his own cabin, Jebb was soaking wet and wrapped in a towel. He had just stepped out of the shower when the phone had rung. He'd picked up the extension that had been located conveniently in the large bathroom. "Dan!" he said, a bit too excitedly. Calm down, he reminded himself. *He's just a guy. A very hot guy, but still just a guy*. "Hey," he added, in a deeper register. "How are you?"

"Good."

"You didn't go into Cannes yet?"

"No, I'm staying on the ship today. I have some work I have to do."

"Well," Jebb said, flirting, "You know what they say. All work and no play makes Dan a dull boy."

Dan actually laughed. "So that's my problem."

"What do you do, Dan? For a living, I mean." Jebb wanted to stretch the conversation out for as long as possible.

"Stocks. I'm a broker." It was a lie, but Dan was so good at lying that it came off as absolute truth. "I have a few clients who are very insistent that I keep in touch with them while I'm on vacation."

"I see."

Dan cleared his throat. "Um, I wanted to…Uh, well, you said something about dinner…"

"Yes! I thought we'd go up to Spencer House. Very posh, as the English say."

The Spencer House dining room was the most exclusive dining room onboard, and not part of the all-inclusive meal plan. Located at the rear of the Compass Deck, its floor-to-ceiling plate glass windows gave its patrons spectacular and sweeping unobstructed views to go along with their five-star gourmet meals. Dinners in the Spencer Room could run up to into the hundreds of dollars as bottles of rare wines and fabulously exorbitant dishes added up to mind-numbing charges. Jebb had heard that there were only 20 tables in the entire restaurant, and reservations were impossible to get after the first day because savvy passengers booked it up as soon as they got onboard.

"Sounds good. When? What time?"

"How about tonight?" Jebb offered, hoping against hope Dan would say yes. "About 8:00?"

"That works," Dan replied, his heart beginning to race. Jebb's deep voice was undeniably sexy and his obvious attraction was clear. It had been a long time since Dan had met a man he wanted to actually date, not just fuck and then hurt. The thought excited him.

Of course, if the date turned into fucking…

No! Dan chastised himself forcefully. Don't go there. You know what happens when you go there…

"Great! Shall I meet you there? The entrance to the Spencer House is up on the Compass Deck, aft of the pools."

"I'll find it."

"Great," Jebb said. He felt like he was flying. It had been so long since he'd even opened up his mind to the possibility of having a date, let alone with a man he was so extremely attracted to, he felt 10 feet tall.

For his part, Dan didn't want to hang up the phone. He wanted to talk to Jebb for hours, but knowing himself too well, he forced himself to end the call. "Well, then," he said, his voice tight with regret, "I'll see you later, 8:00."

"I'll see you then. Bye, Dan."

"Bye, Jebb."

After he hung up the phone, Jebb almost did a happy dance. If all went well, he'd be rolling in the sheets with one hot motherfucker before this night was over.

On the Sun Deck, Jorge swaggered out into the sunshine, squinted, and slid on his Tag Heuer sunglasses. He had heard there was going to be a "hottest tan line" contest in the next few days, and he was determined to win it.

He'd been to Cannes and Monaco the previous year courtesy of a closeted young actor he'd met while the star was on location in Miami making a movie. They'd stayed at the Carlton Hotel, fucked repeatedly, and even had lunch with a low-level member of the royal family of Monaco. He didn't need to go back on a tour bus. He'd decided to stay onboard the *Diana* and work on his tan.

He walked down through the rows of vinyl and steel chaise loungers that the Lassiter Line used instead of the old-fashioned wooden deck chairs of yore. He was well aware of the glances he was getting as he passed the other men who had also decided to stay on the *Princess Diana*. Dance music was blasting from the speakers, making the Pool Deck feel like an outdoor disco.

Wearing only his white flip-flops, a sheer multicolored sarong tied loosely around his hips and a neon yellow Dolce and Gabbana bikini swimsuit, Jorge sashayed a little bit to the driving beat of the music, until he found an empty chaise near the pool's edge that pleased him. It was in the direct center of the pool area, for maximum observation, and close to the cooling waters of the good-sized saltwater pool.

He threw his Bain de Soleil oil and sunglasses down on the chaise, went to the towel bin, and picked up a couple of the oversized towels. Back at the chaise, he carefully laid the towels out and finally, much to the relief and excitement of all the men around him trying hard not to stare, he untied the sarong, and let it drop to the teak decking. The bright yellow of the swimsuit made his already deeply tanned skin look even darker, and his unbelievably tight body flexed and constricted with his subtle movements.

He settled down on the chaise, on his back, and began to apply the suntan oil. Sensually gliding his hands over his body, rubbing in the creamy orange-tinted oil, he knew his every movement was being memorized for future masturbatory sessions by the men around him. Finally done coating his body in the slick, fragrant oil, he reclined, put his sunglasses back on, and closed his eyes.

The sun felt good. Hot. It warmed up his skin quickly and Jorge found that he was soon sweating.

His sexy body also had another reaction to the heat.

He started to get a hard-on. The swelling cock in his bathing suit was barely contained by the stretchy Lycra. Men suddenly found reasons to have to pass by his chair, and took in his perfection with hungry glances.

Jorge zoned out. He allowed himself to drift off, to that delightful state between consciousness and unconsciousness. A slight breeze kicked up, and it felt good scuttling over his body.

He slowly became aware that there was a shadow falling over him. Opening his eyes, he was surprised to see a statuesque woman in a white Versace string bikini and white Manolo Blahnik mules standing next to him. She was holding a large Louis Vuitton tote bag with the highly coveted and rare graffiti pattern on it.

"Is this chaise taken?" she asked in a lightly accented voice, indicating the empty lounger next to him. Under a wide brimmed straw hat, she had long red hair tumbling chicly down past her shoulders. There was not an ounce of fat on her tall, luscious frame. She had pushed her white Chanel sunglasses down with her finger to better drink in the fine figure of manhood below her.

"Uh, no. Help yourself."

"Grazi." She looked over at a pool attendant and snapped her fingers. Instantly towels were brought to her and the attentive crewmember leaned over and spread them out expertly on the chaise. "Renaldo, bring me a Martini," she said to him. She then looked down at Jorge again. "And what would you like?"

"Um, the same."

Donnatella nodded at the waiter. "Duo. Grazi, Renaldo." She settled herself down into the chaise. She pulled out a bottle of sunblock and the latest James Patterson novel. She carefully applied the lotion, letting Jorge get a good look at her sensual contortions. She had a knockout body, she knew it, and she enjoyed showing it off. Not that it would do her any good on this trip, but still.

"I'm Donnatella," she ultimately said, the lilting cadence of her slight accent making her seem impossibly chic.

"I'm Jorge. I'm from Miami. Wow. Donnatella. Like Versace, huh?"

Donnatella curled her nose distastefully. "Yes. I get that a lot, but I'm the other Donnatella. I'm Donnatella Lassiter. My husband's family owns this ship."

"No shit? Really? Wow!"

"No shit." It came out as *no sheet*.

"Donnatella. Wow. That's such an exotic name. Not like mine. 'Jorge.'" He smiled at her. "Your name fits you."

Donnatella's eyes drifted down Jorge's body. She drank in the taut, sinewy muscles under his brown, glistening skin. The toned and built up arms. The perfect six-pack abs. Sucking in her breath, she then saw the hard cock tightly confined by the hot yellow swimsuit.

"And I see that your bathing suit barely fits you. You're driving the men on this deck crazy with that hard package of yours. Me as well, I think, damn you."

Jorge was stunned at the chic woman's directness.

"But I suppose that's the whole point, isn't it?" she added, smiling.

Jorge had to laugh.

She looked him up and down again. "Mmm. Such a waste," she sighed.

"Oh, honey," Jorge said airily. "I don't waste it. Believe me."

Now it was Donnatella's turn to laugh.

"I like making them all squirm," Jorge admitted proudly, waving a limp arm in the general direction of the panting men around them. He would have to have been blind not to see the commotion he was causing. "Makes me feel…"

"Powerful?" Donnatella interrupted.

Jorge nodded. "Exactly. Fuck them all. Let 'em dream about gettin' this piece." He grabbed his crotch and squeezed it playfully, causing one older gentleman, who had strategically positioned himself in a lounger directly opposite the hot stud so he could watch his every move, to drop his cocktail.

"They can dream, but they can't have?" Donnatella asked.

"Oh, if they're hot and I'm horny, they can have, all right."

Renaldo returned with their cocktails and nervously set them down on the small table between the two chaises. After he left, Donnatella raised her glass in a toast, which Jorge joined in on. They clinked glasses.

"To dreaming," Donnatella suggested.

"To dreaming," Jorge smiled.

They clinked glasses and then took long, deep sips. Donnatella sat up, and with a quick flick of her wrist, untied her bikini top and let it fall away. She didn't want tan lines. Her perfect breasts were as dark as the rest of her flawless body, and now, feeling relaxed and comfortable, she settled back into the chaise.

Jorge glanced over, and grinned. "Nice rack. What'd they cost?'

Without batting an eye, Donnatella replied, "Ten thousand. And worth every euro."

"No doubt."

Donnatella allowed her eyes to lazily cast about the pool area. She could not believe the amount of gorgeous man flesh strolling, lying and walking about. It was as if the world's complete collection of genetically gifted men were all here today, for her personal viewing pleasure. These gods preened and strutted their stuff completely for the benefit of others, the small, multicolored Speedos they sported giving a slight, bright break to the deeply tanned skin that had been worked out to perfection.

But no one—and Donnatella took her time to gaze about and make sure —absolutely no one was as sexy as the confident young man lying next to her. And in some small way, even though she was a figure of some importance in the world, just being next to Jorge from Miami made Donnatella feel special and privileged.

15

St.-Jean-Cap-Ferrat, France

The bus was driving down some of the scariest roads Zack had ever seen. They had just passed by the stunningly beautiful bay of St.-Jean-Cap-Ferrat, and the views from the coach's windows were jaw dropping. To the left, there were countless large villas nestled smugly in the rolling hills. The cliffs off the right side dropped down hundreds of feet to the rocky surf below. One wrong turn of the coach's big steering wheel, and the bus was going over the edge.

Trying to keep his mind off the winding turns and the very narrow road, Zack engaged his fellow travelers in conversation.

"So, Kirby, you're a trainer in Dallas, right? Hayden here is a fellow Texan, from Houston."

"Really?" Kirby asked. "What part?"

"I grew up in Tanglewood, but when our parents died, my brother and I moved to the Montrose area."

"Oh, I'm sorry about your parents."

"Thanks. It's okay now, I guess. I still have Clay." He noticed Kirby's confused look. "Clay is my twin brother," he explained.

"I keep forgetting that you and Clay are twins. You're both so different," Kurt joined in from the front seat. "I've always thought it would be cool to have a twin. You'd always have someone to talk to."

"Yeah. What's that like?" Zack asked the new man in his life.

"Actually, it's pretty cool. He's my best friend. Always has been. It's like you have that, a built-in best friend for life, you know? It sucks that he's so far away now, but we talk by phone and e-mail all the time. I do miss him, though," Hayden said with a trace of longing in his voice.

"Did you have to share toys and stuff?" Kirby asked. As an only child, he was constantly fascinated by siblings and their complicated relationships.

"Yeah, but it was cool. I was just always glad that we weren't identical, and didn't look the same. That would have been weird."

"I think I've seen his show, like, only twice," Zack admitted.

Hayden's brother Clay was one of the superstars of daytime dramas. His television show, *The Insiders*, was the number-one rated soap opera, and Clay had the lead on it. He was a two-time daytime Emmy winner, and was waiting for his first major motion picture to open.

"I never get to see it!" Hayden complained. They don't air it in Barcelona, I don't know why. We get his old show, *Sunset Cove*, but not the one he's on now." He shrugged. "He does send me DVDs of what he thinks are his best episodes, though."

"I'm very close to my brother, too," Kurt offered. "I think it's really important to have family. Park, that's my brother, and his wife Dru are, next to Rick, the most important people in my life. Oh, and our goddaughter, of course!"

Rick nodded. "That's true. I think we spend more time with Park, Dru and little Sydney than we do any of our gay friends, except Clay and Travis."

Kurt pulled his wallet out and showed the men on the bus his strikingly pretty niece. "Isn't she cute? This girl is going to knock 'em dead when she's older," he said proudly.

"Wow," Zack said. "How old is she?"

"Three and a half going on 28."

Rick laughed. "And she has this one," he pointed at his lover, "wrapped around her little finger. It's hilarious to watch. Anything she wants, he gets for her. All she has to do is bat her baby blues and bam, he's scrambling for the closest Toys 'R Us."

Kurt shrugged. "That's what us godfathers are for." He shot a quick look at Rick. "Besides, it's good practice for when we have our own."

Hayden jumped in. "Oh? You two want kids?"

Kurt took Rick's hand in his own and nodded happily. "We're discussing adopting. I think Rick would make an amazing dad." He looked at his lover with complete adulation.

Rick blushed, but didn't say anything. He didn't know what his new job offer would do to their plans for a family. It was one of the reasons he hadn't broached the subject yet.

"Did your brother always know you were gay, Kurt?" Kirby asked from across the aisle.

"Oh, yeah. I told him as soon as I figured it out. He's always been totally cool with it. In fact, before I met Rick, he set me up a few times."

Hayden giggled. "In college, Clay once set me up with a guy he had just split up with. He said he thought we'd get along better than they did. It didn't work out. I just felt weird being with a guy I knew my brother had slept with."

"Did Clay ever tell you that I once had a huge crush on him?" Rick asked, turning around and looking at Hayden.

"No," Hayden said, surprised.

"Oh, yeah, I was so into him," Rick nodded. "But he was with Travis, Mr. All-American TV star. Then I met Kurt. All men faded from view when I met my Kurt."

"Awww…" Kurt beamed, giving his lover a warm hug.

"Wait. Travis? Not Travis Church!" Kirby asked, shocked.

"Well, yeah. They've been together for years now. It's not widely known, and I'd appreciate it if you didn't repeat it," Hayden quickly said.

"Oh, sure, no problem. Wow. Travis Church is so hot!" Kirby's head was spinning. He'd had a crush on Travis Church for a while, ever since the actor had been on *Us Two*, Kirby's favorite sitcom. Now a bona fide movie star, Travis had scored several leading roles in some hit movies. He was the definition of sexy. And he was gay!

"Clay and I knew we were gay from the time we were, like, twelve," Hayden continued, grinning. "I think I told him I liked boys first. Then he had to jump on the fag bandwagon. Fuckin' copycat."

"I knew I was queer in high school," Rick said. "I found I was more attracted to the coaches than the Home Ec teacher. I didn't act on it until I went to college. My first roommate. He showed me the light."

Kurt's face clouded. "I think I knew when I was younger, but didn't acknowledge it until I was in boarding school. And I ended up fucking the coach."

"Jesus!"

"No kidding?"

Kurt nodded. "Swear to God. After that, I was balls out gay and loving it. I wouldn't want to be straight now."

"Me either."

"Not me!"

"I couldn't be straight if I tried," Hayden cracked. "And I don't want to try. I find it so interesting that both my twin brother and I are gay. I know we had a gay uncle, too. And they say it isn't hereditary. Please."

"If you look out the left side of the bus," Gabrielle's voice interrupted their discussion. "You can see Le Rocher, or The Rock. That is where the

Palace of the Grimaldis is."

The lush countryside beyond the coastline was jaw dropping. Small villas with million-euro views were snugly nestled up the hills and got more concentrated as they got closer to the principality of Monaco.

The principality itself was situated on top of a craggy cliff that towered over the coastline. A natural defensive point, a structure had been built in some fashion or another on top of it for over 3,000 years.

"The principality of Monaco is only 1.95 square kilometers," Gabrielle continued to explain, as all the men on the bus stared out the windows of the coach at the imposing buildings regally situated on top of the cliff. "And is home to over 30,000 people, but only 4,800 of those are true Monegasques, or natives, and with Monaco's liberal tax laws it's easy to understand why."

Gabrielle told the enthralled men about the royal family, the Grimaldis, and their history. She told them how the first Grimaldi managed to overpower guards and take the rival castle, the Ghibelline Fortress, by dressing as a monk. That was why there is an armed monk on the family's coat of arms.

"I know what I want on our coat of arms," Rick whispered to Kurt. "A cock and balls. I think that would say it all." Kurt had to stifle his laughter.

The bus continued to climb up the hillside, finally come to a stop in a vast parking garage next to several other coaches that were also discharging tourists. Glad to be able to stand up and move, the men of coach four gladly rose up and climbed down and out onto the concrete. Cameras were checked and everyone got ready. Gabrielle then led the large group to a long escalator bank and up they all went. Zack was standing behind Hayden on the escalator and lovingly poked him in the ass.

"Don't do that unless you mean business," Hayden warned.

"Oh, I mean business, all right. Just wait until we get back on the ship."

"Hot damn!"

At the top, they all went to a large bank of elevators and, splitting up into two groups, they got in and ascended to the very top floor, which was actually the ground level of Le Rocher.

Exiting the elevators the two groups merged back together and followed Gabrielle through the narrow streets toward the old buildings that lay ahead.

"This whole area is known as Monaco-Ville," Gabrielle said, leading the group into a warren's nest of narrow alleyways. The centuries old buildings were no more than five or six stories tall, but had been built right up against each other. They were painted all the different colors of the Mediterranean. Blue, Yellow. Pink. For the first time Zack understood the basis for where all

Mediterranean-themed furnishings came from.

Some of the windows and balcony doors were open and crisp lacy curtains would billow out into the late morning air. There were very few locals around, though several other large groups of tourists could be seen wandering through the streets. Some of them were even from the *Princess Diana*.

The cobblestone streets were uneven, but extremely quaint. The streets and alleys seemed to go on for a block, then suddenly dead end, or they turned sharply and rambled back onto themselves. It was a confusing layout, and it reminded Hayden of those villages he'd seen in old Frankenstein movies. He half expected to see a crazed, shouting mob of villagers carrying lit torches come racing down one of the streets.

The gay men were charmed by the city, however, and they all whipped out their digital cameras and started snapping away.

This part of Monaco-Ville was full of small restaurants and quaint tourist shops. The men all knew they'd have time after the guided tour to explore Le Rocher for themselves, so they waited to do their shopping until then.

"I can't believe I'm here! This is so cool!" Kirby excitedly said to no one in particular.

After a brisk five-minute walk, the group ended up in front of an ornate cathedral. Before going in, Gabrielle gathered all the men of her tour into a loose circle.

"This is a very solemn place we are entering," she said in a respectful tone. "Many from the house of Grimaldi are buried here. Both Prince Ranier and Princess Grace's tombs are inside. When he was alive, Prince Rainier would have a fresh bouquet of flowers placed at the Princess's grave every day." Gabrielle sighed softly. "Anyway," she continued, "the Cathedral was built in 1897 and has many priceless and beautiful works of art. We can only go in single file, one after the other. So, let us go in."

She walked into the quiet church, and the men lined up and followed. Zack, Hayden and Kirby fell into line and began to walk through the roped off area.

Rick took a hold of Kurt's arm and pulled him back outside.

"Do you really want see the prince and princess's burial plots?" he asked, with a mischievous glint in is eye.

"I've been here before. You haven't. I thought you wanted to see all of this."

Rick leaned in close to his lover's ear and whispered, "There's something else I'd rather see...and feel."

"Oh, yeah? What's that?" Kurt whispered back in reply.

"You. Inside me. Now."

Kurt's eyebrows shot up. "While I'm always interested in that, I don't see how we can accomplish it here in the middle of the kingdom of Monaco."

"Then you haven't been paying attention," Rick said mysteriously. He then reached out, took Kurt's hand and began to back up. "Come with me, baby."

"Another martini, my dear Jorge?"

Jorge rolled his head over and opened his eyes. "Sure. I never much cared for them before, but now I kinda like 'em."

Donnatella raised her arm and, spying Renaldo, snapped her fingers. He rushed over.

"Duo. Grazi," she said raising her empty glass. How many had that been already? Three? Four? She couldn't remember.

Fuck it, she thought hazily. *I'm on vacation.*

"So, Donnatella, tell me, what the hell are you doing on this cruise?" Jorge slurred. He was feeling no pain and liking it. "It's not like you're gonna get laid, you know. We're all fags onboard! Everywhere you look, cocksuckers!" he giggled.

Gazing at his flawless body, she nodded her head. "Don't I know it."

She lay back down on the chaise. "My husband dragged me on this trip. He is simply terrified that you gay boys are going to ruin his precious ship." She suddenly spat at the ground. "He cares more about this damn ship than he does his own wife!"

Jorge was surprised at the sudden venom in her voice. "Trouble in paradise?" he asked lazily.

Catching herself, Donnatella regained her calm demeanor. "Not trouble. Not nothing. No lovemaking. No love. I don't know why I stay with him."

"'Cause he's worth, like, twenty kabillion dollars?" Jorge stated frankly, as he stretched his lean body.

Donnatella knew she should act outraged at such a statement. She knew she should slap the cheeky man who made such a disparaging remark.

But she didn't.

"You're damn right!" she said forcefully. "I invested too many years to walk away with what I agreed to walk away with in that damn pre-marital. How you say, um, screw that!"

"Atta girl!"

Renaldo returned with the cocktails and handed them off to eager hands, doing his best not to stare at Donnatella's exposed breasts.

Just as Donnatella was taking a sip of her delicious cocktail, she happened to catch a glimpse of a dark figure on the wraparound-deck above them. Forcing herself to focus, she saw it was Rex, dressed, typically, in a suit, staring down at her, shock and disdain on his tight face.

"Oh, look. There he is. My husband. My hero." She pointed him out to Jorge, and then they both waved merrily at him.

This seemed to shock him even more. Rex turned bright red, spun around, and huffed off.

"Excuse me," said an unfamiliar voice.

Jorge and Donnatella looked to their left and saw a drop dead gorgeous man in a teal blue bikini bathing suit standing there. He was probably in his late 30s or early 40s.

"Yeah?" Jorge asked drunkenly.

"I've been watching you from afar, and I wanted to come over and invite you to join me for dinner tonight." The man smiled brightly, showing even white teeth. Jorge looked him up and down. He was built, and built well. Tanned, tall and hot. Jorge then looked at Donnatella. "What do you think? Should I have dinner with this man?"

Jorge had actually turned down three other dinner invitations for this evening. He was hoping to run into the hot man in the black box-cut swimsuit he had spied up on deck yesterday and have dinner, and more, with him. But so far, Jorge hadn't seen him again.

The man before him now was hot, not as hot as black box-cut guy, but definitely hot, and worth a tumble. Jorge already knew he'd say yes, but he wanted to tease the guy a bit first. "Should I, Donnatella?" he asked his sunning companion again.

"Hmmm…" Donnatella pretended to ponder. She too gave the hot stranger the once over and paused. There was something just off about him, something she couldn't put her finger on. "I was hoping you dine with me tonight, Jorge…"

Jorge looked back at the handsome guy and smiled. "See? I already have plans…It would take a lot to get me to break that very important engagement…" he said, suggestively.

The man squatted down next to Jorge and put his face only inches away. His dark eyes were hypnotizing. "What if I told you that after dinner," he said slowly and softly, "I'd give you the fucking of a lifetime. I've got nine, count 'em, nine real inches packed away in here." He sensually rubbed his own crotch. "And they're all yours."

Jorge, stunned, looked at Donnatella. "Chica," he said dryly to her, "how can I pass up nine, count 'em nine, real inches? I'm gonna have to jump on that!" He giggled at his own pun. "We can do drinks tomorrow, can't we? At which time I'll tell you all about it."

Donnatella smiled tightly, never taking her gaze off the man.

"I guess you have a date then," Jorge said.

"Great. My name's Seth. I'll pick you at your cabin at 8:00."

"You got it, Papi."

Seth just smiled, his face a mask.

"I'm on Pearl Deck, 4116," Jorge said, straining to look once more at Seth's well-packed basket. Jorge was an expert at gauging a man's size by his package. What he saw encased in teal Lycra was indeed awe-inspiring. There actually was nine inches in there!

Seth rose to his feet. "I'll see you at 8:00."

Donnatella and Jorge watched him walk away.

"Jorge," Donnatella said hesitantly, mindful that her intuition about people was seldom wrong, "be careful."

"Oh, I always make 'em slip on a condom, so don't worry." The studly young man reclined back into his chair and closed his eyes. He was going to have a memorable night, no doubt about it.

Geoff was having no luck at the poolside bar. Even though men kept coming up to him requesting his autograph, offering congratulations and asking him the same *RAW* questions that everyone asked, he still hadn't been able to score. He was actually getting frustrated. He'd managed to get a pretty fair blowjob last night up on the Compass Deck, and, surprise of surprises, had given that stud Jorge from Miami amazing head up there as well. But he longed for a real old-fashioned roll in the hay with some hot guy.

"Say, excuse me, but aren't you Geoff Corbin? From *Race Around the World*?"

Geoff was about to tell the voice to fuck off when he noticed who was speaking to him.

"Why, yes. Yes, I am." He gave the bikini-clad man opposite him the quick once-over. Good face with a strong jawline. Not too tall, not too short. Good shoulders. Hot chest. Nice flat stomach. Full crotch. Beefy legs.

Yes, indeed, Geoff thought happily. *He'll do nicely*.

"I'm Andy," he said, holding out his hand.

Geoff shook it. "Geoff," he stated the obvious.

"Yeah, I know," giggled Andy. He caught Geoff looking down at his crotch and was glad he'd slipped on the cock ring before heading up to the pool area. It always did wonders for his pouch.

"Enjoying your cruise?"

"Oh, yeah! My lover and I have been on three of these Titan cruises so far. They're just the best!"

"Oh," Geoff said dejectedly. "You have a lover."

"Yeah, he's right over there," Andy pointed to a strikingly handsome board shorts-wearing black man stretched out on a chaise lounger. He was well built and had incredibly pumped up pecs. He waved at Geoff. Geoff halfheartedly waved back.

"You know," Andy said conspiratorially, "I shouldn't be telling you this…"

"Yes?" Geoff was already disinterested. He looked over Andy's shoulder at another good-looking guy who was lounging on a float in the pool.

"Well, when your show was on, Frank and I always thought you were so damn hot. We always said that if we met you, we'd invite you to join us…you know…sometime."

Geoff was suddenly all ears. "Oh, really?"

Andy glanced briefly at Frank, then leaned in close to Geoff. He began whispering into Geoff's ear. When he was done speaking, Geoff pulled back and looked him squarely in the eye. "Then what are we doing wasting time up here on deck for?" he asked, grinning slyly.

Rick led Kurt quietly past their bus driver, who was dozing on a bench by the elevator that went down to the parking lot. Giggling like teenagers ditching class, the two men rode the elevator down and snuck back on their parked bus. Finding the vehicle completely empty, they wandered towards the rear of the coach and began to passionately kiss. Kurt pulled Rick to the last seat and threw him on it. He tore at Rick's clothes like a man possessed. Rick greedily grabbed at Kurt's khakis.

"You want me? Huh? You want me to fuck you?" Kurt sexily grilled his lover through barely parted lips.

"Oh, yeah!'

"Then get ready, baby, cause I'm gonna give it to you good!"

"God, I love you," Rick sighed, lifting his butt so Kurt could slide his pants off.

"I love you, too," Kurt said passionately. The two men then kissed with such tenderness it almost made Rick cry. "I love you so much," Kurt repeated over and over between kisses.

16

Diamond Deck, *Princess Diana*

Rex Lassiter opened his stateroom door and quickly stepped in. Even though he had just seen Donnatella on deck chitchatting with some young faggot, with her breasts hanging out for all the world to see, he still called out to the empty stateroom. "Hello? Anyone here? It's me. Rex."

Expecting, and receiving, no reply, he casually reached up and rotated the dial that was positioned under the message sign that was mounted next to every stateroom's door frame on the ship. He continued to spin the small dial, until the visible message window changed from "Welcome" to "Do Not Disturb." Other options, if needed, included "Make Up Cabin," and "Turn Down Cabin." He then shut the door and bolted it. Satisfied he could now move in peace, he shed his suit jacket and loosened his tie. He walked down into his sunken living room and went to the heavy sofa.

Not the usual lightweight mod-style sofa found in most of the other cabins onboard, this sofa was from Rex's own home in London. Made of thick, carved mahogany scrollwork and crushed crimson velvet, it set the style for the private stateroom, which was one of grand ocean liners past.

The cabin was decorated in a rich and somber Edwardian style. When guests or visitors entered the suite of plushly decorated rooms for the first time, they had the unnerving feeling that they had somehow stepped back in time, into a cabin on the legendary ocean liner *Olympic* or *Mauriatania*. Heavy woodwork. Deep walnut paneling. Thick damask draperies. Expensive oriental carpeting. It was a stark contrast to the glossy and modern decor of the rest of the *Princess Diana*.

Rex gritted his teeth and with surprising ease, pulled the massive sofa away from the wall. Hidden down low to the floor was a small door hidden in the intricate detailing of the rich paneling. Applying light pressure allowed the door to pop open. Rex reached into the compartment concealed there and dragged out a large Louis Vuitton keepall bag. He wiped the perspiration from his brow and hunkered down to his knees on the floor. Taking a deep breath, he unzipped the bag and spread it open. Inside was another bag, this one a plain navy blue canvas duffle. He unzipped this bag as well, and gazed at its contents. Everything was still inside. Safe and secure.

The dull black metal of the casing units looked just like they had when he'd packed the bag two days before. Getting the canvas duffle onboard had been child's play. As president of the line, he had simply thrown the Vuitton, with its concealed canvas bag, over his shoulder and walked up the gangway, Donnatella in tow. No one had dared to inspect *his* luggage.

There were three of the black boxes packed tightly inside the bag. The activation indicators were still and non-functioning.

For now.

Rex allowed himself a rare smile as he imagined the destruction the devices were going to bring. He didn't know why he'd had to look at them again. He'd just been compelled to.

He carefully zipped both bags closed and gently placed them back into the hiding space. With little effort, he shoved the sofa back into place against the wall. Standing tall, he glanced into the gilded mirror that hung over the sofa. His hair had become mussed, and he gingerly brushed it back into place using his fingers.

He began to whistle to himself as he strode over to the elaborate and obscenely expensive stereo system he'd installed in the suite. Punching a few buttons, he was soon rewarded with the rich, lifelike surround sound of Verdi's *Aida*. Settling down into his lush sofa, Rex allowed his mind to clear. This was one of his favorite pastimes - being alone, relaxed, listening to excellent music. It was when he did his best thinking. Now, loosening his tie even more, he went over the plan in his mind for the thousandth time.

The *Diana* would sink. The bombs would take care of that.

Rex suddenly had a brilliant thought. What if he could get Donnatella to be near one of the bombs went it went off? That would tidily take care of that problem, too.

Realizing that this would require some more thought, he closed his eyes and let his mind wander. He knew it was only a matter of time before the answer would reveal itself.

17

Le Rocher, Monaco

'm starving. When do we eat lunch?" groused Kirby after Zack and Hayden joined the group outside.

"Actually, I'm hungry, too," agreed Zack.

"Hey…" Hayden looked around the area. "Where are Rick and Kurt?"

"I saw them leave before we went into the cathedral," Kirby replied. "Oh, the group is moving again. Let's go."

The three men merged back into the larger group and followed Gabrielle through some more winding cobblestone streets. They finally entered a large plaza with an imposing structure facing them across the open space.

"This is the Palias du Prince, the home of Monaco's royal family now led by Prince Albert," Gabrielle lectured, leading them closer to the buff-colored building.

"Doesn't look like a palace, does it?" asked Kirby.

In fact, it did not. Originally built in the 13th century as a Genoese fortress, the buff-colored royal palace had seen many additions built on over the generations. The newer section was probably three or four stories tall, with an elaborate entryway topped by the Grimaldi family crest.

The palace looked more like a Moorish-style municipal building than the residence for one of Europe's more glamorous families. A low, flat wall with small peaked windows fronted the courtyard. High, wide, arched windows covered the upper floors, letting sun into what had to be fabulously decorated public rooms. The back part of the palace was the older part, with ancient-looking rough stone blocks as the chief architectural element.

A simple black chain roped through squat black pylons was all that kept the general public away from the palace's walls. Well, that and two heavily armed guards dressed in crisp whites standing stiffly by the entryway.

A square tower complete with clock face anchored the right side of the compound. A barren flagpole stood sentry on top of the tower.

"When the Prince is in residence," explained Gabrielle, "the royal flag is raised. As you can see, there is no flag. The royal family have many summer homes, and the Prince is probably at one of those."

"Why would you leave this?" Zack whispered to Hayden, pointing to the Moorish styled palace.

"Oh, I'm just so tired of Monaco," Hayden joked, affecting a faux-European accent. "I think I'll summer in Capri…Caroline, Stephanie! Pack up the minivan!"

Zack grinned, playfully shoved Hayden, and returned his attention to the royal residence.

There were several small black cannons situated in front of the palace, and there were neatly stacked piles of iron cannonballs nearby. Gabrielle explained that the cannons were a gift to the principality as her charges snapped shot after shot of the palace and surroundings.

"Now you all have one hour to explore on your own. We will meet at the bus at…" she glanced down at her watch. "At 1:20, okay? Meet at 1:20 at the bus. Then we go down into Monte Carlo." She smiled brightly and the group split up into small cliques.

"Let's go find some food," Zack said to Hayden. "Hey, Kirby! Let's go eat."

Kirby nodded and snapped one final picture of the palace. He put away his digital camera and joined Zack and Hayden. They went back into the alleys of the old quarter looking for a suitable place to eat.

Walking down the quaint streets, the trio spied a small creperie that looked like it had been carved out of the rock itself. A few small tables were outside and already filled, so they went inside. Settling down at a long table on some hard benches, they each picked up a menu and began to pour over it.

A gangly teenage boy came over and took their drink order. The men decided on what they wanted, and when an older woman came over, they gave her their lunch order.

"I guess the boy is her son," mused Hayden.

"He's adorable." Kirby eyed the young man who was no more than 16. He had a body that was showing his change from boy to man. A slim, sinewy torso and arms were set on top of long, growth-spurt legs. His sun-bleached hair was parted in the middle, and he kept looking shyly back at the table of handsome men.

"Notice how he keeps staring at us?" Zack observed. "I think he's a 'mo."

"I think so, too. He stared so hard at your ass when you sat down, I thought his eyes would pop out," Hayden smiled.

"Jealous?"

"You bet. That's my ass!" Suddenly realizing that he sounded a tad possessive, and fearful it would make Zack back away, he forced a laugh.

Surprisingly, Zack only smirked, and slid his hand in between Hayden's knees.

"Hey! Look who it is!" Kirby was pointing to the doorway.

Kurt and Rick were outside looking at a menu, deciding if they wanted to eat there.

"Hey! Kurt! Rick!" Hayden called out. The two bodybuilders looked up, grinned, and came in to join them.

"Hey, boys!" Kurt said happily.

"Hi, guys," echoed Rick, also beaming. "Can we join you?"

"Sure. Park it." Zack scooted over and the two bigger men sat down. Soon they too had ordered, and the conversation turned to Monaco and how beautiful it was.

In minutes their food arrived, delivered by the shy, gawking lad. He now couldn't stop staring at Rick and Kurt, obviously not having seen such built men before. You could see the lust and awe he felt written all over his smooth face.

"Oh, my God! This is amazing!" Zack had ordered a cheese crepe, and it was phenomenal. The creamy cheeses practically melted in his mouth, and the crisp crust was perfection. It was so good as to be almost sinful.

"Mine's absolutely incredible, too," Hayden nodded, chewing a mouthful of heaven. He had gotten a small margarita pizza that he was splitting with Kirby because it was so large. Fresh chopped tomatoes sitting in a dreamy tomato sauce were covered with smooth, melted cheese. And the crust! It was so crisp and light!

Kurt and Rick each had ordered a vegetable crepe and were enthusiastically digging into it as well.

Soon all five men were oohing and aahing over their exquisite fare. They managed to eat every bite. Nothing was left over but crumbs.

The young boy eventually brought over the bill and lingered at the table, picking up the cleaned plates.

"What's your name?" asked Hayden.

Startled, the boy answered hesitantly. "Uh…Franz…Bonjour…"

"Bonjour, Franz. The food here was amazing! Does this place belong to your family?"

Franz nodded vigorously. "Oui, oui. My mama and I run it," he said proudly, in surprisingly good English.

"Well, tell your mama, she can cook!" Kurt said, wiping his mouth with his napkin.

Franz stole a look down at Kurt's lap and saw that Rick's hand was lovingly rubbing his upper thigh. Franz's eyes grew large, and he almost dropped the pile of dishes he was carrying.

"Hey, Franz," whispered Kurt, crooking his fingers, signaling Franz to lean in close. The young man did, and Kurt leaned up to his smooth cheek. He kissed him lightly, then said in a gentle low voice, "You like boys, don't you? It's okay, you know. Don't feel alone, because you're not. There's nothing wrong with you."

Franz drew back slowly and shot a glance at his mother, who was busy in the restaurant's small kitchen and partially hidden from view.

"I think about boys all the time. It's like I no can turn it off!" he blurted out, blushing deeply.

"I remember," Rick said, smiling compassionately.

"Me, too. I was a walking hard-on every time I had to go to gym class," Hayden recalled.

"There's a boy in my school…Jean-Claude…He's the soccer captain…" Franz said, eyes downcast.

The five men glanced at each other and smiled. They saw that Franz was in the throes of his first big unrequited crush. Each of them had gone through the very same thing in their school years. The star pitcher of the baseball team. The captain of the football team. The center of the basketball team. Even the coach himself. And except for Kurt's, nothing had ever come of these schoolboy crushes.

"He is so beautiful," Franz said, a dreamy look coming over his face. "The way he kick and run. I can watch him play all day long."

"Franz!"

All the heads at the table jerked up. Franz's stern mother was staring at him sharply, and beckoned him to hurry up. She went back into the kitchen.

Franz quickly picked up one last plate and turned to leave. He stopped and leaned back down to the table.

"Jean-Claude, he kiss me last night!" he quickly said, and smiling broadly. He ran off to the kitchen.

Well," Zack said after a beat. "You go, Franz!"

"He's going to be a heartbreaker, that one," Kurt said rising. The friends all got up, and pooling money, paid the bill and left a 50-euro tip for Franz.

The fair young man peeked out from the back of the restaurant and waved at them as they left.

Jebb and Nick were feverishly working by the pool, trying to get everything in order. The famous Dog Tag T-dance was set to start in just a few hours, and they had so many details to go over. At first, Jebb couldn't find the boxes of thin metal dog tags with the Titan logo on one side. They finally turned up in Clive and Baldwin's cabin, having been placed there during boarding. Now he and Nick were going through them trying to untangle the heaps of metal chains.

The point of the Dog Tag T-dance was this: each partygoer got a dog tag, and he could put a red sticker on it if he was unavailable, a green sticker if he was single, or a yellow sticker if he was partnered but playing. Then guys could see at a glance who was available and who wasn't. It was a Titan tradition to have the Dog Tag T-dance the first night out so guys could hookup from the start, if they so choose.

So now Nick and Jebb were scrambling to get the tags in order, get the rolls of colored stickers ready, and make sure the DJ had the right power sources, the usual endless list of details required to run a party.

"Okay, I talked to DJ BamBam, and he says he wants two mikes, one for him and one he can pass around the crowd for open-mike karaoke," Nick said as he pulled hundreds of dog tags out of plastic bags.

"That's cool. I have a spare."

"So, did hottie man call you back yet?"

Jebb grinned. "Yes. Dinner tonight."

Nick nodded wisely. "Told you so."

"Yes. Yes, you did."

"Any run-ins with Lassiter, lately?"

"No, thank God. He's been remarkably low-key today. I see his wife is in fine form, though." Jebb motioned to the poolside where a group of ten or so men were clustered around Donnatella Lassiter as she regaled them with hilarious stories of royal dinner parties and such. She had the waiters running, making sure everyone's cocktail was always replenished. A natural-born hostess and storyteller, she had the group spellbound and laughing.

"Yeah, she's totally cool, unlike her stick-in-the-ass husband," Nick said, putting down the box. "I'm gonna go find more stickers. I think I left a roll in my cabin. I'll be right back."

"Okay."

Jebb continued to fiddle with his piles of dog tags and found they were hopelessly tangled. Sighing, he dropped the box. Nick was so much better at this sort of thing. He looked up and saw the zaftig figure of Garrett Gardner wandering across the Pool Deck looking for an open chaise. The comedian was clutching a thick book, and he waved in a friendly fashion to the men who called out hello to him. Jebb quickly went to the star's side.

"Hey, Garrett! Is everything okay? Is your cabin satisfactory?"

"Oh, yes, it's wonderful. Fabulous! I love it," Garrett said jovially. At 320 pounds, he was dressed in a large pair of blue cargo shorts and a huge orange tee-shirt that had "Can Be Used As A Flotation Device" written on it. His shaggy blonde hair and broad, unlined face hid his true age of 55 and made him appear much younger, something that thrilled Garrett to no end.

"Good, good," Jebb nodded.

"Now I'm just looking for a nice chair to lay in so I can read my book," Garrett said, scanning the deck area.

Jebb spied one a few rows away and help Garrett to it. "Everyone's really looking forward to your show," he said, as he waved a waiter over to get Garrett a drink.

"Me, too," Garrett nodded, as he lowered his girth into the chair. "It's been a while since I've done it. I just hope I remember it," he laughed.

"I'm sure you'll do fine," Jebb encouraged. "Well, let me know if I can get you anything. Anything at all."

"How about that man over there? Can you get me him?" Garrett asked, half-jokingly and pointing to Jorge.

"That, I leave up to you," Jebb answered.

A muscular young man with the thickest, sexiest eyelashes Jebb had ever seen walked up to Garrett and held out a piece of paper and a pen. "Can I get your autograph, Mr. Gardner? I'm a huge fan of yours. I read your column in *OutPride* magazine every month!" he gushed.

Garrett gave the young man the once over. He was probably only about 22 years old, and had a hard swimmer's build complimented by a rich, dark tan. Garrett, however, was more intrigued by the promising bulge in his neon green swim trunks.

"Please, call me Garrett," he said smoothly. He reached for the paper and pen, and managed to brush the young man's crotch in the process. He didn't seem to mind. "What's your name?"

"Toby. Gosh, I can't wait to see your show! I was so excited when I heard you were onboard!" He jutted his hips out a tiny bit.

"How excited?" Garrett asked suggestively as he scribbled his signature.

Toby placed a warm hand on Garrett's knee. "Very." There was no mistaking his intention.

Garrett smiled. It was so good to be a gay icon.

"Well, that's my cue to leave," Jebb said. He patted Garrett on the back and went back to the boxes of metal dog tags.

Sighing, he dug up a handful and began to try to sort them apart.

Back on the bus, Zack and Hayden gawked out the windows just like everyone else on the slow-moving coach. They were on a twisting, winding road leaving Le Rocher and heading down into Monte Carlo. The glittering city was amazingly small and amazingly tall. High-rise buildings seemed to sprout up from every square inch of space, and more were under construction. Since Monaco was so tiny, apparently the only place to go was up.

"This area, the marina area, is called La Condamine," Gabrielle said into her microphone as the bus picked its way down the dangerous road. "It links Monaco-Ville with Monte Carlo."

Below the descending bus, Zack could see the beautiful marina complete with a park-like setting that boasted an Olympic-sized swimming pool. Sleek, beautiful yachts and a few lowly fishing vessels were docked side by side in the marina. The most glamorous yacht, a huge white vessel with multiple decks, looked more like an ocean liner than a private yacht. Gabrielle informed the tourists that it was owned by a famous Greek shipping tycoon.

"The road we will be on, and the main road you can see cutting through the city, is part of the Monte Carlo Grand Prix, one of the world's most famous races," she continued as the bus reached entered the actual city. "You can see the race markings painted onto the pavement. As you know, we will again be parking in an underground area and take elevators up to the casino."

True to her word, the bus went into a wide tunnel and eventually stopped in a vast underground parking lot. Trouping off the bus yet again, the group went to the elevators and rode up in separate groups, just like before.

Coming together at the top, Gabrielle began to lead them up a slight hill, and they could see the Monte Carlo Casino above them.

Hayden was attracted to a large, heavily filigreed building to their left on top of the hill.

"What's that?" he asked the pretty tour guide.

"That's the Hôtel de Paris, one of the most famous hotels in the world," Gabrielle responded brightly.

"It's beautiful," Hayden whistled. Zack was already shooting picture after picture of it with his digital camera.

Within minutes, the whole tour group gathered near the front of the casino. A Belle Époque building with twin turrets capped by tiled domes, the casino was not as large as Zack had imagined it would be. There was a wide entrance and several severe-looking doormen inspecting each person that entered. Bags and backpacks were not allowed and could be checked just inside.

Gabrielle told the group that they now had a free hour to do what they wanted in the picturesque city. They all just needed to meet in front of the casino in 60 minutes in order to board the bus and drive back to the ship in time for departure from the port at Cannes.

The men began to walk up the short flight of stairs to enter the casino. When Zack and Hayden got to the doors, the doorman pointed at them and shook his head. Zack's clothes didn't pass muster. The Place du Casino had a strict dress code, and tank tops and shorts were prohibited.

Upset that he couldn't enter, Zack frowned and sulked back down the steps. Hayden followed him.

"Hey," Hayden called. "Wait up!"

"This is so stupid! I just wanted to peek inside," Zack said, cross at himself. "Sorry. You go on and poke around. I'll wait out here." He sat down on a wrought iron bench that was situated in front of a beautiful flower-filled square. In the center of the square was a stunning fountain built in the shape of a cross.

Hayden looked at him. "Do you really think I would go in there and leave you out here alone?"

Zack snorted. "Sure. Why not? Bayne would."

Hayden was startled to hear that. "But, I'm not Bayne. You don't go in, I don't go in." He sat down next to Zack. After a minute, he picked up Zack's hand and held it.

Up on the steps of the casino, Kurt saw what had happened and wanted to go join them. His lover put a hand on his shoulder.

"No. Leave them alone. I think they need a minute," Rick whispered in his ear. "Besides, I want to see the casino, okay?"

Kurt smiled. "Sure. Let's go in."

They entered and nodded at the doorman who looked blankly at them.

They entered the main casino space and both were stunned at the relative quiet. Used to the loud clanging and roar of Vegas, the sedate, serious gambling atmosphere here was completely different.

They were staring at the gilded mirrors when a man from their tour group came over to them.

"Pretty fancy, huh?" he said. He was probably 50, balding, but he took care of himself. Trim and tall, he was dressed in a pale green polo shirt and spotless khakis.

"It certainly is," agreed Kurt, as he pointed out a fabulous crystal chandelier to his lover.

The man from the tour squinted at the couple for a second. "You're Rick Yung, right?"

Rick, a local celebrity in Los Angeles, was surprised someone recognized him halfway around the globe. "Yes, I am."

"Hi, Rick! I'm Ted Hester," the man said, holding out his hand. "I'm a segment producer for the UBC Network News. I hear you're coming our way and joining us in New York. We're all very excited to have you become a member of the team!"

Rick shook Ted's hand, but seriously wanted to strangle him. He still hadn't thought of a way to broach the subject with Kurt.

"What?" Kurt said, looking at Rick with shocked eyes.

"Rick here is one of the best news talents I've ever seen, and they want him in New York as soon as possible. I was glad when I saw you on the bus, so I could say hello before we meet in the workplace." He leaned in close to Rick and said in a low voice, "I didn't know you were gay!"

"Um…I haven't really decided if I'm accepting the job yet, Ted," Rick fumbled. Oh, this was bad, he silently fretted.

"Are you kidding? You have to accept! You'll never get a better offer from UBC," Ted pointed out. He turned his attention to the hunky bodybuilder standing sourly next to Rick. "Hi, I'm Ted."

Kurt numbly held out his hand and they shook. "I'm Kurt, Rick's partner."

"Nice to meet you, Kurt. My lover, Sam, is way over there by the roulette table," Ted said, vaguely pointing to a silver-haired man who was watching the spinning wheel attentively.

"Well, thanks, Ted. Uh…it was certainly nice to meet you." Rick took Kurt by the arm and tried to lead him away.

Kurt wouldn't budge. "So, Ted," he said, steel in his voice. "What happens if Rick doesn't accept this position?"

Ted began to look uncomfortable. He was beginning to realize that he shouldn't have broached the subject. Rick obviously hadn't told his hot boyfriend he was thinking about moving. "Well…uh…honestly, I…"

"No, really. What would happen?" Kurt pressed. He glanced at Rick who looked like he wanted to die.

"Well, You just don't turn down a job offer like the one Rick got. Not if you want to advance in network news. I've never heard of anyone turning down a network position." Ted began to back up. "Well, it was great to meet you! See you both on the ship!" He practically ran away.

"Kurt...I was going to talk to you..." Rick tried to say, but Kurt cut him off.

"When? When were you going to talk to me about this? Jesus Christ! I hear this from a complete stranger? What the fuck, Rick?" Kurt was so angry that the big veins in his neck started to swell and pulsate.

"Baby, I know you..."

"Don't you 'baby' me! You knew about this and you said nothing? How long? When did you get this offer?" Kurt jammed his hands on his hips and glared at his lover.

Rick knew he had to come clean. "Three weeks ago. I have to let them know when we get back to L.A."

"Fuck!" Kurt said with such force, that several people turned around and stared at him.

"Let's go outside, honey," Rick soothed. Kurt spun on his heels and stomped out of the casino. Rick caught up to him on the steps.

"Look, I know I should have talked to you about this sooner, but you're behaving like a baby!"

Kurt looked at Rick like he was an alien. "A baby? Fuck you!" He was shaking with rage. "I just find out, from a fucking stranger, that my lover, my partner, the man I love and want to spend the rest of my life with is thinking about moving 3,000 miles away and didn't think it important enough to discuss with me!"

"I'm sorry," Rick said, his heart sinking.

"You're sorry? Jesus, Rick! What the hell are we gonna do? Are you seriously thinking of going? What about our plans to start a family?"

Kurt looked at Rick with such intensity and hurt it wounded the anchor. "Kurt, I...I...I've been working for this opportunity my entire life. It's what I always wanted..."

"I can't believe I'm hearing this."

"How can I not think about it," Rick continued, holding his shaky ground. "It's everything I've worked for. But I love you. My life is with you, and I don't want that to change in any way. I don't know what to do!"

"You tell them no, goddammit. Our life is in California!"

"No, *your* life is in California," Rick softly pointed out. "And I respect that, and forgive me for asking this, but isn't New York also the publishing capital of, like, the world? Wouldn't it make sense for you to move your company there?"

Kurt was so taken aback by this suggestion that he couldn't speak for a minute.

"I mean, that way we both could do what we love," Rick continued.

"Are you crazy? The charm of my publishing company is that it isn't based in New York! I can't believe you'd even think of such a thing!"

"And I can't believe that you feel what you do is more important than what I do!" Rick hotly retorted. "I did have a career before I met you, you know."

"That's not what I said!"

"You don't have to. It's obvious what you feel."

"This is insane!" Kurt spat out. "Will you be out as a gay man there? Or, are you going to pretend you don't have a husband?"

"What?"

"It'll be much more political there. Being gay is going to hurt you at that level, you know that! So, are you willing to play straight for this job you want so damn much?" Kurt asked archly.

"Where is this coming from? I haven't even thought about that! I am who I am…"

"And the baby? Do you not want to have a child now?"

"Kurt…" Kurt's eyes were blazing with hurt and betrayal, but Rick forged ahead. "Maybe we could wait a year or so, you know? Let's get more settled…"

Kurt simply couldn't believe what he was hearing. "More settled? You know, I don't really want to be with you right now." He stormed off, heading across the square towards the Café de Paris, a large pavilion full of tables and chairs. Kurt disappeared into the shadows of the many umbrellas that covered the tables.

Rick, angry and dejected, headed in the opposite direction, towards the Hôtel de Paris.

Zack and Hayden, sitting at a table in the pavilion drinking ice-cold lemonade, had watched the entire scene.

"Wonder what that was all about?" Hayden said.

"I don't know," Zack replied. "But it sure didn't look good." He took a sip of his drink. "Listen, Hade. I'm sorry I said what I did earlier about Bayne. You're right. You aren't him, thank God. You're such a better man than he could ever hope to be, and I…I…"

Hayden's heart soared to hear these words. He knew he was on dangerous ground. He knew he could easily fall in love with Zack, if he hadn't already. And he wasn't that cavalier with his feelings, so it said a lot that he felt this strongly about a man he had so recently met.

Zack still tried to form a coherent sentence. "…I…I am so glad I met you, Hade. And last night…my God, I haven't felt that kind of passion in years."

"Me, either," Hayden admitted.

"So, I'm just trying to work through some shit now…please understand, okay?"

"Oh, baby, I do." Hayden leaned in close to Zack. "I completely understand. Everything's happening so fast for me too, and I don't want you to feel pressured at all. But I'd be less than honest if I didn't tell you that I think I'm falling for you." He looked at Zack and held his breath.

Zack blinked. "Me, too," he finally admitted out loud, smiling shyly.

18

The *Princess Diana*, Mediterranean Sea

It was a night of 1,000 climaxes. Everywhere onboard the *Princess Diana*, men were getting off with each other. If the sexual energy that the randy passengers generated could be corralled into power, it would have been enough to light the city of Marietta, Georgia, for three days.

In Andy and Frank's cabin on Deck 4, the Pearl Deck, Geoff Corbin was yet again slamming into the supple ass of Frank as Andy urged him to "Do it harder!" They had been down there all afternoon and had only left the cabin for an hour or so to check out the Dog Tag T-dance, then quickly returned to continue their marathon three-way.

Now Frank's legs were held high in the air by Andy's strong hands, conveniently parting them up and out of the way of Geoff's relentless drilling.

"Oh maaannn…fuuuuckk meeeee," Frank moaned loudly.

"Yeah! Give it to him! Hard! He loves it hard!" Andy panted.

Frank could hold back no more and opening his mouth wide to shout out his pleasure, ejaculated all over Andy.

"That's what I wanted to see!" Andy grinned joyously.

In Garrett Gardner's stateroom up on Deck 7, the Diamond Deck, the famous comedian was furiously bobbing up and down on young Toby's mammoth cock. They had spent the afternoon together, and had even danced together for a bit at the T-dance, though Garrett never danced.

Garrett was a legendary Hollywood cocksucker, and his list of conquests was not only impressive, but downright astounding. He had a knack for being in the right place at the right time. Many a "straight" male star feared for the day Garrett should decide to write his memoirs.

Doing what he felt he did best, Garrett was busily slithering up and down Toby's porn-star worthy dick and watching the young man twitch in response. Toby had never received such an awesome blowjob before, certainly not from a famous person, and in a geyser of milky white, he came so hard, and with so much volume, it literally took Garrett's breath away.

In his plain, single stateroom down in the crew quarters located near the bow of the ship, on Deck C, Klaus Jergin, the ship's first officer, was waiting nervously. He couldn't believe he was going to do what he was about to do. He had even had to knock back two shots of tequila in order to calm himself down.

Tonight he was going to cross a line, a line he had only dreamed of crossing. A line that had tempted him for too long.

He glanced down at his crotch and found that he was flagpoling in anticipation. He tried to adjust his black dress slacks to make the erection seem less noticeable, but it was useless. He was a large man there, and he wasn't hiding it. He quickly checked his breath to make sure it was okay. He planned on kissing his partner tonight.

A lot.

At the precise minute that his guest was due, there was a solid knock at the door. Gulping, and unconsciously smoothing down his crisp shirt, he crossed the small space to the door.

"Good evening," he said rather stiffly. He stepped back so the handsome man could enter.

"I rather like what you've done with the place, Klaus," joked his guest, who looked around at the neat compartment.

"I try. It's small, but it's home."

"I know what you mean. I'm sorry we couldn't meet up in my…cabin. There would be the distinct possibility of an interruption, and that could prove…disastrous." Klaus's guest went to peer out the tiny pothole bolted into place on the metal bulkhead.

Unlike the passenger cabins several decks above their heads, the crew quarters were almost spartan in design. Industrial beige paint coated everything, and exposed conduits, pipes, and electrical junction boxes were not hidden from view. Still, the cabin was spacious enough for two people, and as a senior officer, Klaus rated a single. There was an adequate closet containing his three uniforms, and a serviceable wood desk piled high with florid romance novels.

The bed, a queen size, was the one luxury that Klaus had insisted on. He was physically too big a man for the standard twin size bed. The bed ate up extra room, but Klaus felt it was worth it. He was glad he had the larger bed now. There was no way the two large men would have fit on a twin.

His guest spun around and eyed Klaus appreciatively. "You look so damn handsome tonight, Klaus."

Klaus, unused to such praise, blushed. "Thank you, si..." he started to say, then stopped. "Thank you, Joseph," he corrected himself, using his guest's first name.

"And I see that you are very excited for me to be here," Joseph smirked. He took two paces towards Klaus, and placed his right hand firmly on Klaus hard bulge and began rubbing it. Klaus shivered at his touch. "Mmmm...It certainly feels like you're packing, Klaus."

"Oh, God, that feels so good," Klaus barely breathed.

"How long have you wanted to do this? What we're going to do tonight?'

"A long time...Oh!....Oh, Joseph...!" Klaus couldn't contain his passion anymore, and he kissed Joseph so hard that Joseph had to brace his feet in order not to be knocked over.

"Slow down, Klaus, slow down. We have over an hour..." He reached his hands up and pulled Klaus into him and the two men began to hungrily kiss, each feeling the other's hard body constrained by clothing.

In cabin 7235, on the Diamond Deck, Zack and Hayden were under the covers of Zack's bed. Hayden was sliding in and out of Zack's ass with long, slow, deep pulses that caused Zack to moan low with each press forward.

After returning from the tour, they had each gone to their respective cabins, showered, and put in an appearance at the T-dance. After dancing together for about 20 minutes, they had then escaped to Zack's roomy cabin to watch a movie on the TV and order room service.

Things had progressed from there.

"Oh, my God...!" Zack breathed deeply, relishing the sensations he was feeling by having Hayden's hard member fill him up. "What are you doing to me?"

"The same thing you're doing to me, baby," Hayden replied softly, thrusting forward again. He was gently stroking Zack's head as he fucked him.

"Ohhhh!...Oh, God, Hayden...Oh, God...!"

"Mmmmm...Is that good?...Is this how you like it?...I just want to please you..."

"Oh, God! Yes!" Zack arched his back up in an uncontrolled spasm of ecstasy that caused Hayden to press in a bit further. "Ohhhh! Oh, God! Oh, God!...Ohhhh!" Zack cried out in a rush.

"Mmmmm, yeah...Let it out...Pump it out, baby..." Hayden whispered sensually, staring with intensity into Zack's wondrous eyes. He felt Zack squirm under him and knew he was coming. Zack's beautiful mouth was slightly parted with amazement, but no sounds came out.

"You are so beautiful when you come," marveled Hayden, again stroking Zack's face.

Zack took several deep breaths, trying to regroup. "Oh, my God! That was so intense," he finally uttered.

"I know…"

"I love you, Hayden."

Hayden blinked. "Wha…what?"

"I love you. I know it. I feel it. I can't deny it." Zack said the words with no artifice, no guile. He was speaking from his heart and it showed.

"Zack…"

"It's how I feel. I just wanted you to know," Zack sighed happily.

Hayden smiled. He traced a finger slowly over Zack's lips and felt his heart swell. "I'm glad you told me. I'm in love with you, too, Zack. I think I knew it that first day, when we toured through Barcelona."

Zack's lip curled up slightly under Hayden's finger at the memory.

"Oh, God, baby…I love you so much, it scares me," Hayden murmured, moving his finger away in time to press his lips to Zack's.

Zack allowed himself to be covered in soft kisses from his new lover whose cock was still lodged firmly in his ass.

He had never felt so complete.

Across the companionway, Kurt sullenly lay in the master suite of his and Rick's stateroom watching the TV. Rick, in the other, much smaller bedroom, was absently reading the new Ben Patrick Johnson novel.

The couple in the cabin next to Kurt and Rick's were going at it hot and heavy, and the dampened sounds of their animalistic lovemaking floated through the thin wall separating the two staterooms. The muted gasps and cries of pleasure from the two unknown men next door were torture for Kurt to hear, because that's what he wanted to be doing with his lover right now. In his frustration, he kicked the towel swan off the bed and onto the floor.

While they had been off-ship touring the South of France, their cabin attendant had come in to clean up the rooms. In what seemed a very personal touch, their attendant had taken two extra towels and ingeniously folded and molded them together to resemble a swan. Upon Kurt and Rick's return to the cabin, both men were surprised by the craftiness of it, and they each thought it was cute and clever. But since they weren't speaking to one another, neither one of them vocalized this.

Kurt had made a mental note to leave a larger tip for their attendant for his thoughtfulness. He had no way of knowing that the towel sculptures were done in every cabin throughout the ship.

Kurt had passed on attending the Dog Tag T-dance, but Rick had gone, dressed up in dark green camouflage cargo shorts and a jaunty black beret, just to prove the point that he could do fine on his own.

Now, in separate bedrooms, barely 20 feet apart, they continued to ignore each other. It was something they had never done before, and it underscored the severity of their situation.

Kurt was furious that Rick would even consider moving and hadn't bothered to discuss such a huge issue with him. It brought up all of his abandonment issues and he was beside himself with sudden feelings of loneliness.

Rick, desperate to make up with his lover, didn't want to be the first one to cave. He needed to know that he was an equal in his relationship, and Kurt's instant dismissal of his opportunity proved that Kurt felt he was "more equal" than him.

Sighing heavily, Kurt threw back the covers and swung his huge legs around. Standing up, he walked out of the master suite to go to the bathroom. He walked right into Rick, who had gotten up to do the exact same thing.

Now only inches apart, they glowered at each other. Then Rick jerked his arms up, and grabbing Kurt's head, pulled his lover in and kissed him. Kurt, relieved beyond words that the spell had been broken, responded, and soon the two built men were rolling on the floor of their cabin, tearing off each other's clothes murmuring "I love you" and "I'm so sorry."

Twenty cabins forward from Kurt and Rick, in the owner's suite, Donnatella arched her back and pushed her head back down into the soft pillow. She moaned low and then gasped. Her left hand reached out and clutched at the rumpled bedding beside her.

"Oh, Jorge…Oh, my God! Yessssss!…Fuck me, Jorge!…Mmmm," she panted, her eyes screwed shut. She felt another coarse of pleasure jolt through her body, and she forced her legs to spread further apart, her heels digging into the coverlet bunched up at the foot of the bed.

He was on top of her, lovingly pushing in and out. Surprisingly tender, yet unabashedly masculine, the Cuban model was giving her the fucking she so badly needed. She felt his hands run all over her taut body, and she quivered under his warm touch. She knew she was going to have him the second she saw his hot body dancing by the pool that first day. He had been so hot, so erotic, shaking his ass, teasing the crowd, and her, with glimpses of the unbelievable body that she was now enjoying...

"Mmmm...Oh, yes, Jorge!...Ohhhh! Oh, my God..." she panted harder, feeling herself getting close. Her nipples were so hard, erect eraser-like nubs begging to be touched, kissed, bitten.

"Oh! Oh!...Ohhhh!" Donnatella gasped, arching her back more as the sweet ecstasy took over. She suddenly came like she hadn't come in weeks. This was a full-tilt, knock-your-socks-off, banshee climax. Wave after wave of wetness escaped her as she continued to cry out, "Ohhhh!...Oh! Ohhhh!"

In seconds, the nirvana was over and she began to relax her body. Her breathing became more regular.

Jorge had certainly done her good.

"God, I needed that," she giggled.

Opening her eyes, she glanced down to her meticulously waxed patch and slowly pulled out the soaking wet vibrator. Her hand was damp and she knew she had also stained the bedding with her masturbation. The sheets would have to be changed before Rex saw them.

Oh, well. Fuck it. That's what the stewards are here for, she sighed to herself, as she stretched catlike to let the pent-up tensions in her body release.

Happily sighing again, she closed her eyes and pretended her imaginary lover was kissing her gently in their afterglow. "Thank you, Jorge, wherever you are," she whispered softly.

Klaus clutched at Joseph's back and dug his fingers into the hard muscle. "Oh Lord!" he cried out. He had the larger man's beautiful big meat sunk deep into his body, and he couldn't get enough. His legs were upraised and pressed back towards his shoulders.

Joseph expertly plowed the first officer, grunting his satisfaction with each thrust forward. "God, I've wanted to do this for so goddamn long," he rumbled, as he watched his lube-slickened manhood slide in and out of Klaus.

"Oh, Lord!...Why didn't you say something...Oh, Lord!...Sooner?!"

"I didn't know if you...I didn't dream that we could...Goddamn, I love fucking you!"

Klaus stared at Joseph's beautifully built up pecs with their light dusting of clipped chest hair. Even though Joseph was in his mid-50s, he obviously took great care of himself. Klaus had seen Joseph in the ship's employee gym on many occasions and was thrilled to find that he was personally reaping the rewards of Joseph's religiously hard work.

Before he could cry out a warning, Klaus ejaculated all over Joseph's chest. The hot come stuck to his body, and Joseph couldn't believe how sexy it felt to have the fluid on him. He shuddered mightily as he climaxed into the condom, buried deep inside the twitching man beneath him.

"Oh, my lord!" Klaus exclaimed, as Joseph slowly withdrew. "What were we waiting for? That was so good!"

Joseph wiped the sweat from his brow and nodded his agreement. He happened to glance at the bedside clock.

"Well, handsome, I'm afraid I have to get going. I have obligations, you know."

"Yes, the formal dinner, I know."

Joseph took a towel from the thin metal rack next to the sink and ran it under the water. He quickly wiped off Klaus' semen from his torso and tossed the towel to the deck.

"We are definitely doing that again," he chuckled.

"And again!" Klaus grinned, watching the well-built man clean up. He moved like a finely tuned athlete.

"Yes. And again," Joseph winked.

The tall man quickly pulled on his clothes, and, watching himself carefully in the mirror over the sink, he straightened his tie. He turned to leave the small cabin, but first leaned over and gave Klaus a passionate kiss.

"I'll see you soon. You're on duty in 30 minutes, correct?

"Yes. I think I need a shower first. I wouldn't want the rest of the crew to know that I just got royally fucked," he smirked.

"Capital idea." He stood up. "Well, see you later, then." He headed for the door.

"Joseph!" Klaus called out.

"Yes?"

"Don't forget your hat."

Joseph jokingly smacked himself on the forehead. "Thank you!" He reached down and picked the heavy cap up off the floor where it had fallen during their frantic disrobing. He glanced in the mirror again, as he carefully placed the hat on, tilting it slightly. He liked the way the gold braid caught the light.

"Goodbye, Klaus."

"Goodbye, Captain, er...Joseph." Klaus giggled.

Captain Joseph Lucard grinned and opened the door. He stepped brightly out into the companionway and shut the door behind him.

19

Diamond Deck, *Princess Diana*, Mediterranean Sea

Jebb…stop…Stop!…I can't….I want to, but I can't." Dan's shirt was pulled open, and Jebb was doing things to him, amazing things, sensual things, that were clouding his mind and threatening to break his steely resolve. *I can't—I won't give in this time*, he thought feverishly. *I will not slip!*

Pressing Dan up against his cabin's door, Jebb pulled back from nibbling on his date's right nipple, and let his hand separate from the hardened package encased by tight denim. Dan's crotch had felt so damn good in his hand that Jebb wanted nothing more than to strip the rest of his dinner companion's clothes off and go down on him. Instead, he looked into his date's eyes. "Why? What's wrong?"

Dan reached out and stroked Jebb's face. "It's too much!…I can't…I…" he panted, trying to focus, and struggled to regain his self control.

"Yes, you can," Jebb murmured as he leaned in and began to kiss Dan passionately.

Dan groaned and his mouth opened wide, allowing Jebb's tongue deep entry. He pulled Jebb closer and began to explore his body with his hands. His fingers drifted south and felt Jebb's hardness. The area was warm to the touch, and the stiffness within felt so good in his hand that he could scarcely contain his desire.

Enjoying Dan's firm grip on his crotch, Jebb reached down and retook Dan's piece, stroking it lightly through the rough fabric of his jeans. "I want you, Dan…"

Dan broke contact again, "Jebb, please. I want you, too, it's not that…"

Confused now, Jebb took a step backward, "Then what? You're hard as a rock! I know I turn you on, so what's the problem?"

Dan's face clouded over and flashed darkly. "Just back off, Jebb," he growled harshly.

Jebb was stunned. This was surreal. It was as if someone else, someone cold and distant, had suddenly taken over Dan's body.

Dan could read Jebb's reaction on his face. He struggled to compose himself. *Keep cool*, he told himself. *Keep cool. Don't blow it.* "Jebb, I just...I'm dealing with a lot right now," Dan said, thinking fast. "I told you at dinner. I'm in a weird place right now, emotionally. I'm new to being gay, and I came on this cruise to get used to the idea of being with men. I just...I just wanted to explore that. Maybe have some no-strings sex...Get my feet wet, so to speak." He wanted Jebb to think he was fumbling for words. "I...I didn't plan on meeting someone like you, someone that I really like. I can't absorb it all right now."

In the back of his mind, Jebb knew what Dan was telling him made no sense. He'd seen the way Dan had shown off his body and flirted with a few of the others at dinner. Dan had behaved like a confident gay man who was well aware of, and well used to, his sexual prowess. But now, after getting snippy, he was suddenly acting like he was a shy, scared virgin. It was a confusing turn of events, but Jebb wanted to believe in his date so badly he allowed himself to buy it. "So, what now?" he finally asked.

"I don't know. I just don't know if I'm ready to have these feelings...I just...I just want to be sure."

"Sure of what?"

Dan looked at Jebb with fierce passion in his eyes. "I like you, Jebb. I really, really do. More than I thought I would. I just don't handle those kinds of feelings well. I don't want to hurt you."

"Hurt me?"

Dan slowly nodded. "Yes. I'd hurt you so badly, and I don't want to do that. You don't deserve it." It was one of the few honest things Dan had said to Jebb during the entire evening.

"I don't understand this," Jebb sighed.

And he truly didn't. Dinner had been great. They had talked and laughed. Dan was a little hard to get information out of, but little by little he had opened up to Jebb.

Dan had been married. He had a 7-year-old son back in Sacramento. He was divorced and just beginning to understand why he had ended his marriage.

All through the meal, Jebb felt his attraction to Dan grow. Simply breathing had been difficult, and it was all he could do to control his impulse to lean across the table and kiss the man opposite him. His dick had been hard for almost two solid hours, and if he didn't do something about that, and soon, he would explode. And Jebb was certain that Dan felt the same way about him. He just knew it.

What Jebb didn't know was that none of what Dan had told him at dinner was the truth.

"I know it's confusing," Dan agreed. "Just give me a little time to sort it out in my head, okay?" He did actually care for Jebb. He was surprised by how much. He disliked lying to him, but it couldn't be helped. He had no choice. He had to cover his ass, didn't he?

He was well aware that falling for Jebb would complicate everything. It would turn focus away from what he really wanted to achieve with this cruise. He needed to end this, not just for his sake, but also for Jebb's. When he said he would hurt him, he wasn't kidding.

Not by a long shot.

"I think I better turn in. This is getting too heavy for me," Dan whispered. He leaned forward, gave Jebb a sweet kiss on the lips, and backed into his cabin, shutting the door behind him.

Standing alone in the corridor, Jebb was at a loss for words. Then he found one. The perfect word.

"Fuck!"

On the other side of the cabin door, heart racing, and watching from the vantage point of the door's peephole, Dan watched Jebb walk sadly away. He turned around and suddenly felt very claustrophobic in his spacious cabin.

He could still feel the wondrous touch of Jebb's hand and his fingers absently began to caress his still hard cock. His physical yearnings threatened to overtake him. He wanted to race after Jebb, throw him to the ground, rip his clothes off, and screw him senseless. Just the thought of having sex with Jebb made his sexual hunger grow.

But he really liked Jebb. He didn't want to do to him what he had done to all the others.

Trying to maintain even breathing, Dan remembered something a therapist had once taught him. He needed to block the thoughts. He needed to work off his tension in a healthy, safe way. A swim. That might work. Maybe he could bring himself under control by swimming a few laps. Or, he mused, conflicted, *I could just give in, and find a hot piece of anonymous ass on deck, and fuck him senseless. That would sure clear my head...*

"No!" Dan said outloud, shocked at how easily he'd been willing to drop his resolve. "I won't do it!" He stripped off his clothes and pulled on a swimsuit. Grabbing a towel from the bathroom, he left his cabin and headed up to the Sun Deck and its two pools, silently praying that he would have the strength to just swim.

Jorge looked down at the water rush by. He was standing on Seth's balcony and deeply breathing in the clean sea air.

Hey, Jorge," Seth slurred, calling from his bed. "Come back inside...I want to tell you something," He snickered and fell backwards. He feebly tried to remove his unbuttoned shirt, but found the task was too hard for him accomplish alone.

Jorge sighed. This evening hadn't gone quite as planned.

Sure, Seth had nine big inches all right. He just couldn't get them hard.

He was too tweaked out on whatever drug he'd taken at dinner. The drugs and the alcohol he'd consumed during the meal had reduced him to a stumbling fool, and Jorge just wanted to get out of here. Seth must have had twice as much to drink as Jorge had, and Jorge had drunk a lot.

His new favorite. Martinis.

"Jorge?" Seth hollered again. "S'come 'ere..."

"I'm okay out here, just now," Jorge called back in.

"Aww, come on, hot stuff...I think I feel something happenin'...Hurry up! I can do it now..." He tried to get to his elbows to see if he'd gotten hard yet, but found he couldn't support his weight. He collapsed back on the bed, giggling. "Man, I am so fucked up..."

"Hey, Papi," Jorge said entering the cabin. "Thanks for dinner, but I'm going to take off." He went to the cabin door and turned to say goodbye, but discovered that the well-hung man was passed out.

Seth was sprawled across the bed, his pants around his knees, his shirt open. His beautiful, big dick lay useless across his left thigh. The cabin attendant would get an eyeful when he or she came in to change the linens tomorrow morning.

Jorge sighed. He had really wanted to get laid tonight. He was buzzed, frustrated and horny.

I wonder where Kirby is now, he thought to himself as he exited the cabin. Maybe he's up on deck...

Jorge took the elevator up to the Sun Deck and began to wander. There were several men in the hot tubs and one or two guys swimming laps in the pool. He could see various male couples canoodling together in the dark niches of the ship, and his desire for sex increased with each step.

He strolled to the railing and, liking the feel of the warm breeze on his body, unbuttoned his shirt so the warm air could wash over him. He stumbled once, then again.

He was beginning to feel the effects of his own drinking at dinner. He looked up and realized he was near the Compass Deck. He'd find some action up there for sure.

So intent was Jorge on picking his way up the slick staircase, he didn't notice the pair of eyes that were watching him like a hawk. Hidden in shadows caused by a decking overhang, the man, tall and clad in only a black box-cut bathing suit and a pair of flip-flops, began to rub himself sensually. After he watched Jorge walk further across the Compass Deck, the man came out from the shadows and slowly climbed up the stairs after the hot model...

20

The *Princess Diana*, Port of Civitavecchia, Italy

Zack reached out and picked up the phone on the third ring.

"Hel…Hello?" he garbled, trying to wake up.

"Good Morning! This is your wake-up call," trilled the cheerful prerecorded English voice. "Thank you for sailing with the Lassiter Line! Have a wonderful day!"

Zack replaced the phone and snuggled up next to Hayden. The handsome man stirred and pulled Zack closer.

"Hey," Zack whispered. "Time to get up. Today it's Rome. In 45 minutes."

"Do we have to? I'm so sleepy…" Hayden yawned.

"Come on! We're in Roma! The Sistine Chapel, the Colosseum, the ruins." There was no response from Hayden.

"Hmm. Okaaay…How about the shops? Prada…Gucci…"

"I'm up, I'm up."

"You fag," Zack giggled.

"Takes one to blow one," Hayden smiled as he rolled over. They kissed for a few moments then reluctantly got out of bed.

Exactly 41 minutes later, they were standing in the line waiting to disembark from the ship. The *Princess Diana* was docked at a long, wide cement pier and Zack could see 20 or so tour coaches lined up alongside the ship.

Some were the really big, long ones like the one they had ridden to Monte Carlo in, and some were jitney-type vans just like the kind of minibuses that car rental agencies and hotels use to pick up and drop off passengers at airports. Zack remembered that he had paid extra for the extended "Best of Rome" tour so they could be in a smaller group. He correctly reasoned the jitneys were for the more exclusive tours.

They left the ship, walked down the ramp and waited on the pier for a few moments to see who else was going to join them. In a short time, Kurt and Rick stumbled off the large liner, obviously feeling the pain of a sleepless evening. Hayden waved them over.

Soon Kirby and Frank and Andy joined them. The men all stood around chatting, not wanting to get into the minibus just yet. Everyone was dressed in long pants and short-sleeved, collared shirts, as a dress code was strictly enforced at some of the sights they were seeing today. Zack was oddly pleased to learn that he wasn't the only one who had been refused admission to the Monte Carlo Casino the day before.

Soon, more members of their tour group showed up. Hayden was happy to see Garrett Gardner join them along with a pretty young man who hung on to the larger man like a suckerfish. Introductions were quickly made.

"I can't wait to see your show, Garrett," Hayden said, shaking the comedian's hand.

"I just hope I can fill up the room," Garrett laughed.

"I wouldn't worry about that. I think everybody on the ship plans to come, and that includes the crew," Zack piped in.

"I think you know my twin brother, Clay Beasley?" Hayden added.

Garrett smiled broadly. "Yes! Of course! We did a benefit together for the Elizabeth Glaser Pediatric AIDS Foundation last summer. We did a staged reading of *Valley of the Dolls*. He played Tony. He was hysterical!"

"He said you stole the show as Sharon Tate's character, Jennifer."

"No, I think Angelina Jolie and her lips being Neely O'Hara was the show stopper," Garrett joked. "So, you're his brother. I don't see the resemblance."

"We're fraternal twins, not identical."

Garrett leered suggestively. "Well, the only way for me to know for sure is if you to drop your pants. Let's see if there's a family resemblance there!"

Hayden put on a shocked face, covered his crotch with his hands, and said in a faux angry voice, "Why, I never!" Then he winked. "At least, not until I've had a few cocktails."

"Bartender!" Garrett called out, holding up a raised finger. Everyone in the vicinity laughed at the routine. Being a pro, Garrett knew when to make his exit. "Well, my boys, I'm going to go find a seat and get out of this hot sun." He bowed slightly, then strolled jauntily to the minibus. At the steps, he turned and called out, "Coming, Toby?" The younger man grinned and raced to join him on the jitney.

Kurt leaned over to Zack and whispered, "I don't think Toby's the only one who's coming." Zack tried hard to stifle his laugh.

Once Garrett and Toby got on the minibus, some of the others followed suit. In a matter of minutes their party was rounded out by the rest of their tour group. Rick was chagrinned to see that Ted Hester and his lover Sam were in their group today, and he caught the rueful glance Kurt gave when he saw them too. Ted, knowing he'd caused friction the day before, merely waved feebly at them, then scurried onto the minibus with Sam.

The last person to join them was Geoff Corbin. He arrogantly strode up into the minibus and plopped himself down next to Kirby.

Geoff barely glanced at Kirby. "Say, aren't you Jorge the hottie's cabin-mate?" he finally asked.

"Yes," Kirby nodded. He was thrilled to be sitting next to the gay celebrity.

Geoff looked around the minibus excitedly. He saw Andy and Frank at the back and nodded to them. "Is Jorge going on this tour today?" he quizzed Kirby hopefully.

"I don't know. I don't think so. He didn't come back to the cabin last night, so who knows."

"Oh," Geoff sighed, crestfallen. Then he gave Kirby the once-over. He was hot, young, built, and even shorter than he was. Not as hot as Jorge, but not bad. "So," he said, putting on the charm. "What's your name?"

Donnatella slid open the bedroom door of their stateroom and found Rex sitting on the sofa, his eyes closed in concentration, a loud opera blasting from the stereo. She idly watched him for a minute, knowing he knew she was there.

He ignored her.

For some odd reason, Donnatella flashed back to the early days of their marriage when they couldn't keep their hands off each other. Now they had grown so distant that snubbing each other had become routine.

"Good morning," she finally ventured.

Rex only grunted a reply, not wanting to break his concentration.

Donnatella felt anger bubble up, hot and bitter. Deciding it would do no good to start another row, she turned her back on her husband and padded back into the bedroom. She opened her closet and pulled out her clothes for the day.

Now done with his meditation, Rex got up from the sofa, and using the remote, turned off the booming opera. "Are you going ashore today?" he called to Donnatella. "I thought we might have lunch with Captain Lucard. It is our obligation."

"No. I want to go shopping."

"Every time we come to Rome, you go shopping. Haven't you bought out the entire Gucci collection, yet?" he asked snidely, standing in the doorway. "What could possibly be left?"

Donnatella turned to face him. "You know, Rex, some husbands like their wives to look pretty. It makes the man feel sexy and virile to know that such a beautiful woman is his."

"Oh, for God's sake, Donnatella. Is this going to be another one of your tedious 'You don't care about me anymore' conversations?"

"I can't remember the last time you and I made love!" she retorted.

"Last week. At the country house. As I recall, you certainly seemed to enjoy it."

Donnatella snorted in contempt. "Oh, yes. How could I forget? Our eight whole minutes of passion was truly staggering."

Rex's eyes grew cold, almost reptilian. "Perhaps if you weren't such a whining bitch all the time, I would feel inclined to lay with you more."

"Lay with me?" she mimicked mockingly. "I don't want you to 'lay' with me, Rex. I want you to fuck me!" She pulled open her robe and showed him her perfect nude body. Her tan was richly dark and she had never looked better. "How about it? Want to have a toss right now?" she asked.

"Good God! Cover yourself up! Suppose someone from the cabin staff should walk in? Isn't it bad enough that you've paraded yourself around the pool without your top on, like some...some cheap trollop?"

Donnatella closed her robe and cinched the belt tight. "If you don't want me, Rex, then there are others who do."

A rare smile flickered briefly across Rex's face. "Our pre-nup is quite clear. Adultery is verboten. You stray an inch, my dear, and I'll divorce you. You'll get nothing."

"You bastard," she seethed. She reached forward and slammed the door shut, missing her husband's highborn nose by mere millimeters.

"Hello, I'm Teresa, and I'll be your guide for the day."

Zack and Hayden looked up and watched the plain, but energetic, middle-aged woman settle down into her front row seat. She was probably around 50 and thin as a whip. Chicly dressed in a thin cotton shift and navy sweater, she had streaked blond hair cut in a long bob.

Several of the men on the bus shouted out hellos to the guide, and then they fell silent as she began to explain the day's events. Her Italian accent was slight, and she actually had a bit of a British lilt to her speech.

She told the excited gay tourists that they were going to go to Vatican City first, and see the Vatican museum and Sistine Chapel. Then, they were going to St. Peter's Basilica and view the wonders of one of the world's largest churches. After that, they would go to an exclusive restaurant for lunch, then to the Colisseum for an inside visit. After that, they would have some free time to shop on the Via Condotti near the Trivoli fountain.

It was going to be a long day.

Hayden shut his eyes, leaned against Zack and promptly went back to sleep as the bus began the drive into Rome.

Rick was thumbing through a travel book on Rome when Kurt nudged him.

"Are we okay?"

"Sure," Rick said, looking up from the pages of his book. "We're gonna have to talk about my job offer some more later, though."

This surprised Kurt. "I thought we settled that last night."

"No, we had make-up sex last night after a fight. We never got around to discussing the actual reasons for the fight."

Kurt looked out the window in frustration. The scenery wasn't glamorous. They were driving through an industrial area heading out of the port city of Civitavecchia. "But, I thought…How can you even consider us moving?"

"How come you can't? Why does it always have to be your way?"

"Always my way?" Kurt said, louder than he intended.

"Don't get upset! But it's true. I sold my house because you wouldn't move out of your penthouse condo. I didn't go visit my relatives last Christmas because you wanted to go skiing in Colorado. Hell, I couldn't even bring my furniture when I moved in! You said it would 'clash' with yours. I can't think of one decision we've made that's affected me where you didn't get your way."

Kurt didn't know what to say. To hear Rick speak, you would think he was an ogre. He capitulated to his lover all the time!

Didn't he?

"I love you with all my heart, Kurt, but you're very rigid."

"Well, fine. Glad to know you think I'm an ass." Kurt pouted, staring out the window.

Rick had to laugh. "I don't think you're an ass. I love you, baby, but let's face it, you're spoiled. You are a rich kid who always got whatever he wanted his whole life, and you tend to see things only through your eyes. This is a serious opportunity for me, for us, and we need to openly consider it. And yes, I should have told you about it sooner. I apologize, but I knew you would freak out, just like you did."

Kurt felt anger rise up, but he knew his lover was right. He *was* a spoiled rich kid.

"And," Rick continued, "As for being 'out' in New York, I guess I would be. Everyone knows at work in L.A., and it hasn't been an issue. I'd be surprised if they didn't already know about me being gay in New York. They checked me out pretty thoroughly, so yes, you would still be my lover." A sly smile spread across Rick's face. "You aren't getting rid of me that easy, partner."

Taking a deep breath, Kurt slowly nodded and couldn't help grinning as well.

Rick then looked his lover squarely in the eyes. "And I do want to have a child with you. I see how you are with Sydney, and you're so great and loving, and the way you treat her is just so amazing to behold." Rick said these words with all the heartfelt honesty he possessed. "I can't wait to raise a child with you, I swear it. But if we have to push that idea back for a year, will it kill us? Let's just deal with this opportunity now, okay?"

"All right. You're right," Kurt said. "I'm sorry. We do need to talk about this seriously. But not now, okay? Tonight. When we get back to the ship."

"Fair enough." Rick reached over and slipped his hand between the bigger man's huge thighs and left it there. He felt Kurt tense the muscles, squeezing his hand. He smiled.

The minibus entered the noisy city proper of Rome. Excitement grew inside as the passengers could start to see glimpses of a ruined column or a disintegrating temple. The sky was cloudy, the sun peaking out now and then, and the gray stones scattered throughout the city turned even darker in the diffused light.

Teresa prattled on pointing out worthy sites as the bus wound its way through the heavy morning traffic. Zack was amazed at how the city was constructed. He was astounded to find that apartment buildings were built right next to a fallen ruin. There seemed to be no real zoning. There were already tourists out, scrambling over collapsed columns and snapping photographs by the hundreds.

The men on the minibus whipped their heads back and forth as each new site was described by their guide. As the bus got deeper into the old city, the bustle of Rome became a crescendo. Little scooters would zoom dangerously close to the van. Everywhere the gay tourists looked, there were colorful Vespas buzzing around. The zippy motorbikes jockeyed for position in traffic alongside scores of economically tiny cars.

Rick thought the small European autos were cool. Some of them, like the SmartCar, a micro-car built by Chrysler-Daimier, were unbelievably cute, but impossibly small. "Honey," he dryly commented to Kurt, "I don't think you could get even one of your legs inside that thing!"

Hayden, looking around, pointed out to Zack that he found it astounding that the city still felt like an ancient place. The majority of buildings were thick stone structures complete with heavily pedimented windows and doorways. They were art themselves.

"No high-rises," he observed, looking out at the neutral-colored stone buildings as they passed by the van's windows.

Every once in a while a wide expanse of green would pop into view. These were open parks that were beautifully maintained and landscaped by the city. Romantic couples could be seen walking hand in hand through them, while old men and women trudged by carrying wrapped parcels for that evening's meal.

They passed next to a twisting, curving river several times along their route. It was the Tevere River. At last they crossed it and were soon driving next to a high, thick stone wall.

"This is the outer wall of the Vatican City," Teresa informed her charges. "We will be parking soon. Please stay in a group with me. We will first go through the Vatican museum, the Museo Pio-Clementino, and then to the Sistine Chapel. After that we'll go to Saint Peter's Basilica."

The bus soon stopped, and the men trouped off. Teresa carried with her a small, paddle-shaped plastic sign, her "lollipop," as she called it. It had a round, flat head with the Lassiter Line logo on it and the number 10. Like the day before at the dock in Cannes, each of the men in her tour had been given a small sticker, this one orange with the number 10 on it.

Teresa lead them through some sleek, stainless steel doors set in an old stone wall, and being the architectural freaks they were, Hayden and Zack loved the way modern touches had been added to age-old buildings. It was all so very Ralph Lauren.

Inside the grand entryway, each man was given a pre-purchased tour ticket, and after a brief pit stop at the men's room, they were off. They passed through the entry turnstiles and had their tickets taken by some very serious looking guards.

They quickly climbed several steep staircases in this wing of the Vatican and passed through room after room of stunning Greek and Roman antiquities, many of the sculptures over 3,000 years old. Teresa would calmly explain what they were seeing, but the sheer inventory quickly overwhelmed the men, and soon they all tuned her out and just wandered down the wide hallways gazing at the treasures.

Other wide hallways led the group through the exquisite artwork of the museum. They passed through the Galleria dei Candelabri and the Galleria Degli Arazzi where they encountered wall after wall covered with beautiful tapestries made by monks and nuns hundreds of years before. Some of these enormous tapestries had real gold woven into the fabric. These tapestries showed famous religious scenes and paid tribute to the various Popes and Caesars of the ancient world.

In the Galleria delle Carte Geografiche, the awestruck men saw beautifully detailed maps of the Papal states that had been painstakingly painted eons before. The colors and technicality of them were a sight to behold. Zack found his mouth hung open in amazement continuously as he and Hayden strolled past the treasures. Rick and Kurt kept staring up at the barreled ceilings.

Overhead, the museum's heavily gilded ceiling sections contained perfectly executed reliefs reflecting the treasures below. Teresa pointed out the astounding fact that the reliefs weren't stone, but actually paintings made to look three-dimensional. These intricate paintings were so realistic that as Zack and Hayden moved around the hallways, they couldn't tell how they had been achieved. It was simply too amazing.

Eventually, Teresa lead them up more stairs and they stood just outside the world-famous Sistine Chapel. She gave them a brief history of the chapel as the men got their cameras ready. She told them that the chapel had been built between 1477 and 1481, and its walls were covered by frescoes of renowned artists of the time, such as Perugino and Botticelli.

Michelangelo was a reluctant participant, she told them, as painting was not his forte. When he was commissioned by the Pope to paint the ceiling, he actually had to learn how to paint before he began the project. It took him four painful years to finish the fresco, and after it was done, he had been afraid it would ruin him as an artist. Quite the contrary, it turned out, as his stunning artwork brought him fame for his day like nothing before. The ceiling had been restored by 1994 and only one tiny section, a corner, had been left untouched. It had been decided to leave this small section in its original state to show the damage that the ravages of time had caused to the priceless work of art.

"The ceiling shows the stories of the old testament," Teresa said, explaining the purpose of the masterpiece. "There is The Separation of Light from Darkness, The Creation of the Heavenly Bodies, and so on. The paintings cover an area of 10,000 square feet and contain over 300 individual characters. When you enter, please notice the enormous fresco that occupies the wall over the alter. That is called 'The Last Judgment.' Michelangelo painted it 22 years after he finished the ceiling. It is a darker painting in tone than those on the ceiling, reflecting Michelangelo's sadness at the geopolitical happenings of the time."

"We will now go into the Sistine Chapel. Please remember to speak very quietly inside. You will have, say…" Teresa looked at her watch. "Twenty-five minutes to look and ponder. I will meet you by the exit doors." She led them through a doorway and there they were. A large crowd was already wandering around the vast rectangular room, and the men from the *Princess Diana* quickly joined them. Cameras were whipped up and soon picture after picture was being taken of the stunning beauty that the Chapel held.

Zack took Hayden's hand, and they strolled to the center to look up at the famous painting of God reaching for Adam's hand. A non-practicing Catholic, Hayden nonetheless felt a rush of religious pride at the artwork soaring above them. Both men's mouths fell open as they gazed up and around at the exquisite beauty of the centuries-old painting.

"I feel so small," Zack whispered.

Hayden looked at him. "I was thinking the exact same thing!"

Kirby was studying a fresco of one of the walls when Geoff pressed up behind him. Surprised by the closeness of the man, Kirby tried to move away.

"It's really quite inspirational in here, don't you think?" Geoff asked.

"Uh, yeah," Kirby smiled feebly as he turned around to get some personal space between him and the TV show winner.

"But as beautiful as it is, it pales in comparison to your ass. Next to your roomie Jorge, you have the hottest ass I think I have ever seen," Geoff winked.

"Uh, thanks…I think."

"No problem. Maybe later, when we get back on the ship, I can see it as naked as that." He pointed up to the nude form of David reaching out for God.

Stunned that he was being hit on in the holiest chapel in the world, Kirby only managed a tight grimace before beating a hasty retreat from Geoff.

In another area of the splendid chapel, Garrett turned to Toby and whispered, "When do we eat?"

21

Rome, Italy

Donnatella got out of the cab, and after thrusting the fare at the surly driver, shut the door and looked up at the dilapidated building she was about to enter. Anxious and excited, she forced her breathing to slow down. She needed to calm herself, and fast.

She walked to the doorway of the building and buzzed number four on the old panel. She looked down at her outfit, a taupe linen miniskirt and a loose, white vintage blouse by Pucci. She looked chic, but casual. Perfect.

A few seconds later she heard the door click, and she pushed it open. She shot a quick look up and down the street to make sure no one was watching her, and then went in.

The building didn't have an elevator, so Donnatella, her heart racing, climbed the two flights of stairs. Her Chanel slingback pumps click-clacked up the stone steps, announcing her arrival.

A door was cracked ajar on the landing and Donnatella, taking a deep breath, pushed it open. The apartments inside were nicer than the building facade would have you believe. Large and roomy, this particular apartment was sparsely furnished with a few good pieces of modern furniture. A Wassily chair here, a pair of Eames chairs there, it was an eclectic mix, the futuristic lines of the modern furniture sitting in classically formal rooms such as these.

A young man with damp curly hair appeared in the doorway to the bedroom. Olive skinned, dark eyed, lean, and wearing only a towel wrapped around his waist, he was striking almost the exact pose of David, the famous statue in Florence. Donnatella's pulse began to race again.

"Bella," he murmured, grinning sexily.

"Antonio."

"You look gorgeous, Bella."

Donnatella felt a hot flush race through her body. Just looking at this sexy man had made her wet. She was that excited.

"Come here," the young man beckoned.

Donnatella's weak legs carried her to him, his strong lithe arms wrapped around her, and soon she was kissing him—kissing him with all the passion that went untapped in her, and in her life.

In moments, with her clothes scattered on the hardwood floor, he slipped inside her. The warm touch of his velvet hands, the soft brushing of his lips on her skin, and the hot hardness of his cock thrusting deep, caused her to hyperventilate. She was afraid she might pass out from the pleasure of it all. Antonio began softly repeating into her ear that she was so beautiful.

It was exactly what she needed.

Rex looked up the companionway one way, then the other. The few passengers who were nearby were going about their business and paying him absolutely no attention, as planned.

The normally immaculately dressed president was now slumming in a set of the gray coveralls that all Lassiter Line maintenance workers wore. He had left his glasses behind, and instead was wearing contact lenses that tinted his blue eyes brown. He had pulled on a black knit watch cap over his ears, and had smeared some black grease on his face in a haphazard manner. He was confident that if anyone saw him, they would simply assume he was an engine room employee making his rounds.

With the navy canvas duffle hanging off his shoulder, Rex reached into his pocket and pulled out a credit card-like security card. Just as he was about to raise his hand to use it on the security box in front of him, a passenger appeared from nowhere and brushed past.

"Excuse me," the passenger said gruffly, looking back briefly at Rex.

"Scusi," Rex said, affecting a thick Italian accent. He held his breath. Rex recognized the passenger as the big man in the small swimsuit who had stood next to him and Donnatella on the Compass Deck the first day of the cruise. Rex prayed that the stern-looking man wouldn't recognize him. It would bring up too many questions.

But the man kept walking and didn't give Rex another glance. He disappeared around a corner.

Exhaling gratefully, Rex hurriedly slid the phony security card through the slot, waited for the "click," pulled open the steel door, and quickly stepped through. There was no one in the empty passageway, as he knew there wouldn't be.

Just prior to leaving London for this cruise, Rex had made a copy of one of the engine room employee's security cards. Secured ID cards were mandatory in certain off-limit areas of the *Princess Diana*, and this section of the ship where Rex stood quietly breathing was one of them. Should anyone run a random computer check to see who had accessed this particular door, they would find the name Mario Sanzazino and not his. Rex's tracks were covered.

This particular area was always unattended during lunch. The engine and maintenance crews would have gone up to the crew's mess and would be gone for 30 minutes. There was now only a skeleton crew stationed in the vital areas of the ship with standing orders not to leave their posts until the full shift came back from their meal break. Rex planned on staying away from those vital areas. He glanced at his watch and smiled. Plenty of time. He shouldered the heavy navy bag and briskly walked down the passageway.

Painted an unremarkable white, like all the crew areas, this hallway was worlds away from the opulence of the passenger areas two decks up. Heavy steel girders and beams crossed overhead, and various pipes snaked along the walls, ceiling and floor, red valves popping out here and there to signify some shut off or another.

He began to move. Rex's footsteps were nearly silent, thanks to the soft crepe-soled leather shoes he had decided to wear.

He stopped in front of the door he had been searching for. He again used his phony ID card to gain access, pulled open the heavy steel portal, and quickly descended down the steep, narrow steel ladder it had concealed. At the bottom of the ladder, he picked his way along a dimly lit corridor until he found what he was looking for. There was a small steel box close to the ceiling that contained some sort of gyro or gear. It would make a perfect hiding place. Rex dropped the canvas bag to the floor and unzipped it.

He pulled out one of the devices and carefully placed it on top of the steel box, where it was hidden in shadow, and pressed down on it. Wide strips of adhesive adhered along the device's bottom kept it in place.

Satisfied the explosive device was undetectable, Rex switched its receiver on, smiled thinly, and continued down the hallway. He found a second junction box about 15 feet away from the first, and hid another bomb.

The third bomb was placed further down, under a long steel shaft that contained a driving rod to God knows where. Rex had chosen this area of the ship's bowels to place his explosives because after repeatedly studying the deck plans and blueprints of the *Princess Diana*, he knew this area was not heavily trafficked, and was well below the waterline. The hallway was also right next to one of the ship's enormous fuel tanks, and the concentrated explosions from the bombs would ignite that fuel tank in a cataclysm that would clearly mortally wound the ship.

With his functionally adequate knowledge of engineering, Rex calculated that a hole about 40 feet long by 20 feet wide would open up in the hull. There was simply no way the big cruise ship could survive such a blow. The pumps, the steel watertight doors, none of the *Diana*'s defenses would be able stop the enormous influx of water that would send her to the bottom.

Rex had also calculated that it would take the ship approximately one hour to sink. More than enough time to get all the passengers off, so loss of life would be minimal. The only people who might lose their lives were crew members, and Rex doubted that at the time of the explosion there would be anyone in the area.

And if there were, so be it. The loss of a few crew members was a small price to pay for the solvency of his company.

Teresa had led her group up some wide stone stairs and past towering terrazzo columns. They silently walked through the huge metal portals and entered Saint Peter's Basilica, the second largest church in the world. In fact, the famous Notre Dame Cathedral of France could easily fit inside Saint Peter's. Teresa huddled up her group and began her speeches. Off to the right of the entry, she showed the gawking men Michelangelo's protected statue of the Pietà, which depicted Mary cradling the dead Christ.

"Michelangelo actually came back after it was completed to sign it," she said, "when he heard people doubted it was his work. You can see his mark going up the ribbon across Mary's breast. It is the only signed work of Michelangelo in the world. It was vandalized in 1972 and repaired. That is why it is behind glass today."

Andy and Frank wandered away from the main group and stared down the enormous length of the Basilica. The space enclosed was colossal. The ceiling soared over their heads easily four or five stories high and the grand length was over 600 feet long. Further down, in the center of the grand hall, there was an enormous bronze canopy, underneath which there was a simple stone alter surrounded by a low balustrade of marble.

They noticed the floor was highly polished marble and laid out in intricate patterns. The walls were heavily decorated and gilded. Everywhere they looked was a new treasure, another architectural wonder. There were stone balconies and other pediments built out and over their heads, and marble columns sprouted at every turn. It was the most elaborate and beautiful place either man had ever been in.

"How the hell did they build this fucker?" marveled Andy.

Frank, shocked at his lover's cursing in a sacred house, nudged him in disapproval.

"What?"

"Watch your language, dickhead!" Frank whispered.

Teresa led the group back out more towards the center of the entrance hall and continued her speech. "This church is built over the grave of Saint Peter, who was one of the Apostles and the first Pope. This is not the first Basilica built. Saint Peter was crucified around 70 A.D. and buried in this spot. Constantine the Great, the first Christian emperor, built the original Basilica on his gravesite in 326. That church was used for over 1,000 years, but was torn down by Nicholas V, the reigning Pope, in 1452. This current structure was started in 1506, and took over 300 years to complete."

"My God!" Zack whispered under his breath. "It's amazing!" He was looking straight up at the heavily gilded ceilings.

"Think of the simple tools and construction methods they had at that time. It's astounding that they could build such a huge place," agreed Hayden.

Teresa led the group further into the Basilica. She stopped in front of the vast bronze canopy. "This is called baldacchino, or alter canopy. Directly above this canopy you can see the magnificent Dome of Saint Peter's Basilica. It is 400 feet high, from floor to ceiling, and directly below the alter," Teresa continued, "is the actual grave site of Saint Peter."

Rick raised his hand. When Teresa nodded at him, he asked, "I see a lot of people in here now. How many people can this church hold?"

"For services and special occasions, the Basilica can accommodate 60,000 people."

"This is all very fascinating," Garrett groused to Toby. "But when the fuck do we eat?"

Donnatella, nude and lying on top of the sweat-dampened sheets, rolled over and lightly stroked Antonio's face. He was smoking, staring idly at the ceiling, and he smiled at her touch.

"Bella, you are a tiger," he breathed.

"It's because of you. You unleash such…" Donnatella struggled to find the right word. "Animal desires in me. Oh, my God, what you do to me!"

"Then marry me!" he urged, suddenly full of heartfelt, righteous passion.

"Antonio, we've gone over this a hundred times. I can't."

"You can. What you mean is you won't," he pouted. He took a long drag on the cigarette.

"I can't. Rex and I have a pre-nuptial contract. If he cheats and breaks the contract, I get his company stock. Ha!" she snorted derisively. "As if he would ever let that happen. The only mistress he has ever had is his damn company, so that doesn't exactly count. If I cheat, I get nothing." Donnatella stared Antonio in the eye. "And I have gotten too accustomed to nice things," she added wryly, "to walk away from my marriage with nothing."

Antonio rolled onto his side and stared at her deeply. "What else do we need but love? From that first time I met you at the store, I knew I was meant to be with you!" His eyes blazed with the tormented desire he felt for her.

Donnatella smiled. Such youthful exuberance, she thought. Antonio was a wonderful man, a talented, extremely gifted lover and full of love for her. But he was clueless as to how the world really worked.

"Love doesn't pay for vacations to St. Biarritz, darling. Love doesn't buy shoes."

"Bah!" Antonio spat out. "I get an employee discount at Gucci! You can have all the shoes you want!"

"I do care for you, Antonio."

And she did. Her steamy affair with the handsome young man was all she had to look forward to these days. She thought of him constantly, ever since she had walked into Gucci's Rome store last spring and he had been her salesman. Within an hour of laying eyes on each other, they had gone to a private dressing room and made love for the first time.

But he was not going to be her next husband. No, if she ever remarried, she would marry well again, and perhaps keep Antonio on the side, like now.

"Just let me get a settlement," Donnatella said soothingly. "I can't believe my husband will hold out much longer. His business is not doing well, and I don't think he'll be sad to see me leave. I simply want to be compensated for what I contributed. For what I have put up with. And I have to play nicely for now to set that up."

"Wait. Wait. Wait! All I ever do is wait," Antonio spat out.

"Just a little longer, darling. Just a little longer." She reached down and grabbed his soft cock. "In the meantime, let me see what I can do with this…" While he groaned lustily, Antonio's beautiful piece instantly became engorged and hard.

Donnatella put it to good use.

22

The Sloan Square Restaurant, *Princess Diana*, Port of Civitavecchia, Italy

Jebb was enjoying a rare quiet moment, sitting by himself in the rambling a la carte restaurant at the rear of the Sun Deck. Jebb avoided room service. He liked to be seen by his guests. He firmly believed that if he was seen out and about, the guests would know he was on the job, taking care of business.

He had finished eating his yogurt, and now he slowly ate a banana, planning his day ahead. Tonight was the famous Mardi Gras circuit party, to be held right by the pool, so there was lots to do in preparation for that.

In addition, Garrett Gardner had asked for some rehearsal time in the ship's Bond Street Theater before he did his act tomorrow night, so Jebb would have to make sure Garrett was well taken care of. Secretly hiring the expensive escort Toby to be Garrett's personal boy toy during the week had been a flash of brilliance. The hot young man kept the comedian happy, and had even reported back that he actually liked Garrett, and probably would have been with him for free.

Thinking about Garrett and Toby had the unsettling effect of making Jebb think about Dan. He hadn't heard from the man since the awkward scene the night before. Jebb wasn't sure what to do about it. His brain said, let it go. Too much drama. His heart, however, was telling him something completely different.

"Mr. Miller?"

Jebb looked up and saw Captain Lucard standing solemnly in front of him. "Yes?"

"I'm afraid I have a spot of bad news. The Italian police just contacted us. A body was recovered early this morning by some fishermen, floating about 50 miles behind us."

Jebb began to sweat. All thoughts of Dan left his mind.

"The man was nude so there was no personal identification, but he had one of your Titan Tours dog tags around his neck. Obviously, he was a member of your group. Has anyone been reported missing this morning?"

"Oh, my God." Jebb was shook. Another death? This had never happened in all the years he had been running these tours. "No, not that I know of. But, let's go to the information desk. They would know."

He got up, leaving the rest of his snack behind.

Zack and Hayden squinted as they emerged from the dark Basilica into the noonday sun. They had lagged behind the rest of the tour group, just wanting a few minutes by themselves. Garrett and Toby straggled along behind them, the large man clearly feeling the effects of all the walking and climbing. He was tired, hungry and *over it*.

Zack looked down at their group, listening to something Teresa was saying, and they had spied several other tour groups from their ship in various stages of discovery. All of them were now standing in the vast open Piazza San Pietro, the main square that is so famous from all the photographs taken during Papal services.

"Look at all the guys from the ship!" Zack said.

"I wonder if they've ever seen this many gay men at the Vatican before," Hayden asked.

Garrett, overhearing, said loudly, "Sure, at last Sunday's 'priests only' mass."

Zack and Hayden burst out laughing as the large comedian puffed down the stone steps to join Teresa.

"...So if you stand on this spot, they all line up perfectly," she was saying when Zack and Hayden rejoined the group.

"What's she talking about?" Zack asked Kirby.

Kirby broke away from the annoying Geoff and showed Zack and Hayden what Teresa had just explained. "See? See how all those columns are lined up in rows?" He pointed to the sweepingly curved colonnade facing them. Like a welcoming arm, it faced a duplicate colonnade on the other side of the piazza. Together they connected to Saint Peter's Basilica and enclosed the open piazza. Probably about three stories tall, and capped by a seemingly endless line of statutes, the colonnades were four columns deep.

"Yeah," Hayden nodded.

"Okay. If you stand on this stone here," he pointed to a round stone set in the floor of the piazza where Kurt was now standing and marveling at the view. "Then all the columns line up and look like just one row."

"Really?"

When Kurt had finished gawking, Zack, then Hayden, stood on the stone and both men were astounded to find that what Kirby said was true. The lines of four columns merged into one. It was unbelievable and again showed a mastery of architecture that surprised them both.

"Now we will go to a Vatican authorized gift shop so you can buy blessed rosaries and other trinkets, then we will get back on the bus and head to the restaurant for lunch," Teresa said, gathering her charges around her.

"Thank God," Garrett muttered.

Rex let himself back into his suite, and after checking to make sure there was no cabin attendant inside, shut the door and locked it. Exhaling deeply, he felt he could finally relax. The worst was over with.

Twenty minutes earlier, he had left the "Crew Only" area and ducked into a restroom. He'd unzipped the Lassiter Line jumpsuit, revealing his regular, priggish attire underneath. Quickly stepping out of the coveralls, he'd stuffed them into the empty duffle, then tossed the bag into the garbage chute. He then cleaned off his face, took out the brown contact lenses and put his glasses back on. Everything had gone perfectly.

Now in his cabin, safe and sound, Rex marveled at his own cleverness.

Mentally replaying his actions below decks, he did recall one odd thing. Just when he had emerged from the bathroom, redressed as himself, he happened to notice the same man who had bumped up against him before he had gone down to plant the bombs, walking up the passageway.

Analyzing this now, Rex realized the man was coming from the other direction and had probably just had lunch or something. The passenger hadn't even looked at him so, satisfied it was merely a coincidence, the pompous owner promptly let the memory slip from his mind.

Happy now, he pulled open a small desk drawer in the antique rolltop desk. Inside was a small silver high-end cell phone. He pulled it out and turned it on. A small green light came on indicating power.

It was actually much more than a cell phone.

It was the remote detonator for the three bombs lying in wait. The phone and the bomb devices had cost Rex plenty, more than he had originally bargained for, but for this kind of untraceable work, money had to be spent.

Rex's source, a former member of an elite and ultra secret sect of the former Iraqi army, had assured him maximum damage with minimum risk. It was too perfect.

After punching in the activation code, which primed the bombs, he carefully closed the flip phone. To detonate the devices, all he had to do was reenter the code. It was so simple, and would be so devastating.

After setting off the bombs, Rex only had to either leave the phone behind on the doomed liner or drop it into the sea from his lifeboat. The fatal explosions could never be traced to him.

He smirked as he realized by simply pressing the "redial" button, which would automatically reenter the secret code, he could blow up the ship right now. He was oddly tempted to do so. It made him feel all-powerful to know he had the fate of thousands of lives literally in the palm of his hand. He was truly the master now.

Feeling superior, he laughed giddily. He then slipped the tiny phone into his jacket pocket.

He let out an explosive sigh and realized he was hungry. He decided to go to the Côte d'Azur dining room and have a good, formal lunch. With luck, he might see Jebb Miller there, and he could show him the latest bomb threat letter.

The pasted-together bomb threats he had sent to himself had been a stroke of brilliance. He'd painstakingly made them the week prior, and had sent them by post in successive days. Once the *Princess Diana* was at the bottom of the sea, those threats would be touted as the proof that the sinking had been an antigay terrorist act. No one would investigate any other avenues. No one would ever associate Rex Lassiter with someone who could be so cold-blooded as to possibly risk the lives of his wife, himself and hundreds of others for his own gain.

Rex knew better.

23

Diamond Deck, *Princess Diana*, Port of Civitavecchia, Italy

L unch for Zack's tour group in Rome had been excellent. The restaurant was down some very winding, claustrophobic roads, and by the time the hungry men trouped out and filed into the hotel that housed it, they didn't care if the place served burgers and fries. To the delight of all, and especially Garrett, lunch had been superb. First, a wonderful salad, then a dish of excellent pasta followed by a simply delicious roasted chicken main course. Even the dessert met with approval from all. Wine had flowed freely and a contented buzz befell most of the group.

Now, sated and happy, the men were on the move again, this time to see the Colosseum. Zack and Hayden were studying the guidebook, boning up on the ancient ruin.

Built in just ten years, an astounding feat considering the limited technology of that era, between 70 and 80 AD, the Colosseum was a testament to the best and worst of ancient Rome. As an architectural feat, it was unparalleled. Its exits allowed capacity crowds of 50,000 to 73,000 people to completely vacate the structure in a matter of minutes.

The phenomenal multi-story structure even sported something called a velarium. This was actually a large canopy, or roof, that was pulled into place by a corps of 200 sailors. The velarium was used to offer the crowds below protection from the sun and other weather elements.

Admission to events in the Colosseum had been free, though a strict chaste system had been enforced. Rich senators and other dignitaries sat in the first, lower tier. The middle class occupied the higher second tier, while the top tier was given to the poor and the women.

Gladiators fought bloody battles inside, and many prisoners and animals were killed by the skilled warriors. Contrary to popular belief, very few Christians were actually killed in the Colosseum.

"They say the heavy pollution of the city is ruining it, and there are fears it could collapse in the next major earthquake," Zack told Hayden.

"Well, if we have a major earthquake while I'm here, the last thing I'm gonna be worried about is the Colosseum!" Hayden joked.

Two rows behind them Kurt was resting his head on Rick's shoulder. He had gotten sleepy after lunch and was trying to catch a quick nap. He was sitting next to the window, with Rick in the aisle seat. Next to Rick, on the other side of the tour bus, sat Ted and Sam. Even as he tried to nod off, he heard Ted call Rick.

"Rick? I've been meaning to talk to you," Ted said haltingly.

Rick turned to him. "What is it?"

"I just wanted to say I'm sorry if I caused you any trouble. I didn't know you hadn't told…well, you know." He blushed slightly.

Rick smiled. "Don't sweat it. How could you have known? I should have told Kurt."

"Have you decided what you're going to do?"

"No, but we've agreed to discuss it tonight. Kurt knows how much this would mean to me and my career. I'm sure we'll work it out."

"I hope so. This kind of opportunity doesn't come along every day. Not for one of us, anyway," Ted grinned, as he patted his lover Sam's leg.

Kurt, his eyes still closed, and listening to each word spoken, found sleep wouldn't come.

One of the advantages of paying extra for the smaller tour group was the fact that the jitney minibus could park much closer to attractions than the larger, full-sized tour buses. The men got off and followed Teresa up a beautiful, wide esplanade of old cobblestones. After a short while the full glory of the Colosseum came into view. Rising up from the well-tended ground, it towered above the open-mouthed men as they all whipped out their cameras and began snapping off pictures. Zack had his digital camera and was making Hayden back up to get a good shot of him and the famous arena. He then asked Kurt to take a snapshot of the two of them.

Teresa let the men take their photographs. In fact, Sam and Ted saw some actors strolling around the grounds dressed in full gladiator garb. They raced over and, after paying them a few euros, had their picture taken with the hunky men. Everyone else in the tour laughed at their eagerness to be next to the powerfully built faux-soldiers.

Rick leaned into Kurt's ear. "Baby," he whispered, "think you can borrow one of those costumes? I'd love to be taken by a gladiator some night."

Kurt smiled. "You would, huh? I'll see what I can do."

Rick playfully growled in his lover's ear, and they returned to the group.

After all the pictures were taken, including several group shots that Zack snapped off, Teresa marshaled the men together and lead them to the entrance. She handed over their tickets and led the group through portals that had stood for over 2,000 years. The men came through the ancient stone archways and stopped inside the Colosseum on a wooden platform. A long, narrow ramp stretched across the open floor so tourists could look down at the exposed catacombs beneath.

Suddenly, it began to rain. Pouring, drenching rain. The men all scampered back to the shelter of the covered arches. Out of nowhere, the faux-gladiators appeared with dozens of umbrellas for sale. The men of the tour clamored around them, buying out their stock.

The small black umbrellas sprouted open, and they again ventured out into the vast arena. Teresa lead them over the walkway, explaining that the open corridors and rooms below had originally been under the arena floor and had been where the slaves, wild animals and gladiators were held before being used for sport.

"It's kinda eerie to be standing down here where the gladiators would have been," Kirby said to Hayden.

"I know. Can you imagine 50,000 people waiting to see you get killed?"

"I don't see any seats, though. Where did everyone sit?" Kirby asked, looking up through the rain at the vertical lines of disintegrated stone climbing skyward.

Zack overheard and answered. "Most of the marble used as seating was taken for use in other buildings and roads during the Middle Ages, when the Colosseum fell out of use and into disrepair. A lot of the churches in Rome owe their grandeur to the pillaging of this place."

Kirby looked at Zack. "How the hell do you know that?" he asked, surprised by the insightful factoid.

Zack grinned and held up his guidebook. "It says so here."

Next, Teresa took them all the way across the arena floor and back into the bowels of the ancient building. To everyone's amazement, there was a huge glass elevator located here. After shaking out their now-sodden umbrellas, the men all got on the spacious car and rode it up several floors, getting out on the third tier. Wandering back outside, the group discovered that the summer shower had stopped, and the sun was valiantly trying to poke through the gray clouds. They strolled over to a viewing area and could now look down into the vastness of the Colosseum floor and see what the view would have been like for a spectator centuries before.

More pictures were taken from here.

Geoff continued to hover near Kirby. He handed his camera to Frank and asked him to take his and Kirby's picture. As the backed up to get into focus, Geoff put his hand around Kirby, then dropped it low and squeezed his ass, just as Frank clicked the shutter. Kirby's look of surprise was now digitally immortalized.

Teresa let the men have a little "Gee Whiz!" time, then corralled them together and led them back to the elevator.

"We'll now go back to the bus and drive to the Trivoli Fountain where we will split up, and you can shop for an hour or so. The fountain is near the Piazza di Spagna, the Spanish Steps, and the Via Condotti, where all the best stores are," Teresa lectured on the way back to the minibus.

"Thank God! Shopping. I'm sick to fucking death of ruins," Geoff bitched. "I need to see some pretty *new* things."

24

Diamond Deck, *Princess Diana*, Port of Civitavecchia, Italy

Jebb and Captain Lucard were in Jebb's stateroom poring over the passenger list, trying to see if the phoned-in description of the drowning victim could be matched to anyone Jebb was aware of onboard. A photograph was going to be e-mailed over any minute so the victim could be identified. If Jebb didn't recognize him, then they would take the picture down to the photo shop and see if they could find the deceased captured in one of the "welcome aboard" photographs taken just before everyone climbed up the gangway and entered the *Princess Diana* on embarkation day. They could then try and track him down from that.

As Jebb was looking over the "C's", Lucard cleared his throat. "You know, Mr. Miller, I have been meaning to tell you. With this one exception, this cruise has not been as bad as I feared."

Jebb looked up from the list.

Realizing that might have sounded like a backhanded rebuke, Lucard quickly added, "I mean, sir, that it's been an…interesting trip. Your guests, while perhaps a little on the loud and cheeky side, have treated the staff better than any other group we've carried. The entire ship's crew has been enjoying this cruise almost as much as your passengers."

"Well, that's kind of you to say."

"It's bloody awful that this…tragedy," he indicated the passenger list, and the unpleasant task they were performing, " has to mar that spirit of *joie de vivre*."

Jebb sighed heavily. "It's just so odd. This has never happened on a Titan outing before. I'm just at a loss to explain it. First, one of our guests drowns at the hotel in Barcelona, now this. If I didn't know better, I'd think it was all so sinister."

"It's tragic, to be sure, but hardly sinister. I wouldn't whip myself against the post if I were you. This sort of thing happens more often than you think."

"What?"

Lucard leaned in close, as if sharing a great secret. "The Lassiter Line loses about one passenger a year in this fashion. Our guests are on vacation. They want to, what is the phrase you Americans use? Cut loose? Sometimes they get a little carried away. Someone has too much to drink, they take a bad step, they slip and they fall overboard. Last year we had a chap climb over the railing and hang over the side of the *Princess Anne*, as the result of some kind of ridiculous drunken dare. Naturally, he slipped and fell to his death."

Jebb's mouth fell open in shock.

Lucard's face arranged itself into a tight grimace. "Not exactly the sort of thing the PR department puts in the brochures, but there you have it." The stern captain then visibly softened as his eyes took on a cast of personal reflection. "People seem to lose all inhibitions on cruises. Surely you've seen this. People do things. Crazy things. Things they may have secretly desired all along, but never dared dream of doing." He sighed. "Especially on this cruise. So charged with a certain…energy." Lucard looked warmly into Jebb's eyes as if he were sharing a part of his soul.

Jebb sensed there was more weight to the Captain's words than showed on the surface.

"It's a liberating feeling, no? A cruise?" Lucard asked, a slight smile creeping across his broad face.

"I suppose so."

"So you see? I'm sure this," the captain again indicated the passenger list and the task they were doing, "is simply an accident. No more. No less."

Jebb nodded in agreement, but he couldn't shake the lingering doubt that something was seriously wrong on this cruise.

Something evil.

Without another word, the two men went back to going over the passenger manifest.

Zack and Hayden were strolling down the wide Piazza di Spagna, the large square that the Spanish Steps flowed into. Tourists were out in full force, yet it didn't seem that crowed. There were a couple of vender carts parked nearby, and the sellers were offering glacés and Italian ices.

Zack took a large slurp from the Coke he'd bought at a huge two-story Burger King they had passed on the way here.

"Are you hungry?" Hayden asked, eyeing the frozen glacé of a passerby.

"Not after that lunch! I'm stuffed."

"I think I want to get one of those," Hayden said, pointing at the glacé cart.

"Be my guest."

Hayden scampered off, and Zack sat down and looked up at the sweeping double stairs that climbed up the hill, resting below a large church. He idly gazed at Hayden paying for his cool treat and had to smile. Where did he pack it away?

Everywhere Zack looked, he saw gay men from the boat strolling around, most carrying bags from the pricey shops of the Via Condotti a block or two over. But, he noticed self-satisfied, none of the men strolling through the plaza now were anywhere near as hot as Hayden. He had won the prize. Finally.

Hayden sauntered back to his side, and in a spontaneous gesture, leaned over and happily kissed Zack. Surprised, Zack giggled.

"What was that for?" he asked.

"'Cause I love you."

"Awww…" Zack said, reaching up and pulling Hayden in for a longer, deeper kiss.

Kirby wandered through the stunning, but small, Gucci store and tried to get the attention of a salesman. Already slightly annoyed because Geoff Corbin had literally shoved him out of the way when they had been climbing up the stairs to the men's department, he was now irked to see the television personality hoarding several styles of shoes and the lone salesman.

Kirby was clutching a black suede loafer he wanted to buy, but the store was so full of gay men on a shopping frenzy that he was lost in the crowd. He glanced over and saw Geoff sitting on a divan, imperiously ordering the salesman around, demanding more shoes be brought out for him to try on.

When the harried salesclerk got up and headed back to the storeroom, Kirby tugged at his sleeve. "Excuse me," he asked gently.

The salesman looked at Kirby and gave a tight smile. "One minute, please," he said briskly.

"I was just wondering if you had this," Kirby held up the shoe, "in a size nine. American size nine, since you're going to the back now anyway."

The salesman sighed and gave a curt nod. "I see what I can do."

Kirby found a seat opposite Geoff, and noticed the TV personality had a pair of the exact shoes he wanted lying on the floor next to him. Along with five other pairs.

After a minute, the salesman came back loaded down with boxes. He put them down on the floor, and after setting five or six aside for Geoff, he pulled a box out and tossed it to Kirby.

"I only have it in a size seven," he said, whipping off a box lid and pulling out a brown leather sandal for Geoff.

"But I'm a size nine. I can't fit in this."

"I'm sorry," the salesman said, grunting as he squeezed Geoff's foot into the sandal. "The only other size nine are these, here." He pointed to the pair lying next to Geoff. "And this gentleman has them."

Geoff looked up, and looked at Kirby. "Oh, did you want these?"

"Yes, please. I've kind of been saving up for a pair of real Italian Gucci loafers," Kirby explained, as he stared at the coveted shoes.

"Oh," Geoff sniffed. "Sorry. I think I'm taking them. First come, first served, I guess."

Kirby got up and looked Geoff in the eye. "Yeah, and you practically knocked me over on the stairs just so you could get up here before anyone else."

Geoff's eyes widened. "Sore loser."

"Loser? Buddy, the only loser I can see is you." With that, Kirby spun around and left the shoe area.

Geoff's face flushed as he noticed the sly grin appearing on the sales-clerk's face. "You gotta play hard to win," he muttered.

Dan moseyed down the passageway on B Deck, seemingly lost in his own thoughts. His gait was slow, but there was a hidden purpose to his walk.

Two laughing guys passed him, and as usual, gave him a lingering once-over, but his tough guy demeanor was a barrier that they were reluctant to break through. They continued down the corridor.

Dan came to a stop in front of the door that he had seen the grungy crewman lurking suspiciously by, a crewman that was no crewman.

Dan had recognized Rex Lassiter the second he saw his characteristic walk. It was something that people who tried to disguise themselves often forgot to alter. Walks are very distinctive—Rex's arrogant stride especially so.

Dan had been rewarded for his sharp observation when he saw Rex leave the "crew only" bathroom after having ditched his disguise. He also knew that Rex had seen him, but Dan wasn't too concerned about that. All would be revealed soon enough anyway, so what did it matter? Dan almost had to grin. Rex Lassiter had his very own personal stalker, and he didn't realize it.

Not yet.

So now Dan was in front of the very same crew door, and wondering what the charade had been about. Why would Rex Lassiter pretend to be a crewman? He had access to every part of the ship he owned. It made no sense.

Dan looked all around the door and studied the keypad. He recognized the brand and knew he could bypass it easily. Dan was a man with many talents.

He was also a man with many secrets, so he could almost understand Rex Lassiter. That the president of the Lassiter Line was up to something evil, Dan was absolutely certain. How Lassiter's odd behavior related to the door was the burning question now.

It was a question Dan would find the answer to. It might prove useful should things go bad for him later on.

Rick and Kurt were strolling down the Via Condotti, not that far from the Gucci store, when Kurt spied what he had been searching for. A small, elegant jewelry store was nestled down a side street, very close to the main shopping avenue, and that was his destination. Grabbing Rick's hand, he pulled him towards the store.

"Hey! What's the rush?" Rick protested.

"I have a surprise for you," Kurt replied, dragging his lover down the street.

They pushed open the old glass door to the shop, and both men were surprised by how contemporary the inside space was. Clean, glass display cubes were positioned about the tumbled stone floor, and subtle halogen lighting made the treasures displayed inside the glass cases glitter and shine.

"Wow," Kurt said. "This is nice."

A smartly dressed woman stepped up. "May I help you?" she asked in a crisp English accent.

"Yes," the big man said. "I'm Kurt Farrar, and I have some things on hold?"

The chic woman nodded. "Ah, yes. Mr. Farrar, I'm Gwendolyn, and I'll get your items. Please, won't you both sit down?"

Kurt and Rick sat down in a pair of lushly upholstered barstools that flanked each display case. Gwen went to the back of the store and quickly returned with two small black boxes. She confidently placed them before the two men. "They're beautiful, Mr. Farrar. Exactly what you requested."

"What in the world is going on?" Rick asked, confused.

Kurt reached over and picked up one of the black boxes. He turned and faced his lover.

"Baby, I want you to do me the biggest honor and wear this," he said, beaming. He popped open the box, and Rick gazed at a handsome platinum wedding band. Kurt took it out of the box, and only then did Rick see that the sides of the ring were studded with small diamonds. It was a very unique design, and he loved it instantly.

"Oh, my God, Kurt! This is amazing!"

Kurt reached down, took Rick's hand and slid the ring on. It fit exactly.

"I read about this jeweler on the Web. These are a one-of-a-kind design that no one else will ever have."

"Wow," was all Rick could say. He leaned over and gave Kurt a loving kiss in gratitude.

After letting the two men have a moment, Gwendolyn subtly slid the bill forward and took a few steps back. Kurt reached into his pocket, pulled out his wallet, and slid over his black American Express card.

Zack leaned against Hayden and both men watched the passing scenery out of the jitney's window. Truth be told, they were both exhausted and glad to be heading back to the ship. Zack just wanted to grab a quick shower and then eat. He was starving. It seemed like lunch had been so long ago.

"I had a great time," Hayden whispered into his ear.

A wave of happiness overcame Zack, and he snuggled up closer to his new love. "Me too," he breathed.

"I'm so glad I got to see Rome with you."

"I just wish we'd had more time by ourselves. It was all so rushed."

"Well, maybe we can see it slower next time," Hayden said hopefully.

"That's a deal."

One row back, Kurt and Rick were admiring their new rings.

"I'm not a big ring wearer," Rick said. "But I really like the way this one feels. And what it represents."

"I'm so glad, baby."

"So...I have a question for you."

"Shoot."

"How about we make it official?"

Kurt leaned over and looked at Rick. "What do you mean?"

"I mean," Rick explained, "We stand up in front of all our friends and family, and we have a ceremony. Just like my sister's wedding last spring. I want that. I want to do it at home, in L.A. I want the cake and the cheesy reception...and all the gifts."

"I've thought about that myself actually. I just didn't know if you wanted it. God, Mother will be thrilled. She'll want to throw the reception for us. Sometimes I think she likes you more than me."

Rick smiled, then looked pensively out the window. "I don't think I ever thought I'd have what we have." He looked back at Kurt and took his hand. "So I'd really like to stand up in front of all our friends and family and commit myself to you for the rest of my life. I want to prove to you that no matter where we live, no matter what life throws at us, I love you, and I will always be your husband."

Kurt squeezed Rick's hand. "We'll do it."

"That makes me very happy."

Kurt smiled warmly. "Well, that's my goal. To make you happy."

Rick pulled off his ring and handed to Kurt. "Hang on to this until you place it on my finger in front of God and every one of our friends."

"Deal." Kurt pulled his off as well and slipped the shiny bands back into the black velvet boxes they came in.

25

B Deck, *Princess Diana*, Port of Civitavecchia, Italy

Oh, my God, I am so hungry!" Zack complained slightly, squeezing Hayden's hand as he led him down the companionway. As they moved deeper into the ship, they would occasionally pass a heavily decorated door. It was something they had gotten used to seeing, and some of the displays were really quite funny.

Many of the more flamboyant passengers chose to decorate their doorways, much the way sorority girls in college do. The taped-on decorations could be anything from photos of the occupants to stickers, drawings, feather boas or even miniature disco balls. Some industrious passengers had even brought along battery-operated Christmas lights which added a festive air to the rather formal corridors.

"I need a nap," Hayden yawned, passing an ornate display on one door that signified the occupant was a "top dog" and looking to play "fetch."

There was a slight rumble under their feet signaling the mighty diesel engines had started, and they knew that the *Princess Diana* was once more underway. Hayden placed a steadying hand on the closest bulkhead to keep from stumbling, and they headed up the staircase to Zack's deck.

Their tour bus had been the last one to return to the dock. As soon as their group had wearily trouped back up through the loading platform, the heavy steel partition had been raised, and the liner was prepared to leave Civitavecchia.

Now, walking down yet another labyrinthine corridor, Zack was relieved to find his cabin door, and he briskly slid in the keycard. He heard the familiar click and pushed open the door. Hayden casually reached up and rotated the message dial next to the stateroom's door. He continued to spin the small dial until the message window read "Do Not Disturb."

Hayden then pressed up behind Zack, and as the two men entered the cabin, they kissed passionately. Zack realized he felt a comfort with Hayden that had always eluded him with other men.

"Maybe the nap can wait," Zack whispered.

"Little Man? Is that you? Surprise!" called out a deep voice from the depths of the stateroom.

Zack and Hayden both jumped at the voice. "What the hell?" Zack uttered, walking deeper into the cabin.

"Hey, Little Man…" A tall, expensively dressed intruder was grinning broadly and holding up a bottle of Dom Perignon.

"Bayne?" Zack felt slightly weak in the knees. "What the hell are you doing here?"

Bayne took a step closer and realized that Zack was not alone. In fact, to his great surprise, a strange man had his hands wrapped around Zack possessively. "Who's *that?*" he asked archly, his broad grin transforming into a petulant frown.

Bayne's normally narrow face became even more thin and drawn now. His slightly long, patrician nose made the well-tended man always seem like he was looking down on whomever he was speaking to. Part of the reason for this was his height. He was 6'3", and his carriage was ramrod straight. His body, lean but hard and worked out, always seemed to be under tight control.

Zack's mind was reeling as he tried to grasp what was happening. In his somewhat confused state, he was dimly aware that this was the first time he had ever seen Bayne look like he was about to lose his self-restraint. "I repeat," he finally said, warily, "What the fuck are you doing here?"

"I flew into Rome this morning. I took the God-awful redeye! I came here to be with you. On *our* vacation. Now will you please tell me who this asshole is who's feeling you up?" Bayne's eyes narrowed further.

"Hey, fuck you," Hayden growled, holding on to Zack more tightly.

"Bayne, you need to get out of here. You don't belong here," Zack said.

"The hell I don't! I popped another ten grand for the cabin upgrade. I'm staying, Little Man." He crossed his arms and looked balefully at Hayden.

"I hate it when you call me 'Little Man.' Stop it." Zack said.

Bayne ignored him. "Little Man, I think you need to tell your trick here that the party's over, and your boyfriend is back." He continued to stare at Hayden. "Did you hear me? Get lost."

"Zack, what is this?" Hayden said, doubt beginning to color his voice.

"I have no idea," Zack answered. "Where's your new boyfriend, Bayne? Is he here, too?"

Bayne sighed and opened his arms in a gesture of helplessness. "I was wrong. He wasn't the man I thought he was. He wasn't…you." He took another step towards Zack. "Little Man, I'm so sorry. I made a horrible mistake. I need you. We belong together." He reached his free hand out and gently stroked Zack's cheek.

Zack shot back as if burned. "Too late, Bayne. Too goddamn late."

"You don't mean that. Look, this is supposed to be a happy occasion. I came back to you! I thought you'd be overjoyed to see me."

"Bayne, I'm warning you," Zack growled through gritted teeth. "Get out of my cabin or I'll have you thrown out."

"But I came all this way to make it up to you! And to admit my…um, lapse in judgment. I was unhappy in our relationship, Little Man. You weren't giving me the attention I need or deserve, all the time with that damn photography class and work. Honestly, how many fucking crap jobs does one person need to have? You drove me to cheat, you really did. And we're apart for what, a week, and you're already fucking some random guy? I'm so disappointed in you. How can you be so ungrateful after all I've done for you? All I've given you?" Bayne shook his head in a flash of disgust, but quickly caught himself and recovered. "But just to show you that I'm the bigger man, I'm willing to forgive you for…for being with this trash." Bayne pointed a perfectly manicured finger at Hayden.

"Forgive *me*? Jesus, you've got some balls. Who asked you to come? I sure didn't! Last thing I recall is you putting me on the plane and telling me we were through because you'd been cheating on me for months with someone else and had fallen in love with him. And now you're trying to make it like I'm the bad guy?" Zack said, his voice rising.

"Zack, let's get out of here. You can stay in my cabin with me," Hayden offered.

"No! This is my cabin! He can go somewhere else!"

"Little Man! Calm down. People will hear…" Bayne said condescendingly.

"I don't give a flying fuck! And stop calling me that!" Zack shouted louder. "Get out of my cabin!"

"Zack, honey, calm down," Hayden soothed. "He's not worth it…"

Bayne turned to Hayden, distaste oozing from every pore. "You shut the fuck up!" he snarled, his hands balling up into fists. "Who the hell are you anyway? Zack is my man, so shove off, you little bitch."

"What did *you* say?" Hayden was stunned. This idiot was goading him into a fight, and by God, he'd give him one.

"Bayne!" Zack screamed. "I'm not 'your man' anymore! You threw me away, remember? Get out!"

A crowd was beginning to gather in the hallway, listening to the brewing fight.

"Zack, let's get out of here before I deck this asshole," Hayden said, staring Bayne in the eye.

"Try it, Mary," Bayne challenged. "I'm a brown belt in Tae Kwon Do."

Hayden's hands balled up into fists. "Yeah? And I'm a brown belt in 'I'm gonna kick your arrogant ass!'"

Jebb walked into the open cabin and placed himself between Bayne and Hayden. "What is going on in here? I can hear you all the way down the hall!"

"This is my ex-boyfriend, and he won't leave my cabin," Zack tried to explain.

Bayne brushed Zack aside. "I'm Bayne Raddock. Raddock Communications? And this is my cabin. Well, mine and my boyfriend Zack's here. We had a silly misunderstanding, and I'm now trying to have a private conversation with my lover, and this asshole won't leave us alone."

"Fuck you!" Hayden shouted.

"Hey!" Jebb said, his voice firm and distinct. "That's enough! From all of you! I'll throw you all off this boat in our next port if you don't calm down right now!"

"Jebb," Zack tried to control his anger and shame. "Bayne broke up with me right before I came on this trip. He dumped me for another man. Now he's shown up here in some pathetic attempt to get back together. This is my cabin, and I want him to leave."

Bayne's mouth fell open in shock. "You don't mean that, Little Man…"

"Stop telling me what I mean! I don't want to see you!"

"Calm down, everyone, okay?" Jebb said, attempting to ratchet down the tension. "So let me see if I understand. You two," he pointed at Zack and Bayne, "booked this cabin together, right?"

"Well…" Zack started.

"Yes," Bayne nodded emphatically.

"Normally I'd say, fine, whatever, and give you another cabin," Jebb said, "and you two could fight it out over who leaves and who stays, but this cruise is completely sold out. I don't have a spare berth. And since we just left Italy and are at sea for the next 36 hours, you'll have to come to some agreement. We don't hit a port again until the day after tomorrow, when one of you can leave if you want. Or not. It's up to you. But I won't have this screaming, do you understand? I won't tolerate it." *I have enough to deal with right now*, he thought ruefully.

"Bayne, you dumped me at the airport! And now you want me back? I'm sorry, but no. You're…I'm not in love with you anymore. I'm sorry. Go home. Go back to your new boyfriend."

"And I suppose you're in love with this?" Bayne arched his eyebrows in scorn, and pointed at Hayden.

Zack looked at his new lover with devotion. "Yes, I am."

Hayden smiled and put an arm around Zack's waist.

Bayne's eyes shifted back and forth, his face contorted in frustration and rage. Suddenly, like a sudden squall that had spent its fury, he grew instantly calm. "Okay. I understand. My bad. Tell you what. There are two bedrooms here. I'll take one, and you can have the other."

Zack looked helplessly at Hayden.

"That's fine, Bayne," Hayden smiled thinly. "But just know that Zack and I are together now, and I'll be sleeping here with him." He wrapped his other arm protectively around Zack.

Bayne's eye's flashed darkly for a second, but he smiled. "No problem."

"You're taking the smaller room." Zack said.

"Whatever you say."

"Good. I'm glad you could handle this like adults." Jebb nodded curtly and left the cabin.

Wordless, but giving Bayne the evil eye, Zack pulled Hayden into the master suite, and then shut the door behind him.

"Do you believe that asshole?" he seethed when he and Hayden were finally alone.

"What does he think he's doing?"

Zack sighed. "Typical Bayne. Only cares about what he wants. Never a thought about the consequences, or how someone else might get hurt."

"I'm so sorry, honey." Hayden pulled Zack into his body and hugged him hard.

"'I won't let him screw this up. We were having so much fun…"

"He's not. Ignore him. He'll get the message. I bet he leaves the ship at the next port."

"I hope to God so. I can't imagine having to share this cabin with him for another five days."

"Hey! I have an idea. We'll ask my roommate if he wants to switch and come up here. He and Bayne can share, and we can take over my cabin," Hayden said.

"Great idea, except Bayne still gets the better cabin. He wins again."

"Oh, baby, who gives a fuck? We'll be together and he won't be around to bother us."

"You're right. Let's try that."

26

Diamond Deck, *Princess Diana,*
Port of Civitavecchia, Italy

Donnatella slipped back into her deluxe stateroom and practically ran to her spacious bathroom. It was a large space, almost as large as some of the inside cabins on the lower decks. Her bathroom offered Donnatella a sanctuary from her husband, who used the second bathroom, on the other side of the cabin. He never bothered her when she was in here, and she gratefully undressed. Her afternoon session with her secret lover had been deliciously satisfying, and she needed to wash his scent off her. She almost hated to do it. She liked the way Antonio smelled and liked to know she carried that small piece of him around.

She deftly turned on the shower's nozzles, and after a moment of watching the water flow, stepped into the large five-by-five foot space, and began to lather up her exquisite body. She could almost feel his touch on her again as she rubbed the luxurious suds onto her skin and, closing her eyes, let her mind drift back to her afternoon of sin.

Rex happened to return to the cabin at this moment, also in need of a shower. He had spent his afternoon tending to yet another matter, an urgent matter, and now needed to clean up from that exertion.

He smiled as he again thought about the chaos and destruction his explosive devices would cause. He was truly sad that he would lose the *Princess Diana*. She had always been his favorite ship, but the insurance money would be more than enough to finish the *Duchess of Balmoral* and the *Countess of Eads*, the two Lassiter superliners lingering under delayed construction at dry dock in Bremerhaven. There was no other way to finish them unless he had the settlement funds from the loss of the *Diana*.

Rex Lassiter was a man who knew how to make the hard decisions. He never let morality get in the way of doing the things that had to be done. He had always been this way. He didn't even question it anymore.

He removed his coat and tossed it over the velvet settee. Just as he let the expensive jacket go, he heard Donnatella begin to sing, something she only did when she was showering.

So. She is finally back, he thought. She had been gone all afternoon. Looking around the luxurious suite, he found it odd that she hadn't brought back any bags or packages. Usually she had bags stacked chest high after an afternoon shopping.

In fact, Rex was so lost in thoughts about his distant wife and her expensive habits that he failed to notice the small silver object slide out of his jacket's pocket and slip under a fringed throw pillow on the sofa. He ultimately shrugged at his wife's odd behavior and went to his own shower to rinse away the sweat of his earlier labors.

Kirby entered his cabin and grew concerned. None of Jorge's things had been touched. It was obvious the hot Floridian hadn't been back to the stateroom all day. Kirby knew Jorge was a grown man, and had probably just simply hooked up with some hot guy and was hanging out with him, but still, the nagging feeling that something was not right continued to bother him. He wondered if he should say something to one of the Titan staff members.

Unable to identify the dead man by his photo, Jebb moved on to Plan B. He headed down to the Photo Gallery. He had in his hand a copy of the photo of the drowning victim, and he had asked Nick to meet him in the shop and help him figure out who the passenger was. He put on his happy face and cheerfully greeted all the passengers he saw on his way down. He entered the Photo Gallery and was slightly surprised to see it was empty. This was good. They could scan the photos in some semblance of privacy.

"Hey, Chief," Nick called out when he entered the large open space.

The Photo Gallery was really a series of hallways covered with grooved walls that could hold the hundreds of photographs taken by the ship's two photographers. These men wandered over the ship at all hours of the day and night taking photo after photo of happy couples, groups and scenes, then developed the prints and hung them up for later purchase by the passengers. Located down on the Emerald Deck, the Photo Gallery was slightly off the beaten path.

"Hey, Nick. Is Raul around?" Jebb asked. Raul was the crewperson in charge of the Photo Gallery, and he was usually found during business hours manning the plum-colored laminate counter that held the cash register and other business tools.

"He said he'd be here in five. Some problem below decks," Nick said. He then took a deep breath. "I've never seen a picture of a dead guy before. Is it gross?"

Jebb smiled tightly. "No, he looks like he's sleeping." He opened the envelope and held out the picture for Nick to see.

"Oh, yeah…I recognize him. Jose or Juan, something like that, I think." Nick stared at the face in the picture. Yes, he knew this guy. He had seen him several times, but had had no direct contact with him. He had been unbelievably hot, though. "He was on the pre-cruise in Barcelona. This is so sad," he mumbled.

"I know. Well, let's look around and see if we can see his face in any of the pictures." Jebb started scanning the walls and searching for the mystery man's face.

"Sorry I'm late," Raul gushed, racing into the area. "One of our film processors broke down. Big mess," he said. "Hello, Mr. Miller. Hi, Nick."

"Hi, Raul," Jebb answered. He held out the picture. "Do you recognize this man? He's our victim."

Raul reached out and took the photograph. The instant his eyes fell on it, he smiled. Then shock registered, and he frowned. "Holy cow! I can't believe it! This guy? He's dead?" He looked at Jebb and Nick like they were playing a joke on him. He quickly saw by their sad faces they weren't. "Man! I can't believe it. He's like the most popular guy on your cruise."

"Huh?" Jebb asked.

"I have a whole section of him over here," Raul said, walking to the back of one of the walls. "See? All him. I've sold more pictures of this guy than any other passenger on the boat. He made me a lot of money."

Jebb and Nick went to where Raul was standing and looked up at the section of photographs he was pointing to. There were at least 20 different shots of a hot, vibrant young man. One showed him dancing by the poolside in a skimpy black Speedo, his cutup body glistening in the sun. A prominent erection could be seen in his brief swimsuit. There were several others, taken as men had crowded up against him, smiling at the camera. The victim had a superior air about him, even in the group shots. Jebb figured these guys had only posed with the man and didn't know him, but at least it was a place to start.

Then one picture in particular caught Jebb's attention. It was a shot of the man lying on a chaise poolside, oiled up and staring frankly at the camera. A slight smirk was on his face and in his right hand was a half-empty martini glass. In the chaise next to him was the beautiful titan-haired Donnatella Lassiter, an upraised martini glass in hand as well. They looked pretty chummy, and when Jebb happened to notice another photograph of a different

204

couple nearby, taken that same day, he saw Donnatella and the dead man in the background, chatting together like old friends.

Well, finally. She obviously knows who he is, Jebb thought.

"I've sold at least 60 copies of this shot," Raul said pointing to the photo of Jorge dancing by the pool. "The guys onboard are nuts for this man. Too bad, huh?"

"I don't know if he made other plans. Let me ask, and I'll call you right back, okay?" Rick asked, checking out his hair in the large mirror by the open closet door. "Great. Call you right back. Bye." He hung up the phone and crossed to the open bathroom door.

He peered in and saw Kurt's massive back standing in the shower, soap and water running down the wide, tanned lats, and draining down into the pale white crack of his beefy ass. Kurt's head was tilted down, eyes closed, and the hot water was rushing like a torrent onto his head.

"Babe?" Rick called in, after taking a few moments to simply stare at his gorgeous husband.

Kurt looked up and shook his head, a cascade of water droplets showering off his soaked hair. "Yeah?"

"I just got off the phone with Ted. He and Sam have asked us to join them for dinner tonight in the Spencer House dining room. Whaddaya say?"

"Isn't that kind of dressy?"

"Yes, but it'll give you a chance to wear your new shirt and blazer."

Kurt weighed the offer. He hated dressing up. Besides, spending an evening with Ted meant the topic of Rick's job offer would be discussed, and Kurt just didn't want to deal with that now, even though he'd promised to talk about it with Rick.

"Do we have to?" he finally said. "I thought we'd eat with Hayden and Zack in the Sushi Bar tonight. You love sushi…"

Rick shook his head. "Come on. It'll seem rude if we don't accept. We've eaten practically every meal with Hayden and Zack. Let them have a night alone for once. After dinner, we'll change for the Mardi Gras party up on deck. Please?"

Knowing nothing good would come of this, Kurt nonetheless agreed, subtly nodding his head. "Okay, fine," he said in a flat monotone.

Rick grinned. "Thanks." He spun around and went back to the phone. He quickly dialed up Ted, told him yes and got the time for dinner.

After hanging up, he looked back in the direction of the shower. Kurt was still in it. Not a good sign. Kurt only took long showers when he was bothered or troubled. Normally he would be in and out in five minutes flat, but when he was upset, he would just stand there, under the jet of hot water, stewing for up to 30 minutes.

Even though he had already showered, shaved and blown out his hair, Rick reached his hands up and pulled off his shirt. Next, he tugged down his shorts and underwear.

Now completely nude, he padded over to the bathroom, and once inside, silently slid open the glass door to the steaming shower. He stepped in and brought his hands up to Kurt's enormous back and began to rub them around, creating a rich lather from the soap already there.

"Mmmm," Kurt sighed, happy beyond belief that Rick had decided to join him.

Rick stepped closer, nuzzling himself against Kurt's body, and gently kissed him on the neck. "I love you, baby" he said softly, his hands snaking around his lover's torso.

Kurt spun around and took his husband-to-be into his wet arms. "Don't you ever forget that, okay?" he pleaded urgently just before pressing his lips against Rick's.

Clive and Baldwin were helping the *Diana*'s crew clear away the deck chairs from the pool area. There was going to be the most extravagant party of the entire cruise on deck tonight, the traditional Mardi Gras party, and the deck space needed to be as empty as possible. In a few short hours, this confined space would be crammed with 1,300 costumed gay men all gyrating and dancing to hot dance and trance music supplied by hunky DJ BamBam.

Clive had a small stack of regular chairs in his arms, and he went to the closed storage locker behind the hot tub. A large, frescoed wall divided the deck here, the bubbling hot tub on one side, a wide-open space on the other, with a shuffleboard game painted on the decking. Clive set the chairs down and pulled at the storage locker door. It opened easily.

Clive screamed.

Inside the locker was the body of a nude young man, his bathing suit lying near his lifeless feet. Sandy-haired and well built, Clive recognized him as a passenger from St. Louis he had helped with a roommate change two days before.

Baldwin and other crewmembers ran over to see what the problem was, each one gaping in horror at the nude corpse laying inside the locker.

Baldwin came to his senses first and leaned down to examine the man.

"Looks like he was strangled! You can see the marks around his neck!" he gasped.

"Please! Close his eyes," Clive begged.

"No!" piped up a crewmember. "We have to call the captain. We can't touch anything until security gets here."

"Oh my God," Baldwin uttered. He leaned over closer, then stiffened. "I'd say our fellow here got a little before this happened. There's semen all over his chest."

27

Sun Deck, *Princess Diana*, Mediterranean Sea

The party was raging, and Zack tried to relax and let go, but it was difficult. Hayden was in front of him, half naked, swaying in time to the music, but Zack's mind was a million miles away.

Fucking Bayne!

Why did he have to be so…Bayne-like? It was typical, classic Bayne for him to show up like this and ruin Zack's trip. Just when Zack had gotten over the man and met someone terrific, he showed up and threw Zack completely off balance.

Feelings of hurt, betrayal, anger and resentment all bubbled just under the surface. Zack wanted to yell and scream and punch Bayne over and over, and he wasn't a physically confrontational man.

And the way Bayne had treated Hayden! Like he was pond scum or something. The more Zack thought about it, the more worked up he became. To spend the next four days stuck on a ship with the man who had not only broken his heart, but also stabbed through it, was intolerable.

And even more disturbing, for the first time in years, Zack felt the pangs of needing a line or two of coke to smooth away his rage. He was craving it actually, and that was bad. Real bad. This desire scared Zack so badly that he had made a call to the purser's desk and was very relieved to discover there was an AA meeting every morning at 8:00 in one of the conference rooms up near the bridge. He would attend the one tomorrow without fail.

"Zack, honey, let it go," Hayden shouted to be heard over the bump-bump-bump of the dance music. He knew exactly what Zack was thinking about. Bayne. "Don't let him spoil this for us…"

Zack smiled weakly and tried to dance a little more energetically.

Hayden wanted to make his lover feel better, but didn't know how. *That fucking Bayne! What an ass*, he fumed silently. He was also pissed at his loser roommate as well. After finally tracking him down in the gym, he and Zack had pleaded with the guy to switch places and move into Zack's share of the luxury suite. The freak wouldn't do it. He said he felt like it would put him in a bad situation, and he hadn't come on his once-a-year vacation to get caught up in some other guy's drama.

Well, fuck him and fuck Bayne harder, Hayden angrily thought, as he refocused on catching the beat of the music and moving in time.

He and Zack were lost in a sea of swaying men, most of them baring more than a little skin, on the Sun Deck. It was after midnight. Titan's Mardi Gras circuit event was in full swing, and the boys had come to P-A-R-T-Y.

Green laser lights cut through the warm night air, and smoke cannons belched out a thick blanket of fog at appropriate intervals. Colored spotlights on motorized tracks bounced up and down over the pulsating crowd, creating a dizzying wash of jewel-toned lights. Titan staff members were dancing and mingling in the crowd, handing out large ropes of colorful plastic beads to every man they could find. As a result, each passenger had anywhere from 5 to 20 multicolored necklaces dangling around his neck.

There were plenty of glowsticks being waved around as well. Small glowing pendants swung on chains, and even smaller ones hung from pierced ears, bellybuttons and nipples, little neon beacons flashing in the dark. There was also a sea of matching neon necklaces, bright yellows, greens and reds glowing brightly and bouncing as the men who wore them danced. And the constant flashes from the digital cameras that were omnipresent added another element of glimmering light to the night. It almost seemed like some men were so busy photographing the party they weren't enjoying the party.

While many of the men had opted to wear cargo shorts or boardshorts, a vast majority of them had gone all out in their costumes for the event. More than one party-goer wore a full-on feather headdress, some easily six-feet high, and these elaborate headpieces bounced with each movement of its owner. Body paint had been used liberally by the crowd, some men wearing little more than that.

Almost everyone was bare-chested and the lower half of their getups were usually shorts of some fashion. These ranged from tight Lycra gym shorts to cargo shorts, but there was also a healthy representation of glittering g-strings being strutted around, and even a few sarong-style wraps through which a muscular leg would dart out during a slick dance move.

And everywhere there were masks. Some simple Lone Ranger types, others decked out with jutting feathers and golden beads. It was a chance for the inner party man to come out of some of the more reserved passengers and everyone's inhibitions had been tossed aside. Men grinded up against, tongue kissed, and groped complete strangers, yet no one was offended. It was a night of hedonism, fun and sexual freedom.

Hayden was in his favorite pair of workout pants, tight black shorts that hugged his ass and showed off his triathlete legs. Shirtless, he had at least nine bead ropes hanging over his sweaty chest. He had brought a mask to wear, but since Zack didn't have one, he had left it behind in the cabin. He studied his lover's face again and saw, with regret, that Zack was still obsessing over his ex.

At least Hayden hoped Bayne was still the "ex." The thought that that asshole had come onboard after all, and was obviously trying to woo Zack back, upset Hayden more than he wanted to admit. He was crazy for Zack—head-over-heels, can't-stop-thinking-about, wanna-spend-every-waking-minute-with-him—crazy. And even though he had initially chalked up their romance to a much-needed vacation fling, he had felt differently for the past few days. He wanted to make this relationship last, somehow.

Sure, he mused unhappily. We live in separate cities on separate fucking continents. How was this going to work?

Zack was clearly dejected as well. Just getting dressed for this party, with Bayne sullenly stewing in the other bedroom, had been torture. He had barely been able to control himself when Bayne had called out a cheery "goodbye" as he and Hayden left for the party. It was all a charade. Zack knew Bayne. He was playing a game, a game where he thought he'd win Zack back.

Bayne didn't take defeat lightly. If he wanted something, or thought he might lose something he believed was his, he would redouble his efforts to get it back. He bulldozed his way through until he got what he wanted. The only problem was, after he got what he wanted, he'd lose interest. It had been that way when they first met.

Zack had been waiting tables at an upscale deli in the Beverly Center Mall in West Hollywood when he had waited on Bayne. Bayne had become entranced with him and pursued him relentlessly. He sent flowers, small gifts and notes in his determined quest.

After Zack finally capitulated and agreed to go on a date, Bayne had pulled out all the stops. They took a private helicopter ride to Catalina Island off the coast of Los Angeles and had a romantic dinner at the cliffside home of a friend, the twinkling lights of L.A. glittering in the far distance. The beautiful house had been filled with flowers, and the dinner, catered from the best restaurant in Avalon, had been superb. The wine, a $500 bottle of red, had tasted like pure nirvana, and soon Zack felt himself giving in to the charming man, figuratively and literally. They had sex that night for the first time on the living room floor of the borrowed house. Bayne had been like an animal, tearing at Zack's clothes, ravaging him, almost devouring him with his overheated passion.

Over the next few months, Bayne concentrated his assault until he had made Zack fall in love with him. He convinced the younger man to move in with him, and then, after Zack had uprooted his life for him, made sacrifices to his own life plan, after all this, Bayne had begun to distance himself. Oh, sure, they had sex constantly. Bayne never tired of Zack's ripe body, but Zack felt that he'd become a possession, something to be shown off and played with, but not taken seriously. They began to drift apart, and over time, Zack couldn't remember why he was with Bayne in the first place.

That's why taking this trip with Bayne had been so important. Zack wanted to rekindle what they'd once had, but the past week with Hayden had shown him what a real love affair was supposed to be.

He didn't want to let that go.

The only ray of sunshine in this whole sorry mess was Hayden. Zack knew he was completely besotted with the man. In fact, Bayne's arrival had only pointed out the glaring differences between Hayden and him. Hayden was the prize. Of that, he was sure, though how this relationship was going to work out was beyond him.

"Are you okay? Do you wanna stop and call it a night?"

Pulled from his thoughts, Zack looked over at Hayden. "What?"

"I said," Hayden shouted, leaning in close to be heard over the deafening music, "do you wanna call it a night and leave?"

"No..."

"Well, you look miserable. If you wanna leave and go be with Bayne, just say so." Hayden's face had a hard cast to it, like he was braced for news he didn't want to hear.

Zack's heart reached out to him. "Oh, Hade," he said, pulling him close. He kissed Hayden deeply, then leaned over to his right ear. "I'm sorry! I'm freaked out by Bayne being here, that's true...But I love you."

Relief flooded Hayden's body. "I love you, too." He looked around and took Zack's hand. He pulled him off the dance floor and wormed their way through the pulsating crowd to the far side of the Sun Deck, near one of the glass walls that acted as a barrier to the open air and sea. "Zack, what do you want? I think we need to face some issues here. I love you, but I don't know what to do about it anymore. I thought this would be some fun summer thing while you were here, but I've come to care about you much more than I thought possible...I...I just don't know what to do anymore..."

Zack nodded emphatically. "I know. What are we gonna do? How can we make this work? We live so far apart from each other..." He took a deep breath. "I love you completely, like I always hoped to love someone someday...But..." Suddenly speechless, he left the sentence hanging.

"Come on..." Hayden again took his hand and led him away from the pool area.

"Where are we going?" Zack asked, willing to follow Hayden anywhere.

"To your cabin."

"Bayne might be there."

"Fuck him! I want to make love to you so badly right now, I can't stand it! I want to be inside you and fill you up and stare into your eyes! I want to show you how much you mean to me..." Hayden leaned back, grabbed Zack by the back of the head and pulled him close. They kissed passionately for several minutes before breaking contact.

Zack's breathing was shallow and his cock hard. "Let's go."

Donnatella was in her bedroom applying the last touches of makeup to her face. She leaned back and gave herself a long hard stare in the mirror.

She looked good.

She was dressed in a sheer, filmy lime-green halter top and matching sarong skirt. It was a Jean Paul Gaultier design she had picked up last year, never knowing when she could wear it. Tonight it was perfect. She had pulled her hair back into a severe, straight ponytail and had carefully painted a generous, though sexy, amount of makeup on. Her deep tan shined thanks to the microscopic flecks of golden glitter in the body power she had applied, and her low Manolo Blahnik sandals were the perfect color-match to her dress.

Tonight she was going to dance and dance and dance. Something she hadn't done in years.

God knows, she mused blotting her lips in a tissue, *Rex's idea of dancing was that odd little foot shuffle he did after a good quarterly report.*

Donnatella hoped she'd see Jorge at the party so they could shimmy together. She knew he'd have on some fabulous outfit. What a sight the two of them would make!

She was just touching up her cheekbones with her treasured sable-tipped blush brush when her phone rang. She reached a delicately manicured hand out and picked up the suite's cordless phone. "Hello?" she said huskily.

"Mrs. Lassiter? This is Jebb Miller..."

"Oh, hello, Jebb! It was such a pleasure to meet you earlier today. Finally," she smiled. When re-boarding the ship after her afternoon with Antonio, she had come to a tight, blind corner in one of the *Diana*'s passageways and had literally run into Jebb. Friendly introductions had quickly followed. "I'm sorry, but my husband isn't here. He's...Well, actually, I have no idea where he is right now." She gave herself one last look in the mirror and, satisfied, she stepped away.

"No, Mrs. Lassiter..."

"Please, call me Donnatella," she said warmly. "My husband is the formal one in this family. Between you and me, I have to tell you, I simply love this cruise! So much better than our usual boring trips. Such beautiful men! I'm heading down to your party right now, and I'm so excited! This trip is so much fun, no matter what my husband says." She strode out into the living room and sank down into the wide sofa.

"Well, thank you, Mrs., er, Donnatella. But I actually need to speak with you. I have something unpleasant to ask you."

"Oh? What is it?"

"I'm sure your husband has made you aware that we've had a couple of untimely deaths on this trip. One of our group fell off the ship the other night."

"What? No! Rex hasn't said a word about this to me!"

"Oh. I'm sorry, but it's true, and it looks like this drowned man may be someone you know. We're trying to identify his...him, and we have a photo of the two of you by the pool."

Donnatella felt a stab of concern.

"We think his first name is either Juan or Jose—"

"No!" gasped Donnatella. Her hand flew to her mouth in horror.

"I'm sorry, but may I stop by and ask you to verify a photograph of the— of him? It would help us so much. I know this is an awful thing to have to ask."

"Do you mean Jorge? There must be some mistake! Jorge? Camarillo? Beautiful Jorge Camarillo? It's not possible!"

"May I please come over?"

"Yes! Of course! Come now!"

"I'll be right over. Thank you, Donnatella." Jebb hung up.

Donnatella clung to the phone for a minute. She set it down and sank back into the lush sofa. Her hand dropped to her side and felt something hard. She dug down under a throw pillow and pulled out a small silver cell phone. She had never seen it before, so it had to be Rex's. She tossed it onto the coffee table.

Jebb sighed. He had never felt like this in all the years he had been running Titan, but he wanted this trip to end now. There was something evil about it. The unthinkable fact that there was a killer running amuck on this ship had to be addressed. The body of Timothy Jacquard found strangled and stuffed into the storage locker proved that.

Timothy's body had finally been removed, after ship's security had heavily photographed the death scene, and placed in a morgue refrigerator located in the ship's hospital. When they docked in Majorca, authorities would conduct a through examination, and the police would take over.

With so many elderly passengers cruising the world, death by natural causes (and the occasional foolish overboard demise, as Lucard had mentioned) happened frequently enough that a whole set of rules and regulations had been established to deal with the storage of bodies at sea, hence the morgue refrigerator. It was just one of the lesser known, grim realities of the cruising industry today.

Murder, however, was not so common, and Jebb was not pleased that it was happening on his charter. He was absolutely certain that whoever was committing these heinous crimes was not one of his guests. It just wasn't possible. No, he reasoned, it had to be a member of the ship's crew. Who, or why, was beyond him.

New, darker thoughts came to Jebb. What about those bomb threats? What if some whack job was seriously going to try and blow up the ship? There were plenty of crazies out there who hated gays and lesbians. What if the suspicious deaths on the ship and those threats were related?

Whoa, slow down, partner, Jebb sighed to himself. That was crazy. No, the bomb threats were just a way to give some lowlife bigot a bit of power. The deaths onboard were the serious issue. This was going to get messy.

Jebb snatched up the photos of Jorge and walked out of his cabin, to see Donnatella.

Jorge Camarillo, he thought. *Well, at least we might have a full name...*

Dan stood in front of the heavy crew door down on B Deck and pulled the cover off the keycard access device. He shot a glance up each end of the brightly lit passageway, but there was no one around. Everyone was up on deck at the Mardi Gras party, the party he had just left.

Unable to get thoughts of Rex and the mysterious crew door out of his mind, Dan had finally given in to temptation and snuck away from the dance. He was allowing himself just a few minutes down here to once again try and figure out Rex's intentions. After that, he would go back up to the party.

He deftly pulled out a few wires from the entry box and found the two he wanted. He touched each one to a different circuit chip and smiled when the heavy steel door popped open, allowing him access to the crew area. He put the pulled wires back, replaced the cover of the access device, and stepped through the door.

Dressed in his body-revealing Mardi Gras attire, a pair of painted-on go-go shorts and an exotic face-hiding mask, he prayed he didn't run into any crew members. It would difficult to explain why a scantily clad passenger was prowling around below decks where he obviously shouldn't be. His rudimentary knowledge of the ship told him that this area was lightly populated by crew, so if he was careful, he could snoop around and get out without being detected.

At least that was his goal. If he was found, he'd wing it. Lord knows he'd winged it countless times before.

Dan quickly walked down the barren passageway, trying to determine just where Rex would have gone. He tried to put himself into Rex's shoes. It was difficult, because he didn't know what the true purpose of Lassiter's secret mission was. But Dan was usually pretty good at this sort of thing. He had a sort of sixth sense when it came to understanding the motivations of others. This sixth sense had saved his ass on numerous occasions.

He came up to a doorway that had another keycard access panel. Dan replicated his earlier effort and gained entry. He carefully opened the steel door and peered in. It led to a paint-chipped ladder that sank down to a lower deck. It was the only door near the access point, so Dan made an educated guess and decided to go down.

He soon found himself walking along yet another companionway, this one, smaller, narrower and filled with pipes, iron valves and other dangerous looking apparatus. Every few feet, above his head were large, jutting box-like shelves. These box-shelves looked like they contained gears or gyros or some such equipment, and they proved uninteresting to Dan.

Stymied, he stopped in the center of the passageway and scratched his head. There was nothing amiss down here that he could see. Whatever Lassiter had been up to, he couldn't tell what it was. It was huge disappointment.

"Overactive imagination, Dan, my man," he said out loud, shaking his head. He suddenly felt very foolish. His sixth sense about danger had failed him twice before on this cruise, and it had just failed him again. It was very upsetting.

Disgusted with himself, Dan decided to give up this wild goose chase and get the hell out of here. He wanted to go rejoin the party up on deck.

It was time to have some fun.

28

Sun Deck, *Princess Diana*, Mediterranean Sea

Kurt and Rick were dancing closely, but there was a mile wide emotional gulf between them. They had selected a spot away from the pool, looking out at the madness around them. Here they joined a large crowd of costumed and plumed men dancing their hearts out. Rick had brought his new Sony micro-camcorder with him to record some of the more outlandish costumes, but so far he hadn't used it, and merely let the tiny device hang from its tether around his neck.

Dinner with Ted and Sam had not gone well.

The underlying tensions about Rick's job offer had come to the surface when Ted again raised the subject and urged Rick to not hesitate and accept the highly coveted position.

Rick, much to Kurt's shock and dismay, clearly indicated his interest in the new job and his willingness to take on the added responsibility. He had even inquired about current housing costs and if there was a real need for a car in New York, and if so, was a Range Rover too much vehicle for such a crowded city?

Now, dressed in their matching tiny and tight purple Lycra gym shorts, white feather boas and coordinated white masks, they danced as though they had not a care between them.

But inside, Kurt's stomach was in knots. He didn't want to lose this man that he loved so damn much, but could he really pack up his life and move from the city that was his home? A city he loved? It was too daunting a thought to actually have to consider. He dreaded the coming conversation he'd promised to have.

He reached down and patted his waistband. Nestled in the hidden key pocket of his tight shorts were the two platinum wedding bands he had bought for him and Rick. For some reason, having them close made him feel better.

Kirby spun around and around, waving his hands in the air in time to the thumping bass of the Gwen Stefani dance track blaring from the speakers. Wearing only Nike Air Presto sneakers, a white visor, and a small blue Speedo with the word "Lifeguard" written in white across his tight ass, he had received over 20 ropes of glittering beads from besotted admirers. But he only had eyes for his dance partner.

He had just met a tall, hot, dark-haired man with the exotic sounding name of "Dante," and now they were doing the gay mating ritual; suggestive dancing, a causal touch here, a more deliberate one there, a quick, hot deep kiss, and a playful push away. All of this was a clear signal to both men that they would be enjoying a hot ride between the sheets in short order.

Dante had on a mask that covered half his face, from his perfect nose up. Feathers shot out from the sides of the brightly painted mask and small ruby-like stones had been glued into a delicate pattern around the eye slits. Even though Kirby hadn't seen Dante unmasked, it didn't matter. The man was smoking hot. Dante's body was like a work of superb sculpture, cut and ripped and bulky in all the right spots. His incredible six-pack bunched up with each dance step he took, and the gold lamé go-go shorts that barely covered his hard ass were more a tease than anything. Yes, Dante was a fucking stud, and Kirby couldn't wait to get him naked in bed.

Several decks down, Geoff Corbin was writhing between Frank and Andy in their cabin. They had started out at the party by the pool, but had quickly become overheated by seeing all the half-naked man dancing and prancing. Each getting the same thought at the same time, they had raced back down to the cabin to fuck again. Their skimpy costumes, not more than gold jock-straps and neon yellow suspenders, were abandoned on the floor under them. As Geoff plunged again into Andy's willing ass, Frank shoved his hard dick into the reality TV star's mouth.

In the spacious and overly decorated Bond Street Theater located in the bows of the *Princess Diana* on the Sapphire Deck, Garrett Gardner stood on the stage lip and peered out into the empty house. He let his eyes drift up the staggered rows of brocade-covered seats where the audience would sit.

Well, he thought, *I've played worse.*

A completely functional theater with a seating capacity of 950, the Bond Street was a mishmash of garish fabric patterns and mirrored walls. It was a two-story-tall space with the upper balcony accessed by a pair of wide double doors on the Diamond Deck. Heavy columns anchored the ornately fili-greed balcony and provided a convenient surface for even more gilding. Small marble tables were anchored to the floor and spaced evenly through the rows of seats, with one table for every two seats. These tables were a handy spot to place a cocktail received from one of the many staffers who constantly offered liquor during the shows.

With a color scheme of peach, coral and orange, the Bond Street Theater resembled a Jell-O dessert, Garrett realized. Unable to stomach the pastel color palette anymore, he refocused on his rehearsal.

Jebb had come through on his promise to get the comedian some time to rework, rehearse, and pace his act on the ship's small stage. The *Princess Diana*'s entertainment review "Film Ladies We Love!" had finished their second and last performance of the night an hour earlier, and now the great, pastel-themed room was vacant except for Garrett and his boy Toby.

The day trips to Monte Carlo and Rome had given the large comedian a lot of new material, and he had been dying to try it out. He knew he'd kill with his "gay pope" jokes.

Toby sat in the front row, the only witness to the weighty man's hilarious set. He laughed and giggled continuously as the comedian cracked him up retelling the events of the cruise.

Garrett stopped talking, took a swig of water from a water bottle resting on a stool on the stage, and made a mental note to keep the Vatican gags, but drop the Grimaldi family jokes. They just didn't work as well.

As he gulped down the cool water, he noticed a couple of large clothing racks positioned just offstage, in the wings. The sturdy chrome racks held the sequined and feathered costumes for "Film Ladies We Love!" Some of them were hysterically over the top, and Garrett got a devilish idea.

"Hey, Toby!" he called out into the house. "Come here!"

Donnatella was about to pick up her keycard from the coffee table when she paused and sighed.

She was terribly upset to have confirmed that Jorge was indeed the poor soul in that awful photograph Jebb showed her. It was a shock. He had been so full of life, so brilliant, that it was hard to conceive of him still and lifeless.

After Jebb left, she had thought of taking off her makeup and just crawling into bed. Wouldn't it be disrespectful to party so soon after hearing about the death of a young man she was so fond of?

But now, hovering over the coffee table, she steeled her resolve to enjoy herself for once. She realized she needed to be out. She needed to see happiness and joy and people not afraid to be who they are. Perhaps it might give her the courage to finally tell Rex she wanted out of their sham marriage.

She again was reaching for the keycard when she spied the small silver cell phone on the table. For some reason it bothered her.

Why did Rex have a secret phone, she wondered. Then like a burst of white light, a new intriguing thought hit her. *Is he having an affair, too?* Was that why he was so distant? His disinterest in her had evolved over the years as his attention to the family business became all-consuming, so Donnatella never really considered the fact that he might be seeing other women. She had always just assumed he was far too uptight for such normal male activity.

Ever the practical one, Donnatella quickly realized that if he was fucking another woman, she could use it against him in a divorce. This changed everything! She snatched up the phone and pocketed it in her bag. She didn't know how, but this was an important discovery.

Where is the asshole, anyway, she wondered as she slid her keycard into her small baguette handbag next to the tiny cell. She hadn't seen her husband in hours. Not that she really cared, but still.

29

A Deck, *Princess Diana*, Mediterranean Sea

You are so damn hot," Dante whispered into Kirby's ear. He pressed Kirby back into the wall and shut the shorter man's cabin door behind them. His hands quickly wrapped around the hot trainer from Dallas, and Kirby readily did the same. Their hands touched, grabbed and felt each other's bodies until they were both gripping each other's hard manhood.

"Fuck! You're driving me crazy!" Kirby groaned, yanking his visor off and tossing it to the floor. "Take off your mask! I want to see your face when I kiss you!"

"Not yet…I think it's sexier to leave it on…" Dante breathed as he went in for another round of passionate necking. His hands dropped low and cupped the hard cheeks of Kirby's luscious ass.

Kirby maneuvered them over to his messy bed, and they tumbled down onto it. The two men could not stop pawing at each other. They kissed, sucked and touched each other with a frenzy that could only be described as animalistic.

Kirby felt his swimsuit being pulled from his body, freeing his steel erection, and he lifted his ass up to allow Dante to pull the small Lycra garment all the way off. In seconds, Kirby felt the naked hardness of Dante pressing against him.

"I want to fuck you," Dante gasped, pulling his lips away from Kirby's for the briefest of seconds.

"Oh, God, yes…Yes!" Kirby groaned. He eagerly spread his sexy legs wide and prepared himself to accept the masked man who had crawled on top of him. "There's condoms in the nightstand…"

My God, this kid is totally turning me on, Dante thought dreamily, as he deftly slid a lubricated Trojan on. *He is so fucking sexy!* Gazing down at the compact trainer writhing on the bed beneath him, urging him to hurry up, he felt only a minor pang of regret. *I'm completely out of control!* He realized sadly. *I can't help myself anymore. I see a hot ass, and I have to have it.*

The condom now on and snug, Dante placed his wide palms on Kirby's hard inner thighs, and pressed them apart. The young man panted in anticipation, and Dante began to enter him. Kirby's groans of pleasure were music to Dante's ears. *Goddamn this kid is sexy,* he thought again.

Almost as sexy as Jorge, the beautiful man he had fucked, then dumped overboard a few nights ago. Definitely sexier than Timothy, the man he had strangled this afternoon. In Barcelona, Rhett had had a sweet innocence about him that he had been sad to snuff out, and of course, all the others before them, but Dante confidently knew passionate, eager Kirby would be the best lay of them all.

Oh, well, he thought matter-of-factly as he began to thrust his hips back and forth, *at least his last moments on earth will be filled with passion.*

Donnatella was standing on the Compass Deck overlooking the pool area and watching with wonder the unbelievable scene below her. Hundreds of practically naked bodies were grinding up against each other, dancing with carefree abandon and having the time of their lives. She was near a large group of men all dressed the same; silver jocks, long multihued balloons fanning out from their backs like the plumage of some exotic bird, and wildly elaborate masks that had smaller balloons swirling around their heads. Ropes and ropes of gold chains hung around their necks, and these chains swayed mightily with their frenzied dancing styles.

These barely clad men were waving gold silk banners around, causing the flags to flutter and snap in time to the music. They had it down to a choreographed routine, like navy men who signal other ships at sea with a series of flag placements that spelled out words in code. As the flaggers performed for the crowd below, Donnatella could hear the shouts and cheers of encouragement for their striking display.

She passed by the flaggers and wandered to the ship's railing to watch the sea far below race past the towering sides of the *Princess Diana*. It was a calm, warm night, and the moon, not quite full, was shining brightly overhead. She leaned back and let the breeze of the moving liner wash over her. Her thin outfit fluttered and floated up around her. It was a perfect night. The booming dance music from the enormous speakers was creating an atmosphere of sensuality and decadence that was intoxicating.

Her mind turned to thoughts of her errant husband. She excitedly considered the idea that she would finally be able to divorce him. If she could prove he was being unfaithful, he would have to fork over millions! She opened her bag and took out the sleek, tiny cell, the key to her future happiness.

I know who he calls on this thing…he calls his mistress, she thought giddily, as she flipped the cover open. Deciding there was no time like the present to find out who the bitch was, she looked at the softly glowing keypad of the phone.

Smiling at her own cleverness, she punched "redial."

30

C Deck, *Princess Diana*, Mediterranean Sea

Nine decks below Donnatella's Manolo Blahnik-shod feet, the electronic devices became activated one after the other. In a matter of split seconds, they each carried out their catastrophic destiny.

The triple blast ripped a hole 22 feet wide by 31 feet long, one deck below the waterline. The cold Mediterranean Sea immediately began to gush through the gaping wound, and the large ship rocked back and forth severely.

Unknown to Rex, large steel retaining walls had been added during the *Princess Diana*'s recent refit. They had been placed to further protect the fuel tanks and freshwater tanks from possible internal ruptures, so the concussion from the explosions was contained to a smaller area. Only one empty fuel tank was breached, its vaporous fumes adding a sizable kick to the explosive detonation of the bombs. Unfortunately, the newer, thicker steel containment below decks meant that the explosive forces of the blasts had no place to go but up.

Twisted iron, tortured steel, bits of paneling, shattered pipes and other debris shot upward, ripping a wide, jagged, raw vertical shaft six decks high. Hayden's empty, original stateroom on B Deck was directly over the blast source and was vaporized in an instant.

One deck above that, and one cabin over, Kirby's stateroom was torn asunder. A jagged hole instantly appeared on the aft side of his cabin, blowing the bed, with him and Dante still on it, flat up against the forward wall where it landed upside-down in a tangle of metal framing and mattresses.

The blast hole extended up another deck into the Côte d'Azur dining room. Mostly void of diners due to the Mardi Gras party up on the Sun Deck, the Côte d'Azur dining room suddenly had a 10 x 12 foot section of floor open up near the wide port side bank of panoramic windows. The 15-foot tall windows nearest the blast force blew outward, throwing a shower of cascading glass down the side of the stricken liner and into the sea below.

The concussion from the blast roared upward, and the huge energy force bounced off the ceiling of the dining room, buckling the structural integrity of the overhead steel rafters. Large chunks of plaster, concrete and steel rained back down.

Where elegant tables and chairs had once rested there was now the steaming maw of the blast hole. The shockwave from the explosion also flattened every other table in the vicinity, shattered the enormous plate glass mirrors that wrapped around the structural columns, and sent waitstaff, crockery, and furniture flying.

Up on the Pool Deck, the sudden tilting of the wounded cruise ship caused most of the dancing men to be knocked down. Sprawling over one another, they now had to contend with shielding off the huge speakers that had been jolted from their mountings and were tipping over onto terrified, screaming men.

DJ Kenny BamBam was tossed out of the gazebo that housed his equipment and into one of the Jacuzzis. The Jacuzzi's water sloshed over the sides and joined the other torrents of water caused by the swimming pool half emptying itself on the now slippery teak decking.

Spotlights, also added for the party, pulled loose of their brackets as well and crashed to the deck, their shattering clamor only adding to the cacophony of noise that the explosions had caused.

All over the ship, men were thrown to the deck as the huge liner rocked back and forth, her innards torn open. The crescendo of noises drowned out any screams, and as the ship settled back to a listing position to port, the sirens began wailing. Emergency lights flashed on and off.

Six decks directly above the initial blast zone, Zack's spacious cabin was a mess. Severe structural damage from the blast had caused this entire section of the liner to drop down about two feet. Because of the wide-open spaciousness of the two-story Côte d'Azur dining room directly below, the buckling was most noticeable here in Zack's stateroom.

While the small entry hallway and second bedroom were basically intact, the master bedroom was directly over the force of the blast. Walls had been torn away from their mounting braces and hung useless over the sagging floor, jagged metal showing where they had torn away. The elegant furniture had been tossed about like dollhouse toys, and the rich carpeting had ripped and torn into many sections, exposing the cracked and crumbling thin concrete flooring under them. Several of the once-hidden support beams were now exposed, bent and screeching, as they struggled to hold their overtaxed stress loads.

Thrown nude from the bed, where seconds before they had been making love, to the sinking floor of the cabin, Hayden and Zack were caught in a twisted pile of bedding, broken furniture, shattered paneling and broken glass. Hayden recovered his senses first. Frantically pulling the tangled sheets away from his lover, he was terrified to find Zack unconscious, a nasty cut across his forehead beginning to bleed.

"Oh my God! Zack! Wake up! Zack!" he screamed, shaking the still man. He hugged the body of his lover close and began to scream louder. "Help! Help! Please, anyone, I need help!"

His voice only added to the chorus of shrieks coming from the wounded all over the listing liner.

31

Sapphire Deck, *Princess Diana*, Mediterranean Sea

Garrett struggled to get upright, but he was caught up in several feather boas and each time he tried to suck in a deep breath, he got a mouthful of marabou. He began to cough and choke on the feathers.

Toby pushed aside the large clothes rack that had fallen on him, and it hit the stage floor with a terrible crash. The exaggerated Joan Crawford wig he had put on was cockeyed on his head, and the heavily padded frock he had pulled on over his tee and cargos had split right up the side. One of the enormous shoulder pads was sticking straight up and kept poking him in the chin.

"Garrett!" he cried out. "Are you okay? What the fuck happened?"

"Help me up! I can't get up!" Garrett bellowed, still struggling to get upright.

"Jesus Christ!" Toby sputtered as he dug Garrett out from under the layers of costumes that had fallen over on him.

When Garrett finally got to his feet, Toby would have laughed if he weren't so scared. A wickedly funny replica of Bette Davis' "Baby Jane" wig, complete with curls and large white bow, was perched precariously on Garrett's head, and the checked pinafore he had slipped on was torn and falling off his large body.

There was a sudden screech of tearing metal, and two heavy spotlights fell to the stage floor with a mighty crash. Garrett and Toby squealed out in shocked surprise and scurried for cover in the wings. Another light fell, then another, glass flying everywhere from the shattered lenses.

"Let's get out of here!" Toby pleaded, feeling the tilt of the deck beneath him for the first time.

"Absolutely!" replied Garrett. He ripped the ruined dress off and pushed Toby ahead of him, towards the exit. They emerged in a wide corridor and quickly picked their way down the main stairwell located nearby.

Garrett got all the way to his lifeboat station before he realized he still had the Bette Davis wig on.

Geoff picked himself up off the floor of the stopped elevator car and reached for the handrail. He didn't know what had happened, but whatever it was, it couldn't be good.

Emergency Klaxons were now blaring all over the ship. The noise of them was deafening.

A mere minute before the explosion ripped through the *Princess Diana*, he had stepped into one of the aft elevators, having just finished his latest session with Frank and Andy. He had pressed level 9, as he wanted to rejoin the ongoing Mardi Gras party.

Since he had been alone in the large elevator car, he had turned around and was checking out his hair in the floor to ceiling mirror affixed to the back wall when everything went crazy, and he was thrown first to one side of the elevator, then to the other.

Now he realized the car had stopped and he was alone. The normal halogen lights had gone out, and had been replaced by dimmer emergency lighting that did nothing for his complexion when he saw his scared reflection in the cracked mirror of the elevator.

A calm, prerecorded masculine voice now came through every loudspeaker on the *Princess Diana*. "Attention! Attention! This is not a drill! Every passenger must report directly to their lifeboat station immediately. Do not go to your cabins! Life jackets will be distributed at your boat station. Please, every passenger needs to report to their lifeboat station immediately." This announcement was repeated every 30 seconds.

Coming to his senses, Geoff reached out and frantically pressed the Open Door button, but nothing happened. He pressed the Alarm button, and again, got no response. He could hear ghastly sounding creaks and rumblings coming from all over the ship, and there was a definite tilt to the carpeted elevator floor.

Fighting his panic, he began screaming for help.

Jebb shook his head several times to clear it and, like men all over the ship, picked himself up and tried to make sense of what was happening. The sudden lurching of the ship had tossed him clear across his cabin, his papers, clothes and personal effects all trashed together on the floor. He could hear the emergency bells bleating throughout the ship, and he knew that this was no drill. Grabbing his life jacket from the wrecked closet, he threw it on and left his cabin to go where he was most needed.

Kurt and Rick were helping the stunned passengers get up. Surprisingly to both of them, there was not much hysteria on the Sun Deck. The party-goers knew something bad had happened, and they were trying to locate friends and lovers so they could go to their boat stations.

The injured were being led to an area under the Compass Deck overhang, where several passengers who happened to be doctors were tending them. Some men had been tossed into the sloshing pool and they carefully pulled themselves out, finding the ever-growing tilt of the deck treacherous to maneuver.

Up on the Compass Deck, Donnatella followed the group of balloon-clad flaggers to the aft stairwell for the climb down to the Promenade Deck where the lifeboat stations were. She could already see crewmembers in life jackets running around herding the passengers down to the boats.

Hidden storage lockers had been popped open and other crew personnel were handing out bright-orange life jackets to the scared men as they filed past. Donnatella gratefully took a jacket from a crewman and joined the growing group of passengers and crew waiting in the designated lifeboat stations. Almost instantly, the heavy, covered boats started to lower from their storage position, and the swelling crowd pressed closer, eager to board them.

Captain Lucard was barking orders left and right up on the bridge. He had ordered the watertight doors shut immediately. The floor plan of the ship that showed the status of the watertight doors—green for open, red for closed—showed every door shut except for a series of three doors on the port side that wouldn't respond to command. Lucard realized that they must have been damaged in some way from whatever had just happened. He quickly ordered a visual inspection.

Klaus, at his station ten feet away, had been on the phone getting damage reports since the instant after the explosions had been felt. He had a slight cut on his right hand from where he fell on a broken glass when he'd hit the deck. Not bothering to wipe off the blood, he ignored the nasty cut, letting it flow. He glanced up and locked eyes with Lucard.

"Klaus," Lucard said evenly. "Get down to the Promenade Deck. Make sure the passengers are bloody well taken care of!"

Klaus nodded. "Yes, Jose-er, Sir." He gulped and smartly left the bridge.

Down on the Promenade, Deck, emergency personnel were readying the lifeboats for launch. Not the old-fashioned open-air kind that had been famous for not being on the *Titanic*, the lifeboats of the *Princess Diana* were in fact large motor launches, the same kind used to tender passengers to dock on port-of-call days.

These enclosed, behemoth boats were virtually unsinkable and could hold up to 90 people each and were hung up over the deck in steel cages that allowed them to be swung out and lowered to the deck below by a system of cables, hydraulics and winches. These lifeboats could be loaded with passengers in lists of up to 25 degrees.

And now, one by one, they were being lowered to "boarding level" to allow the growing number of passengers to enter them.

"Help! Is anyone there?" Hayden yelled louder, hoping against hope that someone was nearby and could hear him. Bayne hadn't been in his bedroom when he and Zack had come back from Mardi Gras, and Hayden was afraid no one could hear him yelling for assistance. He was terrified that everyone from this passenger deck was still upstairs on the Sun Deck where they had been dancing at the party, or down on the boat deck escaping whatever had happened to them. With each passing second, his panic ratcheted up another notch. "Help!" he screamed again.

"Hello?" called out a faint voice from beyond the bedroom door.

Immensely relieved to hear a reply, Hayden screamed even louder. "Help! In here! We need help!"

The split door to the bedroom creaked open about a foot, and a clearly disheveled Bayne stuck his head in. "Zack! Are you…Where's Zack?"

"He's here!" Hayden indicated the unconscious form of Zack under the sheet. "He's hurt! I can't get him to wake up. Help me get him out of here!"

Bayne tried to push the door open further, and succeeded in getting it to go another six inches, but that was all. Standing in the ruined but intact small hallway of the once luxurious suite, he looked into Zack's demolished cabin and saw his ex-lover lying on the sinking, crumbling floor of the master bedroom. Hayden, still naked, slipped his arms under Zack's and pulled him to his feet. His dead weight was hard to handle, and Hayden sensed an odd movement under his feet. It felt like the floor was sinking down further, collapsing in the center of the room. He even noticed some small objects roll towards the growing depression in the center.

Realizing he needed to get out of here, and fast, he dragged Zack's limp body to the doorway, now four feet above where it had been before the disaster. "Reach down, Bayne. Take his arms and pull him up," he ordered, straining to push the dead weight of his beloved upward.

Bayne braced his feet and reached down. He grab at one of Zack's hands and pulled him up slowly, finally getting his hands under Zack's armpits, and thereby getting a much better hold.

Hayden, underneath, was sweating from his exertion. He strained to push Zack up, and felt Bayne inch him higher and higher. This task was made more difficult by the fact that the floor kept getting lower. Cracklings, the sound of tearing metal, and loud snaps were a constant presence, and Hayden was terrified he wouldn't get Zack out of the sinkhole in time.

Finally, Bayne heaved Zack backward, and the unconscious man's feet finally cleared the doorway. He dropped Zack down to the ground, and reached over to a pile of clothes that had fallen on the floor. He snatched up a pair of sweatpants, and struggled to pull them up over Zack's beefy legs in an attempt to cover his nakedness.

"Hey!" Hayden yelled up. "Help me up!"

Bayne ignored the request and continued to pull the sweats up his former lover's legs. He wasn't about to take Zack to the lifeboats with his dick hanging out.

"Bayne! Help me up!" Hayden repeated.

"Help yourself up," Bayne called back churlishly.

"What? I can't! The floor is collapsing! Give me your hand!"

Bayne peeked back through the doorway and saw that the floor was indeed another foot shorter. Hayden was trying to get a handle and pull himself up, but couldn't get a good grip on the doorframe.

"Hang on a minute. I need to get Zack up," Bayne said calmly.

"There isn't time! Help me up and we can both get him out of here!"

"No."

Hayden didn't think he heard right. "What did you say?"

"Shut up! I'm busy!" Hayden snapped. He slipped his hands under Zack and began to get him up.

"You son of a bitch! Help me!" Hayden screamed, jumping up to try and get a hold of the ledge.

Suddenly, there was a loud cracking sound, and the floor dropped down a full three feet. Hayden was knocked on his ass, and slammed up against a broken chair, a new sharp pain stabbing him in the back. A metal wall beam fell across his chest, pinning him in place. He struggled to get free, but found he couldn't.

"Bayne! I'm trapped! Come help me!"

Bayne set Zack back down on the floor. He looked around and noticed the list was getting stronger. It now took effort to stand upright. There was no mistaking it. The fucking ship was sinking!

Bayne returned to the cabin doorway and looked down at Hayden, who was trying to lift the piece of steel off his chest but failing. Hayden, terrified, glanced up and saw Bayne peering down at him. "Please!" the trapped man pleaded. "Get down here and help me get this thing off!"

Bayne's menacing eyes narrowed. "You know what? I think the *Princess Diana* is in serious trouble."

"No shit! Get down here!"

"Fuck you."

Hayden did a double take. "What?"

"I said fuck you. Get your own ass out. Or don't, I couldn't care less. I got what's important to me." He glanced briefly at Zack's unconscious body. "You're on your own."

Horror crossed Hayden's face. "You can't be serious!"

"Oh, but I am. You think I'm going to let you take Zack away from me? This is a golden opportunity. I'll tell him I saved him. He'll think I'm his hero again. You," he laughed tightly, "You will be but a dim memory. Goodbye, trash."

"For the love of God, you can't do this."

Bayne's eyes narrowed to slits. "Watch me."

With that, he turned away, shut the door, and slipped his hands under the slack form of Zack, getting him to his feet. Hayden's shouts dimmed as he dragged Zack away. He reached into one of the numerous closets and pulled out two bulky, orange life vests. He quickly pulled one on himself, and then loosely attached the other one to Zack's slumped form. He then dragged Zack out of the stateroom. Once in the hall, Bayne shut the cabin door, making sure it was locked. He listened closely to hear if Hayden's constant screams for help could be heard in the hallway. They couldn't.

Smiling broadly, Bayne began to pull his boyfriend down the hall when he met a ship's officer whose wounded right hand was wrapped in a bloody bandage. The officer was also decked out in a life vest and leading a group of frightened passengers down to the boat stations.

"Do you need help?" the burly officer asked.

"Yes! Oh, thank God! He's injured! He's out cold."

Klaus slipped one of Zack's arms over his thick shoulders, and Bayne did the same with the other arm.

"Anyone else need help around here that you know of?" Klaus asked, as they started down the passageway.

"No," Bayne replied. "Thank God."

32

Pearl Deck, *Princess Diana*, Mediterranean Sea

B loody hell!" shouted Dante as he struggled to get out from under the tangle of sheets and the upturned mattress. Kirby, slightly dazed, stirred but clung to the floor. The sound of hissing steam and rumblings from somewhere deep in the belly of the ship sounded awfully loud and close, and Kirby kept his eyes shut tightly. He couldn't understand why he felt the hot moisture of escaping steam on his body.

"Help me get the damn mattress off," Dante ordered brusquely as he gripped the overturned bed. Kirby didn't respond. "Hey!" Dante shouted. "Move your ass!"

Kirby finally pulled himself up into a crouching position, and when he opened his eyes what he saw was way worse than what he had imagined.

His cabin was gone. In its place was a huge, jagged, gaping hole in the floor and also above where the ceiling used to be. Grimy oil and other rank fluids coated the scant pieces of cherry wood paneling that remained on the fractured walls. He and Dante were perched on a small outcropping of cracked flooring that was only about two feet wide by eight feet long. There were chunks of wall material scattered around them, and even an oily piece of pipe, bent at a sharp angle. The mattress resting on top of them had snagged on a spike of steel jutting out from the shattered wall. One good kick from Dante and Kirby tore it loose and sent it tumbling down into the hissing void below them.

"Bloody fucking hell!" Dante swore again, as he looked down into the pit below him. He could see down several decks, with each successive level having more damage than the one above. At the bottom of this otherworldly cavity, he could hear water rushing in, and he knew precious time was slipping away.

Looking up, Dante could see that the damage extended up past one of the dining rooms, which was located directly above them. He shouted up for help, but either no one could hear him or no one was going to come near the hole.

"Wha...what happened?" Kirby asked, nervously peering over the edge of the ledge as well. This was his worst nightmare come to pass. He looked down and couldn't believe that he was in this situation. Looking around the destroyed stateroom, the frightened young man saw that there was no way to get off the ledge.

They were suspended over the hole, separated from the cabin's door by a space of about nine feet. The cabin's metal door was creased and buckled forward, clearly jammed in the doorframe. They wouldn't be leaving that way.

Dante ignored Kirby as his mind raced to make sense of the situation. He needed a moment to figure out his options.

"What happened?" Kirby asked again.

"Shut up! I'm thinking!" Dante snapped.

Kirby, shocked at the outburst, studied his sex partner more closely. Dante's nude body was streaked with grime and oil, as was his own. The exotic mask Dante had worn earlier had blown off and for the first time, Kirby got a good look at the man's anguished face.

"Hey," Kirby whispered. "I know you, don't I?"

Dante, pulled from his thoughts, looked at Kirby with disdain. "What?"

"I know you! You're the guy who owns this ship, aren't you? We all saw you on deck one day, and someone pointed you out as the owner. You're Rex Lassiter."

Rex's face turned into a sneer. "So?"

"What's with the name 'Dante?' Oh, wait. Isn't your wife on board, too?"

Rex snorted. "Not if I'm lucky. Hopefully, she was right above us."

Kirby was too stunned by Rex's reply to respond.

"I can't fucking believe this!" Rex shouted into the void. "It blew early! It fucking blew early! Goddamn it!"

"What...what are you talking about?" Kirby began to fear the man who was hunched over a few feet away from him and screaming into the hole.

Rex settled back and coolly stared at Kirby. He began to laugh. "Well, we're fucked my little friend. Completely fucked! It wasn't supposed to happen this way, don't you see? It was supposed to happen later, when I could get the hell off this boat!" His shrill laughter began to overtake him as he dissolved into hysterics. "Now I'm trapped by my own bombs!" he spat out between guffaws.

"I...I don't understand..."

"No, of course you don't," Rex snorted. "You're just a little piece of ass. You're nothing! You don't know anything...You don't know what I've had to do to save my company..."

Kirby began to get a sickening feeling in the pit of his stomach. He inched away from Rex. "I know that we need to get out of here," he weakly offered.

"Well, you're right about that. *I'm* going to get out of here," Rex nodded. "Sadly, you won't be joining me."

"Wha…what?"

"I'm sorry, Kirby, I really am," Rex said curtly, as he leaned forward. "But no one knows I fuck men. It would ruin me with my family. My wife would use it to get my money in a divorce. And now that you know I planned this little disaster, well…I just can't have you telling anyone about this."

"I…I won't tell anyone," Kirby said, backing up a few more inches. He had reached the edge of the ledge, and there was nowhere else for him to go.

"Sorry, but I can't take that chance. I will tell you this, though," Rex moved closer, his hands opening wide, reaching for Kirby's neck. "I've fucked the hell out of several men on this trip, all of whom met an early demise at my hands." He snickered evilly. "But you were the hottest fuck yet. Even hotter than that that pretty boy model I threw overboard. You should be proud of yourself." He quickly lunged forward and gripped his strong hands around Kirby's throat.

Gasping, and too stunned to move, Kirby felt the fingers tighten around his neck, all air cut off. He struggled as much as he could, given his precarious position and as the blackness began to overcome him, he found the strength for one last effort to ward off Rex. He kicked his right leg up and connected solidly with Rex's knee. Rex grunted in pain, and for a brief instant his fingers loosened.

It was enough. Kirby jerked back, air once again flowing into his lungs. He brought his own hands up and knocked Rex's away.

Rex howled an inhuman cry and lunged forward again. Kirby bent back and ducked down just enough to cause Rex to miss. Kirby shot his hands back up again and gripped Rex's forearms. He pulled the crazed man forward.

"No!" Rex shouted, not believing the kid was fighting back. No one had ever done this before, and for a moment, Rex was stymied.

"Fuck…you!" Kirby grunted, as he twisted his body around and shoved Rex's body forward. Rex's left foot slipped off the jagged edge of the ledge and the shards of torn metal sliced into his leg. He squealed in pain and struggled to get his balance. He managed to hop back and pull his wounded foot up on the ledge again. Blood flowed out of the nasty, deep gashes and slowly began to pool on the ledge.

The enraged owner used his body to slam back into Kirby in an attempt to knock the smaller man off balance. He almost succeeded.

Kirby felt himself slipping over the edge into the black hole, but at the last possible second, he reached his hands back for stability and happened to find them resting on the piece of broken pipe. Gripping it firmly, he suddenly swung it up and around, connecting solidly with the side of Rex's head.

A satisfying "thunk" reverberated through the steel pipe into Kirby's arm. Rex instantly reached up to rub his head in a slight daze. Kirby took this opportunity to begin kicking his beefy legs.

Rex tried to fight off the repetitive thrashing he was getting from Kirby's strong limbs, but he was confused from the blow to his head, and the blood on the small ledge caused him to slip. He stopped trying to get at Kirby, and now concentrated on saving his own hide.

Kirby, sensing he was gaining leverage on the larger man, continued to kick and thrash at Rex as he brought back the pipe for another swing.

Rex tried to stand, his plan being to jump on top of Kirby and subdue him that way. He just hadn't planned on Kirby's incredible leg strength. The fast moving legs kept hitting at him, painfully, knocking him farther and farther back towards the lip of the craggy protrusion they were on.

Suddenly, there was a muffled explosion from below, and a hot gust of air blew up, catching Rex unaware. The strong current of wind then suddenly sucked back down.

Rex lost his footing, and he felt the shattered cabin spin. He tried to catch himself, but it was too late. He flew over the side of the ledge, his arms uselessly pinwheeling as he futilely tried to grab at any protrusion.

Kirby watched in fascinated horror as the evil man was sucked down into the hole, all sounds he shrieked lost in the rush of strong wind. Dropping the pipe and gripping onto the ledge for stability, Kirby saw Rex's body slam into several obstructions before splashing into the gathering oily water at the bottom, where he floated, face down.

"Oh my God," Kirby gasped, his strength almost gone. He fell back against the wall and tried to let his breathing return to normal.

Bayne and Klaus continued to drag the bleeding Zack down the sloping stairwell. The going was slow as crowds of men from the party were also pressing forward, all of them trying to get to the boat deck.

Klaus kept calling out encouraging words, keeping the frightened men calm. This was difficult for him to do, as the ship kept moving beneath them, listing far to one side, then settling slowly back to almost even. The downward tilt towards the bow was becoming more pronounced with each minute and panic was brewing in the frightened passengers.

Zack felt himself come out of a fog. Light filtered through his eyelids, and he concentrated to open them. Finding it hard to focus at first, he blinked rapidly, getting the fuzzy images to come in sharper. He felt himself being carried and finally when it all made sense, he began to help, moving his feet.

"Zack? Are you okay?" asked a familiar voice.

"Wh…What?" Zack asked hazily, looking towards the source of the utterance.

"Zack? Wake up, Little Man…Come on, wake up."

"Bayne?" Zack asked, now clearly focusing in on his ex-lover.

"Yes! Oh, thank God, you're okay."

"What's happening? Where's Hayden?" Zack tried to pull away from Bayne and the other man who held him up.

"There's been an accident. I don't know what happened, but we have to evacuate the ship," Bayne said calmly. "Do you understand? We have to abandon ship."

"Where's Hayden?" Zack's memory was coming back. He had been in the cabin with Hayden, making love, when there had been a weird sensation of flying.

Bayne faltered for just a moment. "I don't know. I haven't seen him. I found you in the cabin, alone and unconscious. He must have ditched you, the bastard. Thank God I came along and found you! You were hurt and out cold. I got you up and out of there."

"But he was in the cabin with me! Did you see him? We have to go back!" Zack began to struggle against the grip of the two men supporting him.

"Hey, hey, calm down," soothed the sturdy man in officer's clothes on his left. "Just relax. We're going to the lifeboats now, okay, sir?"

"No! I have to go find Hayden!"

"Zack!" Bayne said sharply. "Actually, I think I saw him head down the stairs ahead of us. He's probably down at the boats now. Let's go down there and see, okay? I'll help you find him."

Zack looked at his ex-lover for a beat. His despair at Hayden not being there with him was palpable, but Bayne's words made sense to his addled mind.

"Okay," he finally said, shaking off the help of the two men and moving himself forward on his own.

Four decks below, Dan moaned softly and began to stir. He opened one eye, then the other. It took a second for his vision to clear and focus. There was an odd, hard pressure on his back, yet he felt like he wanted to roll over on his side.

When all his senses completely returned, he tested his body. He could move his fingers and toes, so no limbs were broken. It was just so damn hard to breathe.

He placed his palms on the carpeted floor and tried to press himself up. He couldn't. Something heavy was pinning him in place. And the pain in his chest felt like hot pokers were stabbing him repeatedly.

He took as deep a breath as he could and again pressed up. This time something shifted. He felt himself push up and as he rose, the heavy, scorched steel door that had covered his back slid to one side and he was free. He got to his feet, gingerly holding his ribs, two of which, he correctly guessed, were broken. He looked around, shock and disbelief flooding his face.

The companionway was in shambles. The carpeting nearest him was scorched and torn. He could hear horrifying tearings and gurgles coming from beyond the shattered doorframe he stood next to. Other doors down the passageway, passenger cabin doors, were cracked or ajar.

As his mind absorbed all this visual information, he began to process it. He had just stepped out of the "crew only" area, and back into the comfort of Deck A, when there had been a stultifying roar, then blackness. It had been an explosion. A bad one.

Dan realized that the steel door, that damn heavy door that he'd had to break into to enter, had been his savior. Somehow, when the blast force raged upward, the door had blown over top of him, offering sacred protection and saving his life.

Grateful that he was alive, Dan now understood what Rex Lassiter had been doing down here. He had blown up his own ship, and Dan had a pretty good idea why.

"Why didn't I see this coming?" he shouted in anger at himself. "Goddammit!" The yelling only served to make his chest burn with fire once again.

It was then that Dan realized the deck was tilting decidedly to port. It was time to get out of here. He wanted to find Lassiter. Once and for all.

33

Sapphire Deck, *Princess Diana*, Mediterranean Sea

Geoff continued to bang on the elevator doors, praying that they would open. No luck. He could feel the strong downward tilt to the ship now, and he thought he could hear water gurgling in the elevator shaft beneath the floor of the stalled elevator car.

Thank God the annoying emergency Klaxon had stopped, he thought. It had been driving him out of his mind earlier.

"No! I am not going out this way!" he finally shouted in frustration to no one. He again gripped at the elevator doors and tried to part them. They wouldn't budge. He needed something to pry them open with, but he had nothing to use. He began to think that he would die in there, drowned like a rat in a cage.

Fighting his rising panic, he pulled open the flat metal door to the emergency call box and again tried the dead phone. As before, no dial tone. He just wasn't getting a break.

He stared at the call box in frustration when he suddenly had an idea. Maybe...just maybe...

He looked around for some sort of hammer. There was, of course, no such tool around, but Geoff was a crafty man. He'd improvised cunning solutions to impossible problems more than once on *Race Around the World 5*, and he would do it here, too.

Thinking fast, he reached down and pulled off one of his new black suede Gucci loafers. He raised it up in his hand and slammed it down on the open emergency callbox door. The one foot square door didn't budge. He began wailing at it, slamming the shoe down over and over, the rubber sole of the shoe splitting and shredding on the hard, thin metal as he banged on the small door.

Finally, he felt the door give a bit, then a little more. He was sweating as he kept smacking down on it until, with a final wrenching tear, it ripped away from its frame.

Geoff dropped the ruined shoe and picked up the flat piece of steel.

"This just might work!" he said to himself.

He gripped the small door and began to wedge its thin metal side into the crack between the two closed elevator doors. He wiggled it back and forth, ultimately feeling it slide in between the tightly shut doors. With a shrill screech, the elevator doors suddenly popped open, revealing the flat wall of an elevator shaft, and thankfully, the top three feet of the outside elevator doors to the deck the elevator had stalled just above.

Geoff sat down on the tilting floor of the elevator and reached down, sliding his hand in between the elevator car and the outside doors. He was blindly searching for the release latch that would open them. He found it on the first try. The doors slid noiselessly open, and Geoff could see the richly carpeted floor of the deck below.

Sweet relief flooding his body. The reality TV star slipped the ruined loafer back on his foot, swung his legs down, and wiggled his body through the opening. He dropped the final four feet to the carpeted deck.

He glanced up at the location map mounted on the wall by the elevator door, and found he was on Deck 8, the Diamond Deck. He looked down the corridor branching away from the elevator bank and saw a couple of men dressed in hot yellow sarongs, black leather vests, and orange life jackets, dragging hastily stuffed suitcases behind them. They looked back and saw him.

"Hey!" one of them called. "Help us?"

Perplexed, Geoff looked at them. "What the hell are you doing?"

"It's all our clothes!" the other called back. "We're not leaving $3,000 worth of leather gear behind!"

"You're kidding, right?"

"No," the other piped up.

"You realize the ship is sinking, don't you? They're not going to let you bring that stuff! Leave it and let's get the hell out of here!" Geoff urged.

"Fuck you," said the first man. "If my chaps and harness don't leave, I don't leave!"

"Oh, my God, you're an idiot," Geoff groaned as he rushed past them, heading for the stairs.

Lucard kept one eye on the gauges and another on the scene below the bridge windows. It was definite. The ship was down at the head. He could tell by the closeness of the calm ocean to the bow. It only confirmed what he already knew in his gut.

How the bloody hell did this happen, he frantically thought. He could picture the end of his career settling into the calm blue water. They always blamed the captain, he knew.

He had done all he could to try to keep the *Diana* on an even keel. He had received reports from all over the ship about the damage she had sustained, and he knew the approximate size of the gaping wound in the *Princess Diana*'s side. As the water rushed in unabated, he had watched the list of the ship grow to port. He knew the lifeboats were extremely difficult to load and release over a list of 25 degrees, so as the port side dipped lower, he would order ballast tanks on the starboard side flooded to balance out the ship. The unfortunate result of this was that more water was brought into the crippled ship, taking her lower into the sea.

Lucard knew the *Princess Diana* would sink. His job now was to delay that as long as possible. He reached over and snatched up the direct line to the engine room.

"Sven!" he shouted into the phone.

"Yes, sir," came the rushed reply.

"Keep the generators going! I need the lights and pumps to stay on as long as possible!"

"Yes, sir."

"The *Enchantment of the Waves* is coming to our aid. They're about 15 kilometers behind us, so they should be alongside in an hour or so." It gave Lucard great relief to announce the imminent arrival of the Norwegian Liner, the *Enchantment of the Waves*. The flagship of the Scandinavian Cruise Line, the *Enchantment* had been cruising just behind the *Princess Diana*, after a day in port at Civitavecchia as well.

"Yes, sir," Sven repeated. Lucard could hear the loud hum of the turbines in the background, and he tried to imagine the chaotic scene below decks.

"Is there water breaching yet?"

"Forward of us. We've lost the desalination tanks. They're underwater now. I shut down air conditioning and diverted that power to the pumps."

"Good. Do what you can. We'll get you all out in plenty of time."

"Thank you, sir!"

Lucard hung up the phone and again pressed the emergency beacon. The *Princess Diana* was equipped with the latest safety devices. Right after the initial explosion, distress signals were broadcast automatically from the bridge. Lucard wanted these signals to continue broadcasting as long as possible.

He raced to the starboard fly bridge and scanned the activity on the boat deck below him. Several of the huge lifeboats were loaded and on their way down to the water, with one or two others holding position out on the calm sea several hundred yards off the bow.

Lucard picked up his binoculars and surveyed the scene a little closer.

Where is Klaus, he wondered.

"Where? Where did you see him?" Zack frantically asked as he whipped his head around trying to locate Hayden on the Promenade Deck.

It was total chaos here. Scantily clad men from the Mardi Gras party were racing around trying to find their original lifeboat stations, their hastily tied lifejackets adding a surreal touch to their already unique costumes. If they couldn't find their assigned station, or got too scared, they simply hopped into the first available boat. Zack also saw that streams of terrified ship employees were coming up from below decks and taking refuge in the waiting lifeboats.

Klaus was taken aback by the amount of luggage that had materialized on the deck as well. Some of the passengers had obviously gone to their cabins and quickly packed their bags, thinking they could take the suitcases with them. He knew it was a pointless exercise. No luggage would be allowed in the lifeboats.

He could see small scenes happening as the bags were taken from the passenger and tossed aside. One man 10 feet away was actually stamping his foot up and down like a spoiled child, screaming he needed his luggage because it had his supply of Rogaine in it.

Through all this craziness, Zack did not see Hayden. It was hard to believe that Hayden would leave him in the cabin. It didn't make sense.

"I don't see him!" he said, his tension mounting.

"Jesus, Zack!" Bayne snapped. "It's a fucking shipwreck! Who the hell knows where he is? Let's just get into a boat."

"Something's not right," Zack spied Frank and Andy sitting in the lifeboat nearest them, both clinging to each other for moral support.

"Sir, you have to get in the boat now," Klaus said. He stood in front of lifeboat number 12, and held out his hand for Zack.

"No!"

"Zack," Bayne gripped Zack's other arm. "Hayden was heading to the boats. I'm sure he's on one, so get the fuck in!"

Zack looked at his ex-lover, a torn look on his face. "No," he wailed.

"We don't have time for this."

"Did you see him or not?" Zack demanded.

"Look, Zack," Bayne lowered his voice. "I didn't want to hurt you, okay? When I got to the cabin, I did see him. He was already dead, Zack. There was nothing I could do."

Zack's eyes pooled up with tears instantly, and a numbness flowed through his body. "What? No!"

"Little Man, I'm sorry! I'm so sorry." Bayne pulled Zack close and hugged him.

"Please, gentlemen, we have to load this boat," Klaus said gently.

"Oh, my God," Zack wailed. He blindly stepped over the gunwale and took a seat next to a man shivering in fear.

Bayne stepped in and sat next to Zack.

"I know it's hard, Zack," Bayne comforted. "I'll help you through this, I swear. He wanted you to be safe though. It was the last thing he said."

Zack looked up. "What?"

"He said to make sure you got into a boat. For me to take care of you."

"But you just said you found him dead! Now you're telling me he spoke to you?" Zack's voice rose in shock.

"Zack," Bayne tried to think fast. "He was hurt, he wanted you out of there."

"You left him? Hurt? Oh, my God!" Zack leapt to his feet and jumped past Bayne. Bayne shot an arm out and grabbed Zack's leg.

"No! Zack, don't you dare leave this boat! There's nothing you can do for him! It's our lives now!"

"Let go," Zack growled with an intensity that his ex-lover had never seen before.

Bayne actually leaned back a bit in surprise. "No!" he finally sputtered. "You're mine! You stay with me!" He let go of Zack's leg and stood, shaking in his rage.

"Is that what this is about? He was hurt, wasn't he? And you left him there to die, didn't you? My God, Bayne!"

"It's too late, Zack. We're safe. He's not. Forget about him." Bayne's eyes were dulled by a coldness that Zack hoped never to see again.

"Fuck...you!" Zack hissed. He drew back his right hand, balled it into a fist, and swung. The punch connected solidly with Bayne's left eye and knocked the larger man backwards into the bare laps of two shocked men.

Zack didn't even bother to watch Bayne fall over. He had already scrambled out of the lifeboat and back onto the sloping deck. He raced against the heavy tide of men emerging from the doors, and he quickly disappeared into the interior of the ship.

Klaus had witnessed the whole scene.

"Rick! Let's get the hell out of here!" Kurt urged. He tried to grab his lover's arm, but Rick shook him off. Rick had pulled up his mini-camcorder and was filming the chaotic scene on the Sun Deck.

"Shh!" he said. He cleared his throat and began speaking. "This is Rick Yung, and I'm standing on the sloping Sun Deck of the RMS *Princess Diana*, where not 30 minutes ago there was a thundering explosion. The ship is in obvious distress, and the captain has issued an order for all passengers and crew to board the lifeboats…"

Kurt couldn't believe what he was seeing. Rick the reporter had suddenly reappeared and was filming the calamity.

"You can see the sharp angle of the deck," Rick continued as he panned the camera across the emptying Sun Deck. Men were leaning into the downward, port side list and grabbing any handhold they could to get down to the lifeboats. "Passengers are trying to fight the steep tilt and get to the lifeboat stations which are…um, three decks below us, I believe."

Rick then raced to the port side of the ship and aimed the small camcorder down the side of the ship. The rows of brightly lit cabins could be seen dipping under the surface of the water.

"Are you insane?" Kurt shouted. "Let's get out of here!"

Geoff was confused and lost. He hadn't been in this part of the ship before, and he didn't know which way was forward anymore. He saw a heavy, steel fire door and decided to try that way.

He pushed open the cumbersome door and found he was in the Côte d'Azur dining room. Tables, chairs, linens, and other restaurant equipment were tossed aside like kindling, and there was a huge smoking hole right under the center of the far wall. The ceiling two stories above the gash looked like it was sagging down, about ready to break free and crash through the gaping hole beneath it.

His curiosity growing, he had to see what had caused the hole. He slowly crept over, knowing this was the single most stupid thing he had ever done. He should be running down the main stairs, just beyond the open glass doors 20 feet away and heading towards the lifeboats.

He peered over the blackened, torn edge and looked down. He could see through several ruptured decks of the ship, and swirling water was slowly creeping up at the bottom of the smoke-blackened pit.

"Jesus Christ," he whistled.

"Hello?" called up a frightened voice. "Help!"

"Is someone there?" Geoff called down. He saw movement on the edge of one of the shattered walls. There was a slight, jagged ledge sticking out, and a man's grime-covered frame could be seen.

"Help me! I'm trapped here! The water's rising!"

"Kirby?" Geoff asked, shocked.

"Geoff? Help me! I can't jump across to the door! It's too far! Throw me down a rope or something and pull me up!"

Geoff looked around. "Okay, hang on!" He frantically twirled around, searching for a rope, but there was none. "Where's a goddamn Christmas tree when you need it?" he mumbled to himself. Looking around, all he saw were destroyed tables, chairs, crockery and linens.

Linens!

He snatched up a long tablecloth and measured it mentally. Far too short to throw down to Kirby, he thought about knotting them together. But that sort of thing only worked in the movies. The knots would never stay together, and if Kirby fell into the pit because of a slipped knot, Geoff would feel responsible.

It was then that he had a flashback. He was in Africa, outside Zimbabwe on *Race Around the World 5*. His task to earn money for the next leg of the game was to wrap natural vines as a bungee cord around his ankles and jump off a tall tree. The native people had done it for centuries as a test of manhood. Geoff had been terrified the fragile vines would snap, but the locals had done something clever. They had braided several smaller vines into a much stronger single vine rope.

He had jumped and lived to tell the tale.

"I have an idea," he shouted down. "Just hang on a few minutes more!"

"Hurry!"

"Is there anyone else with you?" Geoff shouted as he began ripping the tablecloth into lengthwise strips.

Kirby looked over the side and into the void. The water was a lot higher, and Rex's body was no longer visible.

"Not anymore," he called up.

There was a sudden crackling sound above Geoff's head. He glanced up in time to see a large section of the bulging ceiling break free and fall down, directly into the hole.

"Kirby, look out!" he shouted, too late.

"Fuck! What was that?" Kirby called back up. "I almost got beaned!"

"The ceiling's breaking apart."

"Hurry up, Geoff! Get me outta here!"

Geoff looked upward again and could see the now exposed steel girders holding the floor above were bent and sagging. He realized that he didn't have much time. Crumbling bits of cement, foam insulation, and plaster were beginning to rain down, and it was only a mater of minutes before the entire ceiling section collapsed. Right on top of him.

Concentrating on the job at hand, Geoff's hands flew. He tore long, thin strips, then knotted them end-to-end. He shredded three other tablecloths and, sweating, knotted those ends together too. Soon, he had three very long sections of knotted fabric. He tied them together at one end and began to twist and braid them around each other.

This just might work, he thought, his fingers becoming numb from the abuse he was giving them. When he was finally done, he had made a section of twisted rope, easily 35 feet long. He tossed one end around a still-standing column and prayed it would hold. Then he tied the end around his waist. He walked over to the edge and looked down.

"Kirby! I'm going to throw this down to you. Grab it, okay?"

"Yes, okay," Kirby said, bracing his sturdy legs and reaching up.

Jesus, he's naked, Geoff thought in a flash, as he dropped the rope down. It dangled right in front of Kirby, who reached and missed, almost pitching himself forward into the hole.

"Watch it!" Geoff shrieked.

Kirby threw his weight against the wall and held on for dear life, his breathing rapid.

"Kirby," Geoff said, forcing himself to be calm. "Just reach up and grab it, okay? Let's try it again…" He pulled the makeshift rope back up and prepared to drop it again.

"I can't," Kirby wailed.

"Yes, you can. Just reach out and grab it. Ready?"

"Um…Okay…" Kirby reluctantly let go of the wall and again braced himself.

This time Geoff dropped it right into his hands.

"Can you give me more room? So I can tie it around me?" Kirby shouted up.

"No, that's all there is," Geoff said, stymied. Then he had a thought.

"Kirby, you ever see Cirque du Soleil?"

"What?"

"Have you ever seen that acrobat group, Cirque du Soleil?"

"Yeah, sure…But what…?"

"You know how they have those acrobats who fly around on the silk scarves?"

"Like, out over the audience and spinning around and stuff?" Kirby looked puzzled.

"Exactly! That's what I need you to do! Take the rope and wrap it around your wrists like they do. I'll pull you up!"

"I can't do that! I'll fall!"

"No, you won't! Wrap it tightly! They do it six times a night in Vegas! Eight, if you count Celine! You can do this, Kirby."

Kirby looked up, then down into the smoking hole. "O…Okay…" He reached up and began to twist the ragged rope around his wrists. It kind of hurt, but he didn't care. He just wanted out of here!

"Ready?" Geoff said calmly.

"Yeah."

"Okay. I'm going to walk forward. The strain on the rope will pull you up. You're going to swing out over the hole so be prepared, okay?"

Just then, another large chunk of ceiling fell down, missing Geoff's head by inches. The piece of debris disappeared into the hole.

"Geoff, I don't think I can do this," Kirby said pitifully. "It's too high!"

Looking up once more at the crumbling ceiling, Geoff growled, "We don't have time for hysterics, Kirby! You can do it. Get ready! I'm starting." He began to walk in the opposite direction of the hole. The braided rope was pulled taut by the pulley-like tension created by the rope wrapping around the column. The torque this action caused began to pull Kirby up.

"I'm moving! Wait! Oh, my God, wait! No! This won't work!" Kirby shouted.

"Too late," Geoff said through gritted teeth. He strained to push forward, and he felt the makeshift rope moving with him.

"Oh my God! Geoff!" Kirby shrieked. "I'm hanging over the hole! Don't let go!"

"If I do, I'm going down with you," Geoff correctly observed.

Kirby shut his eyes. He didn't want to see anymore. His arms hurt like hell, but he felt himself rising. He was dangling just off-center of the wound, inching up foot by foot.

He cracked open an eye and saw that the ceiling was much closer than it had been. "It's working!" he shouted.

"I know!"

Kirby got closer and closer to the top. He could almost reach it.

In a minute, it was over. Kirby, dirty, naked and sweating, was lying on the carpeted floor of the dining room pulling off the twisted tablecloth from his reddened wrists.

Geoff stood over him panting from the exertion. "Hey," he said slowly. "I finally got to see your ass."

Kirby looked up at him, laughed, and then gave him a huge hug.

Geoff smirked, sighed and shook his head. "Now let's get the hell out of here."

34

Sapphire Deck, *Princess Diana*, Mediterranean Sea

Zack raced through corridors and up stairwells, occasionally reaching a hand up to wipe blood out of his eyes. He knew he had a bad cut on his forehead, he just didn't care how bad. It seemed to take forever to get back to his cabin.

He was going against the tide of men heading down to the lifeboats, and more than one good-intentioned passenger had tried to stop him and make him go back down as well. Zack shook off their hands without comment and continued his trek up to his cabin.

Panting, he finally reached the door and was surprised to see it closed and locked. He patted down the pockets of the sweatpants he was wearing, but there was no keycard.

"Hayden?" he shouted at the door. "Are you in there?" He pressed his ear to the door, but heard no reply. "Hayden!" he shouted even louder. He looked around the companionway and found he was alone.

Not to be deterred, he stepped back and kicked at the door with all his strength. He heard a crack, but the narrow door didn't budge. It took three more hard kicks to finally pop the lock and open it. Pushing the busted door all the way open, Zack raced into the entryway of his shattered cabin.

He was stunned by the destruction. Debris and clothes were thrown all around, and through a few twisted wall beams. He could see the hole that had been his bedroom. His heart sinking, he realized that Hayden wasn't anywhere to be found. He must have left.

"Is someone there? Help me!" called a voice from somewhere below him.

Zack picked his way over to the doorway, opened the door, and looked down. He gripped the doorframe for support when he saw Hayden struggling to get out from under a fallen girder.

"Hade!" he shouted.

"Zack? Oh, my God! Are you okay? Bayne took you out..."

"Never mind about that, are you hurt?" Zack looked for some way to climb down into the sinking space.

"No, I'm just stuck! I can't get this damn thing off me, and the floor keeps sinking..."

"I'll get you out! Hang on," Zack said, determined.

He stripped off his life jacket and tossed it aside. He then gripped the doorframe and stepped down onto a slight protrusion from the floor. He picked his way down carefully, almost falling twice. Hand over foot, he climbed down the broken and twisted remains of his stateroom to where his lover lay. He could feel the floor swaying under his added weight, and the holes in the floor seemed to be getting bigger. Zack knew in his gut that they didn't have much time before the whole thing collapsed downward.

Finally, he could touch Hayden. In an instant he was straddling over his beloved. He leaned down and kissed the trapped man repeatedly.

"I was so scared I'd lost you," he said between lip presses.

"I thought you were gone!" Hayden replied.

Zack stopped kissing his lover and straightened up. "Okay, let's get this off you." He reached down and took a firm hold of the girder. "Push up as I pull," he instructed.

Hayden placed his hands under the beam and on a count of three, they began to strain. Surprisingly, the beam gave way instantly. It was made of aluminum, not steel, and the combined strength of the two men did what Hayden himself could not. With a loud screech, it bent up and Hayden wasted no time in scooting out from his former position.

"Oh, my God! I thought it was over," he whispered, so thankful to be able to move freely again.

"Let's get out of here," Zack urged as he felt the floor shudder underfoot once again.

"How?"

Zack looked up and found he was in the same position Hayden had been in before. Getting down there had been hard, but getting back up looked almost impossible. "We'll climb. Just like Shelley Winters would."

Hayden looked at Zack dourly. "She died at the end."

"Yeah? Well, we won't. Let's move!" He led Hayden over the cracked paneling to the place he had climbed down. The handholds and footholds were much trickier to grasp from the underside, and Zack strained to pull his weight up. Slowly, he retraced his steps. "Follow where I went," he advised Hayden.

"You got it."

The two men began to pick their way up. When Zack was holding onto a bent girder, he felt a big shaking below and looking back, he saw the center section of the flooring give way. The very spot where Hayden had been trapped disappeared into a gaping hole that went down several decks past the dining room below them. A blast of rushing air shot up, and dust and grit swirled around them. Hayden held on to his handhold, a pipe jutting out, and miraculously, both men stayed where they were.

Now that there was a major breech, larger chunks of the floor began to give way.

"We have to move faster, Zack," Hayden quietly urged.

"I'm trying, but there's no other handhold! I'm just two feet from the doorway, but I can't reach it!"

"Try!"

"I am! There's nowhere to go. We're stuck!" Zack's heart fell. He was glad that he had gotten his lover out of the pit, but his rashness to get in there to reach him had caused him not to plan an escape route back. "I'm sorry. I fucked up," he wailed.

"No, you didn't, baby. You saved my life!"

"But now we're both trapped." Hayden looked up and wished as hard as he could for a miracle.

Geoff and Kirby flew down the stairs and exited the heavy glass doors out onto the promenade of the Emerald Deck. Kirby had wrapped a tablecloth around his waist sarong-style, and the beige fabric flapped in the breeze. To their surprise and dismay, all the boats on this side, the starboard side, were gone.

Geoff gripped the handrail and spied the tiny crafts bobbing in the water about 200 yards away.

"Fuck!" he shouted.

Jebb and Nick, who had stationed themselves here, saw the frantic couple and quickly came over. Jebb informed the two panting men that there were plenty of boats still boarding on the port side. Clasping Kirby's hand and pulling him behind, Geoff raced back inside to cross to the other side.

With a tinge of envy, Jebb watched them go. He wanted nothing more than to get off this sinking ship, but he felt it was his responsibility to make sure every one of his charges got off first. He had met Nick on the boat deck, and together, they had taken a position here, by the main entrance to the boat deck with the express purpose of directing passengers to the other side.

After watching Geoff and Kirby run off, Jebb decided that Nick needed to get to the boats as well. He didn't want to be responsible for Nick staying on the *Princess Diana* any longer than necessary.

"Nick, you go on," he said, pushing his assistant towards the doors. "Go get in a boat."

Nick shook his head. "I'm not leaving until you do, Chief."

"Nick..."

Nick held up a hand. "You can talk all you want, but I'm not leaving without you."

"What is this? You're pulling an Ida Strauss? Get moving!" Jebb ordered. Nick shook his head again and folded his arms across his chest in a pose of challenge.

Stubborn fool, Jebb fumed. He took a deep breath and softened his voice. "Look, I'll only wait here another ten minutes or so. Then I'll go get in one myself."

"Jebb!"

Jebb and Nick looked aft and saw the bedraggled form of Dan Smith moving slowly towards them. Shirtless, and in tattered shorts, he was holding onto his chest and looked like he was having enormous trouble breathing.

It had taken Dan all this time to get to the boat deck. He kept having to stop and catch his breath. It was so damn hard to inhale. He had only been able to inch along a few feet at a time. Now, finally on the boat deck, he was relieved beyond belief to see Jebb.

"Dan?" Jebb said, incredulous at the strong man's weakened condition. "Are you okay?"

Dan reached the two men and grabbed on to Jebb's shoulder for support. "No. I have a couple of busted ribs."

"Oh, my God!"

"I'll live. Have you seen Lassiter? Rex Lassiter?"

Jebb didn't think he was hearing correctly. What did Dan want with that asshole? "What? No. Why?"

Dan puffed in another shallow breath. "It's a long story. I'll fill you...in on the complete details, later. But for...now...Brian Bainbridge. That name...mean anything to you?" The effort to talk was sapping Dan's strength. He had to focus hard, just to be able to speak.

"Brian Bainbridge?" Nick took a wobbly step forward. "Wasn't he that boy band singer who died last year? At a hotel in New York, I think."

"Right," Dan nodded slowly, grimacing. "Rex Lassiter killed him."

Jebb's mouth fell open. "What?"

Dan's words came in stuttered short bursts. He just couldn't get enough air in his lungs. "Look, there's no…time to explain. I need…to find Lassiter. Make sure he…doesn't get…away with this…"

"Nick," Jebb said, turning to his second-in-command, "Let's get Dan to a boat." They surrounded the wounded man, and each threw an arm around him. "We're going take you to the boats, Dan."

"No…I have…to find…Lassiter! You…don't understand…"

But Nick and Jebb were already moving, practically dragging Dan along for the ride. The pain the big man felt was intolerable. He began to think he might not survive this after all.

As soon as Geoff and Kirby burst through the doors on the port side, Geoff was relieved to find that they were indeed still loading boats. There was an orderly chaos to the whole scene as the hushed crowds nervously waited for their turn to step into the massive, hanging lifeboats.

To their right, an exorbitantly dressed group of partygoers waited impatiently to board a lifeboat that was being readied by crew members, but there seemed to be some sort of delay. As Geoff and Kirby got closer, they saw what it was.

A man in full Marie Antoinette drag, including a lavishly decorated 17th century, wide hoop skirt and towering powdered wig, was trying to get into the boat without ruining his costume. Unfortunately, his wide ruffled skirt was making the going extremely difficult. Finally exasperated by Marie's inability to move along, the man behind him, dressed like the Phantom of the Opera, complete with half mask, stepped forward.

"For Christ's sake, Steven! Get in the damn boat!" he snarled as he reached down and lifted the entire hoop skirt up, exposing perfectly pressed crinolines beneath. Now free to move, Marie Antoinette/Steven nodded gratefully and dropped into the boat, scooting over to allow other passengers to board.

Among the passengers waiting was a man clad only in a long sleeve dress shirt. The cargo shorts wearing, buffed-out guy next to him nudged him.

"You are so Stella Stevens right now."

The man in the shirt looked at him for a beat, then he lifted the shirt to reveal he was wearing nothing underneath and grinned. "At least she had panties."

The men in the immediate vicinity nervously laughed.

Geoff pulled Kirby to another lifeboat station two boats down where there seemed to be another problem. A passenger, tall, thin and carefully coifed, in khaki shorts and orange life vest, was struggling with a stockily built, swarthy ship's officer. They both had their hands on a huge vintage Louis Vuitton trunk that looked quite heavy.

"Let it go!" the passenger screamed.

"Sir! You cannot bring luggage with you!" answered the officer, again trying to pry the trunk from the hysterical man's hands.

"It was my grandfather's! I can't leave it behind. My mother would kill me!"

"Sir, I'm sorry, but you can't bring this! Let go!" The officer managed to pull hard enough to get the trunk away from the passenger. With a mighty heave, he swung it around and tossed it over the railing, where it sailed out into the air, before dropping from view.

"Now you can get on the boat," the officer said. "Sir."

"Jesus Christ!" screamed the passenger. "I'll sue! I'll sue!"

"Be my guest," snarled the fed-up officer. "Now get your ass in this boat and shut the fuck up!" He reached over and grabbed the stunned man's arm and practically threw him on the boat.

"Did you see that?" The passenger yelled to the half-filled boat. "That officer just assaulted me! You're my witnesses!"

A chorus of "fuck you" and "shut up" was his answer.

The officer continued to load the boat.

Geoff noticed that most of the people getting on the boats now were ship's staff. There seemed to be very few passengers left to evacuate. Laundry, kitchen and housekeeping crews from below decks were filing in, nervously chattering among themselves.

"Geoff, look!" Kirby yelped, pointing off into the dark night.

Geoff looked out and could see the lights of another large cruise ship bearing down on the *Princess Diana*. The unknown ship chose that moment to blast her deep basso fog horn, and a mighty cheer went up on the *Diana*.

"You can see the lights of a rescue ship. I don't know the name of her yet, coming to our aid," Rick said. "Terrified survivors of the *Princess Diana* are obviously overjoyed at seeing her emerge from the darkness." Kurt swung the camcorder away from his lover and out over the open water. The blazing lights of the approaching cruise ship lit up the viewfinder. He panned back to Rick.

"The Sun Deck, where we have been this entire time, is now clear of passengers and crew, so I'm going to go down to where the lifeboats are," Rick explained for the camera. He turned away and motioned for Kurt to follow him down. Before leaving Kurt panned over the now empty deck. Crushed speakers and other debris littered the teak decking. Kurt could make out feather boas, discarded masks, ropes of plastic beads, cups, glasses and the odd shirt here and there.

"Follow me down the stairs, okay? Keep the camera on!" Rick urged as he lead the way to the aft stairwell.

Kurt sighed, but did as his husband requested. He couldn't believe he was still on the sinking ship.

Earlier, Rick had flat out refused to leave, instead begging the body-builder to man the video so he could report the tragedy on-camera. Kurt knew his husband was a reporter, and in a situation like this, his reporter instinct took over. There was no force on earth that could have pulled the determined news anchor away from this unfolding story. So, instead of fighting him, Kurt had grabbed the camcorder and began taping him. It took Kurt's mind off his fear.

"You can feel the tilting of the ship as she sinks lower by the minute," Rick said calmly as he went down the steel steps. "The announcements for evacuating the ship have stopped, and it seems most passengers have gotten off the *Princess Diana*."

There was a loud roar and a muffled explosion that shuddered under the decking beneath their feet. Rick had to brace himself by placing a hand on the stairwell wall. Kurt almost stumbled, but he managed to keep his footing.

"That was another ominous explosion coming from below decks. The entire ship just moved," Rick duly reported. "I think we had better hurry to the boats now, Kurt," he added, as the gravity of the situation finally seemed to dawn on him.

"Thank fucking God!" Kurt agreed.

"Stop," Dan protested as loudly as he could, which wasn't very loud. His chest felt like it was splitting in two, and the constant pulling of Jebb and his cohort was killing him. He felt his strength seeping away rapidly, and he could no longer even help by moving his feet, He was basically being dragged across the carpeting now. The pain he felt was unbearable. "Jebb…" he gasped out, "Jebb, I can't breathe…I think…I'm going to…pass out…"

Jebb tried to keep his voice calm. "I've got you. Don't worry, Dan, I've got you."

Jebb's mind was reeling. Here he was, smack in the middle of a horrible disaster, carrying the first man he had actually been truly attracted to in months, and that man was hurt, perhaps dying. On top of that, his entire charter had just gone to shit, and his passengers might be dying as well. It was simply too much to have to deal with at a time like this.

The three men were halfway across the landing of the main staircase, heading towards the open door on the port side. Beyond that door were the remaining lifeboats. It was only about 60 feet away, and Jebb knew that their forward motion was harming Dan. But Jebb had no choice. He had to get the hurt man to a boat and into medical care. So he kept moving as fast as he dared.

"Jebb," Dan croaked, his voice barely above a whisper. He was determined to use the last of his strength to get out what he needed to say.

"Yes?"

"Lassiter…he…he…bombs! He blew…up the…ship…" Dan's vision became cloudy, then light, then dark, and he felt himself drift away. He felt like he was floating. His pain suddenly ceased to be a problem and he felt warm and safe.

As his body relaxed and became dead weight, it became harder for Jebb and Nick to maneuver him through the doors to the other boat deck.

"Jesus!" Nick gasped, struggling to carry the heavily built man, "Is he dead?"

"No, he's unconscious. Nick, we have to get him to a boat, fast!"

"What did he say? Lassiter blew up the ship? That's crazy talk…"

Jebb shifted Dan's body weight around to get a better grip. "I don't know what he was saying. He was out of it. It's not important now. Let's just get him some help."

As the three men stumbled through the port side doors and out onto the boat deck, two officers quickly stepped up and helped them with Dan. In moments, the unconscious man was placed carefully in a lifeboat, number 14.

Nick and Jebb clambered in after him.

Another sudden movement of the ship almost caused Hayden to lose his grip. "Zack!" he called up. "We have to do something. I don't think I can hang like this for much longer."

Zack looked back up and tried to judge the distance to the threshold of the doorway. Could he jump and make it? One quick glance down as the now gaping, splintered hole in the cabin's floor made him rethink the possibility of success.

"Hang on, baby. Just hang on!" he said.

There was a crashing sound above him, and he thought another section of the cabin had disintegrated. Afraid to look up, he forced himself to, and was rewarded with seeing the concerned face of the ship's officer who had been with him and Bayne down by the boats.

"Help us!" he shouted out quickly.

Klaus quickly assessed the scene and did some fast thinking. He had watched this determined man, Zack, leave the safety of the lifeboat to come back and look for his partner. He realized that the other man, the weaselly looking man named Bayne, had lied to him. He had deliberately left a hurt passenger behind.

After making sure that the lifeboat was full and lowered, Klaus had then taken off to come back up to this stateroom to see if there was anything he could do to assist. Zack's obvious love for his missing partner had touched Klaus, and he wanted to help.

So here he was, standing in the wrecked cabin.

He cleared some paneling shards away from the torn carpeting beneath his feet and sank to his knees. He then lay down and bent over the threshold, his body extending into the crushed stateroom. The officer bent down and reached his hands out, bandages and all. "Take my hand. I'll pull you up," he instructed in a calm, firm voice.

"Zack, be careful," Hayden said as he watched his lover reach up and take hold of the ship's officer.

Zack gripped Klaus' thick, muscular forearms and felt the strong hands lock around his. Klaus began to scoot his body back, pulling Zack upward. Grunting from the exertion, the officer continued to pull himself backwards, and as soon as he could, Zack let one hand go, and he clutched at the doorframe. He pulled himself up and over the threshold.

Panting, he quickly turned around and bent over to help Hayden. He shot a look back at Klaus. "I'm sorry, what's your name?"

"Klaus, sir. I'm the *Diana*'s first officer."

"Well, thank you, Klaus! Now grab a hold of me and help me pull!"

"Yes, sir," Klaus said as he wrapped his arms around Zack's waist.

There was another terrifying rumbling as the ship tilted over to the port side. It didn't swing back. Hayden scrambled as best he could up to Zack's old position on the wall and reached a hand up. Zack flattened himself down and stretched out into the open space. In his total concentration of saving the man he loved, he was only dimly aware of the loud cracking sound. Hayden had just barely let his fingers touch Zack's arm when the floor completely caved in. The wall section Hayden had been perched on fell away as well.

In a snap instant Zack arched forward and grabbed Hayden's right wrist.

With shocked terror, Hayden yelped as he swung out and away from Zack, over the collapsing floor. His kicking feet swung over the hole and his left hand reached up towards Zack, but he grasped only air.

Zack shut his eyes and forced all his strength into his grip of Hayden. He would not let go no matter what! He felt the slight tug of the ship's officer trying to give him stability.

"Zack…" Hayden said softly, as he dangled helplessly over the dusty, jagged hole. "Don't…let… go…"

Gritting his teeth, Zack strained and struggled to pull Hayden up. "Hayden," he grunted. "You have to…grab my arm with…your other hand…"

Hayden, feeling his strength draining fast, nonetheless took a deep breath and swung his body up. To his amazement, he managed to do it, grasping Zack's arm just above the wrist. Klaus began to drag Zack back and in moments, he and Hayden were hugging furiously and kissing each other repeatedly.

"Gentlemen, if I may suggest," Klaus gasped, catching his breath. "I think we need to get away from here now."

"I'll second that!" Hayden stood up.

"Here, sweetheart," Zack said, picking up a pair of dusty Seven For All Mankind jeans off the cabin floor and tossing them over to his naked boyfriend.

"Thanks," Hayden blushed. He quickly pulled them on, only to find they were Bayne's, several sizes too large.

Zack was about to rise when he noticed, under a shattered piece of paneling, his digital camera. Snatching it up in an impulse, he got to his feet and slipped the tiny camera into the pocket of his sweats. He picked up his life vest and handed it to Hayden. Rapidly rooting through the busted stateroom, he found another one under Bayne's bed. Pulling it on, he followed Klaus and Hayden, leaving his destroyed cabin for the last time.

35

Lifeboat Number 11, Mediterranean Sea

As dawn began to tint the night sky with dusty hints of blush and orange, Donnatella watched the scene playing out before her with an odd detachment. Sitting in one of the lifeboats gently bobbing at sea, away from the *Princess Diana*, she just couldn't completely grasp the magnitude of the situation.

From her sheltered spot in the lifeboat, nestled between one of the balloon-clad partygoers and a man dressed in silver lamé drag, she gazed out at her husband's favorite ship. She was so used to seeing the beautiful cruise liner floating commandingly at sea, that she had a hard time adjusting to the distressing vision playing out in front of her eyes.

The *Princess Diana* was far down at the head, and her rows of lights were tilted down at an absurd angle. She now had a strong list to port, so she was also tipping over as well as going down—a very unglamorous position for the beautifully designed ship. There was a lot of debris floating in the water near the stricken liner. Deck chairs, luggage, bits and pieces of the ship, and evacuating lifeboats all bobbed up and down on the gently heaving surface. Water was now swirling over the forecastle of the *Diana*'s bow, and it was apparent to all who saw her that she would not be afloat much longer.

The passengers in Donnatella's lifeboat were generally sitting in numbed silence. There was very little talking, and several couples clung to each other for support. The initial shock of the disaster had worn off, and now that they were reasonably safe, they had nothing to do but reflect on the events of the evening.

When the majestic *Enchantment of the Waves* had appeared, lights ablaze and blasting her horn, it was as if a great weight had been lifted from the subdued survivors in the lifeboat. Everyone on the tiny craft cheered and whistled, Donnatella included, much to her surprise. The crewmen who manned the lifeboat's large diesel engines, quickly spun the boat around and headed towards the newly arrived and gleaming cruise liner.

All the other lifeboats did the same. The small flotilla began to converge near the now stopped rescue ship. The *Enchantment* blasted her foghorn again, and to the joy of the *Princess Diana*'s passengers bobbing in the water, bright shafts of light appeared on her side, where her loading deck began to lower.

A boarding deck just like the one on the *Diana* was quickly locked into place and readied for the *Diana*'s survivors. Huge floodlights were turned on, and the entire area was bathed in light as bright as day.

The *Diana*'s lifeboats began to queue up and get in a circular order. Donnatella's lifeboat was the first one to unload. As the sturdy craft bumped gently up against the loading platform, several of the survivors began to cry from sheer relief.

An officer of the *Princess Diana*, the man in charge of this particular lifeboat stood up and informed the survivors on the proper way to exit the lifeboat. He asked them to leave one row at a time. He wanted no rushing, pushing or loud talking. Everyone would get off the boat as soon as possible, he added. They were safe now.

As the survivors carefully got up to exit the lifeboat, Donnatella happened to look upwards at the rows of *Enchantment* passengers eagerly leaning over the railings of the decks above. Much older than the *Princess Diana*'s passengers, and obviously straight, they watched in stunned fascination as they participated in a rescue at sea. They pointed to the sinking *Princess Diana* not more than a half mile away. They snapped hundreds of photographs, the small flashes from their cameras like the blinking lights on a Christmas tree. Many camcorders were aimed down at the disembarking survivors.

As the first survivors boarded the *Enchantment of the Waves*, a man at an entry computer would quickly ask for their name, and then type it in, creating a list of survivors. The survivor was asked if he or she needed medical attention, and if not, then another crew member would place a Scandinavian Cruise Line blanket carefully around them. Then the survivor was whisked away to the main dining room of the *Enchantment* where food, coffee, and stronger beverages were waiting.

As the feather-clad and sequined men of the *Diana* began to step off the lifeboat and onto the *Enchantment*'s platform, Donnatella watched the faces of the staid passengers and crew of the rescue ship turn from extreme concern and interest to shock. She began to laugh quietly. *The old farts have no idea what they're in for,* she thought.

When it was her turn to step off the *Diana*'s boat and onto the *Enchantment*, a rugged crewman reached out for her hand. "Hold on to my hand, ma'am," he said in a kind way.

She grasped it and pulled herself up out of the lifeboat and into the bright light of the landing platform. Instantly recognized by the crew as the wife of the president of the Lassiter Line, a respectful silence befell the *Enchantment*'s rescue crew.

"I'm Donnatella Lassiter," she said softly, stating the obvious. "I don't need a doctor, but I do need to get to a phone." She held up Rex's small silver cell phone. "This one must be broken. It doesn't work." With a sigh, she tossed it into her purse.

"Uh...Yes, ma'am!"

A kindly stewardess wrapped a warm blanket around her shoulders and led her away. As Donnatella stepped into a waiting elevator, she idly wondered for the first time since the explosion where her husband was.

Zack, Hayden, and Klaus dashed down the tilting main staircase as fast as they dared. They had to get down three decks, and since the footing was really tricky, they each had to hold on to the handrails to keep from tumbling forward and falling. The pronounced list of the ship seemed to become greater with each step they took.

The huge pieces of artwork that hung on each deck's landing were straining at their bolts to break free. Every now and then, an ominous crashing sound would come from somewhere else on the ship, the signal that something heavy had broken loose.

Klaus, breathing hard from both the exertion and fear, wondered how much longer the *Princess Diana* would remain upright, and he hoped that Joseph had left the bridge.

At last they got to the Promenade Deck and emerged through the plate glass doors onto the teak decking that was littered with discarded luggage, abandoned life jackets and lost articles of clothing.

There were no more boats here.

"The other side," Klaus said briskly, and he led them back into the ship.

Kurt and Rick were standing on the port side of the Promenade Deck as Kurt videotaped one of the lifeboats being lowered into the water. There were still two or three boats left, and empty boats were returning from dropping off their survivors with the rescue ship. There was no need for them, however.

The *Enchantment of the Waves* had trained amazingly bright floodlights on the *Princess Diana*, and the entire Promenade Deck was illuminated. By now there were only about 50 people still milling about, waiting to get into a lifeboat, and easily 90% of them were crew. Everyone on the deck was wearing a life vest, with an open locker nearby holding more, for anyone who should arrive without one.

Helicopters began to appear in the lightening sky, their flashing safety lights blinking. First there were two, then three, then six. They hovered over the rescue scene as the news media inside taped the horrible action beneath them.

Some of the helicopters were equipped with large floodlights, and they had trained those on the *Princess Diana* as well, adding more brightness to the scene. When it became clear that the last remaining survivors on the *Diana* were clustered near the last few lifeboats on the port side, all the news helicopters focused their attention there.

On the *Princess Diana*'s Promenade Deck, the swarthy, handsome crewman, the one who had not allowed any luggage into the lifeboats, began calling for people to enter another boat. The survivors clustered around this boat and, single file, hopped across the spreading gap between the *Princess Diana* and the lifeboat. The list of the *Diana* was making the lifeboats swing further away, and each second brought another fractional increase in the gap.

As soon as the survivors entered the lifeboat, they were shown to a seat by another crewperson. There was very little hysteria.

"The last few boats are boarding and preparing to lower, and it appears to me that everyone will be off the *Princess Diana* in a matter of minutes," Rick said to camera. "I will try and stay until the last boat is lowered."

Kurt peered out from behind the small video screen and looked at his lover with dismay.

"If we tilt the camera down this way," Rick continued, indicating for Kurt to move, "you can see the water has flooded over the bow of the ship."

Kurt moved woodenly and aimed the camera past Rick towards the front of the sinking liner. In the bright, artificial light he could see seawater sloshing around the lower edges of the balconies off the cabins of the Pearl Deck below them. Metal and plastic chaise loungers were clanking into each other as the water lifted them up, floating, from the disappearing deck.

Kurt realized that in only a matter of moments the water would be creeping its way up to the very deck they stood on. It was not a thought he relished.

"The tilt to the deck is steep and loading the boats has become more dangerous as the gap between the *Princess Diana* and the lifeboats gets larger."

Rick reached up and took the camera from Kurt's hands. He ran over to the loading boat near them and showed how survivors had to jump about two feet over the open sea to get into the boat.

"Gentlemen! I need for you to get in this boat now," called out the swarthy seaman in charge of the loading lifeboat. Rick and Kurt looked up and saw the darkly handsome crewman holding a rope and motioning for them to get in the loading boat.

"Not yet! We'll take the last one," Rick said.

"I said now!" ordered the crewman. "All passengers are to evacuate!"

"I'm a reporter. I need to stay until the end—" Rick began.

"I don't care who you are! This ship is going down. This might be the last boat we can safely lower! Get on, now!"

"Rick, let's go," Kurt said quietly.

"No! We'll take the next one."

"Rick," Kurt moved towards his lover. "This is crazy. The ship is sinking! Let's go." He gripped his lover's arm tightly and squeezed. "You got the story. You're risking our lives now."

Rick's face went through several emotions, before he finally nodded. "Okay," he said. "You're right. I'm sorry."

Just then, Zack, Hayden and Klaus stumbled out the glass doors and wandered onto the sloping deck.

"Hayden? Zack!" Kurt called out, stunned to see them.

Just as Zack was about to reply, the *Princess Diana* took a serious lurch. The ship rolled over a full ten degrees, causing everyone and everything on the slippery deck to fall and slide down, towards the railing, the only barrier between the *Princess Diana* and the water. A couple of tumbling women from laundry services tripped over some abandoned luggage and went sprawling over the railing, screaming hysterically on their way to the cold water 30 feet below.

The heavy, passenger-filled lifeboat that had been loading just a moment before swung out far, and then crashed back into the side of the *Diana*. The survivors inside screamed in terror as they were tossed about the interior of the covered boat.

Zack shot a hand out and grabbed Hayden as they slid down the deck. Hayden managed to brace his feet against a small bolted protrusion, and he and Zack stopped sliding. Zack clutched at Klaus' life vest with his free hand and caught him as well. Kurt and Rick ended up against a railing, and to Kurt's horror he could see the dark ocean swirling directly below him.

The crewman who had yelled at Rick and Kurt miraculously held on to his rope, and he swung out and back with the lifeboat. He was able to climb up, hand over hand, and eventually swung himself over to the open hatch of the lifeboat where he nonchalantly dropped in.

"Jesus!" Hayden gasped, holding his breath, as he waited for the ship to capsize and flip all the way over.

She didn't, but she didn't right herself either. The *Princess Diana* stayed heeled over, the angle of her list almost beyond reason.

"Lower away!" called out the swarthy crewman in the dangerously hanging lifeboat. The davit motors kicked in, and the small craft began to sink from view.

"Jump into the water and swim to a returning boat!" he shouted out to the few remaining people on the Promenade Deck who were now clinging to each other and the railings. "We can't lower any more boats!"

Zack looked up and watched in fascination as, one by one, the crew and staff still on deck timidly climbed over the railing and, holding hands, began to drop into the sea. The returning lifeboats quickly realized the situation and motored closer, crewmen inside them yelling encouragement to the jumping survivors. As soon as the people hit the water, they began swimming towards the approaching lifeboats. Zack suddenly realized that his small group were the only passengers left on the *Princess Diana*.

Horrific crashings and rumblings could be heard from the interior of the ship. Somewhere the crescendo of massive amounts of shattering glass was almost drowned out by another demonic metal-tearing screech.

"I think we'd better jump," Hayden said, stating the obvious.

Zack looked back at him and nodded. Klaus let go of Zack's hand and allowed his body weight to carry him, sliding down the rest of the way to the railing.

"Come on! Let's go!" he shouted back to Zack and Hayden. He quickly clambered to the edge of the railing and waited there for his two charges.

Zack and Hayden looked at each other, kissed tenderly, and then let themselves slide the rest of the way to the railing.

"Zack!" Rick called out from his place on the same railing, about 20 feet away. "See that boat there?" He pointed to a lifeboat that was positioning itself about a hundred yards away. "Let's make for that one!"

"Okay!"

Kurt forced his hands to let go of the railing, and he edged his way up, preparing himself for the long drop to the water.

"This is gonna smart," he grimaced.

"We're going to be fine, I promise," Rick said encouragingly. "Baby, I'm sorry we didn't get away sooner."

"Yeah. We'll talk about that later!" Kurt nervously laughed. He then watched in amazement as Rick pulled a small Ziploc bag out of his gym shorts. "What are you doing?" he asked.

"Saving the camera!" Rick dropped the small camcorder into the bag, closed the zipper and then tucked it back into his shorts.

"You found a plastic bag?" Kurt asked, flummoxed by this.

Rick just grinned and reached out for Kurt's hand. "Let's do it, baby."

Kurt took a deep breath, and clutched his husband's hand. "Okay. On 'three'…"

"One," Rick began.

"Two," Kurt said defiantly, working up his courage.

"Three!" they shouted together as they let themselves push out and fall.

Hayden had watched this scene wide-eyed. He turned back to Zack and was stunned to see him snapping off pictures with his digital camera.

"Zack! What are you doing? Let's go!"

Zack palmed the camera and nodded. "Just like them. On 'three.'"

"I love you, Zack."

Zack's eyes threatened to fill with tears. "I love you more."

Hayden took a deep breath. "One."

"Two."

They edged foreword and both yelled "Three!" Zack felt the rush of air, and his grip of Hayden slipped. Hayden had jumped a split second behind him, and that slight difference broke their contact.

They fell and fell and fell until Zack felt a hard whomp as he hit the surface of the ocean. He held his right hand high, the hand holding his digital camera. The bulky life vest stopped him from going completely underwater, though his splash was tremendous. Salty seawater splashed up on his face and head, the stinging pain from his forehead cut making him see stars for a few seconds. Quickly recovering from this, he began flailing about in the water, trying to get a purchase in the gentle heaving of the sea with his left arm.

"Zack!"

He looked over and saw Hayden treading water calmly, about five feet away. "I'm okay," he called back. Zack then heard a mighty splash behind him, and turning around, was relieved to see Klaus pop back up and easily swim to Hayden's side.

The three men began kicking their powerful legs in the chilly water as they slowly swam away from the *Princes Diana*.

36

The *Enchantment of the Waves*, Mediterranean Sea

In the *Enchantment*'s Enchanted Forest Dining Room, Geoff and Kirby were standing in line waiting to get a hot cup of coffee. Kirby, now dressed in a pair of borrowed and too-large sweatpants, had not left Geoff's side since they had stepped onboard.

Geoff walked up to the huge metal urn and was handed a warm mug by an elderly SCL employee who looked at them quizzically.

"Yes?" Geoff asked her, his eyebrows raising.

"Oh, I'm sorry. I've just never seen so many...well, your kind, you gay fellows, in once place before."

Geoff followed her gaze and looked around the spacious dining room. Everywhere he looked he saw subdued gay men from the cruise, still dressed in their Mardi Gras finery. In the harsh, bright light of the two story forest-themed dining room, the wild costumes many of them wore looked all the more exotic. Most of the men had wrapped themselves up in the blankets they had been given upon stepping aboard the *Enchantment*, but there were still enough bare asses casually strolling around to shock and titillate.

While many of the *Diana*'s survivors had gone back to the upper outside decks to watch the continuing tragedy at sea, more than a couple hundred had had enough and were content to sit huddled in the garish dining room. Geoff himself was torn between watching what would surely go down in history as a famous shipwreck and staying down here with Kirby, who absolutely refused go up to witness the beautiful ship's death throes.

Geoff couldn't really blame his handsome rescue victim. Kirby had been through so much in the past few hours that he needed some time to decompress. The game show winner was surprised to find he now felt very protective of the younger man wrapped tightly in a SLC blanket, standing so close to him.

Continuing to gaze around the dining room, Geoff noticed a large contingent of the *Enchantment*'s passengers were watching the scene as well from behind a roped off area. The Captain of the *Enchantment* had ordered that the survivors of the *Princess Diana* be given some privacy, and not be disturbed by his own passengers. So the *Enchantment* passengers weren't allowed into the large dining room, and it was killing them.

Even at this early hour, quite an assortment of elderly passengers from the *Enchantment of the Waves* had congregated here. Dressed like typically tasteless American tourists in loud aloha shirts and pastel polyester pantsuits, they whispered among themselves, pointed to the outrageously dressed men of the *Diana*, and generally looked stunned at what they had picked up at sea.

"Well," Geoff said to the lady behind the coffee urn, who had commented on the 'gays,' "Get used to it. I think we're here to stay for a while."

"Excuse me, young man! Yoo hoo!"

Geoff looked to his left and saw a senior woman dressed in a smock-style housecoat and loose Capri pants waving at him. Shrugging at Kirby, Geoff went to her side, the thick velvet rope separating them. Other *Enchantment* passengers leaned in to see what she was going to say and to look at a *Princess Diana* survivor up close.

"Yes, ma'am?" Geoff said politely. "Did you need something?"

"They say the ship that's sinking out there was one of them homosexual cruises. Is that true? Are you one of them gay boys?" The rural lilt to her terse voice gave away her Southern origins.

Geoff was not about to be insulted by some old crone after all he'd been through. "Yeah, I'm one of 'them gay boys.' What about it?" He planted his feet firmly and placed his hands on his hips in a threatening pose. No matter what awful, derogatory thing she said next, he would defend himself and the other proud men of the *Princess Diana*.

The woman sheepishly looked to her left and her right. She then dug into her smock pocket and pulled out a photograph. "Are you single?" she whispered. "I have a grandson, so nice. He and his boyfriend broke up two years ago. He's a doctor!" She shoved the photo at Geoff who glanced at it. The grandson was, to put it kindly, large, and definitely not Geoff's type. "Would you like to meet him? I'm sure I could arrange it," she said hopefully.

For once in his life, Geoff Corbin didn't know what to say. He certainly didn't want to hurt the old lady's feelings.

Kirby, who had come up behind his suddenly silent rescuer and heard the exchange, cut in. "I'm so sorry, ma'am, but Geoff and I are together." Geoff shot a quick look at him and Kirby just smiled.

The woman's face fell for just a beat. "Oh. Well, do you have any single friends?"

Geoff smiled kindly and spoke automatically. "I'll ask around for you."

The woman beamed. "Oh, thank you! My grandson Hiram is such a catch! He owns his own home, two acres! He drives a Porsche, and his last boyfriend told me that he's hung like a horse and hot in the sack, so spread the word." She winked at Geoff.

Nonplussed, Geoff backed away and went back into the dining room with Kirby. They wandered back to the large coffee urn to fill up Kirby's empty cup. The urn lady watched them, a clear look of unease on her face.

"Thanks for saving me from that," Geoff said, nodding his head in the direction of the proud grandmother.

Kirby smiled. "That was kinda cool. She loves her grandson. I just didn't think you wanted to get fixed up by Gramma."

"Well, thanks."

The two men fell silent as Kirby poured out a cup of joe. When he finished doctoring it with cream and Sweet 'N Low, he turned to Geoff. "Listen, um…," he said, stopping midway through swirling his plastic spoon around the cup rim.

"Yes?"

"I just…I just want to say thank you again. You saved my life. I'll never forget that." Kirby looked up at the older man, unabashed admiration spreading across his handsome features.

"Don't sweat it—" Geoff started to say offhandedly. But when he saw the complete idolization in Kirby's face, his cocky attitude evaporated. "I'm glad I did," he said softly, gently stroking Kirby's face.

"You know," Kirby grinned. "There are times when you're not such a complete dick."

The corners of Geoff's lips curled up slightly. "Oh?"

"Yeah." The built young man leaned up and kissed Geoff on the lips. Gently at first, then pressing harder, his warm tongue darted forward and explored Geoff's mouth. Geoff responded happily in kind.

A loud crash was heard, and both men broke away and turned back to see the coffee lady staring at them, horror on her face. She had dropped ten stacked cups in shock when she saw the two men make out in her dining room.

Geoff and Kirby started to giggle, and then they began to laugh out loud.

Geoff placed an arm around Kirby's shoulder and led him away, over to an empty table. Just as they were about to sit down, Kirby happened to see a ship's officer with a lot of gold braid on his shoulders talking to a small group of Titan staff. Remembering his ordeal with Rex, he quickly crossed to the gathering.

"Excuse me?" he said softly. "Are you the captain of this ship?"

Captain Ramon Estevez, in the middle of giving important directions to the Titan staff, stopped in mid-sentence and stared at his newly acquired guest. "Yes?"

"I need to talk to you. I think I know what happened on the *Princess Diana*."

The captain, not wanting to appear rude to a survivor who had just been through a terrible ordeal, nonetheless didn't have time for a chat. "I'll be glad to speak to you later, young man, but right now, I'm very busy, and…"

Kirby wouldn't be brushed off. "It's about Rex Lassiter. I think he blew up the ship."

A tall, striking redheaded woman whirled around and stared at Kirby.

"What did you just say?" Donnatella asked.

37

Lifeboat Number 14, Mediterranean Sea

Zack, soaking wet and shivering, had his arms around Hayden as they tried to get warm. Standing together by the gunwale of the lifeboat, they watched in numbed silence the unbelievable scene before them. Kurt and Rick were nearby, with Rick narrating into his small camcorder as he filmed the spectacle 100 yards away.

Just behind them, Jebb sat with the still form of Dan, hoping that the big man would pull through. Dan had an oxygen mask over his face, pumping pure air into his abused lungs. Luckily, one of the rescued passengers on boat 14 was an emergency room doctor from Atlanta, and he was monitoring Dan's vitals. He had assured Jebb that Dan's injuries, while severe, were survivable. Nick, sitting next to Jebb, had tears seeping from the corners of his eyes. He eventually buried his head in his hands.

Not ten minutes earlier, Zack, Hayden, Kurt and Rick had been pulled aboard the sturdy lifeboat, dragged, soaked to the bone, from the cold sea. They had collapsed in relief at being saved.

Klaus had waited until everyone else was taken out of the water before allowing himself to be brought aboard. As soon as he was aboard and looking back at the stricken *Diana*, he was stunned to see four officers from the bridge scamper down to the boat deck, Captain Lucard included.

Lucard carefully scanned up and down the boat deck while the other men jumped overboard. He shouted loudly for all to abandon ship, yet he got no response. Safe in the belief he was the last man aboard the *Princess Diana*, he jumped into the dark water and was now swimming slowly towards lifeboat number 14.

Klaus leaned over the gunwale of the lifeboat and screamed encouragement for Lucard who, because of the enormous strain he'd been under the past hour, was lagging. Klaus kept shouting, letting Lucard know he didn't have much farther to go.

When Lucard was about 30 feet from the lifeboat, flailing away at the water and not getting any closer, Klaus impulsively jumped back in. He quickly covered the short distance to his new lover and grabbed Lucard's life jacket. He kicked hard and dragged the exhausted captain to the lifeboat.

Many hands reached out and pulled Lucard up and into the boat. He was then laid on the bottom of the craft, spent. Klaus climbed back aboard and scrambled to Lucard's side. One of the lifeboat's crewmen stripped off his jacket and handed it to Klaus who tenderly covered Lucard with it.

"Oh my god! She's going over!" Kurt sputtered excitedly, pointing at the *Princess Diana*.

All heads snapped up and stared at the sloping ship.

Rex fought off the waves of nausea and the feeling that he was going to black out, and forced his left hand to inch up the banister and pull his weight up another riser. He knew he only had about four more risers to go until he was on the Promenade Deck.

The sharp angle of the listing liner made his progress painfully slow.

Rex tried to make his mind focus on escape. He knew he could do it. He just had a few more steps to go, and then he was safe.

His right arm dangled uselessly, it being broken in three places. His right side hurt like a motherfucker from where he'd hit a protrusion on his fall into hell. The deep gashes on his left thigh and calf had been seeping blood constantly, though the impromptu tourniquet he'd fashioned out of a rag he'd found had staunched the flow somewhat. He also knew he had a concussion, and possibly a skull fracture.

Fucking Kirby! The pipe he'd hit him with had done damage. Rex's head throbbed with intense pain, but he knew as long as he felt pain, he was alive, and that was all that mattered.

Rex had been surprised by the turn of events with little Kirby. The sudden fall into the pit had been terrifying, and he had blacked out after hitting something hard with his right side. Sputtering, he had come to, floating face down in the rising water near the explosion sight. Barely able to keep his head above water, he had clung to a broken tabletop that had floated up as the water rose. Too weak to yell for help, he kept passing out and waking up.

He had finally managed to climb off the tabletop and onto a destroyed landing. Fumbling his way through deserted, sloping hallways and corridors, he finally had stumbled to the main staircase and had begun his assent up one deck to escape the destruction he himself had wrought.

He had to stop for a moment, as the blackness threatened to take him once again. Feebly shaking his head to ward off unconsciousness, he gripped the banister tightly.

The *Princess Diana* kept moving under his feet. He could actually feel the growing list to port.

As he made himself breathe deeply, he listened to the crescendo of sounds that assaulted his ears. There was the not-to-distant roar of water that he knew was claiming this beautiful ship. Somewhere a horrible crashing sound indicated a large, heavy object tearing loose of it's restraining bolts. Earsplitting screeches of metal giving way. A hundred dishes crashing to a hard tile floor nearby. Loud creaking of wood snapping, stressed beyond its limits. A horrific jangle as the slot machines in the casino began to tip over, crashing to the flooring, coins busting loose. The splash-splash-splash of 20 computers sliding from their carrels, pitching over the brass and glass railing, and falling four stories onto the flooding Grand Atrium floor.

He forced his eyes open and stared at the landing. So close. He gripped the handrail, and willed himself to move up another step. He tried to focus on the portrait of Princess Diana that now hung at an absurd angle. It barely registered, when, with a slight tearing sound, the heavily-framed portrait came loose and fell down the stairwell. It came to a rest halfway under the lapping water that was slowly creeping up the stairs.

Just one more riser, Rex thought hazily.

All at once, there was an odd movement under his feet, and he felt like he was flying. He was suddenly plunged into darkness, and had the dim sensation of sailing over the stairs and tumbling headlong towards the heavy glass door that was the gateway between life and death. Life, waiting outside the tempered plate glass doors. Death, being trapped behind them, inside the sinking liner.

"My God," whispered Zack.

Hayden stood slack-jawed next to him as they both watched the *Princess Diana* begin her final roll. The crisp, clean superstructure of the cruise liner was slowly burying itself into the water. Almost completely on her left side, the *Diana's* lights suddenly went out, plunging her into an eternal darkness. Though the sun was just minutes away from rising, it was the floodlights from the *Enchantment of the Waves* and the helicopters above that kept the *Diana* illuminated as she continued to roll over.

More horrible crashing sounds rumbled forth from her as her deck chairs and a multitude of other loose items slid down the perpendicular decking, and fell into the sea. The two immense radar spinners on top of the bridge wrenched free from their mountings as the wires on the radar mast broke free. The loose wires whipped through the air, each one snapping lethally with a loud crack, as the hurtling spinners crashed with a mighty splash into the sea.

A dark movement against the white superstructure caught Zack's eye. "My God! Look! There's someone still there!" he shouted.

Klaus stumbled over to his side. "What? Where?"

Zack pointed to the boat deck, the area they had abandoned not that long ago. "There! See? By that pillar?"

"My God, Zack's right!" Hayden excitedly yelled.

Lucard, hearing the conversation, struggled to his feet. Unnoticed by the other men, he picked his way over to stand behind Klaus. He too could now see the lone figure struggling to escape the ship.

"I thought everyone was off..." he muttered. "I was sure everyone was off."

Klaus turned to the voice behind him and saw Lucard. He put a comforting arm on his shoulder.

"I'm so sorry, Joseph."

Jebb looked over in the direction that everyone as pointing at. He saw a dark figure holding on to something, but just then, Dan coughed twice and his eyes flew open. "Dan!" Jebb cried. "Dan...hang in there...you're going to be fine."

"Wha...what's...happening," Dan asked weakly through the plastic mask over his mouth and nose.

Jebb smiled. "Relax, baby. Everything's going to be okay. Just relax."

Horrible memories flooded back to Dan. "Lassiter..." he mumbled.

"Shhh..." Jebb soothed. "I'm sure he's fine."

Kurt gripped Rick's shoulder tightly. He was focused completely on the struggling figure on the *Princess Diana*. "Why doesn't he jump?" he asked. "Jump!" he shouted over the water in a futile attempt to make the faraway man hear him.

Rex was clinging to a railing by the glass doors and trying to clear his head. The noises around him were deafening. With an inhuman screech, the glass doors behind him suddenly blew apart, sending a shower of glass pebbles spraying outward. Hurricane-like rushes of compressed air fleeing from deep within the doomed liner escaped through this new breech, whipping past Rex with the force of a tornado, and almost knocking him off balance.

He knew he had only a few more feet to go, and then he could jump overboard. He didn't have much time, but the constant noise, rushing air and shifting of the ship confused him, keeping him rooted in place.

"Jump!" Hayden shouted as well. Soon almost all the men on lifeboat 14 began shouting, trying to spur the man into action. The helicopters had also spotted the lone man and trained several spotlights on him.

The crew of lifeboat number 14 were torn. Number 14 was the boat nearest to the *Princess Diana*, and they wanted to move in closer to make the distance between the man and the lifeboat shorter, but if they got too close to the sinking ship, they might put themselves in danger. This quandary resulted in no decisive action being taken, though the other lifeboats that had returned for survivors were quickly leaving the immediate area, giving the doomed *Princess Diana* a wide berth.

The *Diana* continued her slow roll over.

Rex felt the deck under his feet completely tip away. He was now hanging from the railing he gripped tightly with his left hand. He was dangling over water, which in his addled state, didn't make sense to him. His natural instincts for survival had kicked in, and he irrationally clung to the railing. He supposed he should let go, drop to water and try to swim away, but he just couldn't get his hand to release its iron-like grip.

The treacherous sea that had snatched ships from mariners for centuries had the *Princess Diana* in its liquid grasp and was now in a great hurry to claim its prize. Water continued to flood the ship through a thousand openings as the beautiful *Diana* buried herself deeper and deeper into the swirling sea. Portholes, windows, open deck doors and companionways were all avenues for the unstoppable tentacles of blue-green water that greedily flooded her, weighing her down, bringing her closer to the bottom with each passing second.

Unearthly sounds continued to issue forth from the stricken liner. It was as if the *Princess Diana* was loudly protesting her fate the only way possible— metal tearing, glass shattering, wood snapping. Great, grinding shrieks and bellowing basso booms rumbled across the gently heaving sea, reaching the ears of dazed survivors watching numbly from their lifeboats.

Now entombed forever in water, the massive generators in the engine room were lifted from their mounting bases and crashed heavily downward, ripping through steel walls and machinery like tissue paper. The remaining bank of 15-foot-high panoramic windows from the Côte d'Azur dining room imploded inward as the unstoppable pressure from the sea claimed the once-sumptuous dining room. Volcanic geysers of air and water began to spurt out from the exposed open portholes, windows and forgotten sliding glass doors of abandoned stateroom balconies on the starboard side of the *Diana*, which now faced heavenward.

This cacophony of deathly sounds terrified Rex. He dangled there, in place, hanging by a railing, as confused indecision kept him suspended over the turbulent waters immediately surrounding the ship. Precious seconds ticked by. He saw the beauty that was the *Princess Diana* crumbling around him, and he resigned himself to the knowledge that he wouldn't live beyond the next few moments.

Rex had fought all his life to get more than his share. He'd taken what he wanted and not cared about the consequences. He'd married a woman he didn't love because she made him look better. In business, he'd cheated, lied, and stolen. He'd given in to his erotic passions and made others pay the cost.

Rex knew what kind of man he'd been, and he wasn't about to make false amends for it now that the end was at hand.

His only real regret now was that this was not the way he had planned on checking out. It wasn't fair! He was supposed to die a rich old man, in bed, after a rousing session of hot sex with a muscular, hung young stud.

He felt the ship continue its roll, past the point of no return.

"Nooooo!" he finally screamed out in frustration, rage and defiance.

"Why didn't he let go?" Hayden whispered, staring in shock as the huge ship rolled over the dangling man, burying him in the water under tons of steel and iron.

"Jesus," Zack breathed.

With an almost graceful spin, the *Princess Diana* continued her roll, the huge white superstructure submerging itself into the whipped up whitewater surrounding it. She hung there, lying completely on her side for a few moments. The remaining water in the swimming pool sloshed out and sprayed over the upper railings. The last lingering chaise loungers and other debris skittered across the perpendicular decks and crashed down.

The *Diana* floated still for a beat, then her bow began to slip further beneath the waves. As this happened, her stern began to rise up. With a mighty roar of protest, the cruise ship rolled the rest of the way over, and showed her vibrant blue hull to the dawn sky for the first and last time.

Her twin propeller pods were still, and as they rose in the air, water cascaded off the enormous brass blades. The *Princess Diana* began a slow clockwise corkscrew, spinning leisurely around as she sank further and further down.

Rick stared in stunned awe at the unbelievable event happening in front of him, his camcorder forgotten in his hand. Kurt, filled with a terrible sadness, pressed in close to him.

Zack hadn't forgotten about his small digital camera though. He quietly snapped image after image as the *Princess Diana* twisted her way into the Mediterranean Sea.

With a mighty gurgle, she slipped away, gone from view, gone forever. There was a sudden, rough turbulence in the sea where she had last been, the flotsam and jetsam being the only marker that she ever existed.

"She's gone," Klaus breathed softly.

"How did this happen?" Lucard said to no one. Klaus turned around and faced his captain. "I'm so sorry."

"They'll bloody well blame me, you know. They'll blame me..."

"I'll be by your side the entire time. This wasn't your fault, Joseph. I'll let everyone know you did all you could do," Klaus said, ready to stand by this man no matter what. "You're a hero."

Lucard blinked twice, then reached out and pulled Klaus close, hugging him with all his strength. Klaus, his heart filled with longing and love for his captain, squeezed back, and before he realized it, Lucard was kissing him. Klaus happily kissed him back, trying to draw the captain's mental pain into himself. Lucard relaxed and allowed his new lover to hold him.

The other men on the lifeboat realized there was more to these two men's relationship than had been thought, and they drifted away, giving them space.

Lifeboat number 14 slowly turned in a wide circle and began the short journey to the *Enchantment of the Waves*.

38

Enchantment of the Waves,
North Mediterranean Sea

Zack leaned up against Hayden and shut his eyes. Bright sunshine poured through the floor-to-ceiling windows of the Enchanted Forest dining room, so sleep was difficult, even though he was exhausted.

Hayden was tired too, but he couldn't shut off his mind. He had just been through so much, and he needed to put everything in perspective. The warmth of Zack's body against his in the faux-leather banquette where they sat felt reassuringly good.

"How's your head, sweetheart?" he whispered to his lover.

"Hurts. Throbs," Zack replied, shifting around as he tried to get more comfortable.

Upon arrival on the *Enchantment of the Waves*, Zack had been whisked to the ship's hospital to have the gash on his forehead checked out. Seven stitches, two shots and one Tylenol later he was out, and he and Hayden were given fresh clothes from the onboard men's shop. They had returned to the large dining room to be with the rest of their group.

Kurt, also wearing new clothes, was passed out on the banquette opposite them, and Rick was nowhere to be seen. Frank and Andy had stopped by earlier to make sure everyone was okay, and then had left to go take a shower in the *Enchantment*'s gymnasium.

Garrett Gardner had positioned himself at a table near the service doors to the kitchen so he could inspect each new food tray as it came out. He was circled by a legion of his fans, and he was entertaining them all by doing bits from his stand up act. Toby sat wide-eyed near him and made sure no one else got too close to the star.

Hayden patted Zack's thigh and let him be, then turned his attention to the view out the large windows. He idly watched the growing flotilla of small boats and ships that were tagging along as the *Enchantment of the Waves* returned to Civitavecchia. The news of the *Princess Diana* disaster had obviously spread, and the jackals were gathering. Captain Estevez of the

Enchantment had imposed a strict news blackout until the ship docked. He wanted to leave the *Diana* survivors in peace for as long as possible.

The passengers of the *Enchantment*, however, had different ideas. Now that everyone from the *Princess Diana* was aboard, and the *Enchantment of the Waves* was underway, the brazen tourists began to filter in and started peppering the men of the *Diana* with question after question. And for the most part, the men of the *Diana* welcomed the attention. They gleefully told harrowing tales of survival and drama, entertaining the older tourists with their stories.

In return, the passengers of the *Enchantment* dug into their own suitcases and began a clothing donation drive. The men from the *Diana* had been rescued with only the clothes on their backs, and seeing as how these were clothes worn for the Mardi Gras circuit party, that meant they were basically naked.

Now they were dressed in a motley assortment of baggy plaid Bermuda shorts, extra large gym shorts, and golf shirts. While these were not the trendy styles the gay men of the *Princess Diana* preferred, they were touched by the generosity of the *Enchantment*'s passengers.

Hayden sighed. It was going to be a madhouse when they docked, he knew. Cruise line officials had already been through, painstakingly taking information on each survivor so that customs in Civitavecchia would go as smoothly as possible, considering not one passenger from the *Princess Diana* had their passport anymore. The cruise line had also taken next of kin information so that family and friends back in their home cities would know that their loved ones were safe. Hayden also knew there would be God knows how many members of the media waiting at the pier, and travel arrangements home would have to be made for everyone.

But that wasn't what was bothering Hayden. He kept trying to think of scenarios that would keep Zack in his life. Long-distance romances rarely worked, and he knew he would not be able to stand being so far away from this man. No, one of them would have to move if they were to stay together. But who? Would Zack willingly give up his life in Los Angeles to move to Barcelona? For a budding photographer, the Spanish city would be an ideal place to start a career.

Or was Hayden being selfish? Why should he expect Zack to uproot his life for him? Would he be willing to do the same? Could he give up his European life and move back to the States?

"What time is it?" Zack mumbled, breaking Hayden's concentration.

Hayden looked at the large, ornate clock hanging on the wall. "About 10:15."

"When do we get to Rome?"

"They said this afternoon. Probably around 2:00."

"Oh."

"Go back to sleep, baby."

"Okay," Zack drifted off.

Hayden felt a warm hand press gently on his shoulder. He looked up and saw Rick dressed in a pair of too large khaki shorts and a loose tee-shirt that read "World's Best Grandpa" standing beside him.

"Hey."

"Well," Rick said, grinning. "As your intrepid reporter, I've been doing a little snooping. You're not going to believe what I've heard. Get this—there was only one death. Every single passenger and crewmember from the *Princess Diana* has been saved and accounted for, except, are you ready for this? The owner himself, Rex Lassiter. He was the only fatality."

Hayden's eyes grew large. "My God, everyone's all right except for him? That's amazing! How is that possible? That hole in the ship was so big."

"Beats me. I guess everyone was up on deck for the party. For once, being the dancing queens that we are saved us."

"So that man we saw, the one who didn't jump at the end, was Lassiter?"

"Yes, and there's more."

Kurt raised a sleepy head. "What's going on?"

"Hey, sweetheart," Rick smiled. He leaned over and kissed his man gently. "I was just filling Hade in on all the news I dug up."

"So…tell us."

"Well, our little friend Kirby hooked up with Lassiter last night."

"What!" Kurt and Hayden said together. This woke Zack up, and as he rubbed his eyes, Rick told all.

"Yes. Apparently Lassiter played both sides of the fence. He tried to kill Kirby! They were trapped in Kirby's cabin after the explosion, and Lassiter admitted to him that he blew up the ship. It seems the cruise line is in financial trouble, and they now believe Lassiter thought that sinking the *Princess Diana* would pay enough insurance to settle his debts."

"You mean to tell me," Zack said, now wide awake, "that I almost lost the man I love, that we all went through this hell because some asshole business-man didn't want to declare bankruptcy?"

"I'm afraid so."

"Jesus Christ," Hayden whistled.

"It gets better, or worse, depending on your viewpoint," Rick continued.

"I don't see how," Kurt added, stunned.

"Trust me. Remember that guy who died at the hotel in Barcelona? The man who drowned?"

The three men listening nodded.

"It looks like that wasn't an accident either. Lassiter told Kirby that after he had sex with a man, he would kill them to keep them quiet. They're trying to piece it all together, but it looks like he killed the guy in Barcelona, and two men during the cruise as well, including Jorge, that hot guy from Miami we had dinner with that first night at sea."

"My God!"

"You're kidding!"

"Jesus! Poor Jorge."

"Lassiter's wife is pretty upset by all this, naturally. They've had to sedate her. Jebb Miller is with her now. Oh, they just had a prayer service for the *Diana*'s crew, and there's going to be one for us on the pool deck at noon." Having spilled his guts, Rick sank gratefully down onto the banquette next to Kurt.

There was a moment of silence at the table as the men all absorbed what they had just learned.

"Zack? Oh, thank God!" called a strident voice, interrupting the quiet.

The men looked to the source, and each one was surprised to see Bayne Raddock hurrying over. Zack didn't know how he did it, but Bayne was dressed impeccably in a crisp pair of pressed khakis and a pale yellow cashmere sweater. He came to the table and stopped, looking at each face hesitantly. His right eye was bruised and blackened, and it distorted his normally perfect face.

"Little Man," he finally ventured. "Thank God you're safe! I have been so worried. You, you freaked out and left me on that boat. I didn't know if you made it off the ship alive or not!"

Zack look at his ex coolly. "Yeah, I made it, as you can see. I'm just amazed you have the balls to face me—to face us—after what you did."

Bayne blushed and stiffened his posture. "I'm sure I have no idea what you're talking about." The pompous man shot a glance to the others at the table, and held out his hand, ready to shake. "Why, hello, Kurt. Hello, Rick! Dreadful, all this, isn't it?"

Kurt and Rick, having been filled in earlier on Bayne's role in Hayden and Zack's harrowing escape, stared dully at him. Bayne's outstretched hand hung alone in space for several beats. When it became obvious that no one would shake with him, he quickly retracted it, his face reddening even more. He decided to ignore the snub, and in a bid to gain control of the situation, he returned his attention to Zack. "Little Man, I don't know what he told you," he said stridently, as he jerk his thumb in Hayden's direction. "But don't believe him!"

"You fucking asshole!" Hayden spat out. "You left me behind, trapped, to die."

"What are you talking about? Zack, is that the lie that he told you? It's not true!" Bayne hastily said. He reached out to touch Zack, and Hayden's hand shot up like a snake, gripping his wrist with viselike pressure. Hayden began to rise out of his seat, his rage barely held in check.

"Hayden," Zack said tightly, reaching a hand up and placing it lightly on Hayden's shoulder. "Don't." Hayden released his hold on Bayne who, even more shocked and embarrassed, just stood there. "You know what, Bayne?" Zack finally said in even, controlled tones as he tried to contain his own rising ire, "Hayden's right. You are an asshole. I guess I always knew it, I just didn't want to face it."

Bayne's face contorted as his anger grew.

"So, yeah," Zack continued, never taking his eyes of his ex. "I believe Hayden completely. You left him behind. It's exactly the sort of lowdown, scummy thing you would do. Now, if you don't mind, I'd like you to get out of our sight before I let my boyfriend loose to kick your ass."

"You're going to take this piece of trash's word over mine?" Bayne sputtered, incredulous. "Don't be stupid, Zack. I love you. Now, let's go."

Hayden strained to jump up. Zack's firm hand on his shoulder kept him in place.

"I'd be careful who I called trash," Zack said, his eyes narrowing. "And this isn't about you being in love with me. This is about you being upset that you've lost one of your possessions. Because that's how you've always thought of me. As a possession."

Bayne couldn't believe what he was hearing. Even if there was a ring of truth to what Zack was telling him, he wasn't going to stand here in front of Kurt Farrar and his newscaster boyfriend and listen to it.

"Well, I did buy and pay for you, didn't I?" Bayne countered hotly, without thinking. "When I met you, you had nothing. Nothing! You lived in a one-room apartment in Hollywood, for Christ's sake! I gave you everything! A beautiful home, prestige, a place of importance in the community as my partner."

Zack sighed. His anger flowed away. Bayne would never get it, so why bother? "Just go away, Bayne. You're not welcome here."

Now Zack was dismissing him like he was an errant maid, Bayne realized, dumbstruck by the notion. "Trash!" he spouted defiantly. "You're both trash! How I even entertained the thought of taking your cheap, Target-shopping ass back is beyond me." He turned to leave, but stopped. Then he looked evilly at Zack and smiled tightly. "You're so pious now, aren't you," he continued, taking one last swipe. "But, in reality, you wanted me to be your sugar daddy. You used me just as much as I used you." The hurt look that flashed across Zack's face made Bayne feel like he'd scored a hit. It felt wonderful. "You, Little Man, will always be a low-class ex-druggie who had no problem living off his rich boyfriend! I'll admit the sex was hot, but that's all you were ever good for. That's your total worth in the world, a hot fuck."

Now it was Zack's turn to try to get up. Only Hayden held him back.

"Sweetheart, let me," Hayden whispered.

He stood up and stared Bayne eye to eye. "You bastard," he hissed.

"Fuck you, trash."

Hayden drew back his fist and solidly connected with Bayne's aristocratic nose. The crunching sound of breaking bone was unmistakable. Bayne's eyes fluttered, and he reeled backward, collapsing in a heap on the floor.

"Oh, my nose!" he wailed, unintentionally mimicking Marcia Brady. He reached up and clutched the bleeding mess. "My nose!" he repeated.

"Get the fuck outta here," Hayden said evenly, "before I kick your ass into next week like I said I would."

Bayne struggled to his feet and shot daggers at Zack. "You're not worth it."

Zack looked at his ex evenly. "You're right. I'm worth more."

"You'd better leave, Bayne," Kurt piped up. "I think we've all had enough of you."

Being put down by his inferior ex and his loser new boyfriend was one thing, but to have the mega-wealthy and socially prominent Kurt Farrar tell him off was quite another. Bayne couldn't believe it. "You're all trash!" he sputtered. "Trash! Fuck you all!"

Kurt got to his feet quickly, and his massive body seemed to swell even larger. "What did you call us?"

Bayne blinked and ran. He stumbled through the crowd holding his broken nose tenderly.

After he left, Hayden returned to his spot next to Zack. He saw his lover was terribly upset by the scene, and he threw his arm around him and drew him close. "Let it go, baby. The guy's a freak."

Zack looked up, his eyes brimming with tears. "How could he say all that? It wasn't that way at all." Zack was humiliated that the core of a relationship he had once valued had turned out to be rotten. Bayne had never really loved him. Zack now saw that he had only had been a prize, a trophy, and that realization stung. Not because Zack loved Bayne anymore, but because Bayne's words demeaned his place in the world in front of the man he now cared so much about.

"Fuck him, Zack. The guy's screwed up in the head," Kurt offered. "You're worth 20 of him, and he knows it. That's why he had to say all that bullshit. He just wants to hurt you any way he can. Don't let him win."

Zack looked up and a trace of a smile started to creep across the huge man's face. "Besides," Kurt continued. "What the fuck is wrong with shopping at Target? I love Target! Bulk toilet paper. How could you not love that?"

It was exactly the right thing to say. The four men broke out into laughter, and the nasty fight was immediately forgotten.

After a few minutes, Hayden rose up again. "I'm thirsty. Anyone want anything?"

"I'll take a bottled water," Kurt said.

"Me, too," chimed in Rick.

"I'll go with you," Zack said, as he got up, too. They left the table and Rick turned to Kurt.

"Hey," he said, "I have something I need to tell you."

"Shoot."

Rick took a deep breath. "When we dock, I have to hightail it to the media trucks. I'm going to do a live report for UBC from there. They're going to air the tape we shot as the ship was sinking."

Kurt's surprise was evident by the expression on his face. "So soon? You're kidding, right?"

Rick shook his head. "Nope. Kurt, honey, we were there! Do you realize what a coup that is for UBC? For me? I got a call in to New York using a satellite phone. It's all set up."

Kurt stared dully at his husband.

"I would have hoped you'd realize what this means for me. For us," Rick said sadly.

Kurt had to face facts. He was married to a reporter. A good reporter. It was what Rick did. It was what and who he was. To ignore that fact would be to deny the truth. To expect him to not want to be the best in his field wasn't fair. Kurt had always been enormously proud of Rick's accomplishments, but last night, watching him keep his cool and report on the sinking as it was happening, had given Kurt new respect for his lover.

Could he, in all good conscience, hold Rick back from seeing just how far he could go?

"Alrighty, " he finally said. "Go give 'em hell! But this doesn't mean I've agreed to move to New York." The big man sighed heavily. "I know we need to come to some sort of decision, but I can't think about that right now. Okay?"

Rick nodded. "Okay."

In the *Enchantment of the Sea*'s sterile infirmary, Jebb sat next to the sleeping bulk that was Dan Smith. A nasty bruise had slowly overtaken the dozing man's right eye, and the wrapped bandages around his muscular upper torso were dazzling white, in sharp contrast to his deeply tanned body.

Jebb arched his back and stretched. He had 1,000 things he needed to be doing right now and sitting by the bedside of a guy he barely knew wasn't even in the top 500.

He looked around the compact but efficient space. The infirmary was composed of four rooms, a small outer waiting room, a pair of hospital-like bedrooms—each with two twin-size beds, now currently occupied by four sleeping *Princess Diana* survivors who had minor injuries, including a heavily sedated Donnatella—and an examination room that also served as lab and operating room. This was the room that Jebb and Dan were in now. There was scary looking stainless steel medical equipment bolted to the walls, and locked cabinets filled with vials and pills.

If the party boys knew about this pharmacy, Jebb giggled, there'd be a line a mile long for checkups.

Deciding he wasn't making a difference just waiting here, Jebb gave Dan another lingering glance, then stood up. *I need to get upstairs and start sorting out the mess,* he thought as he reached for the oversized sweatshirt with a Christmas tree emblazoned on it that he'd been given by a well-meaning *Enchantment* passenger.

"Where you goin'?" Dan croaked.

"You're awake!"

The injured man blinked a few times, then forced his eyes open. "Yeah. I have been for a few minutes. How long you been sitting here?"

Jebb blushed. "About two hours. Not long." He moved closer to the bed, his face just inches from Dan's.

"The ship?"

"Gone. Sank."

"Lassiter did it."

Jebb sat down again. "Yeah, we know. How do *you* know that? You said something about that when we were trying to get you off the boat."

Dan tried to sit up, but a flash of pain kept him rooted in place. His ribcage wasn't quite ready to move, apparently. "I guess I owe you an explanation."

"That would be nice," Jebb said, giving Dan a dour smile. "Let's start with, what's your real name?" The surprised but guilty look on the injured man's face told Jebb volumes. "We've made up a list of passenger's names for the American Embassy to use so they can rush through temporary passports and visas. There's only one Dan Smith from Berklawn, California, your so-called place of residence. And, unless you're an 87-year-old African-American, that ain't you."

"Dan is my real name. Only it's not Smith. It's Scarpetta. And I live in L.A."

"So, why the fake name? Are you married or something? Taking a gay cruise for a few kicks before heading back to the wife and kids?" Jebb's clear eyes clouded for just a moment as he braced himself to hear the bad news. It would just be some gigantic cosmic joke if he'd fallen for a straight guy who was just "experimenting." It was a hassle he just didn't need.

Dan laughed, and then quickly stopped. It hurt too much to laugh. "No, Jebb," he said. "I'm not a divorced stock broker. I had to lie about that to keep up my cover. I'm a private investigator. An out gay private investigator."

Jebb's eyebrows shot up. "A private gay dick?"

"Careful, now," Dan said smiling, then grimacing. "I was hired by the family of Brian Bainbridge, the pop star. He was found dead in a hotel jacuzzi last year."

Jebb nodded. "I remember."

"Brian was gay. It was a tightly held secret. His record label didn't think the 12-year-old girls would buy CDs from a homo, so it was all kept very hush-hush. The police ruled he died from an accidental drowning. There were clues all over the scene that that wasn't the case; poppers, sex toys, lube, condoms, you name it. Apparently it was easier for the cops to conclude he was some one-man faggot freak show who got carried away while jerking off than to do some actual police work. I mean, Christ. Who needs condoms if you're only jerking off?" Dan scoffed with disgust. "I believe Brian's record company put some pressure on the detectives in charge to come to a 'safe' ruling. Remember how the Back2Boyz's record sales shot up after his death? No one wanted to mess with the cash cow by admitting Brian was gay and killed while getting royally fucked up the ass in a hotel hot tub. Case closed."

"Jesus," whistled Jebb, engrossed in the story.

"Brian's parents hired me to dig a little deeper. After a lot of false leads and legwork, I found out that Rex Lassiter was staying in the same hotel that night. I did a little more digging and discovered that were a string of 'accidental' gay deaths that all had one thing in common. Rex Lassiter was staying in the same hotel as each victim. When I pointed this out to the lead police investigators in each case, they all brushed me off. No one was particularly concerned about solving the murders of a bunch of faggots. Rex Lassiter is a powerful and formable man, and no one believed him capable of it—or believed he was secretly gay."

"So all that gay bashing that asshole spouted, that was an act?" Jebb gasped, thunderstruck.

Dan nodded slightly. "You know he was in financial trouble, right? He figured that by sinking the *Princess Diana*, he'd save his ass. And since the ship was going down during a gay cruise, he could protest and rant and rave about all the queers, and then have a little fun on the side. Who'd ever suspect, right?"

"My God!"

Dan's features set into a hard mask of contempt. "I was following him as closely as I dared, but I got distracted, partly by you, and he got away from me a couple of times. You know what happened then."

"The man in Barcelona, Rhett? Jorge? Timothy? All killed by Lassiter?"

"I believe so. I can't prove it, but I know I'm right. And I'll never forgive myself for not stopping him sooner."

Jebb digested this information. Then he looked Dan right in the eye. "What about us? What happened between us? I didn't imagine that. You were into me."

Dan slowly reached a hand out and gently squeezed Jebb's arm. "No, you didn't imagine that. I am into you. But, Jebb...you see..."

Christ, he's not single, Jebb thought. *Can't I get a break?*

"I'm in recovery for sexual addiction."

Jebb actually laughed out loud. Then, catching himself, he quickly apologized. "I'm sorry! I don't mean to laugh, but..."

"I know, I know," Dan sighed. "Trust me, I've heard all the jokes." He sighed again heavily. "The thing is..." he continued, forcing himself to sit upright. It hurt like hell, but he wanted to explain himself to Jebb on a physically level field. "I want sex all the time. But once I sleep with a guy, I'm over it, and already looking for the next one. I'm in intensive therapy for it, and it's brutal. The good news is that I'm learning to control my urges and impulses, but it's a daily struggle."

"So, what? You can never have sex again?"

Dan laughed, despite the pain. "Yes, I can have sex. It's just that I'm really working hard at changing my pattern of behavior. I'm only going to sleep with a man I think I stand a shot of going the distance with."

"I see." Jebb hung his head and stared at the checkerboard floor.

"I think that might be you, Jebb."

Jebb looked up, surprised.

Dan gave a lopsided grin. "Don't look so shocked. You're an amazing man. I knew it the second I met you."

Jebb beamed at the words.

"I just need to take it slow," Dan continued. "I don't want to fuck it up like I usually do. I don't want to hurt you. I like you too much to do that."

Jebb leaned over and tenderly kissed him. "Thanks for telling me. But I think I'm willing to take my chances with you."

"I'm really sorry I lied to you before, but I was on the job…"

"Then you owe me, and I intend to collect." Jebb winked and rose to his feet. "Listen, I have a million things to do. I have to get back to work. It's crazy up there." He pointed to the ceiling, meaning the survivors of the *Princess Diana.*

"Okay."

"We'll be in port in a few hours. Now that you're all wrapped up, the doctor thinks you'll be fine. They're taking you to a hospital in Rome, just in case. As soon as I can get away, I'll come see you. We'll have dinner together."

Dan smirked. "It won't quite be the Spencer House, will it?"

Jebb leaned down close to the investigator's face once more. "It's not the place, studly. It's the company."

Dan welcomed the passionate kiss.

39

Sports Deck, *Enchantment of the Waves,* Mediterranean Sea

Jebb cleared his throat and tapped the microphone. A loud *thump, thump* blared out of the Sports Deck speakers. "Gentlemen!" he said into the mike, his voice coming through loud and clear.

All heads turned up. The Sports Deck of the *Enchantment* was covered with the solemn survivors of the *Princess Diana*. There was hardly a spare inch of space as the 1,300 men stood here silently watching Jebb. Wearing their newly borrowed garb, they were a colorful, if not hilariously dressed crowd. It looked like a passle of senior citizens had drunk from the fountain of youth, suddenly turning young and buff.

Above the milling *Diana* survivors, hundreds of the *Enchantment*'s passengers and crew had also gathered. They were crowded around the Vista Deck above the Sports Deck watching as well.

Jebb was standing on a small, tightly conformed deck that went around the outside of Sherwood's, the *Enchantment of the Waves*' nightclub. He was surrounded by the entire Titan Tour staff, several ranking officers from the *Princess Diana*, including Klaus and Captain Lucard, as well as a smattering of officers from the *Enchantment*.

"Gentlemen of the *Princess Diana*," Jebb said loudly, then, in recognition of the Enchantment's passengers and crew, he added, "And ladies and gentlemen of the very beautiful, and very timely, *Enchantment of the Waves...*"

There was laughter at this and a spontaneous, loud cheer went up from the *Diana*'s survivors. The cheer grew into a roar as the survivors clapped their hands and stomped their feet in a show of gratitude for the assistance they had received.

Jebb waited several minutes for the din to quiet. "We have been through a harrowing ordeal," he said, as the crowd finally settled down. "We have been through a test, and come out the other end all right. By the mercy of God or Buddha, or Allah or Jennifer Lopez or whatever higher power you believe in, we have come through intact!" There was another thunderous cheer.

"Now, I'd like for all of us to take a moment of silent prayer," Jebb continued. "I'd like for each of us to take this time to personally say thanks to our higher power for our safe delivery from disaster." He bowed his head solemnly, and every head below him followed suit. Even the passengers of the *Enchantment of the Waves* bowed their heads and joined the group prayer.

Jebb's personal prayers included thanking God for bringing the hot hunky man resting in the infirmary below into his life. After a full minute, he looked up. "Amen!" he said softly.

The voices of over 2,000 people repeated, "Amen!"

Jebb smiled broadly. "Okay," he said. "Now, let me take a few minutes to fill you in on what will happen when we arrive back in Italy. We have completed a full registry of all passengers from the cruise. When we disembark in Civitavecchia, each of you will be briefly questioned by the Italian authorities. Don't worry, it's only a formality. Representatives from both the American and Canadian consulates will be there as well to help you replace your travel documents and to help you with any other questions. If you're a guest from a country other than America or Canada, please notify me or any other member of the Titan staff so we can get documentation help for you as well. There will also be representatives of the Lassiter Line who, along with your Titan Tours staff, will make your return travel arrangements to your point of origin. The Lassiter Line representatives will also have all the forms you'll need to put in claims for your lost belongings and luggage. Each of you will be given 500 euros to buy whatever immediate necessities you need. Complimentary hotel rooms are being arranged now, and you'll be informed of where those are when you disembark."

Jebb paused and looked over the crowd. They were listening and seemed to be okay with what he was telling them. He knew there would be problems galore later on, but for now, everyone seemed calm.

"Now, the media will be out in force," he continued. "And you are free to talk to them, ignore them, whatever, it's up to you. We will not allow them into the areas where you will be going through your disembarkation process. If you wish to avoid them, there will be alternative exits made available. So," Jebb said, taking a deep breath, "now that that's all said and done…" He looked to his left and saw DJ Kenny BamBam standing near the *Enchantment*'s portable DJ station that had been hastily set up next to the *Enchantment*'s outdoor bar. BamBam gave him the thumbs up and took his place behind the CD changers.

"…And now that we're all okay," Jebb grinned, "I think it's fitting that we celebrate the way we, as gay Americans, celebrate best! We have so much to be thankful for, least of all the fact that we all made it out alive."

DJ BamBam, who had snuck several of the CD albums full of his best tunes into his lifeboat by hiding them under his bulky life vest, flipped a few switches and suddenly, a distinctive and well-known disco bass track thumped out of the *Enchantment*'s speakers. After a few beats of intro, a strong, lone female voice rang out through the air.

The hundreds of men standing below Jebb looked at each other in confusion as the song began to pick up tempo. Suddenly, as if on cue, each and every *Princess Diana* survivor recognized the song as Gloria Gaynor's dance classic, "I Will Survive." They began to shout and yell in approval. The older passenger's from the *Enchantment* couldn't believe what they were seeing.

Thirteen hundred voices began to sing along with the song. As the music kicked into its famous chorus, the men clapped, cheered and started to dance. The level of enthusiasm was unbelievable.

One of the *Enchantment*'s officers, shocked by what he was seeing, pushed through the collection of Titan staffer's surrounding Jebb. "Sir, this isn't appropriate! I thought this was going to be a solemn ceremony! You've made this into a celebration and a party!"

"With all due respect," Jebb replied evenly, "As a minority, gay men and women have seen so much death and destruction in the past two decades that we've learned how to celebrate life. And life *is* a party!"

By now the men of the *Princess Diana* were dancing their asses off. Zack, Hayden, Kurt and Rick were in a tight cluster near the edge of the pool, their arms around each other's shoulders, singing along with the crowd. Kirby and Geoff spied them, and shimmied over, happily joining the group.

Many of the older, stodgy passengers of the *Enchantment* also seemed to have gotten into the groove. Hips that three years before had been replaced, began to sway in time to the music. Some of the more adventuresome souls went down and joined the party happening on their large pool deck.

The men of the *Diana* welcomed them with open arms, pulling them joyfully into the dancing crowd. Soon, the entire two sun decks of the *Enchantment of the Waves* were one big disco, the sadness of the lost *Princess Diana* fast fading.

Alone together in a crowd of thousands, Zack reached his hands up and snaked them around Hayden's neck, attempting to draw his handsome lover in close.

Hayden reluctantly pulled back. "I love you so damn much," he choked out, struggling not to cry, but failing.

Zack suddenly felt the seemingly hopelessness of their situation in the depths of his being. The hard, cold truth was they lived continents apart. It was nice to pretend that they would be together forever, but in the harsh light of day, the reality was probably vastly different. "Oh, baby, you know I feel the same way! I don't want to let you go, but what the fuck are we gonna do?" Zack stared at Hayden with desperate longing, and didn't even realize he'd begun to cry as well.

Since neither man had an answer to Zack's question, they simply clutched each other tightly, and swayed together gently, lost in a sea of dancing, swirling revelers.

As the *Enchantment of the Waves* steamed her way back to Italy, surrounded by an army of smaller craft, the party on the Sports Deck continued. Eventually, there was a total blurring of lines as *Enchantment* passengers and *Diana* passengers were completely mingled together. They danced with each other, accepted each other.

With the possible exception of Zack and Hayden, no one was afraid to have a good time, and everyone felt the waves of love and compassion that flowed freely. Young and old, gay and straight, they were now one group.

This was what the Titan cruise had been all about. Camaraderie. Sharing. Acceptance. Being safe among friends. Even the loss of the beautiful ship and personal possessions hadn't dampened this genuine spirit of the cruise.

These wonderful feelings would be remembered, and cherished, by the survivors of the *Princess Diana* for the rest of their lives.

40

Port of Civitavecchia, Italy

All hell broke loose when the *Enchantment of the Waves* finally docked in Civitavecchia. It had been a particularly slow news week, and the media glommed on to the sinking of the *Princes Diana* with a fervor that approached hysteria. Over 5,000 people were crowding the pier, waiting for the *Enchantment* to dock at the port, and it seemed as if 90% of them were reporters. Everyone wanted to get a glimpse of the survivors from the first major shipwreck of the 21st century.

At the Lassiter Lines Terminal, each *Princess Diana* survivor disembarking through the main set of doors was assaulted by an onslaught of cameras and reporters all jockeying for a piece of the story. All of the Titan Tours men had become mini-celebrities in the eyes of the world, and no story about the *Princess Diana* disaster was left unturned. While many of the passengers basked in their 15 minutes of fame and gave harrowing details of dramatic rescues, the vast majority of the *Diana*'s passengers simply wanted to go check into their hastily arranged hotels, call their families and get some sleep.

Upon their arrival in Civitavecchia, Rick and Kurt had dashed off the *Enchantment of the Waves* to find the local UBC contact. A hastily set up camera crew had been waiting, and Rick was on camera within 15 minutes, giving the world the incredible story of the sinking of the *Princess Diana*.

Rick's professionalism and composure during his instant on-air reporting from the Lassiter Line pier did wonders for UBC's ratings. His personal videotape shot from the sloping decks of the sinking ship was played and replayed almost every 20 minutes on C-UBC, UBC's 24-hour cable news channel. His compassionate interviews with other survivors, his diligent determination to get the facts straight, and his general good looks all helped make him the "face" of the story for UBC.

Quickly realizing that his presence on a gay cruise obviously meant he was homosexual, Rick came out during his first broadcast. Kurt, who was one of the first people Rick interviewed on air that night, was surprised to later find out that the kyron scroll on the screen that gave his name and hometown, also identified him as "Rick Yung's Husband."

These facts did nothing to dissuade the brass at UBC from doggedly pressuring Rick to accept the network position in New York. Thinking that money was the issue, they boldly doubled their offer. Added perks such as permanent substitute hosting duties on UBC's morning show, *Wake Up, America!*, were also thrown on the table.

Sensing Rick's rising star status, ABC and Fox both offered Rick a contract that actually surpassed what UBC offered. UBC quickly came up with an even better offer: in addition to weekend anchor, Rick could assume one of the primetime anchor slots on the Wednesday night broadcast of *Up Close*, UBC's nighttime magazine show that was challenging NBC's aging *Dateline*.

Both Kurt and Rick understood the time had come. A decision had to be made.

Zack and Hayden, sadly realizing their time together was fast coming to an end, collapsed in emotional exhaustion in their hotel room. They placed the "Do Not Disturb" sign on the door, and attempted to seclude themselves away from the media frenzy that surrounded all the survivors of the *Diana*.

Ultimately giving in to Rick's incessant prodding, Zack released the digital photographs he had taken during the *Princess Diana*'s death throes. The starkly graphic pictures were immediately splashed on all the front pages of the world's leading newspapers, and also on the cover of *Time* magazine. There was talk he would be a shoe-in for a Pulitzer Prize. Rick then pulled a few strings and got Zack an interview with Time-Life, Inc.'s L.A. bureau for a staff photographer position.

The job interview was set for the week he got back to L.A.

The investigation into the sinking began almost as soon as the *Enchantment of the Seas* docked. Kirby found himself being interviewed by the Italian police for over six hours regarding his near fatal run-in with Rex. Word quickly leaked out that the president of the shipping company was the prime suspect, calming the world's fears that terrorists had struck again.

The stark fact that there was only one confirmed death due to the sinking of the *Princess Diana* did nothing to stop the media's hyperbole. The American news magazine shows played up the disaster like it was the *Titanic II*. While the gay angle to the mega-story sometimes proved too good to pass up, gays and lesbians everywhere were actually surprised by the way the media sensitively handled the subject. While some ultraconservative newspapers and magazines wasted a lot of ink commenting on, and condemning, the role homosexuality played in the disaster, the more responsible press chose to take little note of it, an encouraging sign that the times, they were a-changing.

Instead of holding the concept of gay-only cruises up for ridicule, the mainstream press instead dove into the background of Rex Lassiter, digging up shocking secret after secret. New information was coming to light regarding his involvement in the death of not only Brian Bainbridge, but also the deaths of several young men throughout London and Paris, as well. The evil man's personal actions became the actual story, and eventually it was but an interesting footnote that the whole tragic saga of the *Princess Diana* bombing had happened during a gay cruise.

In fact, during the Inquiry hearings held almost one year to the day after the sinking of the *Princess Diana*, the phrase "gay cruise" was used exactly ten times, and all ten times it was uttered by Jebb Miller when he testified about Rex Lassiter's actions during the voyage.

After a month of testimony, The Board of Inquiry rightly laid the entire blame for the *Diana* sinking at the hands of Rex Lassiter.

Rex's beautiful widow, Donnatella, was secreted out of the Lassiter Lines terminal immediately upon the *Enchantment of the Waves*' arrival there. She let the media know through her press secretary that she was in mourning, and in seclusion in Rome, and not granting requests for interviews. The widow of the most hated man in the world since Bin Laden quietly negotiated behind the scenes for a quick resolution for her share of her husband's estate, which was much more meager than she had expected. When she was spotted by the press, which was very rare, she was always in the company of a handsome young Italian man who, it was said, had once worked at Gucci.

Captain Joseph Lucard announced his retirement from shipping in a short statement given to the press by a Lassiter Line representative. During the Board of Inquiry meetings, he was to become a much-loved figure as he calmly and matter-of-factly explained his and his crew's actions on the fateful night of the *Diana*'s sinking.

Heavily burdened by a personal feeling of guilt, he was extremely relieved to hear several Inquiry investigators highly commend his actions of that awful night. When the Board released its findings, Captain Lucard was exonerated of any and all blame for his ship's loss.

In the only interview he ever granted about the tragedy, he claimed that the events of that night had changed him forever. He no longer felt like he was part of the sea. He was now looking forward to the future, and all the promise that future held.

He also mentioned he was opening a bed and breakfast in London with his partner Klaus Jergin, and would happily remain landlocked for the rest of his life.

Lassiter Lines ultimately declared bankruptcy, and soon was in the throes of a buyout by Scandinavian Cruise Lines. The lawsuits and legal wrangling from lawyers representing passengers and crew from the *Princess Diana* would last for years to come.

Jebb Miller was slightly taken aback by the instant fame thrust upon him and his company in the wake of the disaster. At the same time he found himself falling headlong into a passionate love affair with Dan Scarpetti. He was being courted by all the networks and news magazines for interviews explaining Titan Tours and what exactly went on during a gay-only cruise. In concise, enthusiastic replies, he quickly downplayed the more sensational aspects of gay travel, and focused his responses instead on the wonderful feelings of inclusion and camaraderie his guests enjoyed.

Titan Tours' next six cruises sold out completely in under three weeks.

Four Months Later...

41

Pacific Palisades, California

The grand house sat on the crest of a slight hill giving it a commanding view of both the city and the ocean. Georgian in design with thick Doric columns anchoring the wide double-tiered porch, it almost looked like a municipal building or courthouse. Proudly out of place with the California contemporaries that were its distant neighbors, the stately home gave off the impression of enormous wealth and protected safety.

Behind the thick brick and wrought iron wall that surrounded the property were vast, immaculately tended grounds with prize-winning flowerbeds placed in perfect proportion to the house itself. Crowding the graveled driveway was a line of cars, delivery trucks and caterer's vans. Valets ran back and forth creating more room for the arriving guests.

Hayden's brother, Clay Beasley, and his lover, Travis Church, both television and film stars, got out of their brand-new slate blue Range Rover Sport, and Clay tossed the keys to a waiting valet. A pretty young woman with a headset on rushed up to them, confirmed their names on the wedding guest list, and directed them into the house.

"Is it straight?"

"Not yet…there. Now it is."

Zack looked back in the mirror and saw that Hayden was right. It was straight. He smooth down his hair and brushed some lint off his shoulder.

"What about mine?" Hayden asked, trying to muscle into the full-length mirror.

Zack turned around and fiddled slightly with Hayden's knotted silk tie before announcing, "Perfect." He grinned. "Why am I so nervous? This is going to be easy!"

Hayden smiled and reached over to brush a stray lock of hair off of Zack's brow. His finger lightly traced the faint scar that was Zack's permanent souvenir from the *Princess Diana* disaster.

He then stood back to observe himself and his lover in the gilded floor mirror. They were in identical Cameron Fuller designed FullJack suits of light gray wool. They both had on navy shirts with matching navy silk ties. The suits had been custom-fitted for them.

The door to the guest bedroom opened and Clay walked in, dressed to the nines in beautifully cut Prada. He smiled when he saw his brother and his lover dressed alike from head to toe, including identical small red rose boutonnieres pinned to their breast pockets.

"Hey," Clay said as he hugged his brother, then Zack. "I was told you two were up here, and I wanted to say hi before the ceremony started."

The handsome actor was the same height as his twin brother, but much blonder. His unbelievably striking face was about to get even more famous when the movie he'd just completed filming opened. It was his first starring role, and the buzz around Hollywood was building. Just two days ago *Vanity Fair* had contacted his manager about a cover shoot.

"I'm glad you did. How do we look?" Hayden nervously adjusted his tie.

"Amazing. Honest. You guys ready?"

"Yup." Hayden smiled and leaned over to kiss his lover.

"Please. Didn't you two do enough of that last night?" Clay groused good-naturedly.

The wedding shower/bachelor party the night before had been insane. Forty-seven guys had shown up to watch the happy couple open up their mountain of wedding gifts. The beer and wine had flowed freely, the strippers—or male exotic dancers, as they preferred to be called—had danced, and by the end of the evening, Hayden and Zack, slightly buzzed, couldn't stop making out with each other.

"I don't think I can ever get enough," Hayden said honestly.

"Me, either," concurred Zack. The two lovers kissed again.

"Get a room," Clay laughed, practically pushing them out the door.

It had taken three long months for Hayden to square everything away in Barcelona in preparation for his move back to the United States. Wrapping up his affairs, quitting his job, searching for and finding a great position in L.A., packing. He had done it gladly, counting off the days until he was back with the love of his life.

While Hayden was busy moving lock, stock and barrel to L.A., Zack had crashed at Kurt and Rick's while he hunted for a new place for Hayden and him. Neither man wanted to have anything to do with the apartment Bayne had picked out for Zack. While doing this, he also had juggled the demands of his newly won position as a staff photographer for Time-Life, Inc. Zack was also assembling and shooting more photographs on L.A. architecture. He and Kurt had grown close over the months since the *Diana* sinking, and after seeing examples of Zack's photography, Kurt had contracted him to do a coffee table book for Atlantis Books.

Despite all the intense obligations on his time, Zack did find a great duplex on La Jolla Avenue, in the heart of West Hollywood. The beautifully maintained, Spanish style duplex was bright, airy and convenient to everything. The wonderful space had a living room complete with wood burning fireplace, formal dining room, spacious kitchen with lots of cabinets, one and a half baths, a master bedroom and a second smaller bedroom that would be used as a home office. The house had more than enough room for the two lovers.

Thankfully, the minute Hayden walked into the newly leased and empty space, he fell in love with it, calming Zack's fears that he wouldn't. After 90 torturously long days apart, the two men happily fell into a daily routine that finally included each other.

Away from the chaos of the wedding, upstairs in the master suite, Kurt watched in amused fascination as the famous iconic fashion designer Cameron Fuller himself adjusted Rick's suit. Cameron's lover and business partner, Blake Jackson, had already made sure Kurt's beautifully cut suit fit perfectly.

Rick and Kurt were dressed in identical black lightweight wool FullJack suits, custom fitted for their built bodies by the designer personally. Crisp white spread-collar shirts and clean dove-gray knotted ties completed the clean-lined look that Cameron and Blake's clothing line, FullJack, was famous for.

"You both look great," Cameron said, standing back and admiring the handsome duo.

"Absolutely!" agreed Blake, who also stepped back. "No doubt about it, you guys rock in those suits!"

Kurt and Rick laughed nervously.

"Well, I think we're done here, so we'll leave you and go find our seats," Cameron said, as he moved towards the door. Blake nodded slightly and followed the designer out of the suite.

"Well," Kurt said, stepping close to his lover, "this is it, baby."

Tears threatened to fill up Rick's eyes. "You've made me so happy, Kurt. I mean that from the bottom of my heart. You've been so great about everything, and I'm just…I just…" He couldn't finish. He was too choked up with love for the man standing before him.

Kurt said nothing, but wrapped his massive arms around Rick and pulled him close. "Don't start that now, or we'll never get through this with dry eyes," he tried to joke, but the lump in his throat gave him away.

"Okay, okay," Rick wiped his eyes with his sleeve, and took Kurt's hand firmly. "Let's go get married."

As one of the ushers, Hayden escorted Maria Chanchez, Rick's former news co-anchor to a seat on Rick's side, then walked back up the wide rose petal strewn aisle. He caught a glance of Travis Church, his brother's equally famous lover, in the shadows of the arbor by the pool. Travis happened to look up and saw Hayden gazing at him. The beautiful actor smiled broadly and gave a happy wave. Hayden waved back.

He went back to the guest line and took the arm of Kurt's mother and followed fellow usher Zack, who was leading Rick's grandmother, back to the front of the seating area and placed them in their proper seats.

"You look awful sexy there, mister," Zack whispered as they walked back to get more guests.

"Not as sexy as you." Hayden sighed briefly when he suddenly remembered Zack was leaving town the next morning for eight long days. He was shooting an ecological summit in Japan for his new job. It was Zack's first out-of-town shoot, and Hayden knew he was slightly nervous about it. *He'll be back soon*, Hayden reminded himself over and over. *He'll be back soon.*

"Zack! Hayden!" cried out a familiar voice.

"Kirby!" Hayden called back, happy to be pulled from his funk. He and Zack went up to the vertically challenged trainer and both men hugged him hard.

"When did you get in?" Zack asked happily.

"Just this morning. I'm sorry I missed the rehearsal dinner and party last night. I left my present in the hall of Tara, there," he pointed back at the grand house. "I was in Vegas visiting Geoff. He's taping a few episodes there for sweeps week, and I barely caught the flight here."

"How is Geoff? We watched the premiere episode of his show, but haven't caught it since."

"He's great! He absolutely loves being the host of his own extreme game show. It's like he was born to do it. The things they make those contestants do…Ugh!" Kirby wrinkled his nose recalling the smell of the boiled horse rectums the contestants of *Face Your Fears* had to eat in two minutes or be eliminated from the game and lose out on the chance to win the $100,000 top prize.

"Well, I think the ceremony is any second, so let me take you to a seat. Groom's side or Groom's side?" Hayden asked, cocking his head to one side and grinning broadly.

"Groom's side, please!"

The music started, played by a severe-looking string quartet off the side of the wedding area, and the guests fell quiet. Not the traditional wedding march, the music was instead Rachmaninoff's "Rhapsody on a Theme of Paganini," more commonly known as the theme to the movie *Somewhere in Time*.

A strikingly beautiful three-year-old girl, Kurt's niece Sydney, carrying a little split-wood basket, strolled up the aisle throwing huge clumps of rose petals on the ground and laughing as she did so. She completely charmed the crowd who all smiled at her as she passed.

Sydney's radiant mother, Dru Parker, stood up from her chair near the front of the seating area and beckoned her daughter to her side. Dru was eight months pregnant with her second child, and glowing with a contented happiness that was palpable to all who were near her. Sydney clapped in delight when she got to her mother, and the assembled group all chuckled at her antics.

The music continued as the best man, Dave "Park" Parker, confidently strode up the aisle to take his place on the right side of the gorgeous floral alter. Park was Kurt's equally handsome half-brother, Dru's husband, and Sydney's father. His obvious pleasure at being a part of his beloved little brother's big day was clear for all to see.

The music changed to a formal, classical-style rendition of "Y.M.C.A." When the crowd recognized the tune, they burst out into laughter. Kurt and Rick then walked up the aisle in perfect sync, side-by-side. When they got to the front, they stopped and, reaching out, took each other's hand, Kurt on the left, Rick on the right.

The reverend, a jolly, robust woman with a severe crewcut who led a gay and lesbian community church in West Hollywood, held out her hands and began the ceremony. Kurt, raised Presbyterian, and Rick, a Catholic, had decided to have a nondenominational service. It felt right to both of them to not make the day about religion, but rather make it about their commitment to each other.

As the two besotted men listened to the reverend welcome the guests, and delve briefly into each of their backgrounds, Kurt realized he had never been so at peace with himself as he was right now. He had thought he'd be terrified by this point in the service, but he was amazed at how natural it felt to stand before his friends and family and declare his intent to share the rest of his life with the beaming man next to him.

He glanced out over the assembled crowd and saw his mother gently dabbing at her eyes with a white handkerchief. He saw his sister-in-law openly crying happy tears. He saw Zack and Hayden holding each other's hand and he wished they would one day soon take the same steps he and Rick were making today. He saw Rick's parents, somewhat stiff and formal in unfamiliar surroundings, but obviously very proud of their handsome son. He saw his brother Park discreetly wipe his damp eyes with his hand. He saw his future husband, standing tall, look at him with all the love and desire he felt clearly written on his face.

I'm such a lucky man, Kurt thought. *I'm surrounded by love*. He looked back at the reverend. She caught his eye and smiled broadly.

"This is not," she was saying, "a legally binding ceremony." She paused, and glanced at the crowd. "Though, undoubtedly," she added with a wink, "that will change soon enough." The assembled crowd laughed and applauded.

"So, while this is not a legally binding ceremony, it is a spiritually binding one, and I have never met two men so committed to being together as Kurt and Rick."

And together they would be. In New York.

After a brief three-day honeymoon in Napa Valley, the couple would fly to New York and begin their new lives. Rick had been working in Manhattan since their return from the ill-fated cruise. UBC had thrust him into his weekend position immediately, not wanting to lose the momentum of his growing renown. Kurt had flown back and forth across the country every five days, settling things in L.A. and getting his new publishing offices on Third Avenue set up. The stunning apartment loft they had bought in Tribeca needed major work, so there would be chaos for a few months until everything settled into a daily routine. One thing both men had agreed on was the need to cement their relationship and get married before beginning this new chapter of their lives.

Just as Kurt had predicted, his mother had begged to host the ceremony and reception. As far as the wedding planning went, both men wanted it to be in California where the majority of their friends and family were. So, with delight, Kurt's mother insisted the event be held at her estate. Rick had interjected his thoughts and wishes as best he could, but Kurt and his mother had truly pulled the whole thing together.

Rick was awed and thrilled by the ceremony and reception plans. It was his dream wedding, and he felt slightly guilty that his major responsibility had been to simply show up. He was only able to take one full week off from his anchor duties, and in a touching show of support, the staff and crew at UBC *Nightly News* had thrown him and Kurt a great shower before they left to come back to L.A. for the event.

"And now," the reverend announced, "the grooms would like to say a few words to each other. Rick, you go first."

Rick cleared his throat and faced Kurt. "I've told you a thousand times how much I love you, but I still worry that you don't know how deeply I hold you in my heart. You are the most amazing, loving, compassionate man I have ever met, and each time I realize that you belong to me, and I belong to you, I want to weep with joy." Rick's vision became fuzzy and he knew the salty tears were beginning to fall, but he didn't care. "I cannot imagine living my life without you, and I don't ever plan on letting you go. You are my best friend, my lover, my partner and the man I most admire. You are everything to me, and I am so, so proud to become your husband. I know that since we've survived so much, including having a ship sink beneath our feet, we can survive anything."

There were a few muffled sniffles coming from the guests, and Kurt didn't even bother to wipe his tears of happiness away.

"Kurt, your turn," the reverend said gently.

"Oh, boy," Kurt said, trying to control his raging emotions. "I hope I can get through this without bawling, but I don't think that's possible." The joyous crowd tittered at this admission, and Kurt breathed in deeply. "Okay. Rick, there is not a day that passes when I don't thank God for bringing you into my life. You give me joy. You give me laughter. You give me love. You put up with my training schedule even though you hate getting up at 5:00 in the morning. You let me have the last slice of pizza. You always let me have the aisle seat. You've shown me the way to become a better man, a man who isn't so self involved. You showed me that the greatest happiness I have ever known comes from giving to you, and that amazes me. I will be there for you always, and I can't wait to see what the future holds for us. I see us as two old men, surrounded by close family, beloved friends, and a whole passel of kids and grandkids."

Rick gasped as he tried to keep a lid on his emotions, but he ached to reach across and hug and smother Kurt in kisses.

"We will have everything we ever dreamed of," Kurt continued, with difficulty, "because we will have each other. And I thank you for that. And I thank you for the life I'm going to have as your husband."

Unable to control himself anymore, Rick reached over and pulled Kurt to him, hugging him so hard that both men couldn't breathe. Kurt squeezed back with all his strength, and the sniffling of the guests grew louder.

The two men, faces blotchy and red, eventually pulled way from each other and sheepishly glanced at their guests. The audience applauded.

"And now, we come to the ring ceremony," the reverend said, breaking the tearful silence.

Park stepped forward and handed the reverend the two platinum and diamond bands that Kurt had bought in Italy.

After getting aboard the *Enchantment of the Waves*, Kurt had discovered the beautiful bands still safe in the key pocket of his torn shorts. Knowing then that he would marry his partner just as he had promised, he never told Rick he still had them. He wanted to see the look on Rick's face when he saw them again on the day of their wedding.

He wasn't disappointed. Recognizing them immediately, Rick's eyes grew large, and he looked at Kurt with a stare of total confusion. "How did..." he started to whisper excitedly.

Kurt silenced him by merely winking happily.

Fresh tears seeped out of Rick's eyes.

"Repeat after me," the reverend said to Kurt handing him one of the shiny bands. "I, Kurtis Parker Farrar, take Richard Lee Yung as my wedded husband."

Kurt's voice was clear as a bell. "I, Kurtis Parker Farrar, definitely take Richard Lee Yung as my wedded husband!" He then proudly slipped the band on his lover's trembling finger while the guests laughed.

"And Rick, you repeat now, I, Richard Lee Yung, take Kurtis Parker Farrar as my wedded husband."

"I, Richard Lee Yung, most definitely take Kurtis Parker Farrar as my wedded husband!" As the laughter from the guests grew in pitch, followed by another round of applause, Rick slid Kurt's ring on his finger.

"Then, by the power invested to me by the West Hollywood Community Church and our higher powers, I hereby declare you husband and husband! Gentlemen, you may now kiss!"

Kurt and Rick just gazed at each other for a beat, stunned that it was over.

"Uh, gents? This is what the crowd came here to see," the reverend joked. "Hot man-on-man action, so pucker up!"

Kurt and Rick embraced and did the audience proud.

"Ladies and Gentlemen," the reverend said, after a beat to the assembled group, "I give you Mr. and Mr. Yung-Farrar!"

As Kurt and Rick still kissed, the crowd got to its feet and began clapping ferociously.

"Hey, Kimosabe," Kurt said as he slid into the elegant slipcovered side chair next to Hayden. The table Hayden was at had places for eight, but they were the only ones sitting down. Everyone else from table number two was out on the dance floor shaking their grove things. Rick, tie and jacket off, was leading the dancing throng through the steps to the regular version of "Y.M.C.A." Zack was next to him, dancing as well, and trying to have a conversation with Blake Jackson. They had become fast friends again since reconnecting during the fittings for the wedding suits.

"Hey, Mr. Yung-Farrar," Hayden replied, giving the large newlywed a big hug. "Beautiful ceremony. And the reception! Damn, your mom outdid herself!"

"Didn't she?" Kurt said, looking around approvingly. The reception was being held in the side courtyard of his childhood home, flanked on three sides by fragrant gardens. A live band played classic disco tunes from the '70s, and the dinner catered from The Ivy had been superb. "Rick and I came to loggerheads a couple of times over some stupid detail, and then she would come in and fix it. She was just amazing throughout this whole thing."

Hayden smiled. "So. Yung-Farrar. That was a surprise. Is that going to be your new last name from now on?"

Kurt nodded. "Yup. I'm officially Chinese-American as of now. Rick's parents are so proud of their new blond son-in-law," he grinned.

Hayden laughed.

"Clay and Travis leave?"

"Yeah, about a half hour ago. They both have early calls tomorrow."

A sedately beautiful woman with champaign-colored hair and dressed in an exquisite Chanel suit walked up to them and put her arm around Kurt. "Everyone is having a marvelous time," she said happily, as she surveyed the room.

"Mother, we were just talking about you! It's all so beautiful...Rick and I, we're both just so grateful for everything."

Mrs. Farrar waved her hand. "Honey, you know I'd do anything for my boys." She turned to Hayden. "And you, Hayden. Can I get you anything to eat?"

Hayden shook his head. "Oh, no, I think I overdid it with the cake. I'm fine. Thank you, Mrs. Farrar."

"Please. I'm Betty. Mrs. Farrar was my former mother-in-law. And I'm glad to say, she is no longer among the living." The merry wink she gave the two men easily conveyed a history of rank contention between the two Mrs. Farrars. "Oh, I just love this song! I think I'm going to go out there and cut a rug. I'll speak to you boys later?" She gave them an airy wave and left.

"Your mother is amazing. Your whole family is amazing."

Kurt beamed. "I know. I'm so blessed."

Hayden looked around and saw Zack bopping by, shaking his head in delight as he danced. "Would you look at that goober I'm in love with?"

"He looks happy. You look happy. Rick and I are thrilled for you both."

"We are happy. Very." Hayden looked down at his dinner plate. "I never knew I could feel this much love for one person, Kurt. It amazes me every day."

"I know what you mean."

"I hate that he's leaving for Japan, though. It seems like I just got to L.A., and now he has to leave. And after this assignment, who the fuck knows where they'll send him?"

Kurt smiled ruefully. "Hayden, old buddy, I'm gonna let you in on a great relationship secret that I learned the hard way."

"Oh? What's that?"

"Don't try to fight it. Zack's gonna need to explore his potential. He's a terrific photographer. This is his time to shine. If you love him, and I know you do, you'll let him wander the world, as long as he comes home to you. Hell, I'm moving away from everything I love to be with the man I know I could never live without, because this is his time, and I have to support him."

"It's just that I finally feel like I'm home. I don't want him to be gone from that."

Kurt rubbed Hayden's knee in friendship. "But he won't be. Not really. He'll be in your heart, on your mind, and I suspect, on the phone. It's not perfect, but fuck, what is? Besides, you just started a new job. Concentrate on that while he's gone. He'll be back before you know it."

Hayden looked at Kurt with admiration. The sometimes petulant man he'd seen on the *Princess Diana* had grown up. "When did you get so smart?" he asked.

Kurt grinned. "Fuck if I know!"

Hayden caught sight of Zack across the floor. His handsome lover was now dancing with Kurt's mom and paying the price with trod-upon feet. Hayden's heart swelled with a rush of emotion.

Kurt noticed the loving change come over Hayden. "What do you say," he said, rising, "that we go out there and show them how to dance? I think your boyfriend is tired of having my mother step on his toes."

Hayden got up and followed Kurt out to the floor. Rick sashayed over and took Kurt's hands. Hayden slipped up behind Zack, and kissed his neck gently.

"Hey," Zack murmured, wrapping Hayden's arms around his body.

"Hey."

"I've been looking everywhere for you! I missed you!"

Hayden squeezed Zack tightly, and pulled him close. "Me, too, baby. Me, too."

Author's Note

Obviously, *SUMMER CRUSING* is a work of fiction.

The odds of a disaster at sea, like the type that dooms the beautiful *Princess Diana*, happening in today's safety-conscious and stringently regulated cruising industry is about as likely as the Reverend Jerry Falwell officiating at a gay wedding. It's theoretically possible, but highly improbable.

I have always been a bit of an ocean liner and shipwreck nut. I can tell you minutiae about the *Andrea Doria*, *Britannic*, *Empress of Ireland*, *Titanic* and *Lusitania* that would make you think I was a complete loser. Yet, I had never taken a cruise. Somehow, dealing with married straight couples from the Midwest, screaming kids and testy grandparents all stuck on a floating hotel wasn't something I wanted to experience.

But, then, two summers ago, I was fortunate enough to be invited along on an Atlantis gay cruise through the Mediterranean. I had the best time on that cruise! I made some amazing friends, saw parts of the world I had only read about and, yes, even got laid a couple of times. Having already finished my second novel, *MALE MODEL*, I was about to start work on my third one, and had been searching for a good "hook" to drive the plot. Then and there, I decided to set it on a gay cruise. I actually started writing *SUMMER CRUISING* while still at sea during that cruise! I told my great friend Bruce Vilanch (I based the character "Garrett Gardner" on him) I was setting my next novel on a gay cruise. Knowing our shared love of ocean liners and shipwrecks, he got a mischievous glint in his eye, and said, "You're going to sink the ship, aren't you?" Frankly, I hadn't thought of doing that. "But you must," Bruce insisted. The original plotline was going to follow our merry band of travelers through the entire cruise and conclude with the end of the cruise. But, the more I thought about it, the more, well, fun, it seemed. *The Poseidon Adventure* is perhaps my all-time favorite movie (and I'm not ashamed to admit it!), and the thought of creating my own little disaster at sea was just too delicious to pass up.

I tell you all this to explain why I sink the *Princess Diana*.

Quite simply, it works as a dramatic device to further develop and explore the complicated relationships and plotlines the characters of *SUMMER CRUISING* are embroiled in. Plus, it was a hell of a lot of fun to write.

However.

In reality, the cruise industry is run by highly dedicated and extremely competent professionals who actually care about your comfort, enjoyment, and most of all, your safety. I can honestly say that on all the gay cruises I have taken, I have never seen so much as a hint of unprofessionalism or possible danger to any passenger or crewmember by any of the cruise line staffers or members of the tour packagers, such as Atlantis (www.atlantisevents.com) or R.S.V.P.(www.rsvp.net). Modern cruise ships have so many safety features and backup safety features and backup safety features for the backup safety features, that the chance of a incident at sea is basically nil.

What I'm saying is, don't be afraid to take a gay cruise! Have a blast (um, the good kind!), see the world, party your ass off, and possibly even fall in love.

What's not to like about that?

Dave Benbow
Los Angeles, CA

About the Author

After graduating from the University of Texas, Dave Benbow left Texas for the bright lights of Hollywood. As an actor he has had small parts on *The Young and the Restless, Days of Our Lives*, and *General Hospital*. But after hearing "no" at an audition just one too many times, Dave left acting behind and began an executive level career in high-end retail and interior design that continues to this day. He lives in West Hollywood, California, with his beloved Golden Retriever, Emmett, and is currently working on his next novel.

Readers can visit his Web site: www.davebenbow.com.

Front and back cover photos © DAVID MORGAN www.dmny.com
Model: Brandon
Grooming: Jorge Vargas
Cover design: Dave Benbow

Fiction

In and Out in Hollywood
(ISBN 1-928662-02-1)

Ben Patrick Johnson
(USA ~~$24.95~~ Hardcover)
Now $15.00!

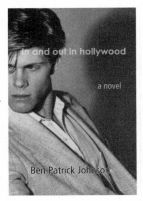

In and Out in Hollywood is a wild ride on the Hollywood highway of fame. A young man named Freddie is plucked from obscurity and groomed to be the host of a new entertainment TV show. But the show's producers and Freddie both learn that altering the package doesn't change its contents. It's all good until an incident at the company picnic. Then Freddie is left scrambling to keep his career on track and his love life in tact.

Potato Queen
(ISBN 1-928662-06-4)

Rafaelito V. Sy
(USA $14.95 Paperback)

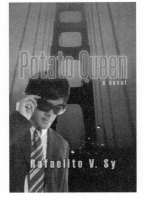

"*POTATO QUEEN* is a novel about East and West, immigration, homecoming and homeleaving, an odyssey in quest of the true sexual self. But most of all, in a world of canned culture and programmed tastes, it is novel about keeping the imagination alive, an accomplishment all readers can celebrate thanks to this remarkable debut by Rafaelito Sy."
— Lamar Herrin
author of *THE LIES BOYS TELL*

Mystery

The Guessing Game
(ISBN 1-928662-00-5)

Ted Randler
(USA ~~$16.95~~ Paperback)
Now $11.50!

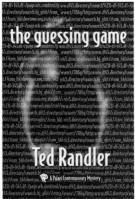

A local television news producer is found viciously murdered in the bathroom of a crowded bar. With virtually no witnesses and ominous blood-painted graffiti as the only suggestion of motive, the media quickly links the murder with two unsolved cases as a "plague of hate crimes" against the gay community. Apparently seducing men by pandering to their erotic fantasies and then ritualistically displaying their corpses, the murderer is seemingly capable of transforming identities and even gender before disappearing without a trace.

BUY DIRECT FROM PALARI

Save with free shipping and other publisher discounts on these titles.

A High Seas SIZZLER!

from Dave Benbow

2006 Release

Summer Cruising
(ISBN 1-928662-07-2)

Dave Benbow
(USA $14.95 Paperback)

Remember FREE SHIPPING when ordered with this form!

Deliver books to:

Name_____

Phone_____-_____Email_____

Address_____

City_____State_____Zip_____

	Number of Books		Total
In and Out in Hollywood . . . $15.00	@_____	=	_____
The Guessing Game $11.50	@_____	=	_____
Potato Queen $14.95	@_____	=	_____
Summer Cruising $14.95	@_____	=	_____

VA residents add 5% sales tax =   _____

TOTAL ENCLOSED =   _____

Order online at WWW.PALARIBOOKS.com
or send check or money order to
Palari Publishing LLP
P. O. Box 9288
Richmond, Virginia 23227-0288